THE PILGRIMAGE OF THE
LYFE OF THE MANHODE

VOLUME II

EARLY ENGLISH TEXT SOCIETY
No. 292
1988

THE PILGRIMAGE OF THE LYFE OF THE MANHODE

Translated anonymously into prose from
The First Recension
of
Guillaume de Deguileville's Poem
Le Pèlerinage de la vie humaine

VOL. II

EXPLANATORY NOTES, BIBLIOGRAPHY, AND GLOSSARY
EDITED BY
AVRIL HENRY

Published for
THE EARLY ENGLISH TEXT SOCIETY
by the
OXFORD UNIVERSITY PRESS
1988

Oxford University Press, Walton Street, Oxford OX2 6DP
Oxford New York Toronto
Delhi Bombay Calcutta Madras Karachi
Petaling Jaya Singapore Hong Kong Tokyo
Nairobi Dar es Salaam Cape Town
Melbourne Auckland
and associated companies in
Beirut Berlin Ibadan Nicosia

Oxford is a trade mark of Oxford University Press

Published in the United States by
Oxford University Press, New York

© The Early English Text Society 1988

All rights reserved. No part of this publication may be reproduced,
stored in a retrieval system, or transmitted, in any form or by any means,
electronic, mechanical, photocopying, recording, or otherwise, without
the prior permission of Oxford University Press

British Library Cataloguing in Publication Data
Guillaume, de Deguileville
[Le pèlerinage de la vie humaine.
Middle English]. The pilgrimage of the lyfe
of the manhode.—(Original series/
Early English Text Society; 292)
I. Title   II. Henry, Avril   III. The pilgrimage
of the lyfe of the manhode
IV. Series
841'.1   PQ1483.G3A6
ISBN 0-19-722294-3

Printed in Great Britain
at the University Printing House, Oxford
by David Stanford
Printer to the University

CONTENTS
VOLUME II

EXPLANATORY NOTES	357
GLOSSARY	509
INDEX OF NAMES	581
APPENDIX: Additional prose and Pilgrim's Lament in MS. M	585
BIBLIOGRAPHY	589

ERRATA IN VOLUME I

p. xxi (in italicised paragraph, 3rd line): *wordly*/*worldly*
p. 3 line 110: hadde./hadde
p. 60 line 2512: hem?"/hem)?"
p. 68 line 2834: And/and
p. 74 line 3074: su*m*f. 6ov]thing/su*m*[f. 6ov]thing
p. 125 line 5228: ffiþe]/[þe]
p. 152 line 6346: Damisele/"Damisele
p. 153 line 6389: and where/"and where
p. 163 line 6784: elles/"elles

EXPLANATORY NOTES

In the absence of any adequate commentary on the text in either language, it has been necessary to include material not only on the translation *per se* but also on the original poem. However, these notes do not pretend to be exhaustive: the text awaits and deserves the attention of scholars in philosophy, history, language, liturgy, art, theology, and literature who will be able to indicate the full extent of Deguileville's originality and traditionalism. References to the Fathers make no attempt to be definitive or to identify the earliest reference to a given idea: they merely serve to show that it was traditional.

Line references to Stürzinger's edition of the French text are prefixed by 'F'. In quotations from Stürzinger, his use of *( )* and *[ ]* has been retained. Round brackets indicate words which 'should be omitted, as inconsistent with the meaning, grammar or metre'; square brackets indicate words 'which for a like reason should be added from other MSS., or as conjectural emendations'. However, his use of italics for 'other words which have been substituted from other MSS. or by conjecture' [for those in his base text *t*], and his use of partial italicisation to indicate expansion, is not retained, as it would create much visual confusion. Umlaut over the 'vowel which in Modern French has disappeared from the pronunciation or spelling or has changed its sound' is also omitted. Where all the MSS are unanimous in a reading rejected by Stürzinger but seen by τ, their reading is given.

In the absence of the source French MS it is often impossible to say whether τ's deviant readings are due to misreading on his part or corruption in his source. Throughout the notes, the phrase 'τ read [the French]' is shorthand for 'τ either read as, or was faced with a French variant'; 'om.' preceding a portion of the French text means 'τ omitted the equivalent of, or found absent in his source...'. Minor deviations from the French, such as the insertion or omission of tags, are omitted. Major corruptions are marked in the text itself (Vol. I) by *.

French variants are preceded by 'var(s).', and followed by Stürzinger's sigils: for example, '*tournelle* vars. *tourelle* MSS *A⁷GM¹*, *tonnelle* MS. *L*' indicates that MSS *A7*, *G*, *M¹* have *tourelle*, while MS. *L* has *tonnelle*. Only relevant F variants are given, but it is not intended to imply that τ saw the MS(S) cited. Sigils of French MSS are italicised to avoid confusion with the non-Greek ME ones, though ME τ, χ, ψ, β, ω are inevitably italic.

Stürzinger collated only MSS *toLTAGHBMM¹*, ten of the fifty-three copies of the *Vie* known to him; two MSS, *D* and *V*, possibly containing the *Vie*, were inaccessible. He occasionally gives the variants of others not consulted throughout. Important among these, because close to or among the MSS used by τ, are *M*, *o* and *A⁷* (see Avril Henry, 'The French Source Manuscript of the Middle English Prose *Pilgrimage of þe Lyfe of þe Manhode*' for evidence showing that none of these can be the single source of the translation).

Sigils denoting the English MSS are explained in the stemma, p. l. In many cases, which I have not distinguished unless important, 'τ' really means 'τ, or χ which may be a level of correction to τ if not an independent manuscript' (see p. lii). Sigil 'S' is sometimes in brackets because it probably derives from G as corrected (see p. lxxii).

Adoptions of alternative readings, and emendations, which in the text are both in square brackets, are not explained here when adequately accounted for in the Textual Variants.

References are cited in full only in the Bibliography, and very long titles are abbreviated even there. This space-saving device has some unwelcome results: for example, the familiar *Analecta Bollandiana* appears in the Notes simply as 'Hooff'.

It has unfortunately not always been possible to refer to one edition of the works of Durandus of Mende. He is usually cited in the Latin (Naples 1859), sometimes in the more accessible French of Berthélemy, and where possible in Neale and Webb's English translation of Book I, and Passmore's of Book II.

Unless otherwise stated, English translations from the Vulgate Bible are from the modernised Douay. Where clarity is so served, the Knox translation has been used.

No attempt has been made systematically to relate images in our *Pilgrimage* to their development in *The Pilgrimage of the Soul* and *The Pilgrimage of Jesus Christ*, although the three original poems were really designed as a whole. Occasional mentions of them are made where they throw light on the *Lyfe*.

1 **hows** F2 *mansion* var. *maison* MS. η. *Hows* was usually used of a house as property or edifice, though it could mean a permanent home. *Mansion* means rather 'home'. John xiv 2 *In domo Patris mei mansiones multae sunt* is discussed by Aquinas, *ST*, 3a Supp., q.93. a.2.

   but introduces an emphatic statement (*MED but* 7b).

2 **as ... Poul** Heb. xi 13, xiii 14. St Augustine developed the Pauline metaphor: *Qui ergo peregrinatur, et per fidem ambulat, nondum est in patria, sed jam est in via* (*PL*, XXXVII, 1640). *Circuimus quoque peregrinationem istius mundi, si intelligentes nos non habere hic 'civitatem permanentem, futuram inquirimus'* (Radulphus Ardens: *PL*, CLV, 1548). Human life as pilgrimage is rare in art earlier than Guillaume (Kirschbaum *pilger, pilgerschaft*; Marle, II, 151–66, Didron, *Annales* give a few earlier examples).

4 **pilgrimes** F6 *Pelerins et pelerines*: τ did not echo the distinction between male and female pilgrims.

4–5 **day** om. F8 *en dormant* 'when I was asleep'.

6 **romaunce** is not *Romaunce* because though MSS referred to as *le romaunt de la Rose* are common, *romaunt* is probably not part of the poem's name, simply indicating a work in the vernacular.

EXPLANATORY NOTES 359

Hultman, pp. 119-36 lists supposed echoes of *Le Roman de la Rose* in the *Pilgrimage*. The convincing examples are cited below.

9-11 **let ... herkne** Heb. x 38-9.

11 **þis** F21 *la vision*.

12 **withouten any owttaken** in view of F22 *sans point de excepcion*, and the fact that at 1451 all the MSS have *exceptinge* or *exceptioun* for F2659 *excepter*, perhaps the reading should be *withouten any excepcioun*, accepting J on the assumption that α and δ independently substituted the native word.

18 **Chaalit** F33 *Chaalit* vars. *Chaaliz, Chaalith, Chalit, Chalict, Caliq*. I have not standardised spellings of this name. Chaalis, 11 k. from Senlis, was a 12th-century daughter-house of Pontigny, itself one of the four daughter-houses of Citeaux (Trilhe, I, xxx; Meer, Map II). Its ruins survive (Seltzer, p. 584; Meer, figs. 70, 73). Jacques de Therines, a leading University of Paris theologian, and abbot of Chaalis 1308-1317 (Faral, p. 6) possibly influenced Guillaume; De Valois gives a bibliography and summary of his major works. By the 1380s Chaalis the abbey was known for its library.

19-21 **I ... aperseyued** F3741 *d'aler estoie excite | En Jherusalem la cite. | En un mirour, ce me sembloit, | Qui sanz mesure grans estoit | Celle cite aparceue* 'I was moved to go to the city of Jerusalem. This city appeared, it seemed to me, in an immeasurably large mirror' (var. for *ce: et* MS. *A*⁷). The var. distorted τ's syntax. The image is not random: it is used at 1740-52, and at 2009-10 Christ is a mirror. It may also suggest divine grace in a temporal context (I Cor. xiii 12, II Cor. iii 18). The mirror also implies that the poem is a *speculum*: Quicherat p. 212 observes that Arras MS. Bib. de la Ville MS. 845 calls it *unz biaux Miroirs de sauvement*. For lists of *specula* see Morrill, pp. xxii-xxiv; Perdrizet, pp. 1-2. Bradley, and Grabes, give accounts of the genre.

22-4 **me thouhte ... gold** F43-6 *Mont me sembloit de grant atour | Celle cite ens et entour. | Les chemins et les alees | D'or en estoient pavees: ens et entour* modifies *cite* not, as τ thought, *Les chemins et les alees* with the awkward result that þe weyes and þe aleyes are outside as well as inside the city wall. The imagery derives from Apoc. xxi 21. *PL*, CCXIX, 114 lists extensive commentary on every part of the city (correct Augustine, *Quaestiones in Apocalypsim* to XXV, 2417 and Bede, *Expositio in eandem* to XCIII, 129). A typical commentary is more accessible in Dulong.

25 **newe** F49 *vives* 'living' var. *noeue* MS. *A*⁷. See I Peter ii 5.

26 **hy wal** Apoc. xxi 26. Hultman (p. 6) suggests an echo of *Le Roman de la Rose* 131 (Lecoy, I, 5) contrasting the New Jerusalem as a life-goal with the Lover's garden.

27-8 **þere ... hadde** in view of F54-5 *La ... Illuec*, C's *þer ... þer* (the unstressed form) is emended to the stressed form *þere*

28 **ioye withoute sorwe** Apoc. xxi 4.

29 **shortliche ... me** F55 *pour passer m'en briefment*: the translation is literal, as at 2359—*OED pass* v. intr. gives no reflexive meaning 'to proceed in narration'.

32 **Cherubyn** was from the 11th century used as a sg. or proper noun (as here) as well as a collective noun: cf. *OED cherub* 1c. (where in *Ancren Riwle* and *Cursor Mundi* it is the same angel's name), and the gloss *Cherubyn sunt judices* in M ff.10^r, 12^v; pl. *cherubims* appears in the 16th, and *cherubim* only in 17th century, when the Hebrew pl. was recognised. Uriel is sometimes called Cherubyn: he is *ignis dei* in Jerome's *Liber de nominibus Hebraicis* (*PL*, XXIII, 1205).

34-5 **with ... turnynge** F65-6 *a deux taillans, / Tout versatille et bien tournans*. *Versatille* has two meanings, the first equivalent to the preceding phrase *a deux taillans* 'with two cutting edges', the second to *bien tournans* 'easily turned' (Godefroy cites the adaptor's gloss to the 1465 prose version of the *Pèlerinage*: *Versatille, c'est a dire muniable*). Gen. iii 24· *Cherubim et flameum gladium versatilem*. Cherubyn appears again early in the *Pilgrimage of the Soul*, when as Porter of Paradise he attends the Pilgrim's Judgement trial (*Guillaume de Deguileville*, f. vi).

35-7 **þere ... be** F68-70 *N'est nul ... / Qui par illec passer peust / Que mort ou navre ne feust* 'no-one could pass that place without being killed or wounded'; G's *ne* is accepted.

36 **kan ... bokelere** in view of F68 *tant sache du bouclier* perhaps JMO's *of* should be accepted in place of *on*, but I have assumed that the former is an up-dating of idiom, accidentally agreeing with F. A *bokelere* is a small round, oval or half-moon shaped shield.

þere in view of F69 *par illec*, C's *þer* is emended to the stressed form (see n. 27-8).

37-9 **nouht ... passage** F71-3 *Le prince neis de la cite, / Pour ce qu'avoit humanite, / Au passage mort y receut*. Many F and ME manuscripts are corrupt here: the correct reading is in doubt. Confusion has been caused by *neis* meaning 'even' or 'not even'. *Le ... cite* might conclude the first idea ('no-one could pass that place ... not even the prince of the city') or initiate the second idea ('even the prince of the city, since he too was human, met his death at the entrance'). G's construction is accepted (*Nowght that the prince ... ne resseyued deþ*—cf. *Nouht þat ...* at 1930, 2747, 3487, 6741, 7138, 7281). C and J clearly rewrote to avoid

EXPLANATORY NOTES 361

confusion. τ perhaps began his sentence at *Nouht*, thinking at first that *neis* was negative, then found it to be positive, and produced an awkward construction, 'Not that the prince (himself) did not receive death'—i.e. he too died. τ's *ne* was then apparently misread as *he* by C and β.

40 **payage** is earlier than any example in *OED peage*.

alþouh should possibly be *þof al* following M on the assumption that this reading in β, which gave JMO's variants, represents τ.

raunsome F76 *treuage*: Christ not only pays the human toll for crossing to the other world but also, being God, redeems man by paying the fine due for sin (*OED ransom* 1, 2b, 3a, 3b). Both meanings fuse in *le treuage de la mort* 'debt of nature, or of death'.

42 **þei ... chalys** Matt. xx 23.

43 **passage** F80 *passer* 'the passing' gives a double sense 'entrance/death'.

43-4 **of ... noon** F81-2 *la porte / Dont le portier nul (ne) deporte* is awkward too: in addition, τ cannot echo the word-play on *port*.

44-5 **I ... blood** F83-4 *Pendans en vi les penonciaus / De sanc rougis, tains et vermaus*: τ om. *rougis* or *vermaus*. A *penselle* was a small flag borne by an esquire. An early commentators (on the Second French Recension) says of the bloody flags: *On y voyit les marques des supplice que l'on fait souffrir aux Martyrs* (Goujet, p. 76).

45 **I sih** om. F86 *sans estre deceu* 'without a doubt'.

46 **entre ... needes** F87 *entrer a force y convenoit* 'of necessity one had to go in there' or 'one had to suffer violence in entering there'.

47 **I ... passe** F90 *Nul mais passer ne veoie*: as at 998, τ misconstrued intensive negative *mais* as 'but'.

49 **he ... safetee** F93-4 *Bien puet son glaive flamboiant / Metre en saif*: the sword is put not where it will be safe but where it will do no harm. Contrast 435-6, where Holy Oils are put in a place of safety, and *en sauf* is correctly rendered *in saaf*. *En sauf* could mean 'in reserve' (Godefroy, Supp. X *en salf* s.v. *salf* adj.) but τ understood the alternative meaning. As O's annotator observes, the point is that Christ's merits made the entrance to heaven easier. The angel who drove Adam and Eve from paradise is sometimes shown sheathing his flaming sword at the Crucifixion (the 13th-century *Figurae Bibliorum*, Eton College MS. 177, f. 5ʳ; the 13th-century 'Good Samaritan' window in Sens Cathedral's North Choir Aisle; the 'Passion Window' at Rouen Cathedral [Cahier and Martin, Etudes XX, XI respectively]).

52 **Seint Austyn** Augustine is mentioned first as the greatest of the Fathers, whom religious Orders claimed as their patron (*CE*, II, 92).

53-7 **semede ... faire** the feeding of birds is an image of religious instruction: *semen* is *divina praedicatio* (*PL*, L, 742) and *locutio oris* (*PL*, CXII, 1048). A gloss to *thaym no movth-sede sewe* in *The Mirour of Mans Saluacioune* (Henry, p. 199) says: *he prechid noght personely to thaym*. The *swete seyinges* (F110 *diz doucereux*) refer to fowlers enticing birds with music, as in *Piers Plowman* (Skeat, B Text p. 468, lines 466-72), and *Kingis Quair* (Norton-Smith, p. 34, lines 939-42). The image relates to Book 4 (6254-69) where souls winged with virtues fly over the sea of the world.

54 **to** om. F105-6 *amorser / ... et apasteler* 'bait and'.

56 **croumede** τ read F109 *enmieles* 'honeyed' as *enmietes* (see n. 6826).

57-63 **many ... citee** birds commonly represent contemplatives. Commentaries on Genesis make this clear: *Quinta die ... Multum etiam sancti quasi aves per contemplationem ad coelestia sublevantur* (Remigius, *PL*, CXXXI, 56); see also Damian, *PL*, CXLV, 813-14, and Hugh St Victor, *De Sacramentis*, I, i, xxvii (see Deferrari); the *Bible Moralisée* (f. 4ʳ) explains: *aues sunt contemplatiui id est religiosi qui amant spiritualia*; *Ancrene Wisse* (Tolkien, p. 69) says : *Treowe ancres beoþ briddes icleopede. for ha leaueþe eorþe ... & ... fleoþ uppart toward heouene*.

Souls, however, rarely appear winged in medieval iconography (exceptions are in Didron, II, 176 and Delisle, *Origine*, pl. 2). Here they derive from the tradition associating virtues and feathers, e.g. the late 12th-century Raoul de Houdenc's *Li Romans des eles* (Scheler, pp. 248-71), where wings of Largece and Cortoisie are feathered with virtues. See 4306-9, where Pride's Mantle of Hypocrisy is feathered.

58-9 **refer to three Augustinian orders**: French Dominicans (*Jacobins* because their chief monastery was Saint-Jacques in Paris), *Chanownes* (Canons Regular of St Augustine, or Austin Canons), *Augustines* (the Order of Hermits of St Augustine, or Austin Friars); see *NCE*, IV, 974; III, 62; I, 1059, 1071.

62 **and ... clymbe** in view of F122 *pour ... monter* perhaps *and* should be omitted.

70 **twelve ... humblisse** derives from Gen. xxviii 12, Jacob's Ladder, which in the *Biblia Pauperum* is one of the Types of Abraham's Bosom (souls taken to heaven in Christ's mantle). Its immediate source may be the Rule of St Benedict (*PL*, LXVI, 371-410 and N.N., ch. vii). Variations on the 'heaven-ladder' are common: St Bernard's *De Gradibus Humilitatis* for example, claiming to be Benedict's steps but in fact a different series (*PL*, CLXXXII, 942-72—see Burch for a translation), and Raoul de Houdenc's *Le Songe de Paradis*, where a pilgrim to paradise ascends by a ladder of eight rungs (Scheler, pp. 222-7). See Martin, pp. 7-8 for other references to the ladder.

EXPLANATORY NOTES

72 **monkes ... greye** 'monk' could apply to Benedictines, Cistercians or Carthusians. The distribution of Orders in 50–78 is maintained here, *þilke þat weren of his folk* meaning those that follow the Benedictine Rule: Benedictines themselves, called Black Monks, and Cistercians (like Guillaume), called Grey or White Monks.

75 **knet** Franciscans enter by the relatively laborious knots of Poverty, Chastity and Obedience (which appear on their waist-cords).

79–80 **of ... names** the awkwardness originates in F156–7 *dont je ne sui pas seurs / De tous les nons vous raconter* which conflates two constructions, *vous raconter* filling the line but not fitting the sense.

81–2 **only ... see** *only* modifies *was*; the dreamer is aware of some methods of gaining heaven: there are others.

84 **a ... streyt** F166 *un petit huis et estroit* is cited (Hultman, n. 6) as an echo of *Le Roman de la Rose* 514–55 *un huisset ... petit et estroit* (Lecoy, I, 17). Perhaps there is an implied contrast with the entrance to the garden of secular love. The image originates in Matt. vii 13 (Luke xiii 24).

85 **equitee** might imply that the entrance was kept impartially, according to the letter of the law (*MED equity* 1), or according to the principles of justice which modify law (ibid., 3). See McCutchan for Equity's modification of Justice.

85–6 **Þe ... Peeter** Matt. xvi 19.

86,87 **triste** perhaps G's form *trust(e)* should be accepted here and at 1512, 1517, 1531, 1833, 2033, 2038, 2052, 2723, 2726, 2727, 4827 (also for *triste* sb. at 4710).

87–8 **he ... noon** in view of F172–3 *ne laissoit ... / Nullui* perhaps C's *ne suffrede* should be retained—but the double negative, though normal, does not appear in the other MSS.

88–90 **þilke ... nedele** Matt. xix 23–4.

93 **þerbi ... cloþed** Eccles. v 15.

93–4 **of ... robes** F184 *des robes le roi*: GJMO's literal *of* 'some of' is partly erased in C, though under u.v. *f* is visible, perhaps changed to *n* to achieve an English idiom. The *kynges robes* (the 'robes' of Christ-like poverty?) are, unlike other material possessions, retained in heaven.

99 **þer is not** F196 *pas n'y a*; C's *þere*, over erasure, is emended to his normal form for unstressed 'there is' (see n. 27–8).

101 **swich a dwellinge** F200 *si bel estre*: τ omits *bel*, and cannot match the subtlety of *estre*, which suggests condition more strongly than location: 'such a pleasant state'; he has the same difficulty at 186.

364   ÞE LYFE OF ÞE MANHODE

102 **for ... saulee** F202 *Pour estre saoul* 'to be satiated': τ used sb., *saulee* for adj. *saoul*; *ful* may be an attempt to keep the force of F.

105-6 **for ... seygh** F207-10 *De la voul estre pelerins, | Se je pouoie a toutes fins. | Ailleurs, voir, si com songoie | Nul repos je ne veoie* 'I wanted to be a pilgrim to that place (at all events, if I could). Indeed, I saw no rest elsewhere, in my dream'. τ om. *a toutes fins* and misconstrued *voir* 'indeed' as 'see'.

106 **Noon reste** *visio pacis* is the traditional interpretation of the name Jerusalem (Jerome, *PL*, XXIII, 830). Alanus de Insulis so calls the New Jerusalem (*PL*, CCX, 76); see also Hugh St Victor, *PL*, CLXXVI, 1159 (cited Gewande, p. 23).

110-11 **As ... bourdoun** The dreamer is aware of the need for pilgrim's equipment *before* his dreamed birth as well as immediately after it: his wish to reach the city results in the dreamed life.

113 **I ysede** the birth image is in powerful contrast to the visionary heights of New Jerusalem, the goal of the pilgrim's life and the end of all temporal life.

116-17 **I wente ... fynde** according to F227-9 *querant aloie | Et (en) plourant me dementoie | Ou peusse trouver*, *seechinge* should modify *wente* so that *where I mihte fynde ...* should modify *bimenynge me*.

118 **of ... fairnesse** F232 *de sa biaute* shows that this is instrumental *of* (Mustanoja, p. 39).

120 **rochet** a long robe fitted above the waist, with long, close sleeves, and commonly closed at the neck by a brooch.

121 **grene tissue** interpretation of medieval colour symbolism is hazardous: perhaps this signifies *la regeneration par les actes, de l'initiation spirituelle et de la Charité* (Gilles, p. 120).

122 **charbuncles** *It shyneth in derke places and it semeth as hit were a flame* (Trevisa, II, p. 839); *C'est le gemme de gemmes. Elle enlumine les euvres par nuit et pars jour* (*The Lapidary of King Philip*, cited Baisier, p. 115). For other lapidaries' treatment of it see Studier and Evans, pp. 49, 89, 110, 139, 175. At 2019-32 it forms the second knob on the Pilgrim's staff, symbolising the Virgin, but 159-61 show that worn by Grace Dieu it means Christ illuminating mankind's darkness. As the fourth stone in the Pectoral of Exod. xxviii 18, the ruby received much exegetical attention. See Rabanus Maurus, *PL*, CXI, 471, or Alcuin *PL*, C, 1106 (cited Baisier pp. 83-4), and Isidore, *PL*, LXXXII, 578 (cited Gewande, p. 17). Hultman, p. 123, contrasts it with Lady Richesse's carbuncle in *Le Roman de la Rose* 1097 (Lecoy, I, 34).

123 **amelle** the first letter, erased in C, was *a*, but in view of F240 *esmail* and the fact that the rest of the word is over erasure, perhaps GS's *emall* should be accepted, in spite of the fact that *MED amal* 'enamel' records no form in *e*- (though there is

EXPLANATORY NOTES

enmailen 'to enamel'). This jewel indicates Grace Dieu's high rank: similar large, brooch-like clasps are familiar on 12th-century sculptured queens (as in Joan Evans, pl. 50).

128 **she ... first** Divine Grace is freely given. The doctrine, founded on Rom. iii 24, v 15 and Eph. ii 8, is developed by Augustine (*CSEL*, LX, 235.24–5): it is not, he explains, truly Grace if it is merely earned (*CSEL*, LVII, 55.6). *PL*, CCXIX, 803–4 has a complete index *De gratia gratis data*. The balance to this view of Grace is given at 2731–6: Grace Dieu will leave the pilgrim if he chooses the wrong way. For the doctrine of Grace see Aquinas, *ST*, 1a2ae, qq.109–14.

134–5 **þe mo ... folk** F261–2 *Plus a le pommier de pommes, / Plus s'encline vers les hommes* is a proverb: see the *Aȝenbite* (Gradon, p. 246, 34–5).

136 **þat ... banere** is not cited by *MED baner(e)* 4d 'symbolic embodiment, object or sign', which is what *banere* must mean here, referring to *Humblesse ... the signe*.

142 **My freend** τ read F275 *Biaus amis* 'dear friend' as *Miaus amis*: at 1488 *Biaus* in this context is rendered by *Goode*.

she F275 *celle* 'this lady' var. *elle* MSS *AMH*.

150 **who ... wite** F289–90 *qui vous estes tout de voir / Voudroie voulentiers savoir* 'I should be glad to know who you really are': *tout de voir* qualifies *estes*, but τ makes *in sooth* qualify *wite*.

152 **she ... seyde** for F293 *me respondi* is a common tautology.

152–3 **In time** τ read F294 *entens i* 'listen [to it]' as *en tens*.

154 **suspeccionous** GS echo F296 *souspeconneuse* in an earlier occurrence of the word than is cited by *OED suspicionous*: CJMO anglicise to forms of *suspeccious*.

156 **nouht ... neede** F301 *Non pas pour ce qu'en ait mestier* 'not that he needs them' var. *Non pas pour ce que ait mestier* MS. *T*.

161 **þo** F309 *ceuz*: perhaps GS's *thilke* should be accepted here and at 168, 292, but in all these cases one must then assume that two scribes (C and β, from which J's *thaye* is a variant) substituted *þo*.

175 **forveied** GS's *forueyed* is accepted because it echoes F334 *fourvoiez* which derives from the prefix *for-* and *voie* 'way'; CJMO's readings show a commoner English participle.

175–6 **I ... folk** F335 *Esloingner ne vueil nulle gent* 'I will turn no-one away': τ perhaps expected the familiar *s'esloingner* 'to turn oneself away from'.

180–1 **riht ... citee** echoes the main sense of F343–4 *mont souvent, / Ains que tu viengnes par couvent* but does not retain a possible pun on *par couvent* 'before you shall come to the city by means of the monastery' (at 6760 the pilgrim enters Citeaux or Cluny).

186 **dwellinge** F354 *l'estre* see n. 101.

191-2 **þilke ... naked** F365-6 *les uns ... Les autres* 'the one ... the other': τ read *uns* as *nus*.

193-4 **ooþere ... vertues** see n. 57-63; *Li Romanz des eles* describes how 'prowess must not be merely brave, but must have two wings of Largece and Cortoisie, each wing is of seven feathers ...' (Scheler, p. 253). Houdenc may have influenced Guillaume not only in this but also in his vision-poems *Songe de Paradis* and *Le Songe d'Enfer* (see Kundert-Forrer, Part III, for the suggestion that Houdenc is after all the author of the former).

196 **assaye** om. F372 *En divers lieus* 'in various places'.

207 **into** in view of F393 *Vers* perhaps G's *to* should be accepted.

210-11 **xiii ... xxx** dates the First Recension of the French poem to 1330.

211 **she wiste** τ read F400 *souvenoit* 'she remembered' as *savoit* (no doubt abbreviated).

213-14 **it ... eerþe** Apoc. xxi 10.

214 **as þouh** perhaps JMOS's *as* should be accepted, assuming that C and G independently added *þouh*, not that S and β independently omitted it.

215-16 **It ... aray** F407-8 *Clochiers i ot et belles tours | Et mont estoit biaus ces atours*: if *ces* is not a form of *ses* 'its', τ read it as such. Alternatively, he wrote *þis*, misread by α as *his*. The reading is in doubt.

217 **a water** the pilgrim approaches Baptism (discussed in Aquinas, *ST*, 3a, qq.66-71). The water surrounding the city may derive from Apoc. iv 6: 'And in the sight of the throne was, as it were, a sea of glass like to crystal', commonly interpreted as Baptism (Alcuin, *PL*, C, 1117, Rupert, *PL*, CLXIX, 1107; CLXX, 314). See *PL*, CCXIX, 159 for a list of other patristic sources for the image; see Maertens for an extended treatment of the rite of Baptism; see *NCE*, XII, 802 for the iconography of the sacraments in general. See Fortescue (1962) for the ceremonies allegorised in Book 1.

220 **þe water** τ read F414 *le lieu* as a form of *l'eaue*.

226 **Þow ... seiste** see n. 3397.

quod she, without precedent in F423 and superfluous after *answerde*, could be omitted on the assumption that χ added it.

228 **passe ... see** F426 *passer i ... la grant mer*: τ om. *i* as on at least six other occasions (listed on p. lxxxvii).

229-30 **of gret ... wyndes** F429-30 *de grant soussi, | De tempestes et de tourmens, | De grans orages et de vens* 'of great care, of tempests and of torments, of great storms and of winds': τ saw var. ... *Et doraiges et de grans vens* MSS *AH¹Hy*, and om. *orages*.

234 **pilgrimage** in view of F436 *pelerinage* JMO's reading is accepted.

| | EXPLANATORY NOTES | 367 |

236-7 **þerforth ... hem** martyrdom is the Baptism of Blood. Aquinas, *ST*, 3a, q.66. aa.11, 12 declares it more perfect than the Baptism of Water.

239-42 **but ... þee**[1] physical washing of the newborn child and its spiritual cleansing in Baptism are intrinsically linked by the fact that Original Sin is transmitted through the flesh: Hugh St Victor observes that divine justice is 'irreprehensible in this but not comprehensible' (Deferrari, pp. 138-9).

243 **for** has no precedent in F452, but var. beginning *Quar* MS. *M* may have been in front of τ, in which case G and δ perhaps omitted *for* after *foorth*.

243-4 **Heerbi ... not** Christ was baptised not of necessity, since he was uncontaminated by Original Sin (*was nouht foul*) and remained sinless (*ne ne misdede not*), but as an example (Matt. iii 15). Baptism is *prima Ecclesiae janua quae per Christam aperitur* (Anselm, *PL*, CLIX, 76).

249 **to baþe ... þee** if not mere repetition, this may refer not only to the immersion but to the touching of the baptismal candidate by the priest to 'signify washing' (*NCE*, II, 56).

251-2 **and for ... enemyes** F469-75 *Pours mains douter les ennemis* / *La crois il te metra u pis;* / *Derriere aussi et sus le chief,* / *Pour pou douter trestout meschief,* / *Il t'enoindra com champion,* / *A ce que tous un grant bouton* / *Tu ne prises tes anemis*; the syntax is ambiguous in F and ME: a sentence could end at *chief*/*heed*. A triple anointing is echoed in a thrice-made assurance that fear will be banished. The baptismal candidate is anointed on breast and back with Oil of Catechumens and then on the head with Chrism. See Aquinas, *ST*, 3a, q.66. a.10 whose sources for the graces conferred by the anointings may be Innocent II (*PL*, CCXV, 285) and Rabanus Maurus (*PL*, CXII, 1176), St Ambrose (*PL*, XVI, 431). Innocent's treatment is fullest.

252 **þine** F469 *les* var. *tes* MS. *A*[7].

a F470 *La*: τ weakened the meaning.

255 **as a chaumpioun** Aquinas (see n. 251-2) cites Ambrose's observation that the first anointing is as if for God's champion: *unctus es quasi athleta Christi* (*PL*, XVI, 419). For the use of *athleta* to mean 'champion' see Dobson, *Moralities*, pp. 96, 176.

255-6 **þou ... bodde** in view of F474-5 *un grant bouton* / *Tu ne prises*, GOS's reading, which omits only *grant*, is accepted. C used a common ME idiom *þou shalt sette at nouht* 'you won't give a rap (for)', but elsewhere retains the F idiom (the only two examples cited by *MED budde* 2c). This is one of the rare occasions when only O in the β-branch agrees with the α-branch's correct reading as preserved in GS. It looks as if β carried the literal reading glossed with the English idiom, and passed both on to δ: M accepted the gloss, J modified it and O retained the original

ÞE LYFE OF ÞE MANHODE

reading. C's reading is the result of contamination from the β-branch.

259 **he** in view of F481 *Cil* (or *Ce lui*) perhaps GS's *thylke* (which C would spell *thilke*) should be accepted, presupposing substitution of *he* by C and β.

260-1 **þere ... þerinne** Baptism by Triple Affusion (pouring of water), Immersion and Submersion was practised in the 13th and early 14th century. The first, probably intended here, is discussed by Aquinas, *ST*, 3a, q.66. a.8.

270 **whan ... cometh** F499 *quant mon point verrai* 'when I see my [right] moment': τ may have read *verrai* as *venra* 'will come'. The time in question does not come until line 1828.

271 **my** is C's normal form before all consonants apart from *h* and in one instance *w* (*myn werching* 855). There is no precedent in F501 for the repetition of the possessive pron. already expressed in 270 *my scrippe*. Perhaps it should be omitted, as if added by χ.

273-5 **First ... lamb** the newly baptised pilgrim sees the great Rood over the crossways of the Church he has just entered. Its centrality is literal as well as metaphorical, since the sacraments, which inform the greater part of Book 1, 'flowed from the side of Christ while he lay on the cross' (Augustine, cited by Aquinas, *ST*, 3a, q.17. a.1) and appear so in iconography (Rushforth, *Antiquaries Journal*). The redness of the cross is appropriate to the association (derived from I John i 7 and Apoc. vii 14) of the Blood and Baptism, and is not uncommon: the late 12th-century main east window at Poitiers (Aubert, pl. VI) shows Christ on a red cross symbolising his blood (Réau, II, part ii, 485).

274 **peynted reed** F506 *Paint*: if added by χ, the adjective should be omitted.

275-6 **þe ... forhed** the Tau leads us from the Baptismal connotations of the Rood, to the second of the seven sacraments, Confirmation, which by the 13th century consisted indispensably of the cross made in oil on the candidate's forehead by a bishop (who enters next). Tau is one of the *Pilgrimage*'s most complex images. Equivalent to the Greek T, it was one form of the Cross by the second century. Associated with God's mercy in Exodus, Ezechiel and the Apocalypse, it suggests the whole of church history from the Passover to the end of the world. In Exodus xii 7, God's mark or seal was made in blood on the lintels of the Israelites, to be passed over by God's vengeance. Exodus does not mention *thau*, but in iconography this mark has become one: the *Bible Moralisée* gives the Passover scene a Latin explanation meaning 'The sons of Israel making tau on their lintels signifies Christians making the sign of the cross on their foreheads.' At 281-2 reference is to Ezechiel ix 2-6, a vision of God's sparing those marked with God's *signum thau* (see n. 281). The blessed in Apoc. vii 14 (and ix 4, xiv 1) are not only washed with the

EXPLANATORY NOTES

blood of the Lamb, they are also marked on the forehead with God's sign, which in iconography (though not in the Bible) is again a Tau. It is a marvellously inclusive image with which to begin this section of Book 1, set in the church/Church. As a seal indicating ownership Tau is linked to the other example of multiple symbolism in Book 1: the Gift of Peace (see n. 1372).

277-80 **a maister ... Moyses** the *maister* is a bishop, *vicarie of Aaron or of Moyses*—themselves Types of Christ (Réau, II, part ii, 176): only he can ordain priests, administer Confirmation and consecrate Holy Oils (289). See Innocent III's decretal on these oils: *In Exodo quippe legitur praecepisse Dominus Moysu, ut Aaron et filious [sic] ejus inungeret, quatenus ei sacerdotio fungerentur* (*PL*, CCXV, 282, referring to Exod. xxviii, xxix). He is *faste by* because Confirmation would be administered under the Rood just mentioned: the Holy Oils were kept locked in the nearby sacristy in a cathedral, or chancel cupboard in a church (see n. 289-303).

279 **a yerde ... eende** Num. xvii 8. Aaron's rod is the Type of a bishop's crook (Réau, II, part ii, 215). It is curved at the top so that 'by consolation the bishop may attract the kindly' says Hugh St Victor (Deferrari, p. 278).

280 **horned** the tradition of Moses horned supposedly springs from a mistranslation in Vulgate Exod. xxxiv 29 of the Hebrew word for 'a ray of light' or 'horn'. When Aquinas explained the apparent confusion, the tradition was well established (Réau, II, part ii, 177). Mellinkoff suggests however that Jerome's use of *cornuta* 'horned' is a deliberate image of strength, honour and kingship. Moses is also horned as a mitred bishop. From about A.D. 1125 to 1200, mitres' two points, technically known as 'horns', were aligned like horns. The image here is archaic, perhaps because of the long tradition allegorising vestments (see n. 340).

281 **Ezechiel** Ezech. ix 2-6: the bishop now becomes Ezechiel's 'man clothed with linen', to whom God said: 'Go through the midst of Jerusalem, and set a mark upon the foreheads of the men that sigh and that cry for all the abominations that be done in the midst thereof', so that these should be spared in the slaughter of vengeance. Tau is thus a superb introduction to the episcopal duties (289-433) in which the bishop will be taught how to be discerning in the execution of God's justice.

285-7 **With ... forhed** F527-8 *Et de ce signe u front seignier / Me fist Grace Dieu et mercier* 'And with this sign Grace Dieu had me marked on the forehead and forgiven': τ om. *Et*, and either renders *seignier* by *blisse*, mistaking *mercier* for *marquer* 'mark', or transposes the infinitives, rendering *mercier* by *blisse*, and *seignier* by *marke*.

288 **neede þerof** F550 *mestier de l'oingement* 'need of the anointing-oil'.

nouht ... congruitee salvation is possible without Confirmation, which is, however, the sacrament of the 'fulness of grace', perfecting Baptism (Aquinas, *ST*, 3a, q.72); *congruitee* is therefore 'correctness' in this context. *MED* gives 'convenience', missing the theological point.

289-303 **Afterward ... oynement** the bishop consecrates the three Holy Oils: Oil of Catechumens and Chrism (for Baptism, Chrism being also used in Confirmation, the 'sacrament of chrism'), and Oil of the Sick (for Extreme Unction); all these he gives to *þe forseide official*, a priest. Details of their composition and use are given in *NCE*, VII, 81, their symbolism in Durandus, *Rationale*, I, viii (Neal and Webb, pp. 161-80).

293 **champiouns** τ om. F542 *Et autre chose n'en feras* 'and you shall not do anything else with them'.

293-303 **Þe ... oynement** after Baptism and Confirmation comes the third sacrament of the three using oil (Aquinas, *ST*, 3a, q.84. a.4). The sick or dying are anointed (Mark vi 13) for sin, as well as for sickness, not all over as *oueral* might suggest, but on eyes, ears, nostrils, mouth, hands and feet (the five senses), and sometimes loins (Aquinas, *ST*, 3a, q.32. a.8).

296-7 **to ... suer** F548 *loial mire leur* 'a true doctor to them': τ untypically added *and suer*.

303-8 **Of ... administracioun** the bishop anoints during Coronation, in consecrating bishops, conferring Holy Orders, consecrating altars, and administering Confirmation (the last and Holy Orders being sacraments, the others sacramentals).

305 **þe boord** (F565 *lestables*) should, strictly speaking, be *boords*, agreeing with *vicaryes* and *leches* as part of a general, not a particular, statement.

307 **withholde to myself** F567 *retien* does not repeat F561 *devers moi*, but τ has *to myself* here as well as *to meward* at 304, where F gives precedent for it.

310 **tweyne** Reason speaks to the two clerics about the difference between mercy and reprobation in their duties, so taking us from the liturgical use of oil to the wider symbol of healing oil, the 'consolation of good hope', and the Good Samaritan. Alanus de Insulis calls oil '*divina gratia*' (*PL*, CCX, 233); other mercy-connotations of oil are listed *PL*, CCXIX, 270, 175, 207).

311 **tour** F574 *tournelle* vars. *tourelle* MSS A^7GM^1, *tonnelle* MS. *L*. F usually means 'a little tower', and may simply derive from *Le Roman de la Rose* 2957 (Lecoy, I, 91), where Reason comes down from a tower (noted Hultman, p. 124, and Stürzinger). But the tower is out of place in a church, and it is not like Guillaume to be visually imprecise. The word and its variants can

EXPLANATORY NOTES 371

carry architectural meanings possibly relevant but unfortunately obscure. Godefroy *tornelette* mentions a framework round the top of a pillar, for people to stand in. Is Reason standing in an early form of pulpit? Godefroy *tournelle* also mentions a spiral staircase: since at 579 Reason seems to preach from the division between choir and nave, it may refer to the staircase which often leads from the *pulpitum*. She returns to her *tournelle* at 813 (F1500), but it is called *tour* almost at once (F1502), and may be referred to again in 816 (F1506).

316 **two** perhaps GS's *twey* should be accepted on the assumption that C and β found it archaic (*OED tway* does not record it after 1499).

317-18 **to¹ ... shitte** F586 *A plaie overte et a close* shows that *opne* and *shitte* are adj., not inf.

319-20 **for ... mysbifalleth** F590 *Quar trop rudesse i mesavient* 'for excessive roughness is most unfortunate': τ was perhaps misread by χ as if *mys* were the subject of *falleth*, necessitating the introduction of *of* at the beginning of what then became an adverbial phrase *of to gret rudeshipe mys bifalleth* 'for misfortune occurs as a result of excessive roughness'.

322-3 **þat ... lyouns** F595-6 *qui sont felons, | Qui sont cruelz comme lions*: τ replaced rel. *Qui* by *and*.

324 **levinge** F599 *lessier*: GS's reading is accepted not because it echoes F more accurately than C's *letinge* (which is arguable) but because it explains JMO (see p. liv).

336 **vengeaunce** Deut. xxxii 35; in view of F620 *vengement* JMO's reading is accepted, but perhaps τ used the pl., and β normalised.

339 **answerde ... seide** F625 *Respondu*: *and seide* is an otiose tag.

340 **whi ... horned** the horns of the mitre usually meant the Old and New Testaments, weapons against enemies. This and the association with Moses are explicit in the episcopal consecration: *Imponimus, Domine, capiti huius Antistitis, et agonistae tui galeam munitionis et salutis, quatenus decorata facie, et armato capite, cornibus utriusque Testamenti terribilis appareat adversariis veritatis; et, te ei largiente gratiam, impugnator eorum robustus existat, qui Moysi famuli tui faciem ex tui sermonis consortio decoratam, lucidissimis tuae claritatis et veritatis cornibus insigniti* (Andrieu, *Le Pontifical*, III, 389 and the *Souvenir of Consecration*, a record of a modern consecration of an Irish bishop). Mellinkoff (pp. 97-98) cites the *Pontificale* and observes that it is still in use. Durandus also said *Duo cornua sunt duo charitatis praecepta* (Avino, p. 12), and Rabanus Maurus called the horns *sancti potestas justorum* (*PL*, CXII, 903). I find no precedent for their being corrective goads: 'only in Deguileville do we find extensive and novel interpretation of the horns of Moses' (Mellinkoff, p. 197).

341-2 **for ... dedes** F629-30 *pour punicions | Des maus faire et corrections*; vars. for *punicions, punicion* MSS. *HH¹GLM¹M*; for *corrections, correction* MSS *HH¹AG*; for *mau faire, maus fais* MSS *H¹A⁷*.

343-52 **prikke ... rigurowse** Durandus' 13th-century 'Pontificale of Mende' gives the ceremony in which a bishop receives his pastoral staff: *Accipe baculum pastorale officij. et sis in corrigendis uiciis pie seuiens iudicium sine ira tenens in fouendis uirtutibus auditorum animos demulcens in tranquillitate serenitatis censuram non deserens* (BL MS. Add. 39677 ff. XXX^r-XXX^v, modern foliation 31^r-31^v; see also Andrieu, I, 149). Durandus' *Rationale*, III, xv, para. 4, referring to the point, shaft and crook of the staff, says *Pontifex debet pungere pigros, regere debiles sui rectitudine, & colligere vagos*.

356 **þouh** Since *all* is present in GSM's *all thowgh* as well as JO's *ʒif alle*, perhaps the reading should be *al þouh*. On the other hand, more than one scribe might have added *all*.

356-7 **þouh ... shuldest** F655-7 *comment cornu soies, | Par justice toutevoies | En ton cuer dois avoir pitie* 'even if you are horned, in the interests of justice you ought to have pity in your heart'. *Par justice* modifies *dois*. τ read *Par* as *Por* 'for', and so regarded *for iustice* as modifying *horned*.

360 **any ... staf** F662 *verge ne baston* leads us to expect simply *yerde oþer staf*, but all the English MSS have an additional word before *yerde* (*any* CJ, *eyther* GMOS). The correct reading might be *either yerde* or *any yerde*, chosen because F661 *aguillon*, which ought to give simply *prikke*, was rendered *any prikke*.

363 **þan ... art** F668 *Que cil dont tu es vicaire* shows that this is one of the rare occasions when only M in the β-branch preserves the original reading apparent in CGS (apart from substitution of *he* for *þilke*). JO mistook a form of *whos* 'whose' for *was*.

365 **made ... passe** Exod. xiv 21-2; perhaps GS's *made Israell passe* should be accepted.

368 **naked** om. F678 *Des cornes* 'of horns'.

375 **þilke** τ read F692 *tel* 'such' as *cel*.

377 **foord** F695 *rivage* 'bank' var. *passage* MS. *T*.

378 **assaye** om. F696 *le passaige* 'the ford', presumably because it occurs, in τ's variant text of F, at the end of the previous line (n. 377).

381 **Pontifex** (? from *pontem facere*, but the etymology is debated) is a Roman or Jewish high-priest, hence also a Christian bishop, bridge between God and man: *Pontifex princeps sacerdotum est, quasi via sequentium, ipse et summus sacerdos, ipse et pontifex maximus nuncupatur: ipse enim efficit sacerdotes atque levitas, ipse omnes ordines ecclesiasticos disponit, ipse quid unusquisque facere debeat ostendit* (Isidore, *Etymologiae*, PL, LXXXII, 291); Ponti-

fex vero princeps sacerdotum est, quasi pons et via sequentium factus (Durandus, *Rationale*, II, ch. xi (Avino, p. 95)).

383-96 **whi ... place** probably refers to a bishop's general guardianship of the Church, but may refer specifically to the dedication of churches, reserved to a bishop. Relevant acts in the ceremony, described by Durandus, *Rationale*, I, ch. vi (Neale and Webb, pp. 111-36), are the expulsion of the devil from the building, the bishop's striking the threshold with his staff and giving the cry made familiar in dramatisations of the Harrowing of Hell: *Attollite portas principes vestras...*, cleansing the church by sprinkling holy water. See Hugh St Victor, *In Speculum*, pp. 711-12.

392 **ysen** F722 *issir* supports GS's *ysene*: C substituted *goon*, though using *ysede, ysinge* at 113, 114, *ysen* at 1214.

392-3 **þe tweyne ... place** (F723 *labelles*) are *infulae* or strips hanging from the mitre of a bishop or archbishop: *duos fimbrias, seu ligulas ... denotantes ejus promptitudinem ad fidei, et sacrae Scripturae defensionem, etiam usque ad sanguinis effusionem*—De Mitra, in *Rationale*, III, ch. xiii (Durandus, p. 119); ibid., para. 4 describes them as two things to be remembered, the acts of God and the wearer's sins, which are to act like the bells worn by Aaron (Exod. xxxix 25), warning that the good are to be received to, and the evil excluded from, the offered sacrifice. I find no precedent for the bishop's winning them, nor for their association with church dedication (n. 383-96). Perhaps this is a heraldic extension of the traditional image of vestments as armour (see n. 397-8): a label is either a band across the top of a shield, having dependent points or tabs, or it is one of those very points (Brault, pp. 223-4). Perhaps *infulae*, hanging over the stylised hood of a cope, reminded the poet of a shield and labels, as in the diagram, indicating the bishop's rank as a prince of the church, or his prowess in spiritual battle. In England the label is the chief mark of cadency, but the French royal family, which usually used the *bordure* for this purpose, also used the label, especially in Normandy (Gayre, pp. 45-51). It might also be an Augmentation of Honour awarded for special service. The two-point label can also be sole charge (Woodward, p. 200; Renesse, III, 171-89; VII, 264).

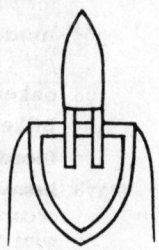

397-8 **Grace ... inne** the bishop should often wear the vestments which are symbolic of past victory over, and continuing struggle against, evil. Equation of episcopal vestments with armour is traditional: see n. 340, and Honorius of Autun (*PL*, CLXXII, 566-7); Durandus, *Rationale*, III, i (Avino, p. 58, or Passmore for the English translation): *vestibus sacris, quasi armis induitur, arma, quibus Pontifex ... armari debet contra spirituales nequitias*

ÞE LYFE OF ÞE MANHODE

pugnaturus.

402 **nih ... newe** the awkward ME is the result of τ's having misplaced *fresh* after reading F740 *pres | De bataillier nouviaus et fres* as if *pres ... et fres* were a divided phrase.

407 **þiself ... hem** at 4914 Avarice shows the pilgrim the king using the bishop's staff to undermine the Church.

410 **hornes ... snayle** the snail signified harmlessness (Randall, pl. LXIV): 'the coward is like those who dare not enter the straight and narrow way for fear of the snail which shows its horns' (Brother Laurent, *Somme le roi* [cited Mâle, *The Gothic Image*, p. 123]). O's gloss *Epī cornua siliā testudini spac*' clearly compares snail-horns and mitre, whatever the last word is (cf. Ovid, *Metamorphoses*, III, 20-1: *spatiosam cornibus altis frontem*). The use of *testudo* for 'snail' is attested by *OED snail* (Ælfric). The 13th-century Cistercian Odo of Cheriton (Vacant, XI, 936-7) uses the word, comparing snail-horns with a mitre: *Testudo duo cornus erigit; sed cum palea vel spina tanguntur, cornua retrahit, et infra testam se includit. Ita est de episcopus cornutis: quando leui tribulatione uel adversitate tanguntur, cornua sua retrahunt, et quandoque fugiunt, quandoque in cameris se includunt, et non opponunt se muros pro domo Domini* (Hervieux, IV, 219-20, and II, 628). For Odo's possible influence on Book 4 see Gewande, p. 38.

412-15 **Seynt ... free** Thomas Becket (c. A.D. 1118 1170) upheld the rights of the Church against Henry II, and threatened England with interdict in A.D. 1169. It is natural that Guillaume should cite this example: during his quarrels with the English king, Archbishop Becket stayed for two years in Chaalit's motherhouse of Pontigny, where he had many books copied for his library, then stayed at the Benedictine abbey of St Colombe, Sens (Robertson and Sheppard, III, 325-476, especially 357).

416-23 **of ... lyfe** St Ambrose (c. A.D. 339-397), Bishop of Milan, refused the Arian Emperor Valentinian II and his mother Justina the use of churches in Milan. When in 385 they tried to force him to surrender the basilica of Portius, outside Milan walls, Ambrose offered his wealth, freedom and life but refused to surrender his church (*PL*, XVI, 997, and Dudden, p. 275).

425-6 **þin ... fynger** F783-4 *ta maison que espouse as | Et dont l'anel en ton doit as* 'your house which you have married, and whose ring you have on your finger'. *Pontifex ergo annulum portat, ut se sponsum Ecclesiae agnoscat, ac pro illa animam, si necesse fuerit, sicut Christus ponat* (Honorius of Autun, *PL*, CLXXII, 609).

430 **goode Moyses** Exod. vii-xii; the bishop must maintain the Church's freedom from evil, as Moses gained and held his people's freedom from Pharaoh, traditionally equated with the devil (*Bible Moralisée*, ff. 36-48). The bishop was merely *like* a representative of Aaron or Moses at 278; here at 430 he is told

EXPLANATORY NOTES 375

he 'would be' *goode Moyses* if he used his authority against evil. By 434 he is Moses, Type of Christ. The section on episcopal duty (304-433) has been cleverly included at the end of the treatment of the first three sacraments, each requiring the use of Holy Oils consecrated by a bishop (the uses of them reserved to the bishop were listed at 303-8). Here at 434-5 the priest takes the Oils away, leaving the bishop listening to Reason while the priest turns to officiate at Matrimony, where the bishop's presence is unnecessary.

431 **with ... mes** F792 *de son bon mes* 'as her faithful spokesman': τ read *mes* 'spokesman' as the cognate word *mes* 'serving of food' or 'company of people eating together'.

436-46 **And ... þens** Matrimony, usually last in the lists of the sacraments, is treated here to allow the final emphasis to be placed on the Eucharist which informs most of Book 1. It is briefly dealt with, perhaps because at it a priest merely officiates: his presence is not indispensable (Aquinas, *ST*, 3a, q.42. a.1). It is also the only sacrament irrelevant to the dreamer's monastic life.

The groom's arrival from the East suggests his association with Christ (Eph. v 25), coming from the sun's rising: Petrus Lombardus speaks of *Matrimonium ... tenens imaginem Christi et Ecclesiae* and Augustine says *Conjugii sacramentum in Christo et in Ecclesia magnum, in viro et uxore minimum* (*PL*, CXCII, 1586 and XLIV, 427 respectively).

437-8 **þe official** F805 *li*: a rare example of τ replacing pron. with sb. for clarity.

439 **togidere** should perhaps be *togideres*, accepting G's reading as the rarer form.

441-3 **Neuere ... Moises** F811-14 *Ja mais en jour de vo(stre) vie | De vous n'iert fait departie, | Se certaine cause n'i a | Et par Moysen* 'separation of you two shall never be made, unless there is good reason, and [unless the separation is made] by Moses'; the ME echoes the awkward syntax, which led C to add *it be do* after *þere*, and M to replace *and* by *foundyn*. The passage refers to 'reservations': to the bishop's authorisation of legal separation, to the Pope's authorisation of dissolution of marriage. Adultery is the only ground for separation (Matt. v 32 and xix 9). A man with evidence of her adultery may forbid his wife his bed on his own initiative, but may forbid her his house only on the judgement of the Church. The wife has similar privileges. Aquinas, *ST*, 3 Supp., q.62. aa.3, 4 gives further details. Neither spouse may remarry (ibid., a.5; I Cor. vii 10, 11). Formal separation does not dissolve marriage. Aquinas, *ST*, 3a, q.67. a.3 discusses Mosaic divorce with great clarity, but ibid. a.2 is cryptic about circumstances permitting dissolution of Christian marriage. The account in *Codex iuris canonici* is summarised in *NCE*, IX, 273: dissolution is 'a matter of law by subsequent solemn religious profession, and by virtue of a dispensation granted by the pope in view of a just cause'. The NT foundations of these laws are discussed in *NCE*, IV, 930. Since they relate to Mosaic Law, *Moises* may appear not only in his papal capacity but as Moses.

445 **þat ... shulden** an example (like 422 and 437–8 but rare) of τ substituting a longer phrase, perhaps finding F817 *ce* 'this' abrupt.

446 **Þe ... ayen** the priest goes back to stand by *Moyses*, the bishop; he is not mentioned again until 534.

went F820 *rest alez* 'went back': τ perhaps wished to avoid repetition after *turnede ayen*.

452–5 **And ... wise** the bishop administers First Tonsure, which admits laymen to the clerical state. This ceremony (not a sacrament) was distinct from and preceded Minor Orders: hair was cut from five places on the head (see n. 486). Hugh St Victor derives the practice from Ezek. v 1 and Acts xvii 18 (Deferrari, p. 260). Further details are in Maskell, III, lxxxiii-xc (the Rite is pp. 144–51); *NCE*, VII, 85.

454 **God ... heritage** 'You shall possess nothing ... neither shall you have a portion ... I am thy portion and inheritance' Num. xviii 20.

458–9 **to feyne folye** I Cor. iv 9–10: 'God hath set forth us apostles, the last, as it were men appointed to death. We are made a spectacle to the world and to angels and to men. We are fools for Christ's sake ...'; the tonsure, originating in the practice of shaving slaves' heads to humble and mark them, was adopted by Christian religious as a sign of humility (*NCE*, XIV, 199d). The Western tonsure was also associated with the Crown of Thorns (Réau, III, pt. iii, 1083).

463 **If ... folie** F851 *Se il ne tient a vo folie* 'if it [this holy folly] is not compatible with your folly'; for the ME idioms *long on* and *long of* see *MED*, *OED long* a²: *long of* is commoner after the 15th century. GS's *long on* is likely to reflect τ (corrupted by C into *long in*), JMO's *long of* being a modernisation. But the ME phrase, unless it carries the unrecorded meaning 'belong to', means 'attributable to' or 'on account of': τ took *tient a* in its other sense 'is owing to'.

463–4 **ye ... me** F852 *vous ne me volez mie*: perhaps G's reading, lacking *haue* (supplied by the corrector), should be accepted as more literal.

465–82 **I ... vices** Reason recommends moderation and rationality to new religious. The theme appears in Plato's *Phaedrus*, where the soul is like a charioteer controlling two winged horses (Fowler, pp. 471–503), in Boethius' *Consolation of Philosophy*,

EXPLANATORY NOTES

III, prose 3, and in Alanus de Insulis' *Anticlaudian*, IV, chs. 2–4, where Reason's chariot to God is pulled by the bridled horses of the five senses.

465 **discerned** in view of F856 *Discerne* GMOS's reading is accepted.

470 **lordes** F864 *seigneur* var. *seigneurs* MSS *AM*.

ye wole F865 *voules*: C altered something to *eyþer* to anticipate *oþere* in 471; perhaps the reading should be *ye wol*, which C has at 464 (*ye wol do* at 1076), but his usual form is *ye wole*.

471 **argumentes ... me** F866–7 *argumens,* | *Sans moy*: if Stürzinger's punctuation is right, the comma should follow *argumentes*.

471–2 **shul ... confusioun** F867–8 *n'arez conclusion* | *Qui ne viengne a confusion* is not in Whiting or Hassell, but cf. Chaucer's *Canon's Yeoman's Tale*, 1082–3 and *A Complaint to Mars*, 257–8.

472 **þat ... come** F868 *Qui ne viengne*; the reading is in doubt, GS's being accepted as more literal.

474–80 **Ye ... Rose** in counselling avoidance of gluttony, anger and lust, Reason may be anticipating her exegesis of the tonsure, following. Paulinus of Nola (c. A.D. 353–431) says: *Peccata nostra, quibus super capillos capitis multiplicatis animam habemus impexam non (e) accisione medii tondeantur, sed ad vivum quasi novacula radente perimantur ... vitamque nostram ... Deo in castitate et parsimona consecremus* (*PL*, LXI, 262).

479–80 **þat ... Rose** Reason is forced to leave the unheeding Lover in *Le Roman de la Rose* 7200 (Lecoy, I, p. 221).

482 **vices** om. F888 *Et de bien se dessaisonne* 'and gives up good', var. om. F888 MS. *A*.

485 **A gardyn** F893 *un courtil* 'a small courtyard', but at this date its distinction from the *hortus conclusus* (see n. 485–6) was fine.

485–6 **A ... wal** Reason's comparing the tonsure to a walled stronghold refers back to her insistence (465–72) on the importance of purity in religious life: the tonsure actually and symbolically surrounds what Rabanus Maurus calls 'the castle of our mind' (*PL*, CXII, 885). The *anima pia* was frequently called a *hortus* — a garden protected from the outside world: Gregory the Great said this *hortus* was *virtutem castitatis per continentiam munitae* (*PL*, LXXIX, 399). *PL*, CCXIX, 171 lists many such references.

486–8 **Þe ... empechement the** tonsured head, the *place within vnheled*, is open to God, symbolising religious' desire for direct access to him. Honorius of Autun (*PL*, CLXXII, 603) and Hugh St Victor explain: 'The top of the head is the top of the mind. The baring of the head signifies the illumination of the mind ... the opening and unveiling of the senses, that is, of the eyes and of the ears, that occupation with earthly things, which are

ÞE LYFE OF ÞE MANHODE

signified by the hair, may not impede him from hearing and understanding the words of God' (Deferrari, pp. 259-60). See Maskell, III, lxxxviii-xc (especially n. 57) and 226-7 for these symbols in English rites.

489 **maketh** in view of F899 *fait*, GJMO's reading is accepted in place of C's *þat maketh* which may account for the alteration in the next line.

þat ye haue in view of F900 *Que... aiez* GMO's reading is accepted; the meaning (from 488 *Þe*) is 'the circle [of the tonsure] makes an enclosure all the way round so that you have...'.

490 **him** F901 *li* refers to *le monde*, so G's literal reading is accepted.

490-1 **ye... parte** Matt. vi 24. F901-2 *vous faut departir, | S'a vostre Dieu voulez partir* var. for F902: *Se auec dieu voulez venir*. τ retained the word-play: 'you must leave the world if you want to leave [set out] with your God'; his source carried the *auec* var.

494 **youre partye** see n. 454.

495 **whan... parte** F910 *quant aucun s'i veult partir* 'when anyone wants to divide [something]' is another play on *parte*.

499 **al þe remenaunt** F916 *un tout* 'an all': τ weakened the meaning 'the part is worth as much as the complete whole', saying the part is worth as much as the rest of the whole.

500 **is** τ did not retain the admonitory subj. F917 *soit* 'let it be'.

501-2 **walleth... departeth** F918-20 *(vous) enmuro | En vous du monde dessevrant | Et vostre part bien departant*: *En* governs *dessevrant* and *departant*, so τ should have used *departinge* instead of *departeth*.

502-3 **is to yow** the impersonal subj. construction F921-2 *aussi vous soit | Bel* confused τ: the tonsure 'ought to seem attractive to you [as a sign of your office]'. As at 500, he weakened the meaning.

503 **ye... heerdes** F923 *bonnes ovailles estes* 'you are well cared for little sheep' (*ovailles* fem. pl. from Lat. *ovicula*): the good shepherd has shorn, not skinned them. These wearers of the tonsure may also be good sheep in that they give 'wool'. J. Evans, *Art in Mediaeval France*, p. 97, observes that Charity's attribute is sometimes a 'lamb, that gives its own wool': see the south porch of Chartres, the west facade of Notre Dame, Paris (Freyhan, p. 13), and Amiens (Mâle, *L'Art religieux du XIII*^{e}, p. 114). To Rupert of Tuy a sheep shows generosity in its sacrifice of flesh, milk, fleece and skin (*PL*, CLXVIII, 1212). But *heerdes* may mean 'flocks (of sheep)' or 'shepherds'. τ either knew that *ovailles* meant 'little sheep' (in which case *heerde* at 504 for 'shepherd' is confusing) or thought it derived from Lat. *ovilio* 'shepherd', and so ignored the sense (religious are not 'sheared' because they are shepherds).

507 **al** τ read F931 *Coustel* 'a knife' as *Tous tel* 'all this'.

EXPLANATORY NOTES

509 **hise** τ read F934 *ces* as *ses* (if *ces* is not a form of *ses*).

509-56 **Whan ... freend** the bishop confers the four Minor and three Major Orders: *ostiarius, lector, exorcista, acolythus, subdiaconus, diaconus, presbyter (et episcopus)* (Isidore, *PL*, LXXXII, 290, 293 my brackets). They are described by Hugh St Victor, *De Sacramentis*, bks. II, III, iv-xi (Deferrari, pp. 261-9). Their rituals of ordination are in Durandus, *Rationale*, II, iv (Berthélemy, II, 181-205), and Maskell, III, 154-225. Commentaries are in Puniet, pp. 122-40, Maclean, pp. 78-82, and Andrieu, 'Les Ordres Mineurs ...'. Many are illustrated in *NCE*, X, 730-4. Examples of the Orders in art are in Cabrol and Leclercq, I, 3207-8 and XIV, ii, 1531-2.

511 **priuees** F938 *huissiers* 'door-keepers' refers to the first of the Minor Orders (see n. 512). One expects *porters* or *vssheres*, used at 693-4 in rendering F1265-6 *Huissier / Du dit passage et portier*. The ME Bible used *keper, vscher*, and *porter* in passages prefiguring or describing Minor Orders, e.g. I Chron. xv 23-24 (Cambridge University Library, MS. Mm. 2. 15, f. 112ʳ), John x 3 (Cambridge University Library, MSS Add. 6684, f. 219ᵛ; Mm. 2. 15, f. 319ᵛ). The office of Porter would be so familiar that I have wondered whether τ wrote *porters*, subsequently altered (since misreading seems unlikely) by χ, thus obscuring the first clue to the allegory of Minor Orders. The variants suggest that τ wrote *priuees* 'personal servants', stressing the privileged nature of the service performed. *OED privy* B suggests 'confidante' but under A2 illustrates the adj. by *priue chamburlaine*, and our text has *[priuees]) of his hous and chamberlaynes* (see n. 512). τ might not at first have realised that the symbolic keeping of door-keys was more important than the idea of confidentiality.

C, consulting a β-branch MS (to check *priuees*?) altered his reading to *princes*. One possible explanation may be no more than coincidence. I Chron. ix (familiar in Aquinas, *ST*, 3a Suppl., q.37. a.2) describing the appointment of Levites as keepers of the temple doors, refers not only to *porters*, but also to *princes*:

> to þes foure leuytis was bytaken [MS bytakem] alle þe noumbre of porters and þei / were kepyng priue housis in þe tresouris ... þes be þe princes of syngers by þe mey/nees of leuytis · þat dwelliden in priue chaumbris · so þat day and nyȝt contynuly þey seruen in þe seruyse þe heuedis of leuytis by her mey/nees princes dwelliden in jerusalem.

(Cambridge University Library MS. Add. 6681, f. 144ʳ,ᵛ). Perhaps β, recognising the general context, recalled this account of 'princes'—people of special responsibility in the house of God— and so misread *priuees* as *princes*, C following suit.

512 **chamberleynes** F939 *chambellans* (see n. 511). In the early church the porter's main function was to guard the church

doors. The lay office became one of the Minor Orders in third-century Rome. A Porter (*chamberleyne*) has access to his master's private rooms: essential to this ordination is the presentation of keys. It is omitted here, perhaps to avoid confusion with 551 ff., where keys (of the Kingdom) are given with the priesthood, last of the three Major Orders. Following Isidore (n. 509-56), Aquinas lists a Porter's other duties: to tend those not yet prepared for communion, to exclude notorious sinners and unbelievers, to ring the bell, open the church, spread the book for the preacher (*ST*, 3a Suppl., q.37. a.2). The passage following shows the increasing dignity of the Orders as they proceed.

513 **sergeauntes** Exorcists, third in Minor Orders though second here: *NCE*, V, 750 gives further details. The *enemyes þat ben in þe bodyes* are evil spirits possessing a human body. The gravity of the exorcist's function and the stringent requirements for those fulfilling it perhaps explain why the poet calls them *sergeauntes*: they were 'managers of the temple of God' (Hugh St Victor, *PL*, CLXXVI, 425), 'temple' here meaning both the church and the body.

515 **his** τ read F945 *saint* 'holy' as *sien*?

515-16 **rederes** Lectors, second in Minor Orders though third here, read the epistles (only in that sense *preche*), and sing or chant some other parts of the Mass (*NCE*, VIII, 601).

516 **candeles** Acolytes, fourth in Minor Orders, assist at the altar, light its candles, pour water and wine, carry the processional candle. At ordination they receive a candlestick with an unlighted candle, and an empty cruet (*NCE*, I, 86).

518 **gilte ... void** the empty chalice given with a paten during the ordination of a Subdeacon, lowest in the three Major Orders, to signify that he may assist at the Offertory of the Mass before wine and bread are offered (*NCE*, XIII, 756 lists other privileges). Rushforth, pl. IX and pp. 93-4 lists examples of this scene in art.

519 **ooþere** om. F954 *sans mentir* (a tag, lit. 'without lying'), as at 657. At 670, where F1221 is emphatic, *sans point mentir* becomes *withoute lesinge*.

520-4 **bodi** F955 *jou* 'yoke' vars. *douz* MSS *oT*, *non* MSS *BH*, *crois* MSS *AH*¹, *cors* MS. *A*⁷. τ saw the last. Even French scribes found the reference (Matt. xi 29-30) difficult. The *jou* is the symbolic stole placed across the left shoulder of a Deacon at ordination: *On place encore l'étole sur l'épaule gauche du diacre, parce qu'il confient d'asservir les choses du temps a celles de l'esprit, ou bien parce qu'il faut que la droite du diacre soit libre et dégagée, afin qu'il assiste le prêtre avec plus de facilité* (Durandus, *De Stola* in *Rationale*, III, v, iv [Berthélemy, I, 233]). Durandus (ibid., p. 190) explains that as Hugh St Victor says 'Whatever labour and patience we endure in this life we bear on the left, as it were,

EXPLANATORY NOTES 381

until we have the [sic] rest on the right, that is, in eternity' (Deferrari, p. 265; *PL*, CLXXVI, 426, 427). Hugh also compares Deacons to the Levites who at the age of twenty were strong enough to carry the Ark and Tabernacle—but no mention is made of the left shoulder. The variant *cors*, giving *bodi*, is an understandable substitution: a Deacon may distribute the Host (*bere þe bodi of Ihesu Crist*). *NCE*, XIII, 722 and IV, 677 give further details.

525 **Whan ... ordeyned** may be a pun on 'arranged' and 'ordained [as clergy]'. The first six Orders have been conferred, but we do not proceed at once to the Priesthood. The allegory now proceeds in a new way, in a kind of slow motion, until the end of Book 1: it is as if the Mass itself were going on, but interrupted on several occasions. The first of these is at 530 (see n.).

526-7 **Þe ... redy** in view of F967 *La table alerent aprester* G's reading is accepted, *bord* being the direct object of *made redy*.

527 **to dine** F968 *disner*: as at 531, 776, the meal is probably breakfast (late Lat. *disjunare for *disjejunare* 'to break a fast').

528 **cloþes** the ceremonial coverings of an altar 'table' (Jungman, I, 53, n. 52 and p. 257) and associated linen (ibid., II, 60).

530 **water** the mingling of water with wine in the Eucharistic chalice originated with the Passover supper. It came to symbolise the union of Christ with his Church, of the divine and human natures in his person, and of the water and blood from his side (Jungman, II, 39-40). The procedure is explained by Ambrose (*PL*, XVI, 465-6) and Aquinas (*ST*, 3a, q.74. a.6). It might occur before Mass, at various places during Mass before the Offertory, or immediately before the Offertory, as it is now (Jungman, II, 60, n.98). Perhaps it is here intended to take us from the initial preparation of the altar (the spreading of cloths and provision of elements) to the Offertory itself, in a sketched allegory of the Mass. If this is so, Moses (Celebrant, Christ-figure and Bishop) reaches the moment just before the Consecration (which only a priest can perform) and pauses to confer the priesthood on others (544-7). The last of the Major Orders and the beginning of an allegorisation of the Mass may thus be skilfully integrated. This is followed by a long allegory of clerical duties: the Mass is not resumed until 776. See Avril Henry, 'The Structure of Book I of Þe Pilgrimage of þe Lyfe of þe Manhode,' for fuller analysis of this formal device, and others.

531 **he wente** F975 *alast*: C's *þei* probably continued the pl. subject of the preceding sentences. Just possibly, he read *he* as the native nom. pl. pers. pron. (OE *heo*)—at this date common in Norfolk and Suffolk, possible in nearby Cambridgeshire and North Essex: a few examples occur in Chambers and Daunt (cited Mustanoja, p. 134).

dinere the meal is the Eucharistic sacrifice and communion (see

n. 527). τ replaced F975 *disner* by a sb., or his *dine* was misread as *diner* by χ, and so should be the reading.

537 **hauteyn** should perhaps be unemended, as *MED hautein* 1c. records variants with the *-aun-* form. However, these occur under the influence of *haunten* v.2, from OF *hontoiier* 'to scorn'. If one discounts *MED*'s citation of this example under 1c, the only *-aun-* form is from *The Pardoner's Tale*, where there are connotations of scorn. There no reliable evidence for *-aun-* forms when the word simply means 'loud', as here.

541-2 **she ledde me** F996 *la [me] mena*: perhaps GS's *me* should read *him*: C's *me* is over erasure, and most French MSS read *la mena* (easily misunderstood as *l'a mena*). But the sense would be poor in F.

542 **whan ... he** F997-8 *quant la vi pres de li, / Moyses* 'when I saw her near him, Moses...'. τ's apparently small modification has damaged the allegory. Here, as at 781, the priest calls Grace at the beginning of the sacrament, but shows no awareness of her, and although she gave him the keys (551) she nowhere addresses him directly. He does not need to see Grace given in order to perform his function.

544 **anoynede** F1001 *enoinst* var. *enioynst* MS. *T*: the ordinand's hands are anointed before being joined. CGJOS's forms of *ioynede* may originate in attraction from *ioynede* six words later, but similar confusion arose in F, whose variant *enioinst* τ may have seen, in which case there should be no emendation. The emendation is in the *an-* form (in spite of F, and the fact that C uses only *en-* forms of the verb) because *enoienen* is rare; but perhaps *enoynede*, or even *enoyntede* (from the commoner *enointen*) should be used.

544-56 **First ... freend** the priesthood, third of the Major Orders, is conferred. The sacerdotal symbols which should be received (the stole on the right shoulder, and the chasuble) are replaced by Sword and Keys, providing an opening for discussion of priestly duties (nn. 551, 580-690). Moreover, the Sword which in the hands of Cherubyn banished man from paradise, and represented Death (32-43), is now, in the hands of priests, the instrument of God's merciful justice in readmitting him (548). The Sword carries connotations of preaching, discernment, discipline and punishment (*PL*, CCXIX, 203) and as 770 suggests, signifies ecclesiastical jurisdiction (*NCE*, VIII, 61-3).

547 **variable** (F1006 *variable*) can mean 'flashing as it moves' or 'versatile': *varie* at 652, where the reference is to a judge's freedom to use point, edge or flat, suggests the latter meaning.

549-50 **wel ... figured** F1010 *Figure bien proprement*: the Sword is well made, but in both languages the participle suggests that this priestly sword was prefigured by Cherubyn's.

550 **he took hem** om. F1011 *moy present* 'while I was there', perhaps

EXPLANATORY NOTES

by eyeskip to the end of the next line, *en fist present*. The omission is not insignificant: the phrase underlines the dreamer's indignation (expressed at 556) at not receiving keys.

551 **a key** F1013 *unes cles* 'a pair of keys' (compare 670 ff.) var. *une clef*. The variant sg. may be due to familiarity with the Key of Ministry (Aquinas, *ST*, 3a, q.17. a.1), distinct from the Keys used in absolution.

552 **hireself** see Godefroy, *acusance* for C's (? 17th-century) marginalium.

567 **þan ... closed** F1041 *Que ne fait fontaine enclose* 'Does it not make a well closed ...'.

568 **dar ... approche** in view of F1042 *approchier n'ose* G's reading (supported to some extent by JMO's *dar come nere*) is accepted.

569 **profitable, so good** in view of F1043-4 *profitable, | Si bonne*, G's reading is accepted, γ and β having smoothed.

571 **goodnesses** F1047 *bien* var. *biens* MSS HH^1: perhaps GOS's *goodschepes* should be accepted on the assumption that C normalised—compare 582 where for F sg. *bienfait* I accept GJMO's *goodshipe* in place of C's *goodnesse*.

578 **counforted ayen** F1059 *reconforte* 'comforted': τ thought there was a verb *conforter*, here with a prefix?

579 **þe chayere** F1061 *prone* 'the grille or railing separating choir from nave, or the space enclosed thereby, where notices were given and addresses delivered'. If τ did not read *trone* 'throne'— at 1572 Wisdom is indeed discovered on her *chayere* (F *cheoire*)— *chayere* may carry its meaning 'dais' (raised front of the chancel) as in *MED chaiere* n. 2b. No throne has been mentioned in the surroundings or in connection with Reason, but she might preach from a raised area such as a *pulpitum* spanning the building at this point (see n. 311).

580-690 **Lordinges ... shulde** this section on the sacerdotal duty to combat evil in the souls of men is contained by the allegory of the Eucharist, celebration of which is the priest's primary function.

589-97 **Þe ... suspeccioun** F1079-93: Gewande (p. 29) notes the similarity here to the 13th-century Renclus de Moiliens' *Roman de Carite* 44.24.

590 **deserueth** F1080 *dessert* 'deserves' or 'executes' is equally ambiguous, but in F the latter is more likely, and at 526 *deserue* means 'perform, execute'.

594 **þe execucioun** F1086 *la discution* 'the discussion' gives good sense, and vars. *distinction, dissention* MSS H, H^1 are technical terms in formal disputation, so their connotations are correct.

596 **surquideoures** the spelling is in doubt. *OED surquidrous* (as distinct from *surquidous*) cites C's reading as 'doubtful', and

cites no other example until Caxton: perhaps G's *suurquiderous* or S's *surquydrous* should be accepted.

598-9 **at þe tastinge** F1095 *a tastons* 'by touching' or 'by feel' refers to the fumbling sword-stroke of a blind man. τ thought the phrase meant 'at a touch'.

601 **meselrie** F1100 *meselerie* 'leprosy' is perhaps used to mean 'disease'.

602 **þe lasse** literal rendering of F1101 *la mendre* would require a superlative (which J has), rare in ME in comparisons between two (Mustanoja, p. 285).

604-5 **departinge of throte** Isidore, *Etymol.* (*PL*, LXXXII, 644): *Proprie autem appellatur gladius, quod gulam dividit, id est, cervicem secat* (noted by Wright). This traditional etymology (GuLAmDIVidit) is extended to refer to the priest/judge's skill in discerning truth from falsehood in what is said—a kind of dissection. See Heb. iv 12-13?

aughten alle juges F1109 *tout juge ... veut* 'every judge should': τ causes confusion by his use of pl. here and sg. in 607-8.

607 **he ... allegge** F1110-11 *allignier | Il a oui* 'he has heard given in evidence': τ copied F's construction (*oir* plus inf.) using inf. with passive meaning and ellipsis of object, common after verbs of perception (e.g. 'I heard tell').

610-11 **wherto ... telle** F1115 *Pour quoi .I. seul pas ne soufist* 'why one alone is not enough': τ mistook negative *pas* for *pas* 'step'.

616 **grete horned** might refer to the bishop (Moses) or, more probably, the Pope, to each of whom absolution of some serious sins is reserved.

617 **And for þat in view of** F1125 *Et pour (ce) qu'* GS's reading is accepted in place of C's *And for as michel as* over erasure of a shorter phrase (the erased annotation in the margin is illegible under u.v.).

622 **þat is ... is** F1122-3 *qui en .II. | Partie est* var. *qui est en .II. | Partie est* MS. *A*. GS's reading, derived from the var., is accepted. Punctuation is G's: as punctuated by CS, with *in tweyne* an adverbial phrase modifying *departed*, the second *it is* becomes otiose. C rationalised, inserting *& yit* in the left margin. Man is in two parts (II Cor. iv 6); *Duplex est autem homo, interior et exterior. Interior homo: anima; exterior homo, corpus* (Isidore, *PL*, LXXXII, 398).

622-3 **withoute beinge tweyne** τ read F1134 *sans entredeus* 'without anything in between', i.e. 'without being separated', as *sans etre deus*.

623 **Hy** see p. lxxii.

Justice F1135 *justicier* is pl.: perhaps JMO's *iugges* preserves

EXPLANATORY NOTES   385

the original reading in this respect at least. The *Hy Justice* was
Chief Justiciar, representing the king as the priest represents
God.

627-8 **wol . . . turne** perhaps there should be a comma after *amende*:
in accordance with F1144-5 *amender | Ne se veut pour amonester,
| Tourner pouez, for amonestinge* might modify *amende* or *mown
turne*.

628 **þe kervinge** F1145 *l'autre taillant* 'the other, the cutting edge':
neither *OED* nor *MED* records *kervinge* in this sense.

630 **cursinge** there are three kinds of ecclesiastical condemnation:
interdiction debars a place or person (especially the former)
from ecclesiastical functions and privileges; anathematization or
major excommunication debars the offender from all contact
with the Church and its members; excommunication or minor
excommunication debars a person from the sacraments. Either
of the last two might be meant: the latter is most common.

632 **perce on him** F1152 *sur soi . . . ruer* 'rush [down on] him': the
ME phrase is inappropriate for the violent action of the sword
blade, specifically distinguished from the blade's point at 592-
608.

635 **flat** should perhaps be emended to *platte*: see n. 637.

637 **platte** although at 635 all the English MSS have a form of *flat*
for F *plat*, at 637, 642, 646 GS have *platte*, accepted in place of
C's *flatte*. At 657 only G echoes F: its reading is accepted even
there.

637-45 **Bi . . . sharpe** Rom. xiii 1-5?

639 **smit** 3 per. sg. as in F1165 *fiert* (*OED smite* v. 1b).

640-1 **þat . . . deth** is not a reference to any opinion of Christ; true
advice and teaching consists of the teachings of Christ: the
antecedents of *þat* are *avisement, amonestinge, prechinge*.

641 **in whom** the antecedent of F1168 *Ou* might be *parole* or
Jhesucrist: τ would have been better advised to use the equally
ambiguous 'where'.

lyth F1168 *gist* and the English vars. suggests that CG's model
had *by*, a misreading of τ's *liþ*.

641-2 **With . . . vsen** in accordance with F1169 *De ce plat user vous
deveiz* GS's reading is accepted. The rarity of the construction
'use . . . with', meaning 'make use of' (*OED use* v. 23b: the
earliest example may be predated by the *Pilgrimage*), probably
accounts for C's erasure of half a line in order to cram in *to smite*
as the object of *vsen*.

643-4 **maketh . . . sinne** F1172 *Fait mainte foyz pechie laissier* 'often
causes the leaving of sin': GS's literal rendering of the acc. and
inf. construction (in which the acc. is understood normally in
F but awkwardly in ME) is accepted in place of CJMO's

normalisation.

645 **ye hauen** F1175 *avez*: the sense in both languages is 'have knowledge' or 'understand' (*MED haven* 7cc), but Stürzinger accepts MS. *A*'s *savez*.

653-4 **is right** F1189 *est droiz*: GS's literal rendering is accepted. CJMO show alteration of normal ME non-expression of *it* in conjunction with an impersonal verb (Mustanoja, p. 143), to the later construction.

654 **effect** (F1190 *effect*) is translated in the Glossary with deliberate ambiguity, as 'effect': the modern sense 'in effect' is uppermost, but the ME is probably the philosophical term meaning 'the manifestation of being in an act'—a sense the modern word still carries.

654-5 **as ... wisdom** see n. 682-3.

655 **deuyne** (G's reading) is without spelling precedent in C.

664 **for** 'in order that' (*OED for* conj. B4).

670 **keys** derive ultimately from Matt. xvi 19 (keys of the kingdom of heaven); compare Dante, *Purgatorio*, IX, lines 97-132 (J.D. Sinclair, II, 122-5) where the Porter of Purgatory bears Peter's keys, one gold, one silver, the latter being the penitent's correct disposition before the gold key's pardon is exercised. Guillaume's are the Keys of Mercy balancing the scalpel-like Sword of Justice (605ff.). They also echo Aquinas' Keys of Knowledge and Absolution (*ST*, 3a, q.17. a.1), and the Keys of Order (proper only to priests), and of Jurisdiction in external Courts (admitted to other Orders too).

673 **men ... men** in view of F1125-6 *on ... on* GMOS's reading is accepted.

674 **maad ... makinge** F1228 *fais et faissiaus* '[big] bundles and little bundles': τ mistook *fais* for pp. of *faire*, and read *faissiaus* as *faissans*. GS's *a makynge* may preserve τ's reading.

680 **seeche** the confessor's questions constitute the 'search' of sinners: F1239 *serchier* is correctly rendered (*OED seek* 10).

681-4 **Alle ... Cherubyn** cf. the weighing of souls by Michael, a cherub?

682-8 **þe ... Cherubyn** *Interpretationes nominum hebraicorum*, a list of pseudo-etymological meanings given to Biblical and other proper nouns, is sometimes at the end of Vulgate MSS. At least seventeen are in the Bodleian, eg. in MSS. Auct.D.3.8 (f. 514ᵛ), Auct.D.4.9 (f. 502ᵛ), Auct.D.5.14 (f. 548ʳ). The list explains *Cherubim: scientia multiplicata seu scientiae plenitudo aut quasi plures scientiae vel intellectus*. Similar explanations are in Jerome (see n. 32), and Isidore (*PL*, LXXXII, 273) through whom the interpretation was familiar to Bartholomaeus Anglicus (Trevisa, I, 73-4).

EXPLANATORY NOTES

687 **penauntes** om. F1252 *Et vous verrez (les) repentances* 'and you shall see the repentances'; var. om. MSS A^7H^1.

tokne F1257 *enseignement* 'teaching' or 'symbolism': τ gives the same rendering at 1243.

689 **þe techinge** om. F1258 *et l'apensement* 'and the thought'.

692 **lust took me** F1263 *Talent me vint* 'longing came to me': just possibly, M's *lust was to me* reflects τ's construction, a verb of motion being omitted instead of altered to *took*.

696 **eende** om. F1272 *Pour ce que avugle est Cherubin* perhaps because of its apparent obscurity: why should Cherubin ('the fulness of knowledge' see. n. 682-8) be blind? Presumably his face covered by two of his six wings (Is. vi 2): even the most complete created knowledge cannot see the future, so mere man has little hope of doing so.

713 **scole** F1305 *l'escole* may refer to a school, to a University School in a Faculty, or, because of its Aristotelian context, to a classical school of philosophy. The implication is that the pilgrim was educated poorly, if at all.

715 **Ad Aliquid** the Predicament *Ad Aliquid* is the fourth of Aristotle's ten Categories which indicate the ways in which Being may be expressed (Cooke, pp. 46-7). The fourth Category is Πρός τι 'Relation': 'Those things which are called relative, which, being either said to be *of* something else or *related to* something else, are explained by reference to that other thing' (Edghill, 6a36-8b24); 'all relatives have their correlatives. "Slave" means the slave of a master, and "master" in turn implies "slave"' (Cooke, p. 49). For further information on the Categories see Rijk, ch. iv.

The pilgrim does not understand the limitations of his humble state, desiring priest's authority when he has not received even the lowest of Minor Orders—indeed not even First Tonsure. Even a full priest may be unable to use the 'keys' until formally given jurisdiction ('faculties': Aquinas, *ST*, 3a, q.17. a.2). The pilgrim receives bound sword and keys as a layman, who in case of necessity may hear confession (Aquinas, *ST*, 3a Supp., q.8. a.2). The power of Keys and Sword remains potential, there being none upon whom he has the right to exercise it. Analysis of human relationships in grammatical terms became commonplace, as in Alanus de Insulis (Moffat, pp. 50-4).

720 **þat**² F1318 *se* var. *ce* MSS $TAGM^1LH$.

720-1 **cleerliche ... withholde** the importance of retaining knowledge is developed at 2659-745, Book 1's culmination in the pilgrim's acceptance of Memory's help.

721 **wel ... withholde** in view of F1320 *Bien retenir et (bien) apprendre* GS's reading is accepted.

721-3 **Whan ... gabbe** the change from God (*Deus*) to Lord God (*Dominus*) occurs in Gen. ii 4, immediately after Creation.

723 **ne gabbe** om. F1324 *me* 'to me', as do MSS $A^4A^7TAMGM^1L$.

724-5 **whan ... lordshipinge** Aquinas, *ST*, 3a, q.76. a.7: a development of Aristotelian concepts (see n. 715).

730 **knyt** F1337 *nee* 'born' is parallel to *engendree* 'engendered': τ read it as *niee* (Greimas *nier* 'to knot in') as if the overall sense were 'Lordship is tied up with the having of subordinates'.

738 **whateuere** F1353 *qui que* 'whoever' var. *quel que* MSS A^7GAH^1.

743-4 **keyes ... hem** F1362-3 *clefs, se les avoies | Descouvertes*: I have taken *swerd naked* and *keyes unheled* as parallel, but F suggests that the comma should follow *keyes*.

744 **folye** om. F1364 *et grant desroi* 'and great haste'.

749 **sum men mihten** in view of F1374-5 *pourroit ... | Aucun* perhaps JO's reading should be accepted, giving *sum mihte* 'some-one might'.

752 **þat ... dores** F1380 *Dont leurs huis (il) deffermeroient* 'with which they opened their doors'.

752-3 **þi ... han²** F1381-2 *tez clefs tex gardes ont | Comme les estranges les ont*: only J, doubtless by intelligent addition, has an equivalent for *tex* 'such' in his *swilke*: without it, the sense is obscured. The *wardes* are the teeth on a key; the meaning is either that the pilgrim's Keys are like those of any ordinary person (anyone may hear confession *in extremis*), or that the pilgrim, were he to lay premature claim to full clerical faculties for hearing confession before his full ordination, would carry 'keys' as an impostor. The latter is preferable since confession *in extremis* is not treated until 764.

759 **þat ende** F1395 *celle fin* var. *ceste fin* MS. *A*: perhaps GS's *thilke* should be accepted on the assumption that C and β substituted *þat*, perhaps feeling *thilke* archaic (see n. 1582).

760-1 **he ... swerd** F1397-8 *Les clefs te puisse deslier | Et le glaive desgainer*: CG³'s *vnsheþe þee þe swerd* has been rejected on the assumption that γ added *þee* to smooth the syntax, repeating the construction of *vnbynde þee þe keyes*: there is, strictly, no equivalent for the second *þee* in F. Possibly CG³'s reading should be retained, β and S having removed a *þee* (as β clearly did in the first instance, giving JMO's *vnbynde the kayes*).

764 **if ... misdoo** F1404 *Se tu ne te veus meffaire* (var. lacks *te* MS. *T*).

Perile ... outtaketh 'he makes an exception only in the event of danger of death'.

766-8 **necessitee ... to¹** see n. 715.

768-71 **Thilke ... him** F1413-20 *Cil a qui ce fait apertient, | C'est cil que nu le glaive tient, | Qui les clefs a desliees, | Nues et desseellees,*

EXPLANATORY NOTES

/ *C'est cil qui juridiction* / *Sur lui et domination* / *A et en est droit relatis,* / *Pour ce qu'a li il est sousmis* 'He to whom this office belongs is the one who carries the unsheathed sword and the loose, bare and unsealed keys—he is the one who has control and authority in the matter of this office, and is directly responsible for it, it being under his control'. The ME shows confusion in the pronouns. τ took F1418 *lui* and F1420 *il*, which refer to the *fait* or 'office', as masculine personal pronouns.

772 **also** in view of F1421 *aussi*, GMOS's reading is accepted.

775 **sheped** om. F1428 *et en fuerre boute* 'and pushed into a scabbard'.

wrapped in view of JM, perhaps the reading should be *wapped* (*OED wap* v²), on the assumption that α and O normalised.

776 **me** om. F1432-3 *Et ce devant fu despechie* 'and the foregoing was concluded' which may be gently ironic: Reason's long account (691-776) of why the dreamer is not qualified for the consecrating priesthood has delayed the consecration about to occur.

776-7 **Moyses ... it was** F1433-5 *Moyses vout aler disner* / *Et son mangier vout aprester* / *Tout autrement que il n'estoit* 'Moses wanted to go to his meal, but wished to prepare it quite differently from the way in which it had been done for him'. G's reading (echoed in JMO) is apparently due to τ's having taken *mangier* as a subject, and not recognised *aprester* as an infinitive. Perhaps τ read *fust (a) prestre* 'was ready' instead of *vout [vult] aprester*. G's corrector, referring to γ, whose reading C carries, made sense of G's strange reading by inserting *haue* before *his mete*, and cancelling *was redy*.

777 **al ooþerwise** should perhaps be *al ooþerweys*, following GO; *otherways* and *otherwise*, though similar, are distinct.

780-1 **þe ... shulde** Gen. ix 4; Levit. vii 26; xvii 14.

788 **alle** Communion was distributed, then as now, first to the officiating clergy: the priest does not turn to the congregation until 1083, and even then distribution is delayed until 1450.

790-2 **Bi ... renown** F1461-4 *Onques ne fu nu[l] tel disner* / *Dont j'aie point oui parler,* / *Ne nulle tel mutation* / *Qui ait si merveilleux renon* 'there was never such a meal that I have ever heard of, nor was there ever a transformation with such a reputation as a miracle'. τ seems to have read *fu* as *pu*, and *disner* as *dire*, so that *pu ... dire* has become *shulde ... kunne telle of*; in consequence he has taken *Dont ... parler* to mean '[to judge] by what I have heard tell' (*Bi ouht ... speke*), and has transposed it to begin the next sentence.

793-1082 **Whan ... suffre** communion of the officiating clergy complete, communion of the congregation should follow, but the short space of time it would take the celebrant to move from sanctuary

> to communion rail (or at least to the junction of chancel and nave) is appropriately filled by the great argument between Nature and Grace about Transubstantiation. The congregation may be monastic. The Cistercian Rite, regulated shortly after A.D. 1119, names the four feasts on which the Community communicated (*PL*, CLXVI, 1437).

803 **ey imaad** should perhaps be *ey maad*, on the assumption that C's *i*-prefix is the result of confusion with *ey*: the prefix is not C's practice. But δ and β could have omitted the prefix, misreading *ey y maad*, or C added it, misreading *eyy maad* in γ.

804 **a pipe** F1484 *un chalemel* 'a chalumeau', a musical instrument derived ultimately from a stem or reed.

807 **nature** is parallel with *vsage*, and since the latter is not personified in the *Pilgrimage*, I have assumed that personified Nature is not intended until 808. The relation between natural causes and the divine will had preoccupied 12th-century philosophers of the 'School of Chartres' (Crombie, pp. 44-6). Ambrose, discussing Consecration, observes: *majoris esse virtutis gratiam quam naturam* (*PL*, XVI, 423). The supremacy of the divine will might have been familiar to Guillaume in the *Anticlaudianus* (Cornog) and *De Planctu Naturae* (Moffat) of Alanus de Insulis.

810 **is** in view of F1496 *est*, GJO's reading is accepted.

813, 814 **tour** see n. 311 (for *tour* 816, too).

815 **alone** in view of F1503 *tout seul* perhaps the reading should be *al alone*, following G's reading in spite of the fact that the other witnesses omit *al*, perhaps by independent eyeskip in CS and β.

818 **vnder her sides** F1509 *sous l'(es) aisselle(s)* lit. 'under her armpits'.

824 **remeve** om. F1521-2 *et muer* 'and alter'.

825 **yow ynowh** GJMOS's reading is accepted in place of C's *jnowh to you*. C might have written the wrong word first, and been obliged to alter the word order. C's spelling is also (perhaps mistakenly) rejected: he does not use *jnowh* elsewhere, and prefers *yow* to *you*.

834 **me and yow** F1541 *moi et vous* var. *vous et moi* MS. *H*: in view of the var., perhaps the reading should be *yow and me*, following JMOS.

835 **mistake** om. the otiose F1544 *n'entrepreissons*.

836 **wheel** in the Aristotelian geocentric universe, the moon was embedded in and carried round by the innermost of seven concentric 'spheres of the planets'; in contrast to the celestial region, the sublunary terrestrial region was subject to various changes and movements (Crombie, pp. 89-93).

840-1 **Venus ... ram** F1553-4 *Venus beste cornue | Ou (de) Mercure*

EXPLANATORY NOTES

une tortue: the *tortue* is a tortoise, not a ram. Mercury and Venus are the two planetary spheres nearest the Moon. Nature is saying that Grace is free in her own celestial realm to be as unnatural as she likes, turning Mercury, the fleet messenger of the gods, into a slow tortoise, and the lovely Venus into a monster. τ may have used the libidinous *ram* for *tortue* because he thought *beste cornue* meant 'cuckold'.

843 **elementes** om. F1560 *Des impressions* 'of the effects [or actions of the elements]'.

843-51 **maistresse ... newe** in Alanus de Insulis' *De Planctu Naturae* the poet addresses Nature: 'whom the heavens befriend, whom the air serves, whom the earth cherishes, whom the wave worships, to whom, as to the mistress of the universe, each thing pays its tribute; who, linking day to night by interchange, dost grant the candle of the sun to day, and puttest to sleep the clouds of night with the shining mirror of the moon ... who changest the face of the heavens, and variest its appearance, and grantest life and population to our airy region, binding it together with law; at whose nod the world grows young, the forest is curled with leafy locks, and, clothed in its tunic of blossoms, the earth exults ...' (Moffat, p. 33). Gewande (p. 56) notes a possible derivation from Aristotle, *Physics*, II, i; *De Coelo*, I, 4.

844 **varyinges** om. F1562 *Et diverses mutations* 'and various alterations'.

847 **The ... robes** F1570 *La terre de mes robes est* 'the earth is robed in my clothes'?

848 **prime temps** F1570 *printemps*: the Gallicism is no doubt due to the absence of an established ME word for Spring.

852-3 **was ... bush** Luke xii 27.

857 **preciows** F1588 *pereceuse* 'lazy' var. *precheuze* MSS $H^1 A^7$ 'fastidious', 'too proud'.

860 **cornes** F1594 *les bles et les fourmens* 'corns and wheats'.

861-2 **me ... me** F1596-7 *Mes avis m'est que (pour) baiesse / Malement me voulez tenir* 'It seems to me that you wrongly want to regard me as a servant-girl': *malement* modifies *voulez*, but τ thought it modified *est*, giving his *me thinketh euele*, with the overall sense: 'I am angry inasmuch as you treat me like a common girl ...'.

861 **for þat for** F1596 *que (pour)*: the phrase is quite grammatical— *for þat* adv. conj. (*MED for-that*) followed by *for* prep.

865 **neuere ... sette** F1604 *onques paine je n'i mis* 'I never involved myself in this': perhaps expecting the sense 'I never baked bread', τ took *paine* (lit. 'trouble') for *pain* 'bread'.

867 **to** in view of F1608 *au*, GMOS's reading is accepted.

870 **It ... nouht** in view of F1612 *Point ne me plaist*, GMOS's reading is accepted.

874-80 **I ... Architriclyn** Nature appears to give simple examples of Grace Dieu's interference with the natural order, but all three are traditional Types of the Incarnation or Crucifixion. In *Biblia Pauperum* the Burning Bush (Exod. iii 2) and Aaron's Rod (Num. xvii 8-9) are Types of the Nativity—the *virgines chyldinge* of 882. The Bush foreshadows the Virgin's remaining inviolate at the conception and birth of Christ, as the bush remained unburned (Honorius of Autun, *PL*, CLXXII, 904). The parallel occurs in Guillaume's own 'Hymn to the Virgin' (5922).

Aaron's dry rod which bloomed signifies Christ's body sprung from the 'rod of Jesse' (Ambrose, *PL*, XVII, 26), or the Cross or Resurrection (Augustine, *PL*, XXXIX, 1805, 1806).

Moses' rod which became a serpent (Exod. iv 2-4: called *serpens Christi sancte* by Augustine, *PL*, XL, 696) signifies death conquered by Christ (Augustine, *PL*, XXXVIII, 61) and again foreshadows the rod or tree of Jesse bearing Christ as fruit. These resonant examples of miracle are appropriately cited in discussion of the Eucharist, in which Christ is both reincarnated and sacrificed. It is surely no accident that Nature's second example from the New Testament, the Marriage at Cana, carries connotations not of the Body but the Blood.

876 **þe ... Aaron** in view of F1624 *Des verges' Aaron*, perhaps the reading should be *þe yerdes Aaron*, following G.

880 **noces** it is clear from F1630 *noches* that the readings of CJMOS are substitutes for or corruptions of this rare word (*OED noces* 'wedding' cites only two examples, *MED* does not record it). Perhaps G's *noses* should be accepted, but in the absence of a recorded form in -s- I adopt the form nearer F. O's *mese* suggests that δ retained *noces* (*noses*?) or corrupted to *neses*, which O misread, and M assumed was an abbreviation of *necessite*.

Architriclyn in view of F1630 *Archedeclin* var. *Archetreclin* MSS *TL*, perhaps the reading should be *Archedeclyne*, following G; but the variant supports C's form, nearer Lat. *architriclinus* 'master of the feast'. The word in the Vulgate account of the Marriage at Cana (John ii 8-9), where the master of the feast comments on the miraculous wine, was sometimes taken as a proper noun. Nature mentions the occasion because, as *Mandeville's Travels* says, at Cana 'dide oure lord the firste myracle at the weddyng of Architriclyn'.

884-5 **ye ... virgine** in view of F1637-8 *virge enfanter | La feistes*, G's reading is accepted, *childe* being the verb. C's sb. *chyld* becomes v. *chylde*.

899 **fersliche** F1661 *fierement*; at 1074 *fersliche* translates *fierement*, but perhaps G's *feerliche* should be accepted as the more difficult reading, *feer* being a correct but rare equivalent of *fers*. It might have been independently read by CSβ as *fersliche*, corrupted further to *fresly* in O. On the other hand, G may simply have

EXPLANATORY NOTES 393

left out *s*. Alternatively, G substituted *feerliche*, intending a form of *OED ferly* adv., 'unexpectedly', a common native word.

905 **niceliche** om. otiose F1674 *Et assez despourveuement* 'and quite rashly'.

913 **gardyn** see n. 485.

918 **halt him oonliche** F1698 *seulement... se tient*: in view of the flexible use of *only*, C's closer echo of F's order is probably accidental.

927-8 **so... acounte** F1715-17 *A fin que huiseuse ne fussiez / Et que de tout me rendissiez / Conte loyal* 'on condition that you are not idle, and that you give me a correct account'.

ye yolden in view of F1716 *rendissiez*, GS's reading is accepted.

trewe acount GJMOS's reading is accepted: having misread *yolden* in 927, C or his model took *acounte* as a verb, and so made *trewe* an adverb.

934 **wil** apparently inserted in C's hand, is suspect, as the only use by C of *wil* for pr. 1 ind. of *willan* (*OED will* v.¹), his normal form being *wole* (*wule* at 382, 473). Just possibly it is part of *OED will* v.², indicating the strong sense 'wish'.

935 **to medle** perhaps GS's *medle* should be accepted as the more literal rendering of F1730 *Mesler*, on the assumption that C and β normalised.

939 **withoute** in view of F1738 *sans*, J's reading is accepted, though possibly an intelligent reconstruction rather than a preservation of τ's reading. However, I have assumed that τ carried an abbreviated form, $\bar{w}^t$, misread by χ as *with*.

941 **to uarie... turne** the planets ('wandering stars') change position relative to the 'fixed' stars.

942 **of heuene** (F1743 *du ciel*) should perhaps be *of the heuene*, following GS on the assumption that Cβ's omission of *the* is more probable than δ's insertion of it.

945 **of** in view of F1749 *de*, GS's literal reading is accepted in place of C's more idiomatic *in*.

949-52 **Aristotle... sunne** *On the Generation of Animals*, II, 3, 4; *Physics*, II, 2; *Metaphysics*, L, 5.

954 **riht nothing** F1766 *rien*: τ's emphatic addition is untypical.

955 **firmament** F1767 *firmament*: In view of the phrase following, *and of the planetes also*, the word *firmament* seems to have the specific sense 'sphere of the fixed stars', contrasted with spheres of the wandering planets. CG's model, apparently not realising this, replaced *firmament* with the native word for 'heavens'.

958 **ylost and abated** om. the otiose F1774 *Et expire*.

961-5 **Isaye** Is. x 15, xxix 16, xlv 9; Rom. ix 20.

963 **axe** Grace glances at the tradition of the axe as symbol of the

394   ÞE LYFE OF ÞE MANHODE

power by which God's will is executed (Carcopino, p. 56)—in this case Nature herself.

964-5 **and asketh ... shap** F1787 *En sa facon li deniant* 'objecting to his shape': τ's copy combined elements of both vars: *Et sa facon lit demant* MSS *tBM*, and *En sa facon li demandant* MS. *H¹*.

969 **ye ... instrument** in Alanus de Insulis' *De Planctu Naturae*, Nature admits 'He is the maker, I am the made; He is the Creator of my work, I am the work of the Creator; He works from nothing, I beg work from another; He works by His own divine will, I work under his name. By his nod alone He orders a thing to exist; but my activity is the mark of the divine activity, and, compared with the divine power, thou canst see that my power is impotent' (Moffat, p. 29).

980 **and þerof** GJMOS's *and* has no precedent in F1817 *De ce*, but is accepted on the assumption that τ added it. Perhaps it should be omitted, on the assumption that G(S)β made the addition.

986-7 **for ... profyte** F1828 *que mieux en vaut le commun bien* 'since the common good is served as a result': the sense may have been obscured by a var. such as that in MS. *o*, where *en* 'as a result' (lit. 'from it') is missing. τ's *abetter* (MSS *a better*) is not recorded: it seems to be ME prefix *a-* + *better*, or a conflation of *better* and *abbeten* or *abet* (*OED better* v. 1, *MED abbeten* v. b; *OED abot* v. 3 is less likely, the earliest instance being 1596).

989-90 **wolde ... do** F1833-4 *rien ne lairoie ... faire* 'I would not fail to do' or 'I would not refrain from doing': in accordance with the conditional, GMS's reading is accepted.

991 **þus** om. otiose F1836 *despute et* 'disputed and'.

995-6 **I wolde** should perhaps be *wolde I*, following GS and assuming that Cβ transposed the words.

997-8 **I ... game** F1846-7 *je tien a gieu | Quanque hui mais dire vourrez* 'I shall take anything you say henceforth lightly; GMO's reading, in which *today more (hui mais)* seems to be analogous to *to-yere more* (*MED more* adv. 5) is accepted. C's *but game* may be the result of *more* having been read as compar. adj. qualifying *game*.

1006 **ye ... bore** F1864-5 *nulle chose nee | Ne devez faire ne muer* 'you would not be likely to make or change anything alive' (lit. 'born', accurately rendered by G's *bore*). The strange reading probably explains β's omission of the word. The critical apparatus is hard to interpret. That τ wrote *remeeve nothing* is clear from GMO's *remeewe nothing*, corrupted in S to *renuwe no thing*, and in J to *neuerre remove*. But from *ne make nothing*, G omitted *ne make* (at the end of a line), writing ȝee scholde remeewe nothing nothing bore. A corrector put *ne make* in the margin to replace the first *nothing*, giving ȝee scholde remeewe ne make nothing bore. G's agreement with C suggests γ lacked the first *nothing*, and either had *bere* which G³ did not notice or did not accept, or

EXPLANATORY NOTES

bore which C misread as *bere* (as did S in expanding and corrupting bore to *incresse and bere*).

1011-12 **men ... hous** F1877-8 *ne peut ouvrer | Ne maison bonne edefier | Le charpentier* 'the carpenter cannot work or build a good house': τ did not realise that *charpentier* is the subject of *peut ouvrir* as well as (*peut*) *edefier*.

1018 **neuer** is (as at 3553, 4297, 4541, 5923) an expansion of *neu* followed by a suspension mark; having no unexpanded precedent, it should perhaps be in C's normal form *neuere*.

1040-1 **as ... hewe** F1928-30 *com le charpentier | De sa coignie a charpentier | S'aide et a edefier* 'by means of his axe the carpenter enables himself to cut and build': τ omits *s'aide*, transposing the infinitives.

1053 **carpentere** F1952 *charpenter*: *MED carpenteren* records only two examples, this and 1367 *carpentered* (F2508 *charpente*).

1055-6 **neiþer ... ooþer** F1956 *Nul charpentier ne neul charon* (vars. *charron* MS. *A*, *charton* MSS *MA⁷*, *machon* MS. *H¹*): 'neither carpenter nor cart-maker'. As Godefroy *charon* shows, the craftsmen were associated in a tag (cf. 'tinker and tailor'): nevertheless, French scribes, as well as τ, did not recognise the idiom.

1059 **filthe** see p. lxvi.

1068 **I ... leese** F1979 *Ne voi que de rien i perdez* 'I do not see that you lose by it in any way': τ omits *i* 'by it' and renders *voi que*, literally, *I look þat*.

1072 **þat** in view of F1986 *Que*, GJMOS's reading is accepted.

1074 **folilich ... fersliche** F1990 *folement | De parler a vous fierement* '... foolishly, to speak to you arrogantly'. τ's omission of *De parler* is hard to explain, and *and* should perhaps not be retained: but G's reading, without *and*, may simply reflect the archetype's omission of *to speke*, by eyeskip to *to yow*. This presupposes an χ distinct from τ (not merely a level of correction of τ), and the independent supplying of *and* by CβS or their ancestors.

1080 **upon yowre eyen** (F2000 *sur l'eul*) *MED eie* 7c(1) cites this single example with the sense 'in mind': I punctuate according to my gloss 'on (pain of losing) your eyes', as if the phrase were analogous to 'upon the pain to be blind' or 'upon your life' (*OED upon* 12), which is how β understood it.

1083 **Whan** the bishop again attempts to distribute communion to the congregation (see n. 793); this long second interruption (1087-1439), by Penitence and Charity, is relevant to communicants' preparation.

1084 **releef** (F2007 *releef*) carries, in both languages, three appropriate meanings: (i) sustenance, especially that given to the poor; (ii) the remainder of a meal; (iii) payment to an overlord by a tenant's heir taking up his inheritance. The first is dominant

ÞE LYFE OF ÞE MANHODE

here, where *releef* and *almesse* are associated; the second is dominant at 1289, where the food is described as remaining from the Last Supper; the third may be implicit in both, since the sacrifice of the Mass is a gift from, and an offering to, God.

1088 **withoute mistakinge** F2014 *sans mespresure* 'without fault' or 'to be sure', an ambiguity present also in the ME.

1090ff. Charity is *mentioned* before Penitence because as the bearer of the 'jewel of peace' (1345-6) she represents the Prayer for Peace, and Kiss of Peace, which in the Mass precede public confession and communion of the congregation: *Domine Jesu Christe, qui dixisti Apostolis tuis: Pacem relinquo vobis, pacem meam do vobis: ne respicias peccata mea, sed fidem Ecclesiae tuae, eamque secundum voluntatem tuam pacificare et coadunare digneris* (see John xiv 27). But Charity is not *described* until after Penitence's sermon (1299). That she is described and speaks after Penitence suggests that love follows voluntary discipline and pain (cf. *Ancren Riwle*'s treatment of love, after six books on discipline and penance).

1096-7 **a ... courreyinge** F2027-8 *Unes bonnes verges cinglans, / Grelles et vers et couroians* 'a good cutting cane [birch], slender and green and good for beating with'. τ omits *cinglans*, perhaps feeling it otiose (but at 1254 it was omitted for other reasons). See p. lvi for J's *wele plyande*.

1101 **for** in view of F2034 *Pour*, GMO's reading is accepted.

1104 **ye biholden** om. F2040 *bien*, doubtless because of *bien* shortly before and after, both translated.

1106 **myn array** in view of F2042 *mon maintien*, GJMOS's reading is accepted against C's *it* over a larger erasure, doubtless made to avoid repetition of *myn array*.

1109 **Penitence** may signify the general need for absolution before approaching the altar, and public confession of the congregation before communion (Jungman, II, 371). She describes the sacrament of Penance (1011-1298) from the point of view not of the confessor (as at 688-755) but of the penitent.

1110 **wardeyn ... hyd** Stürzinger's MSS have (note *erratum* on his p. vii^b) *Penitence sui apelee / Gard(ienne) de l'ille celee* (var. for *de l'ille*: *de lis la* MS. *o*). This is a crux: the sense 'island' for *ille* is inappropriate (could *li(e)ue* 'place' have been corrupted to *l'ille*?). Lydgate thought *l'ille celee* (in the Second Recension) was man's inner heart: *thylke yle most secre / The wych (who espye kan,) / Ys yhyd with-Inne a man*, marking the last couplet *Verba translatorys* to show that it was a gloss (Furnivall, p. 107). The sense 'place' for *yle* is possible (*MED ile* 2.a 'domain, realm, province'), but *ille celee* seems to refer to a place which may be entered only when sins have been purged. Perhaps Penitence, standing between celebrant and congregation, guards the chancel or sanctuary in which the mass took place, and from which communion was distributed. Confession was often heard at the

EXPLANATORY NOTES

junction of nave and chancel (Feasey, p. 32), which may have been permanently screened (Bond, *Roodscreens*, p. 78) or, like the sanctuary, curtained off. Durandus mentions curtains between sanctuary and choir, or choir and nave (Berthélemy, pp. 57-8). Hugh St Victor may explain *hyd*: 'the curtain between choir and nave signifies the veil of the letter by which the truth of the Gospel was still covered for those under the law; the one between sanctuary and choir signifies the veil of mortal nature by which the secrets of heaven are still hidden from us even when we are in a state of grace' (Deferrari, p. 318).

1113 **contricioun** carries its literal meaning 'crushing' as well as 'repentance' (Aquinas, *ST*, 3a Supp., q.1. a.1; q.2. a.1).

1117 **juse ... appel** the apple here representing the stubborn soul crushed to contrition becomes Christ in Book 4 of the *Soul*: the fruit of the Green Tree (the Virgin), crushed to refresh man.

come out F2063 *Issir ... et hors saillir*: τ omits the otiose *Issir* (at 1129 he renders *issir* by *ysen*, *saillir* by *come out*).

1121-2 **Peeter ... been** F2070-1 *Pierre et amoliai / Qui si dur Pierre avoit este*: Matt. xxxvi 75. The pun is more obvious in F.

1126 **Magdaleyne** Luke vii 37, 38.

1132 **I ... ayen** F2089 *Ʒe les requeil*: with excessive fidelity, τ rendered the *re-* of *requeil* by *ayen* (cf. 578); at 1431 he simply translated F2624 *requeillis* by *gadered*.

1133 **bowkinge** is the earliest record of the word (*MED bouken*), meaning an alkaline lye or solution, usually a mixture of wood-ash and water, for bleaching clothes. *OED bucking* claims that the process, rather than the solution used in it, is meant.

1134 **tere** F2093 *lexive* 'laundering-water' (Lat. pop. *lexivum*: Greimas, *lessif*) var. *lerme* 'tear' (Lat. *lacrima*) MSS AA^7.

1135 **so¹ ... defamowse** om. F2095 *tant viez* 'so old', but it is not otiose—Repentance must be able to obliterate not only sin but the stain of that which is ingrained.

1139-40 **Þe ... pot** Lanfranc, speaking of the holy vessels carried by Subdeacons, says: *Vasa, corda significant ... Subdiaconi itaque vasa Domini lavant, cum conscientias mundant* (*PL*, CL, 629, cited by Vogel, p. 160, who provides a useful guide to patristic writings on penance).

1140 **pot of eerþe** F2104 'earthenware pot' rather than 'pot full of earth'.

1143 **þat is þat** F2109 *C'est que* 'this is because': τ understood *que* as *qui*, his second *þat* being rel. pron. 'who', obscuring the sense.

1146 **contrite** F2115 *le contris* 'I crush it': *contris* is pr. 1 sg., and so apparently is the ME though *MED contriten* does not record this part of the verb, and though *it*, the equivalent of *le*, has been omitted, perhaps by error in χ—*it* after *contrit(e)*—in which case the reading should be *contrite* [*it*]. This would imply an independent χ, as opposed to its being a level of correction to τ. This is an earlier example of *contriten* meaning 'crush' as opposed to 'reduce to contrition' than any in *MED* or *OED*; here it means both (see n. 1113).

1148 **if...wel** F2119 *se (bien) ne le contrisoie* 'if I did not crush them thoroughly' (with the connotation of contrition): var. *se bien le connissoie* MS. *A⁷*. τ's source seems to conflate the variant reading and the negative construction of the other MSS: 'if I did not know them well'. To suggest the original pun, I gloss the phrase 'if I did not examine them thoroughly'.

1151-87 **Now...cleped** Examination of Conscience, the first stage in Penitence, is explained. Contrition is followed by Confession (1188-1240) and Satisfaction (1241-77): cf. Chaucer's *Parson's Tale*.

1159-60 **swich...Moneday** F2139-40 *lors feis tu ainsi / A tel dimenche, a tel lundi*: F and ME mean 'you did so-and-so then, on such-and-such a Sunday, on such-and-such a Monday' (unusual ME examples of the demonstrative adj. used without a preceding prep. such as *at* or *on*, and earlier than any with this sense in *OED such* dem. adj., or pron., 16).

1164 **litel...purchasedest** F2145-6 *peu luitas / Ou tu la luite pourchacas* 'you struggled little, or you yourself brought about the struggle': the pilgrim hardly resisted, or actually invited, temptation.

1165 **to breke** om. F2148 *et depecier* 'and smash'.

1170 **þat** F2156 *cel*: CG's *þilke* could be τ's reading, or reflect γ's Southern preference for using it 'of individual shaped things [such as this pot] while *that* and *this* are used of formless substances in the mass, such as flour, milk, marble' (*OED thilk*). At 1165 CGS have *þilke foule uessel* for *Cel ort vaissel*: on the other hand *þilke* is used at 1134 *þilke tere*.

1173-4 **þe...conscience** Is. lxvi 24; Mark ix 43-8; not the faculty of distinguishing between right and wrong (which Penitence would not, of course, destroy) but the effect of this capacity, i.e. remorse (St Bernard, *PL*, CLXXXII, 838). Its brief appearance here is a prelude to its part in the Judgement which constitutes Book 1 of the *Soul* (*Guillaume de Deguileville*, f. xv^r-xvi^v), where the worm blames the Pilgrim for its teeth having been worn away by fruitless attempts to bite him into penitence, and where its tail is swollen with poison because the Pilgrim would not beat it with Penitence's *yerde*.

1177 **astone** F2166 *assoumast* '[might] strike': τ understood the word in its later, metaphorical sense 'stun, astonish' (*MED astonen* shows the metaphorical meanings dominant in ME).

it...rounge F2167 *rungier ne fineroit* 'it might not stop gnawing': that τ wrote *rounge* is evident not only from the α-branch

EXPLANATORY NOTES 399

corruptions but also from JMO's *frete* 'chew'. *OED rounge* cites this line as it appears in Wright's diplomatic edition of C, but gives '*rounge* [printed *raunge*]'; in fact the MS does have *raunge*, echoed in G³'s marginal correction to *Raunge* of G's meaningless *Renge*. Probably χ used a form such as *roūge*, which G misread as *renge* in spite of its incomprehensibility (as he retained *mugos* at 2666). γ falsely emended to *raunge* 'hunt about'. See p. lxxiii on S's reading.

1179-80 **I sle...astone** F2171-2 *le fiere et estonne | Et (que) le tue et (que l')assome*: τ om. *assomme* 'beat', and alters the order of the other verbs (assuming that *sle* renders *tue*, and *smite* renders *fiere* — *astone* certainly renders *estonne*).

1197 **sum anglet...cornere** F2201-2 *aucun anglet. | En aucun destour ou cornet*: the correct reading may be CGS's ... *crook or cornere* or, as I have assumed, JMO's ... *crookede cornere* (ignoring their addition of *sum apere* before *crookede*). Either way, τ made a rare addition (either *crook* or *crooked*). It is against JMO that β was rewriting here, as *sum apere* shows, and that *crook* 'nook, corner' is rare, and might be misread, or prompt substitution. It is against CGS that τ's additions (as at 226, 274, 307, 339, 442, 445) are usually of small words or minor adjectives. In lists of nouns he tends to cut, not add (p. lxxxvii).

1198 **heled or heped** F2203-4 *(re)celee, | Reposte ou amoncelee*: τ omits either *(re)celee* or *Reposte* 'concealed', avoiding repetition.

1200 **seyd of** F2208 *dite de* 'called': the ME equivalent is *seyd* (*OED say* v.¹1e, or B2e 'named after'); *of* is over-literal here and in 1200-1.

fisshes F2208 *poisons* 'poisons' var. *poyssons* MSS *oT-AGLM¹H¹H*: Stürzinger oddly accepted the minority reading, although he gives the note *porta piscium* (see n. 1200-4).

1200-4 The Gate of Fishes (II Paralip. xxxiii 14; II Ezdra iii 3, xii 39) and the Gate of Dung (II Esdras ii 13, iii 13) are in Jerusalem's wall (see Hastings, p. 476 for a complete list). The site of Jacob's Dream is called the Gate of Heaven (Gen. xxviii 17). The Gates of Hell are in Matt. xvi 18, those of Brass (and Iron?) in Ps. cvi 16 and Is. xlv 2, the Iron Gate in Acts xii 10.

1201 **bras** is not the modern metal (basically an alloy of copper and zinc): it might mean copper, or a copper/tin alloy such as bronze.

1204 **þe...felthe** is probably at the SW of the SE hill of Jerusalem (where the Tyropoeon and Hinnom valleys meet): an outlet to the refuse dump there might well be called Dung Gate (Brockington, pp. 131-2, n. 13).

1209-13 **yates...filthe** the image of senses as openings admitting pollution to the soul is commonplace (Isidore, *PL*, LXXXIII, 628, cited Gewande, p. 18, and Hugh St Victor, *PL*, CLXXVI, 899), deriving from Jer. ix 21, which actually refers to Jerusalem (see n. 1200): *'ascendit mors per fenestras nostras, ingressa est domos nostras'*, where *mors* is interpreted as sin.

1210 **þe ... in** in view of F2224 *l'ordure dedens va, þe* (omitted in JMO) is retained, but JMO's sg. is accepted.

1217 **That** C tends to avoid using capital thorn (the *th-* form of *that* occurs only at the start of sentences, e.g. 4250, 4654, 5083, 7103)—but it does sometimes occur (e.g. 3761 Þe).

1225 **al to sweepe** in view of F2249 *pour tout balier | Housser* GJMOS's reading is accepted. τ om. the otiose *Housser* 'to brush': at 1237 he similarly om. *housse*.

1226 **I wole** in view of F2253 pres. ind. *veul*, GJMS's *wull* is accepted.

1228 **My ... palet** F2255-6 *Mon balai si est ma lengue, | Mon fourgon et ma palengue* 'my tongue is my broom, my ash-rake and shovel'.

1232 **withoute outtakinge** F2264 *sans ... deception* 'without any deception': τ's source apparently had *exception* for *deception*, but the correct reading is in doubt (see p. lxiii). Variants at 12 suggest that there τ used *owttaken*, only J substituting *exceptioun*; but at 1451 τ did use *exceptinge* for *excepter*.

1237 **wel** see n. 1225.

1240 **swept** F2278 *baliee*: the correct reading might be CGS's *kept*. The ambiguous evidence is among the strongest for the existence of α. JMO's reading is accepted on the assumption that F is from *balier* 'sweep', as in 1225 *to sweepe* (F2249 *balier*), 1229 *I sweepe* (F2257 *baloie*), 1237 and 1252 *swept* (F2271 and F2298 *balie*) as well as 1228 and 1235 *beesme* (F2255 and F2267 *balai*). In this case α misread *swept* as *kept*. But F could be a form of *baillier* 'to guard', though at 866 *I deliuerede* (F 1605 *je baillai*) and 1550 *taken to* (F2844 *baillie*) F has *-ll-* and the specific sense 'to hand over to be guarded'. In this case CGS are right, and β, influenced by *swept* in 1237, misread *kept* as *swept*.

1241 **Now ... herd** F2279 *Or [s]avez vous ainsi* vars. *auez vous oy* MSS GBH, *Oit aues ainsi* MS. H^1; τ follows the *GBH* variant (which, however, omits *ainsi*).

1243 **and** F2283 *Si*: possibly *now* is the correct reading, so varied are the meanings of *Si*.

1246-9 **I ... hem** Is. lxv 20: *Non erit ibi amplius infans dierum, et senex qui non impleat dies suos: quoniam puer centum annorum morietur, et peccator centum annorum maledictus erit.* For some reason, this is often cited in the form *puer centum annorum maledictus erit* (W. O. Ross, pp. 119-20; Pope, p. 623) with the sense explained by Dan Michel (Gradon p. 259): the curse is deserved by a man who remains a sinner into old age.

1249 **I ... awaite** om. F2294 *Volontiers* 'willingly' or 'quickly'.

1254 **yerdes** see. p. lxxvii.

1257-8 **I ... ayen** F2309 *lui (re)fas dire* 'once again I make him say':

EXPLANATORY NOTES

ayen should modify *make*.

1260 **ne ... þee** F2314 *Ne que pour vous ose pechier* 'nor, because of you, shall I dare sin'.

1260-1 **I make to preye** F2315 *le fais prier* var. *lui fais prier* MSS *HH*[1]. GJM have *y make hym to preye*, but *hym* is an insert in M, and in G is marked with a cross and subpuncted by a corrector. In view of this and C's reading it looks as if, in spite of F *le*, χ did not have *hym* (perhaps τ misread *le* as *ie*), and that it was supplied by GJM to improve the sense, just as S supplied *þee*.

1262 **needy** om. F2317-18 *aus souffraiteus* 'to the suffering'.

1263 **mendivauns** F2318 *mendiens*; G has *mendiuauns*, or possibly *mendinauns*: see *OED* and *MED mendina(u)nt, mendivaunt* for the difficulty in distinguishing them.

1267-9 **to þat ... sinne** F2330-1 *Pour qu'il ne s'amorde mie | De retourner a son pechie* 'in order that he will not be at all anxious to return to his sin': *s'amordre* means literally 'to bite oneself'. The error may be due to misreading *s'amorde* as *l'amorde* and *De* as *Ne*: τ's reading would then be literal, though wrong. Annotations to CG show that reference to the gnawing Worm of Conscience (1171-83) was understood.

1268-9 **his ... purged** ME awkwardness echoes F2332 *son pechie | Dont il s'est gete et purgie*, where two verbs taking different contructions are made to take *Dont*: sin is cast out of the sinner, not *vice versa*.

1278 **maad yow sermoun** (F2347 *fait sermon*) should perhaps be *maad sermoun*, following MO as a literal rendering rationalised in CJ.

1282 **partere** F2355 *chancelliere* 'a senior ecclesiastic's (female) deputy'. In context, F means 'controller', but *OED chancellor* derives the word from Lat. *cancellarius*, one whose place in court was at the screen between officials and public; thus *chancelliere* may refer not only to Penitence's judicial, controlling function, but also to her penitential position at the chancel screen. τ may have tried to suggest both 'controller of communion' and 'one who stands at the division of chancel and nave'.

1284 **ye wole** in view of F2358 *vous voulez*, *wole* is based on GMOS's *wulle*.

1284-5 **to fooles** F2359-60 *a garconner | A coquins* 'those of low intelligence and scoundrels'.

1287-9 **of ... allegeaunce** F2365-6 *Du quel qui gouste dignement | Ne peut qu'il n'ait alegement* 'anyone tasting it in the proper manner cannot but receive relief'. The ME vars. suggest that τ had CGS's literal reading, JMO supplying *it* before *may* as idiom requires, but perhaps the reading should be not *may* but *it may*, following JMO's correct rendering of *Ne peut*.

1289 **releef** see n. 1084.

1290 **cene** Matt. xxvi 26. *MED cene* does not cite this example.

ceened is a very rare example of S's reading being accepted, because nearer F and *cene*—but perhaps G's *s*- form, recorded in *MED*, should be retained.

1292 **quikned** F2372 *ravive* 'brought to life again' var. *auiue* MS. H.

1295 **but if** F2376 *Se ... n*': GJS's accepted reading is that of all the ME MSS at 1294 (again for *Se ... n*').

1296 **eche ... himself** F2379 *s'i gart chascun endroit soi* 'may each man look after himself properly in this matter': *soi* is reflexive, *s'* merely emphatic. τ took *s'* as reflexive, giving the redundant *him*. Cf. 1410, where F2585 *endroit soit* is also translated as *for himself*.

1300 **ooþer ladi** refers to Charity, whose name is 'explained' by Isidore: *Charitas Graece, Latine dilectio interpretatur, quod duos in se illiget. Nam dilectio a duobus incipit, quod est amor Dei et proximi, de qua Apostolus: Plenitudo · inquit · legis · dilectio* (*PL*, LXXXII, 296). The derivation of *dilectio* from *duos + illigere* hence 'join two' explains why it is Charity who presents the p.a.x. representing the soul's love of its neighbour and of God (n. 1372).

1311 **Seint Martyn** of Tours: see Réau, III, part ii, 900-7.

1313 **osteleer to pilgrimes** of the personifications in Book 1, only Grace and Charity reappear in Book 4. Charity, hostess to travellers as well as the greatest of the virtues, is seen first in the monastery, and her appearance in Book 1 is recalled (6808-12).

1316 **þat þat** apparently τ had in front of him *ce que* ('him whom'), a conflation of F2414 *Ceuz que* 'those that', and var. *Ce qui* MS. H.

1319-21 **þilke¹ ... ooþere** I Cor. xiii 4-7?

1320-1 **þat² ... ooþere²** may be one of the rare occasions where only M in the β-branch preserves τ's reading. It is more likely that J and O misread *ooþere¹* as a form of 'oath', than that M should have noticed and corrected this error.

1321-2 **nouht for þanne** except in this phrase (also at 1477, 1548, 2055), the scribe uses *þan* for the dem. pron. Perhaps he uses adverbial *þanne* here because it is in an adverbial phrase.

1322 **I ... misdoinge** τ struggled to echo the word-play of F2425-6 *ai je fait | Aucuns maus fait*. The ME accurately echoes the paradox: 'I have, without doing anything wrong, caused some harm to be done'. As God's love, Charity has caused Christ suffering: she is sometimes shown assisting in the execution of the Crucifixion (Schiller, II, 137-40, plates 448-54; Katzenellenbogen, pp. 38-9, figs. 40-1).

1328-30 **I ... nailes** F2437-40 *Les bras li (fiz) en crois estendre, | (Li) despoulier, le coste fendre, | Les piez et les mains atachier | Li fiz et*

EXPLANATORY NOTES

de gros clous percier 'I caused his arms to be extended on the cross, [I caused] him to be stripped and his side opened, I caused his feet and hands to be fastened down, and pierced with great nails'. τ did not treat the acc. + inf. construction consistently.

1333 **descenden** om. F2445 *pour ces maus* 'as a result of these evils': the Passion resulted in the redemption of those in Limbo. Perhaps τ saw the meaningless var. *par ces maus* 'by means of these evils', and omitted it. Alternatively he understood *ces maus*, and found 'his evils' inappropriate to Christ.

1336 **leue** (F2449 *laissier*) may be in C too, rather than *lene*.

1339 **testament** this is an example of the literary type known as Christ's Last Will and Testament (Spalding, p. viii, see also Perrow, and Jones). It differs from Testaments in which Christ leaves his mother to St John (John xix 26-7, see Langkammer), or which, like the OE example printed in *An English Miscellany*, pp. 357-62, are admonitions to Sunday Observance, and from those consisting of the reproaches from the Cross. Spalding distinguishes Guillaume's Testament even from the Charters which are Christ's dying bequests in legal form. Guillaume's Testament does not draw on their metaphor of Christ's body as the parchment, his wounds the letters, and so on ('Long Charter', in Spalding's Appendix, and in Furnivall, *The Minor Poems of the Vernon MS.*, pp. 637-57.) However (*pace* Spalding) Guillaume's Testament shows other elements of the type. Latin ones often include formulaic 'headings' (perhaps echoed here) beginning *Ego Jhesus* ...; they promise an eternal inheritance, provide the Eucharist as indenture, seek co-operation from man as in a covenant, use images of the seal and Cross. Charters cited by Spalding are 14th- or 15th-century, but the one which could have influenced Guillaume is Rutebuef's version of the deed granted Theophilus (see Faral and Bastin), a 'real' deed, not a metaphor. Guillaume may have been as original in use of the *carta* convention as he was in handling *tau* and *pax*.

1342 **I Ihesus** F2459 *Je Jhesus*: if C does preserve the original reading (see p. lxxvi), Gβ must independently have omitted *I*. This is more likely than C's having supplied the pronoun, though conceivably he recognised the formal opening of a Will, or the *carta* form, and so emended intelligently. In this is case, the reading should be *[I] Ihesus*.

1342 **weye ... lyf** John xiv 6.

1343 **nyh** F2461 *prochaine*: possibly C's *niht*, though not recorded in *OED nigh*, should be retained as a legitimate form (cf. 14th-century *neythe*, 15th-century *ney3t*, 16th-century *neight*, *nyght*).

1343-4 **laste testament** Matt. xxvi 28, said at the Consecration of the Wine (which was at 783).

1344 **leeue** ('leave') should perhaps be emended to *leue*, C's *leeue* being reserved elsewhere, with one exception, for 'believe' (see

n. 5125).

1344-5 **þe ... weepinge** *valle lacrymarum*, Ps. LXXXIII 7; an echo of the hymn *Salve Regina*, dating from at least the 11th century, and familiar to Guillaume, for Cistercians chanted it daily (*NCE*, XII, 1002).

1346 **jewell** F2467 *jouel*: the dominant meaning seems to be 'precious object' rather than 'gem'; Godefroy *joiel* suggests 'gift' but cites only two examples, one in this text and both unconvincing. The sense 'gem' may be present, because the *pax* symbol is a notary's sign (see n. 1406), the jewel thus resembling a seal-stone.

and þe faireste F2468 *et plus bel* 'and fairest' var. *et le plus bel* MSS AH^1BM.

1352 **hadde had** in view of F2480 *eusse*, GJMOS's reading is accepted.

1358-9 **to have ... had it** F2492-9 *de li avoir.* / *En bail l'ont eu* 'to have it. They have had it in trust.' CJMOS begin the new clause at *þei haue had it*, as if *in havinge* modified *to have*. G, unpunctuated here, is assumed accurately to echo F, *in havinge* modifying *haue had*.

1359 **oonliche ... it** F2493-4 *seulement* / *Pour rapeler*: inf. with passive meaning, giving 'only [for it] to be recalled'.

1367 **carpentered** see n. 1053.

1367-9 **withoute ... vnmaken** the implication is not simply that peace cannot be made noisily, but that the silence of prayer produces *pax triplex*.

1369 **tobreken ... it**[3] F2512 *le despiecent et deffont*: perhaps the first *it* should be omitted, following GS on the assumption that their reading is nearer F's use of a single pronoun.

1372 **carpenteres sqwire** *pax triplex* is the book's most complex symbol. It is related by its position to the Mass's Rite of Peace with oneself, God and one's neighbour (n. 1090), of which its form is a diagram, echoing the triple structure of Penance, just examined (n. 1151). In one 12th-century Mass this Rite is followed by prayers for exactly the triple peace (Simmons, pp. 48-52). *Pax triplex* is found in Augustine, *PL*, XXXIV, 72; Alanus de Insulis, *PL*, CXX, 156; Aquinas, *ST*, 22ae, q.29.2.3; Albertus Magnus, p. 24; Bernard, *PL*, CXXXIII, 754. But association of *p.a.x.* with *proximus* (*prochain*), *anima* (*âme*), and *x* for the first sound (χ) in *Christus*, as well as with a carpenter's square, seems to be original. This 'jewel' is precious to God (1346), created by him (1366), and the instrument of his building of his kingdom, for it is the attribute of the medieval master-mason (Lethaby, fig. 90). It also suggests the Crucifixion (1354-65), *Christus* being set above mankind *in scaffold* (1382). This bequest, read before the altar, forms a meditation on the Eucharist (see 1365-6): the congregation confess and receive

EXPLANATORY NOTES 405

communion when Charity finishes (1440-64).

first should perhaps be *[firste]*, used everywhere else by C for adj.

1374 **wel a poynt** F2521 *bien a point* 'right' or 'exactly': G's literal reading is accepted against C's *in þe poynt*. The variants show that τ wrote *a point*, not *apoint* (*MED apoint* adv.).

1379 **writen** om. F2529-30 *Par les trois letres que j'ai dit* 'in the three letters I have described', avoiding repetition of *These thre letteres*.

1380 **to thre thinges** F2532 *a trois choses* 'in three respects'. The translation, retained in CGS, is literal and clumsy.

1382 **x ... I am** χ is the first letter of CHRISTOS in Greek.

1385-8 **Afterward ... pes** F2543-7 *A pres a l'anglet bas assis | Et ou est anichie et mis | A, par qui entendue est | L'ame qui en humain cors est, | Doit aussi avoir bonne pais* (var. for *bas*: *bien* MSS tBM). τ saw the var., giving the general meaning 'next, placed right in the corner where it is set and nestled, 'a' (by which is understood the soul in the human body) should also enjoy true peace'. τ confusingly rendered *est anichie* (referring to fem. *âme*) by *she is sett*.

1393-5 **to ... inne** F2557-61 *a son prochain, | Qui par le P du bout derrain | Est entendu, doit pais avoir, | A quoi le doit mont* [recte *mout*] *esmouvoir | Le mesme degre ou il est* 'with his neighbour (who is meant by the 'p' in the very end) he should have peace, to which he should be greatly prompted by being at the same level'. t awkwardly echoed F's syntax.

1395-6 **it is** the subject of F2562 *est* is either *degre* 'level' or *il* 'he'. The sense is that man and his neighbour should be at peace, as equals.

1397 **whan ... made** F2564 *Quant les crie, fourme et fis* 'when I created, formed and made them' var. *Quant lescript ie fourme et fis* MS. M. The sequence of creative verbs resembles that at 1046.

dedliche F2565 *mortex* supports CGS's reading.

1397-401 **Alle ... hole** the primary meaning is that all men, whatever their status, are mortal. But *worm* carries many connotations. Men become worms in the grave, the *oon hole* which all, like worms, enter; like worms, men are essentially naked and worthless—Griselda begs 'Lat me nat lyk a worm go by the weye' (*Clerk's Tale*, 880). There may be an echo of 'Ego autem sum vermis, et non homo' from Ps. xxi 7, quoted by Christ on the cross, sharing humanity's humiliation.

1401 **hole** F2569 *pertuis* 'crevice' is a more vivid metaphor for the grave than *hole*.

1405 **and ... figured** F2576 *Et qui la pais a figure* 'and which represented the peace' var. *A qui la pais ai figure* 'by which I have represented the peace': τ seems to have seen a text something like *Et la pais que ai figure*.

1406 **notarye** GJMOS's reading, accepted here, is an attributive use of nom. *notarye*. A notary authenticating a document would mark it with his sign, which might resemble a carpenter's square or other geometric figure, much as masons' marks do.

1411 **in** F2586 *a*: CJ's *to* may preserve τ's reading, rather than showing normalisation.

1413 **rested** F2590 *recite* 'recited': if τ wrote *resited*, misread by χ (in which case this may be evidence for a physically distinct χ), the reading should perhaps be [*resited*]. But it is possible that on re-reading, τ was aware of *þanne she bigan ayen* coming next, and made a false correction to *rested* (in this case χ would simply be a level of correction to τ).

1419 **with** om. F2600 *tout* 'all'.

1430 **wole** the subject of F2623 *Veut* is *Jhesus* (F2615); Christ, not the jewel, wishes the soul to receive communion: to stay away from it can therefore be culpable (1431-2).

1441 **were encline** F2642 *furent encline*: C originally had *encline* rather than G's more literal and uncommon *weren enclyne* (*MED enclin* adj.), accepted here.

1454-6 **riht ... elded** I Cor. xii 29.

1455 **dong-hep** om. F2668 *ou d'un bourbier* 'or from a pile of mud'.

1456 **elded** F2670 *avillis* 'dishonoured' var. *auieillis* MS. *H*.

1457 **alle ... kamen** F2671-2 *touz fameilleus | S'en revindrent* supports GJMOS. As in F2669, where *Touz noirs devindrent* was rendered by *al blac þei bicomen*, *touz* might be a pronoun, giving 'all returned hungry', or an adverb, giving 'they returned, totally unsatisfied'. If τ understood a pronoun, *alle* is simply over-literal, but the sense suggests adverbial emphasis on hunger rather than the number of sinners, so the form should perhaps be C's usual adverbial *al* (*all* at 1092, 2533, rarely *alle* as at 851, 1979). Cf. 1461.

1459 **obley** a thin cake or wafer, probably made without fat or yeast. Altar-bread was usually but not invariably made the same way.

1460 **þere** see n. 27-8.

1461-2 **of ... fulfilled** F2679-80 *dont il ourent tous, | Si remplis furent*; the grammatical function of *tous* (*alle*) is not clear: perhaps the comma should follow it. If it is an adv. (*il ourent, tous | Si remplis furent*), then the meaning (suggested by CG's punctuation and by the context, which contrasts fulfilment with the emptiness of evil communicants) is that good communicants were so satisfied that they desired nothing else. But *tous* (*alle*) might be adj.: 'all of them were so filled', emphasising the sacrament's infinite capacity for distribution rather than on its virtue. Literal rendering of *dont* by *of whiche* left *hadden* unidiomatic. CS

EXPLANATORY NOTES 407

normalised.

1466 **I wole telle** CJ's *wole I* might be correct.

1467 **abashed** (F2689 *esbahir*) should perhaps be *abashe*, following G as more literal.

1472-3 **not² ... fulfilled** F2700-2 *plainement, | Non pas un seul, mais eus trestous | En furent remplis* 'not merely one alone, but all were fully satisfied': *plainement* modifies *remplis*. τ needed *fulliche, not oon* ... for a literal if awkward rendering.

1478 **she ... hire** in view of F 2711 *elle (s')estoit acoutee*, CG's reflexive *hire* is accepted (*OED lean* VI, 2.b).

1479 **þe releef ... almused** F2714-15 *donner | Le dit relief et aumosner* is either 'the giving of the said relief and its distribution as alms' (where *aumosner* governs *relief*), or the more likely 'the giving of the said relief and the giving of alms' (where *aumosner* is absolute, without an object). τ omits *dit*, and for verbal nouns *donner* and *aumosner* substitutes the normal ME idiom in past participles. Replacing *donner* by *yiven* was easy, but for *aumosner* he had to assume a verb **almuse(n)* based on ME *almus*, sb., a variant of *almes(se)*, with a pp. *almused* (cf. G's *allmused*). C's *al musede* suggests that he took *al(l)* as a noun, *mused(e)* as a preterite: 'pondered everything'.

1486 **swich ten** om. F2726 *tans* 'so large'.

1488 **Goode** F2729 *Biaus*: see n. 142.

1494 **þou seye** F2740 *tu veis* I reject C's *sigh*, in spite of the fact that it is equivalent to G's *seye* 'you saw'. It is over erasure, and C uses *seye* as often.

1497 **I ... þee²** F2746 *Je t'avise et si te somme* supports the accepted readings.

1502 **Doted** F2755 *esbloie* 'blinded' var. *esbahys* MS. *A*.

1503-7 **But ... cleerliche** F2757-62 *Mais le sens d'ouir seulement | En enfourme l'entendement; | Celui a tast ici endroit | Odourement, goust et veoir, | Cetui connoist plus soutilment | Et apercoit plus clerement*, clarified by *Celui, Cetui*, for which τ finds no equivalent, means that only the sense of hearing instructs the understanding in these matters: 'In comparison with the senses of touch, smell, taste and sight, it comprehends more subtly and perceives more clearly'.

1506 **Þis** F2760 *Cetui* supports GS's reading. Harking back to *heeringe* in 1504, γ and β clarified.

1508 **Esau** om. F2765-7 *Quar Ysaac mon bien cuida | De Jacob qui l'apastela | Que ce fust son fil Esau* 'for Isaac really thought about Jacob who fed him that he was his son Esau'. Gen. xxvii 1-29. Independent eyeskip in α and β could explain the omission, but it looks as if τ's eye leapt from *Esau* to *Esau* at the end of F2764 and F2767. The missing passage is in the margin of C in a late medieval hand.

1512 **leeve** F2776 *apuies* 'lean': that CGJMS have *leeve in*, not *leeve on* suggests misreading of τ's *leene on* by χ (cf. 1832 *lenede to* for F *apuia*), but as with all these instances seeming to demonstrate independent existence of χ, the reading might be the result of τ's making false correction. Alternatively, *leeve in* 'believe in, rely on' is a rational substitution for 'lean on' (*MED leven* v. 4b gives examples of *leeve . . . to* 'pay attention to').

1515–16 **þe . . . wittes** F2781–2 *le voir n'en aras | Par ces .IIII. sens ne saras* 'you will never have the truth, nor learn it from these four senses' vars. *Par ces sens ne ne saras* MSS *oTABMH*.

1517 **leeue** F2783 *apuier*: see n. 1512.

1522 **spreynt** F2792 *cruentee* 'made bloody', not merely 'sprinkled'.

1523 **clepe . . . wurþilyche** F2794 *Bien dignement et apeler* shows that *wel* should modify *wurþilyche*: τ wrongly added *and* after *wel*.

1523–6 **Bred . . . man** John vi 35, 51.

1527 **with . . . aungeles** Ps. lxxvii 25; on *panis angelorum* see Petrus Lombardus, *PL*, CXCI, 1617.

1531 **þe . . . oonliche** 'only the hearing teaches you'.

1534–51 **Charitee . . . hoper** Paulinus of Nola calls this world a mill grinding (unspecified) wheat for our eternal consumption (*PL*, LXI, 194). That Christ is grain and bread is implicit in John xii 24, explicit in vi 51; in I Cor. xv 37 Paul's *nudum granum* may be the origin of Christ's 'naked body' in our text. General equation of Christ's life with the preparation of bread is common: *La Bible Moralisée* f. 59ᵛ, illustrating Lev. ii 1–9, interprets Jews baking bread as his conception, and the placing of bread in the pan as his Scourging. The image of his body milled is, however, rare at this date. Kirschbaum, *Mühle, mystische*, and Réau, II, part ii, pp. 420–1, cite no pre-15th-century examples (Réau's from the *Hortus Deliciarum* in fact illustrates Matt. xxiv 41. Further discussions of the Mill (offering no clearer precedent) are in Lindet, and Alois Thomas. Vloberg, pp. 172–83, discusses and illustrates *Le moulin et le pressoir mystiques*: no pre-15th-century example shows Christ ground up, but the destroyed 12th-century window of Saint-Denis not only showed the familiar 'OT ground into the NT', but also referred to *perpetuusque cibus noster et angelicus*, a eucharistic reference. The nearest example I know is a 12th-century literary Mill of the Passion: *Granum, autem per trituram de theca sua excutitur contumelis et approbriis arefactus, a Judaeis, et gentibus, quasi duobus lapidibus, flagellis atteritur, cribatus conspersus compastinatur, dum a suis separatus, sanguine proprio perfusus cruci compingebatur, in qua quasi panis in igne passionis excoctus in immortalitatem mutabatur* (Honorius of Autun, *PL*, CLXXII, 544). Perhaps Guillaume's

EXPLANATORY NOTES

image was itself influential.

1536 **greyn** F2817 *grain*: wheat, the noblest grain, was used for altar-bread (Jungman, II, 31-5): *Þæt clæne hwætene corn, þe Crist þa embespæc, tacnæþ hine sylfne* (Balfour, p. 75); *Þe vble ys made of whete, / Þe louelyest corne þat men ete* (Furnivall, *Robert of Brunne*, p. 315, col. 1, line 10092).

1538 **heete of sunne** F2821 *chaleur de soleil* somewhat supports G's reading, accepted on the assumption that CJMOS's is the result of independent smoothing in β, and SC (possibly influenced by β).

1539 **made berne it** F2823 *engrangier le fist*: one of the rare occasions when O alone in the β-branch agrees with the α-branch and F. *MED bernen* cites only this example.

1543-4 **was naked ... born** F2830-1 *nu fu et desnue. / Au moulin apres porte fu* may be punctuated in two ways: *nu* and *desnue* 'naked and stripped' may be parallel, or *desnue* may qualify the subject of *porte fu*. τ understood F in the second way, using *naked* twice.

1544 **disgisyliche** (F2832 *desguisement*) 'in strange attire' (suggesting the disguise of Christ's body in grain), also 'strangely, monstrously' or perhaps 'exceedingly' (*MED disgiseli*). There being no modern punning equivalent, I gloss it 'horribly'.

1545 **hoper** F2833 *balestes* var. *aulnes* MS. *A*. I gloss this 'machinery', with deliberate vagueness. 'Hopper' is not sense in context, since grain is not ground in a mill-hopper (essentially a container, as at 1551, where it stores flour) but is merely fed by gravity through it to the mill-stones. *Balestes* [Lat. *bal(l)ista*] usually means some kind of missile-throwing weapon. If it does mean 'hopper' here, perhaps it is because stones, before being discharged, were held in the 'bucket' of a *ballista* as grain is held in the feed-hopper.

in ... cloth F2834 *Ou il n'avoit pas dras de lin* is obscure too. If F's construction is personal, *il* refers back to *le grain*, and the reference is to Christ's being stripped. But τ clearly thought the construction impersonal, the *balestes* having no linen cloth. If he was right, the image might be one of four:

1. a cloth screening the grain-hopper against extraneous matter;
2. a cloth 'sleeve' at the end of the shute bringing grain from the upper floor down to the grain-hopper—lifting the end of the sleeve cuts off the supply of grain very precisely;
3. the filtering of flour through increasingly fine grades of linen in the flour-hopper;
4. the surrounding of the mill with curtains during almost liturgical preparation of altar-bread: under Cluniac reform 'wheat had to be selected kernel for kernel; the mill on which it was to be ground had to be cleaned, then hung about with curtains; the monk who supervised the milling had to don alb

ÞE LYFE OF ÞE MANHODE

and humeral' (Jungman, II, 35).

All these imply that the grinding of Christ was not a refined or refining process, but crude and cruel.

1546 **grounden** om. F2836 *trible* 'tortured'.

1547 **was ... wynd** F2837 *fait a vent estoit* 'was made to be turned by wind'.

1548 **nouht for þanne** see n. 1321-2.

1548-9 **þis ... softe** F2839-40 *ce moulin moles / Avoit qui n'estoient (pas) moles*: τ could not echo word-play on *moulin/moles/moles* 'windmill/millstones/soft' (noted by Mrs Walls).

1552-3 **bakere ... bred** F2847-8 *fournier / Pour pain faire et boulengiere* 'oven-cook and baker to make bread': *fournier* and *boulengiere* are parallel. τ mistook the latter for *bouleter* 'sift'.

1554 **so it is** F2851 *tant y a* 'it is so big': GMOS's reflection of an inaccurate translation is accepted against C's rationalisation.

1555 **cowde not turne** the verb (F2851 *tourner*) suggests both the movement of shaping bread, and the change of substance which Charity produces without the aid of Sapience (who may represent not only the wisdom of philosophy but Christ himself: see nn. 1572, 2009-10).

1557-8 **She ... maistresse** F2856 *D'une mestresse li souvint*: perhaps JMΩ's *of* should replace *on*, but *of*'s apparent closeness to F may be the accidental result of substitution.

1559 **Sapience** Wisdom here is God the Son (I Cor. i 24); the frequency of this identification (based on free application of the book of Wisdom to Christ) is apparent in ME literature (see Frances Smith).

1563-4 **in ... oxe** F2867-8 *dedens l'escaille d'un euf / Meist bien tout entier un buef*: this is not the result of ignorance about reproduction in oxen. French idiom associates *oeuf/boeuf* to represent small and large objects, e.g. *faire d'un oeuf un boeuf* 'make a mountain out of a molehill', also *donner un oeuf pour avoir un boeuf* and *qui vole un oeuf vole un boeuf*.

1572 **chayere** F2883 *cheoire* usually means the throne of the pontiff, or the bishop's throne in a cathedral. The dignity of Wisdom's seat shows that like Grace Dieu she represents an aspect of the deity (*OED wisdom* b,c), and may be identified with Christ by her part in transubstantiation.

1574 **book it** om. F2888 *et le moula* 'and moulded it'.

1582 **eche ... partyes** F2900 *chascune partie* var. *chascunes des parties* MSS *tBGM¹LA¹MH*: in view of the ME vars., perhaps this should be *eche [one] of þilke partyes*. However, uncorrected G also omitted *one*.

þat bred F2904 *du pain* var. *de ce pain* MSS *tBGM¹LA¹MH*: perhaps, as at 759, GS's *thilke (bred)* should be accepted.

EXPLANATORY NOTES

1585 **hire þat chidde** refers, as CG's commentators remark, to Nature. Grace has been speaking since 1488, and recalls the long argument between herself and Nature which began at 821, when Nature was indeed annoyed by the supranatural qualities of consecrated bread. Then, Nature's own objections merely underlined her subjection to Grace, so that the implication was *quid queris naturae ordinem in Christi corpore, cum praeter naturam sit ipse natus Christus ex Virgine*? (Durandus, *Rationale*, IV, xli, para. xxvii). Nature now tries logic, not law.

1585-6 **it ... hire** in view of F2910 *l'en pesa* GJMOS's reading is accepted.

1590 **Aristotle** is called to Nature's assistance as an authority on the relation of parts and wholes. *Metaph.*, VII, x-xi (Rose, II, 1024^b-1037^a) does not, of course, show the simple-minded approach attributed to him in our text, where he represents the inadequacy of philosophy to explain divine power. See Aquinas, *ST*, 3a. q.76. aa.1-4.

1601 **on ... side** this phrase occurs repeatedly (1617, 1926, 2058, 2355, 2363, 2541 *passim*), translating *d'autre part(ie)*. It means 'besides' or 'moreover' not, as in *OED* side sb^1, 'on the other hand'.

1606 **disgise** in view of F2944 *desguises*, GJS's reading (*MED disguise* adj., *OED disguisy* adj.) is accepted against C's *disgised*, erroneous rationalisation to the pp. of *disguise*. The sense is multiple: the bread is not changed in appearance, but it is 'elaborately prepared' and 'extraordinary' (see n. 1544). The spelling is C's at 1609, 4842, though he uses *disgisee, disgisy(e)*. Contrast 4858, 6171.

1607-8 **þat ... it** F2946-7 *Qui ou monde pas ne pourroit / Ne pas le ciel ne soufiroit*: the meaning, clumsily expressed, is that neither heaven nor earth can accommodate the nourishment offered by the Eucharist. The object of *suffice* should be 1616 *þe feedinge* (F2945 *la paisture*).

1610 **hep** F *masure* 'mass'; C corrupted this to *hopp* 'something circular' (whch *MED hop* unfortunately cites).

1613 **merveile hire** F2958 *s'en esveille* 'should grow angry at it' var. *si sen merveille* MS. A^1L.

1619 **withoute ... divininge** modifies *wisten* in 1618.

1622 **an al** F2977 *un tout* supports GJMOS's reading, accepted against C's *al*, which is perhaps the result of not having realised that the indefinite article is essential: 'a whole ... greater than a part'.

1638-9 **lilyes ... violettes** F3008 *Lis et glais et violetes* 'lilies, irises and violets': τ saw something like var. *Lis glais roses et violetes* MSS *HM* (his text had *gais* for *glais* or he thought it did).

1640-1 **þee ... argue** F3011-12 *(j')enseignoie / L'entendement et (l'en)*-

fourmoie 'I instructed the understanding and taught it to argue' (vars. *j*' om. in MS. *L*; ... *et le fourmoie* MS. *o*). All the ME manuscripts are corrupt. G's uncorrected *the y towghte the vnderstondinge and enfoourmed the to argewe* is accepted; though F gives no precedent for 1640 *þee* (G's *the*¹)—unless *j'enseignoie* [*i'enseignoie*] was misread as *t'enseignoie*—it is supported by GMO: MO's model rationalised to *þe I taught vndirstondynge*, and J rationalised to the ambiguous *I tawght the vndyrstandynge*. CG³S's *þere I taughte þee vnderstondinge* was a rationalisation by γ. Second, F gives precedent for 1641 *þee*. τ did not recognise the masc. pron., agreeing with *entendement*, at the beginning of *l'enfourmoie*. Perhaps, having read *t'enseignoie* at the end of F3011 he expected *t'enfourmoie* at the end of F3012.

1643 **canoun and lawe** F3016 *canon et lais* 'Canon Law and Civil [Law]'; in the var. *canons et loys* MS. *H*, *lais* was apparently mistaken for *leis* fem. pl. 'laws', and *canon* made *canons* to agree. τ probably mistook *lais* for *leis* too, but made it sg. to agree with *canon*. Wisdom, representing (*inter alia*, see n. 1572) revealed Christian knowledge, so develops Aristotelian thought that it becomes the basis for civil law and ecclesiastical law laid down by Papal Decrees and Councils.

scoole om. F3017 *deputee* ... *et* 'intended and'.

1651 **told** C uses *tolde* for pa. t., and *told* for pp. Here, *told* pa. t. may be due to elision of final *-e* before a vowel, or be an error, or be a variant form, for C is not always consistent: *tauht*, for example, is often pa. t. (6464, 6909) as well as pp.

1675 **bi ... discrecioun** modifies *arguest* in 1674.

1692 **apparence** F3108 *apparence* 'appearance': CGS have forms of *aparisaunce*, which could be correct—but *MED* cites only this example, deriving it from OF *aparissance* 'outward show or display'. JMOF make better sense in a discussion of the relation between the Accidents or appearance of the Host and its invisible actuality or Substance.

1694 **Yit** C has *Zit* (the same *Z* is last in the *ABC*, f. 115ᵛ). The other ME manuscripts have 3 or 3. C does not use either, so one would expect *Y* (quite clear at ff. 13ᵛ, 25ʳ, for example). The scribe's guide-letter to the rubricator is not visible here or in the *ABC*, but the error (repeated at 1727) is probably the rubricator's.

1696 **it is** F3116 *est*: in view of the likelihood of *it* being accidentally omitted before *is*, GS's *it is* is accepted. But CJMO's *is* may echo τ's literal rendering, and could be retained, assuming that G(S) smoothed.

1697 **deuynale** G's spelling is retained as it explains the corruption. C has no precedent for this form, the nearest being 1619 *divinynge*. The sense is that one should believe the Mystery of Transubstantiation without undue struggle to lay intellectual hold on it: while not irrational it is inapprehensible.

1706 **a kyte** (F3135 *un escouffle*) perhaps used here with the general sense 'bird of prey'. JMO's *glede* also carries both meanings. The English version of Albertus Magnus refers to: '*Milvus*, a Kite or Glede' (Best and Brightman, p. 58). The rare kite was once a common scavenger. It was probably *Milvus milvus* (*Milvus ictinus, regalis, vulgaris*) the Red Kite (D. W. Yalden, 'Bones of Scavengers,' *The Daily Telegraph*, 12 Sept. 1981, p. 16). The image is of a portion so small that it will not even satisfy an already glutted bird.

1708-9 **with ... fulfilled** F3139 *sa capacite*: it is not like τ to translate 2 words by 8, and it is hard to see why he did not use *capacitee* here as at 1772; however, *MED capacite* has no example earlier than A.D. 1425, and the word is glossed *desyr* by G's corrector, so perhaps τ felt paraphrase necessary at first.

1713-14 **filling to suffisance** in view of F3148 *remplage a soufisance* 'a meal sufficient to satisfy hunger', GJMOS's *fullynge* 'a fill of food' is accepted (with C's spelling, on the assumption that both are from *OED fill* v.²) against C's *fulfillinge* 'repletion' (*MED fulfilling* b). GS's *suffisance* is accepted because unlike C's *sufficience* it derives from OF *soufisance*. Another possibility would be to give the word C's usual *-aunce* ending—but C does use *-ance* at 198, in *aqueytance*.

1714 **be** F3150 *Soit* supports GJS's reading.

1714-15 **commune ... spred** F3150 *autorite vulguee*: τ rendered *vulguee* by both *commune* and *þat is wide spred*: a rare case of his hedging his bets.

1716-17 **in ... empty** Aristotle, *Physics*, IV, vi-ix (Rose, II, 213ª-217ᵇ).

1719 **god ... sovereyn** the *summum bonum*, that which men desire above all else: Aristotle, *Nicomachean Ethics*, I, 1,2 (Ross, IX, 1094ª). By development from *Nicomachean Ethics*, Xd, 8 (Ross, IX, 1178ᵇ) where contemplation is presented as the most perfect way of life, the *summum bonum* came to be identified with God.

1726-7 **shal ... false** F3172 *sera faus tes dis* var. *seront faus tes dis* MSS *BL*; perhaps *seyinges* should be sg. not pl., following JMO, since though *tes dis* might be sg. or pl., the verb is sg. However, I have retained CGS's reading on the assumption that τ saw the var.

1727 **Yit** C has *Zit*: see n. 1694.

1728 **Grece** F3175 *Romme* var. *Grece* MSS to*BMGM¹H*. Stürzinger's reading, from his MSS *TA*, is because of F3180 *les citez* (1731 *þe citees*) and F3193 *deux cites grans* (1739 *tweyne grete citees*).

1728-31 **Grece ... ben** Augustine said of the capacity of the mind to retain large images: *Meministine tandem urbis Mediolanensis? ... recordaris quanta et qualis sit?* (*De Quantitate Animae*, I, v; *PL*, XXXII, 1040, cited Hultman, p. 99 with a wrong reference).

1730 **how ... ooþer** F3178 *Combien l'une et l'autre contient* 'how much they both contain': the reason for mistranslation is unclear.

1736 **I...hem** F3188 *mis les ai* supports GJMOS's reading. In addition, G's omission of a line between *put* in 1735 and *put hem* in 1736 suggests that his model had *put* in both places, causing eyeskip.

1737 **Oo...Sapience** F3189 *A Sapience respondu* 'Sapience replied': τ mistook auxiliary *A* for 'Aah!'—an understandable error in view of *Haa* at 2064 and 2075, correctly rendering *A* (F3789 and F3809).

1740-3 **In...apertliche** Durandus, *Rationale*, II, XLI, para. xxiv, explains the Eucharist: *Le huitième prodige, c'st que son corps, qui est immense, se trouve contenu dans si petite hostie; on en peut donner cette raison, que la pupille de l'oeil, qui pourtant est bien petite, ne laisse pas que d'embrasser une vaste montagne* (Berthélemy, II, 267). Voragine, VII, 244 uses the same image. Augustine used the pupil analogy of the memory: the quotation cited in n. 1728-31 goes on *aut nunquam in pupilla oculi alieni faciem tuam vidisti?*

1743-4 **looke...shap** the mirror analogy is questioned by Aquinas, *ST*, 3a, q.76. a3 (Gilby, LVIII, 103).

1746 **maxime** appears to be one of the occasions when JMO preserve τ's reading (see p. lxiii). The form given is C's at 1621, where all the English MSS have *maxime*.

1748 **tobroken** om. F3210 *et rout* 'and broken'.

1750 **þi...apertliche** F3214 *Ta face* gives no precedent for *apertliche*; perhaps τ wrote *þi visage al* 'all your face', and then χ took *al* to modify not *visage*, but some missing adv., and so supplied *apertliche*.

1753-68 The sequence *localliche / virtualliche / ymaginatyfliche / representatyfliche* and then *bodilich / rialliche / presentliche / verreyliche* may originate in an untraced patristic treatise on Modes of Being in the Eucharist (e.g. *PL*, CCIX, 787, 857-8). Cf. similar contrasting adverb-groups in the Council of Trent, A.D. 1551, *signo / figure / virtute* and *vere / realiter / substantialiter*: an observation I owe to Fr J. Crehan S.J. Aquinas, *ST*, 3a, q.75. aa.1-2 and q.76. aa.1-7, dismisses the idea that Christ is present locally in the Sacrament, but he does not use these adverbs. The main point is that Aristotle is trying to blind Wisdom with philosophy.

1754 **þat...put** F3223 *Soient mises toutes ces* gives no precedent for *þat*[1], subpuncted G³ and omitted in C, whose reading should perhaps be accepted on the assumption that Gβ independently smoothed.

1754-5 **put...enclosed** F3223-4 *mises... / Es lieus qu'avez dit et (en)-closes* 'put and enclosed in the places you have mentioned' is followed too literally by τ.

EXPLANATORY NOTES

1758 **ymaginatyfliche** F3230 *imaginaument*: *MED imaginatifliche* cites only this example.

1760 **it ... anoon** 'it is not necessary to bother to understand all this at once'.

1775-6 **litel ... hath** F3263 *petit pain a* 'there is a little bread': τ was over-literal, or understood F3261 *le cuer (herte)* as the subject of *a (hath)*.

1776 **if ... ynowh** F3264 *Se assez veut*; *assez (ynowh)* is either adverbial or an adj. used predicatively: 'if it [the heart] wants sufficiently' or 'if it wants there to be enough'.

1782 **I ... answere** the ambiguity of *shulde* leaves the force of F3275-6 *je ne doi ... respondre* 'I am not obliged to answer you' unexpressed.

1783 **if ... summething** F3277-9 *se faire (je) ne savoie / Ou en nul temps ne faisoie / Aucun(e) chose*: F's conditional construction, two imperfects, *savoie (faire)* and *faisoie* followed by conditional *seroie* in F3281, means 'if I did not know how to do something or sometimes did not do it, then ...'.

1788-9 **for ... can** F3289-90 *Pour Charite tous jours ferai / Quanque je plaire li saray* 'I will always do for Charity whatever I know will please her' var. for F3290: *Tant que lui plaire je saray* MS. *A* 'I will always do for Charity as much as I can to please her': τ saw something like the var.

1795 **ayens** F3298 *contre*: I accept GJO's reading (of which S's *ageynst* is a var.) because everywhere else in Book 1 C uses *ayens* for 'against', and *ayen* for 'again'.

1814-15 **I seide þee** at 139-46 the pilgrim was not given Faith and Hope, the staff and satchel later to support him, because he had not received the instruction to enable him to support them.

1819-20 **Withoute failinge** like the ME, F3344 *sans faillir* might modify either what precedes or what follows it, so perhaps the previous sentence should end with *failinge*.

1820 **þe ... burdoun** these were the object of Pontifical blessing when a pilgrim set out on a journey: see the unpublished version of the 13th-century Durandus' *Pontificale of Mende*, BL MS. Add. 39677, ff. CXLI^r-CXLII^r (modern ff. 142^r-143^r).

1825-6 **Me ... forthward** (F3355 *Mont* [recte: *Mout*] *m'est tart que meu soie* 'It seems very late for me to be on my way') is idiomatic.

1826 **fer þilke citee** in view of F3357 *loins la belle cite*, GS's reading (corrupted in JMO to *for ...*) is accepted against C's *fer to þilke citee*; *þilke* may originate in corruption of *belle* to *celle*.

1831-2 **so ... to** is one of the occasions when MO preserve τ's reading (with a variation in J, which nevertheless retains *bare*). CGS omit *bar* (see p. lxii).

1840-66 The bells are inscribed with a Creed, the elements of which are here printed bold to distinguish them from phrases not in the Nicene, Apostles' or Athanasian Creed (see n. 1916). However, these articles do not correspond exactly with any of the major Creeds, where belief in the Spirit is 8th not 3rd. *PL*, CCXIX, 919-28 is an index to exegesis of the Creed. Durandus' *Du symbole* explains each article (Berthélemy, II, 156). Literary Creeds are discussed (in the context of a well-known one by the 13th-century Joinville, whose text is in Friedman, a commentary on it in Langlois, 'Le Credo de Joinville') by Lozinski, who on his pp. 179-82 lists 12th- to 15th-century French prose and verse Credos which show similar amplification.

1844 **thinges** F3389 *cloches* 'bells' var. *choses* MSS *toBM¹LM*.

1844-5 **michel ... dredinge** F3389-90 *mervelleuses / Mont me furent et (fort) douteuses*: difficulty has been caused by *fort douteuses* 'terrifying' or 'very uncertain in meaning', sometimes suggesting uncertainty in size (Greimas *dotos* s.v. *doter*, *MED doutous* 1.a.3). The sense 'very puzzling' suits the deliberately impossible-to-visualise image of three bells sharing a clapper. G's *muchull wonderfull and gretleche dredynge*, supported by MO (and J, with minor variations) is accepted. τ correctly took *fort* as adv., understanding *douteuses* as 'terrifying' (*MED dreden* v., 6.a). But terror is not appropriate to the Mystery of the Trinity, which may be why γ, puzzled, referred back to the French, as shown in CG³'s readings (see p. lxxvii).

G's corrector marked *gretleche* and *dredynge* for gloss and tried a new translation. Unfortunately he compounded confusion, unnecessarily subpuncting *muchull* (F *mont*), taking *fort* as adj., and failing to elucidate *douteuses*. At the bottom of the page he wrote the whole clause to which C's reading is related: *but thyse thre thynges weren to mee wonderffull and [erasure] and hard and doutous*.

1845 **of so nyh** F3391 *(de) si pres* 'so closely': cf. Caxton, '*The deth that of nyghe foloweth them*' (*OED of* 64b).

1846 **alle be oon** in view of F3392 *tout(e) une estre*, GMO's reading (corrupted in JS to *alle but ane*) is accepted.

1846-7 **þat ... claper** F3394-5 *Quar seulement es trois ne vi / Que un martel qui y estoit*, words in square brackets are supplied from G, variations of which appear in all the MSS except C (see p. lxiv).

1849-55 **descendede ... sett** grammatical functions are elusive, perhaps confused by F3399-411's awkward mixture of transitive and intransitive verbs throughout its participle constructions: *descendus, conceus, fait, ne, tourmente, mis, navre, mort, ensevlis, Descendu, Susite, monte, assis*. If τ echoes F in the use of participles or adjectives, 1849 *descendede* (G's form too) may be a scribal error for pp. *descended*, to which it should be emended. But perhaps τ tried unsuccessfully to echo the Latin Creed's

EXPLANATORY NOTES

mixture of preterites and participles. In this case 1849 *descendede*, 1852 *descended* (both Lat. *descendit*), 1854 *sussited* (Lat. *resurrexit*) are pa. t. sg. (for which C uses both *-ed* and *-ede*). However, 1854 *steyn* is certainly pp., whereas the Latin has *ascendit*.

1851 **nature** τ misread F3404 *navre* 'wounded' as *natvre*, preserved in G (and clearly repeated in the catchword). C(S) emended to *naturelly*.

1852 **helle** F3406 *l'infernal palu* 'the infernal mire'.

1859 **þe¹... cristenynge** the Creed notes an effect of Baptism: remission of original and actual sin, and of punishment due because of them.

1869 **tre of Sethim** wood of the acacia or shittah-tree: shittim wood. The Ark of the Covenant was made of this fire-proof and rot-proof wood (Ex. xxv 10-15, xxvi 15). See Bartholomaeus Anglicus, p. 1048, and Durandus, *Rationale*, I, Chap. 1, para. 13.

1883-4 **Nothing... it¹** F3463 *Rien en li ne me desplaisoit*; with no F precedent for *þere* 'that place', I retain C's *þer* on the (perhaps mistaken) assumption that it is unemphatic (see n. 27-8).

1884 **yrened** F3464 *ferre*: MED *irened* translates this example 'made of iron', but the word is used of horses' shod hooves, and a pilgrim's staff would be tipped or 'shod' with iron, not made of it.

1885 **me¹** om. F 3466 *tel* 'like this'.

1895 **þe... scrippe** Rom. i 17; Heb. ii 4, x 38: visible only under u.v. is *Iustes ex fide sunt* at the bottom of M's f. 25ᵛ.

1898 **greenesse... sight** *Carystei viriditas reficiat oculos. Nam et qui nummulariam discunt, denariorum formis myrteos pannos subiciunt, et gemmarum sculptores scarabeorum terga, quibus nihil est viridius, subinde respiciunt, et pictores idem faciunt, ut laborem visus eorum viriditate recreent*: Isidore (*PL*, LXXXII, 240), cited by Bartholomaeus Anglicus (Trevisa, II, 1290); *Ancren Riwle* says *grene ouer alle heowes frouređ meast ehnen* (Tolkien, p. 97).

1901-2 **she shal neede þee** F3493 *elle t'ara mestier* 'it will help you' refers to *la verdeur*: τ, understanding the alternative meaning of the construction *avoir mestier*, translated *elle* literally.

1902 **to... wey** om. F3495-6 *A ce que loing tu voies | Le pais ou tu t'avoies* 'so that from a long way off you should be able to see the country in which you may live.' Either τ misunderstood the previous construction and so did not recognise a reference to Hope given by Faith, or his source lacked F3495-6 by eyeskip (*voie adrecier... voies... avoies*).

1903 **for... God** F3497 *or* 'now' or 'but' var. *pour Dieu* MSS *tBGM¹LMH*.

1904 **atached** in view of 1330 *tacche*, the reading could be *[atacched]*.

1904-5 **þe thre ... claper** patristic similes and metaphors of the Trinity abound (e.g. Augustine, *Sermo de Symbolo, PL*, XL, 1195). I have not found a source for this image.

1908 **þe** F3508 *Ceste* 'this'.

1908-9 **withoute ... belles** F3507-8 *sans sonnetes* / ... *et sans clochetes*: τ could not echo the puns on *sonnetes* 'chants' (the phrases of the Creed written on the bells) and 'little bells'. *OED ringer* omits this sense 'little bells'.

1913 **elded** F3518 *avillie* 'dishonoured' var. *aviellie* MS. M^1.

1914 **þe bewte** F3519 *sa biaute* 'its beauty' var. *la beaute* MS. *T*.

1916 **þe twelve Apostles** for the apocryphal attribution of each article to an Apostle see *The Book of the Vices and Virtues*, a translation of *Somme le roi* by the 13th-century Lorens d'Orleans (Francis, pp. 6-9). Durandus, *Rationale*, IV, XXV, paras. 6, 7, gives the three major Creeds, the tradition by which Apostles contributed their articles, and each attribution. See Jauss, II, 21-2 for Creeds in prose and verse. For the tradition in iconography see, e.g., contemporary Calendars described by Joan Evans, p. 200, and reproduced in Morand.

1919-26 **Þese ... þee** the Creed is to echo in the mind. In a sermon on the Creed, Augustine explains Jer. xxxi 33 'I will put my law in their inward parts, and write it in their hearts' by *Hujus rei significandae causa, audiendo symbolum dicitur: nec in tabulis, vel in aliqua materia, sed in corde scribitur* (*PL*, XXXVIII, 1060). I have found no source for articles as bells (but *PL*, CCXIX, 919 may well conceal one). Aquinas, *ST*, 2a2ae, q.1. a.9 dicusses Creeds: as well as being a bulwark against heresy, they are for those 'busy with other matters [who] cannot find the time for study' (cf. 1924).

1920 **heere** F3529 *si* 'therefore' or, as τ thought, a form of *ci*.

1923 **for ... belles** F3535-6 *Pour nient (en) guise de clochetes* / *Ne sont pas mie* 'they are not put there like bells for nothing' is the reading of all Stürzinger's collated MSS except *L* (which he accepts).

1924 **if ... writinge** (F3537-8 *se de veoir es escris* / *Estoies trop lens ou remis*): *leftest* is in doubt. The accepted explanation of the variants is that τ took F3538 *remis* 'idle, negligent' for 'you delayed', and wrote *leftest* (*MED leven* v.¹ 1c), corrupted in χ to *lestest*, and altered by G to *lested* (cf. *listed* S), perhaps with the mistaken sense 'you wished' (*MED listen* v.¹), while β, taking it as a form of *list* 'to please', substituted *lyste nouȝt*, trying to make sense; finally it was correctly emended in γ back to *leftest*, whence CG^3. Another possibility is that τ, correctly understanding *remis*, wrote *lechese* 'remiss', which though unrecorded is a plausible form in view of *MED laches(se)* adj., and *leche* cited under *lache* adj. He uses this word at 6881, 7003. In

EXPLANATORY NOTES 419

this case, χ miscopied *lechese* as *lestest*.

1926 **Poul** Rom. x 17.

1928-9 **so ... scrippe** F3545- *Si ques la cloqueterie | En l'escherpe ne nuist mie* 'so the ringing in the satchel does no harm [i.e. it does good]' var. *... ne mist il* MSS *BMM*[1].

1930 **bileeue** F3548 *Dieu croire* 'believe in God' var. *croire* MS. *M*[1].

1933 **bred** F3553 *pain blanc* 'white bread'.

1937 **in soothnesse** F3562 *en unite* 'in unity' var. *en verite* MSS *BLM*.

1937-8 **God ... it is** F3563 *Dieu seul es trois personnes est* 'one God is in three persons' var. *Dieu seul et* .... See Isidore, *PL*, LXXXII, 271 (cited Gewande, 17).

1941-2 **for ... vnderstant** F3569-70 *Quar des douze tout se depent | Qui a son droit tout bien entent* 'for everything hangs on the twelve, if one understands everything properly'.

1946 **meevede al my corage** F3578 *mon courage tout esmut* is ambiguous: *tout* may be adj. or adv.; if it is the latter the sense is 'completely upset me [my mind]'.

1946-7 **I hadde ... bifore** F3579-80 *autre fois veu | Ne l'avoie n'aperceu*: τ omits *n'aperceu*, destroying the parallel between *veu ... n'aperceu* here and *veoie ... apercevoie* in the next line (1947 *I hadde seyn and apperceyued*).

1947-8 **I ... scrippe** F3581-2 *l'i veoie | Encore et apercevoie* 'I often used to look at it there, and give it my attention': the dreamer wonders how he could have missed blood-spots on such a familiar satchel. In F, contrast between pluperfects in F3579-80 (see n. 1946-7) and these imperfects expressing habitual past action distinguishes 'it' (that the satchel was blood-spotted) from 'it' (the satchel). ME tenses could not equal these subtleties, so τ replaced the second F pron. by *þe scrippe*, producing an apparent contradiction.

1954 **þat highte ... scrippe** F3594-5 *Qui en jeunece Estevenin | Ot non qui l'escherpe portoit*: Acts vi 8-vii 60. It is more likely that *en jeunece* modifies *Ot non* than *portoit*: 'who in his youth was called Stephen, and carried the satchel'.

1956-7 **peyneden hem** F3599 *se penerent* supports GJMOS's reading. C's *him* may be by attraction from *him* four words later.

1960-1 **men ... stoned him** F3604-6 *on le tuast. | Toutevoies (il) le tuerent. | (Et) murtrirent et lapiderent*: perhaps the second *sloowen* means 'beat' rather than 'killed'—a sense possible in F too.

1962 **bidropped and aproved** F3607-8 *goutee | ... et esbouciee* 'covered with drops and spattered' vars. *esconciee* MS. *B*, *ensanglantee* MS. *A*, *coulouree* MS. *L*. F has the same participles at 1973 (F3627-8) and 1983-4 (F3645-6), giving *(bi)dropped* and *preuued*.

It is hard to see how *esbouciee* could give *aproved/preuued* 'confirmed/approved'. Did τ see *esprouvee* in all three places, or did he associate blood-sprinkling with sanctification or authorisation (as if the Satchel were sealed with a red mark, like a document)?

1965 **his bleedinge** F3614 *l'ensanglantement* 'its [the satchel's] bloodying' var. *le sanglantement*. It is uncertain which MSS have the var.: Stürzinger is inconsistent here.

1967-8 **defende ... it**² F3619 *la deffendre et garder*. It looks as if JS's reading, accepted against C's *defende and keepe it*, was the reading in G's model, *defend it* being misread as *defendit*, giving G's *defended* (the final *d* of which G³ subpuncted, inserting *it* after it). But perhaps C's reading, nearer F, is correct.

1968 **þei ... hem** F3621-2 *Eus despecier et desmemberer* / *Se faisoient* 'they caused themselves to be cut up and dismembered' var. *Se lessoient* MS. L. The ME inf. is the object of *suffreden* (Mustanoja, pp. 533-54). τ omits the otiose *despecier et* 'to be broken up and'.

1968-9 **and ... peynes** F3621 *paines souffrir* var. *et paines souffrir* MSS *otM*¹: τ saw the var., but replaced *souffrir* by a pa. t., altering the construction and sense.

1969 **tormentes** F3621 *tourmenter* is passive inf., parallel with F3620 *desmemboror* : τ makes it a noun parallel with *peynes* (see n. 1968-9).

1972-3 **bidropped ... preeued** F3627-8 *goutee* / ... *et esbouciee*; see n. 1962.

1973 **it ... thing** F3630 *Ce n'est pas chose* supports GMS's reading.

1974-5 **to ... michel** which C omits by eyeskip from *michel* in 1974 to *michel* in 1975, is supplied in accordance with F3630-1 *a prisier;* / *Quar n'i a goutte (si) petite* / *Qui (assez)* from GJMOS.

1975 **þat nis:** absent in C (see n. 1974-5), the reading is G's (echoed in S); but if χ had an uncontracted form (reflected in J's *þat it ne es*, MO's *þen it is*), the reading should be *þat ne is*.

1975-6 **þat ... preciows** F3632-4 *Qui (assez) miex de [une] marguerite* / *Ne vaille et (que) plus precieuses* / *Ne soit et (tres) plus vertueuse*: τ omits the last four words 'and much more powerful'. He may omit all F3634 (F3635 begins similarly): *Ne soit* is unnecessary if you take *precieuses* as parallel with *miex*.

1982-3 **dropped ... preeved** F3645-6 *goutee* / *De sanc et si esbouciee*: see n. 1962.

1986 **þee**¹ om. the otiose F3651 *et mort souffrir*.

1991-2 **she ... it** F3661-3 *elle me plaist* / *Et rien en li ne me desplaist,* / *Si la penrai* 'it [the satchel] pleases me, and nothing about it offends me, so I will take it'.

2002 **burdoun** Ps. xxii 4.

2009-10 **The ... spot** Ambrose (*PL*, xx, 22) speaks of Christ as *speculum Dei majestatis*, echoing Wis. vii 26, and perhaps I Cor. xiii 12. The conceit of Christ or Mary as a mirror is common in art: *Speculum sine macula* is one of Mary's titles (Crisp, figs. 68, 70). In *La Roman de la Rose* 17,425-53 (Lecoy, III, pp. 23-4) God sees all things in the mirror of Himself.

2014-15 **Lene ... poyntes** F3701-2 *Toi apuier i de touz poins | Et fort aherdre t'i aus poins* 'you must lean on it with both hands, taking hold of the knobs firmly' or 'you must lean on it at all times ...'. τ omits *de touz poins* (but at 2605 [F4774] he correctly translates *de tous poins* by *of alle poyntes* 'of everything' or 'completely'); he could hardly have echoed the play on *poins* ('handfuls' or 'points in time' and 'pomelles'). Perhaps he also read *poins*² as *points*, since he uses *poyntes* instead of his usual *pomelles*: but he may have meant to clarify the allegorical sense 'hang on to the main things in life (i.e. Christ and Mary)'.

2020 **þilke** om. F3710 *Dont vint, dont fu et* 'from whom he came, from whom he had his origin and'.

2022-6 **charbuncle ... ouerthrowen** see n. 122.

2023 **distracte** F3716 *eschampes* means 'escaped, broken loose' rather than 'distracted' (the ME carries modern connotations of distress as well as failure in concentration).

2026 **graffed** may mean that the lower hand-hold is grafted, not merely joined, suggesting the Virgin's place on the Tree of Jesse: for a moment the staff, Hope, is identified with God's design for salvation as represented in that tree which, rooted in Isaiah's prophecy of the rod of Jesse, blossoms into Mary and then Christ (see Watson).

2029 **eche** F3727 *Pour ce que chascun* 'because each ...': τ omits *Pour ce que*, but *for* (as supplied by J) would have been clearer.

2035 **hyere** F3738 *pas si bas* 'not so low': a rare deviation in τ.

2043 **redy I was** F3751 *apreste estoie* supports GJMOS's reading.

2068 **were** om. F3796 *bien* 'well'.

2069 **I speke þis** F3798 *En parle je* 'I speak of it' supports GJMS's reading (*OED speak* v. 27).

2070 **burdoun is not** F3800 *bourdon n'as pas* 'you do not have a staff' var. *bourdon nest pas* MS. *M*.

2071-4 **if ... þee** F3803-7 *se tu dis que (toi) deffendre | [Te] veuz sans plus, (sans) point offendre, | Armes dont bien te deffendras | Et dont tes ennemis vaincras | Assez tost je te baillerai* 'if you are saying you only want to defend yourself without using violence, I will give you armour with which you will be well able to defend yourself, and overcome your enemies at once'. τ misplaces *withoute offence* (which in F modifies *deffendre*, not *deffendras*), so losing F's double meaning: by wearing Grace's armour instead of using his staff in battle, the dreamer would defend himself

422 ÞE LYFE OF ÞE MANHODE

without using violence or offending Grace.

2072 **armures** Rom. xiii 12 and Eph. vi 13-17. Armour acquired different meanings in chivalry: Cohen, *Histoire*, ch. 16, gives an account of this symbolism, and in ch. 20 gives the associated ceremony.

2079-80 **bihold ... with** F3815-17 *regarde, dist elle, en haut | A celle perche, s'il me faut, | Pour querir armes, loing aler* 'Look up at this rack, she said, [and see] if I have to go a long way to look for armour!' τ, if not using a corrupt MS, did not notice *s* 'if', and took *querir* with *faut*, and *aler* as inf. of purpose, as if F were . . . *il me faut | Querir armes, pour loing aler.*

2081 **helmes** etc.: armour of the relevant period (to A.D. 1330) is described in Martin, pp. 41-9 and Pls. 29, 30, 39-42, 44, 45, 52, 148; in Blair, pp. 37-52, 197, 207; in Leloir, pp. 164, 208, 214, 228, 332. None of the technical words can be dated with sufficient precision to give the translation's date: mostly they appear in the late 14th century—many are much earlier. Each piece of armour will be discussed at the line where it is donned by the pilgrim (since he puts it on in the correct order), not that in which Grace discusses it. For *helm* see n. 2460, *haubergoun* n. 2184, *gorger* n. 2459, *jakke* or *doublet* or *pourpoint* n. 2091, *taarge* n. 2463.

2090 **but if** perhaps GS's *butt* should be accepted: Cβ might have added *if* to clarify *but*.

2091 **a doublet** F3837 *un gambeson*: a close-fitting tunic or *gambeson*—the same as *jakke* (2082) and *pourpoint* (2111). At 2132 the pilgrim complains of its weight, so the poet may have meant the type reinforced by metal rings or plates. It is also heavy because of the allegorical anvil at its back (the armour is otherwise realistic).

2093 **an anevelte** F3843 *une enclume*: a rare occasion (see 2193, 2711) on which O is alone in the β-branch in agreeing with the α-branch, at a point where F offers no guide to the correct reading, the ME variants simply being synonyms for 'an anvil'. JM have *a stithe*, O has *an anueld id est a stethi*, so that the β-branch readings are explained by *anueld* glossed *stithe* in β, both reading and gloss being incorporated into O. For association of Fortitude (here the doublet of Patience) with an anvil, see Tuve, p. 166, fig. 15, who cites no example earlier than Guillaume.

2097-8 **a pile** (F3850 *un pel* [Lat. *palus*] 'a stake') 'a stake used in practising swordsmanship' (*OED pile* sb., 3c). The image is of a man handicapped in self-defence by being not only without hands and feet but also tied to a stake designed to receive swordblows. *Pel* was also used of the Cross (at 2118-20 the tied figure becomes Christ crucified).

There are three possible explanations for CJMO's *pileer*. *Pile* being rare, Cβ may independently have misread it *pile* as *pile*er,

EXPLANATORY NOTES

or independently have substituted an expected image: the pillar to which Christ was bound for his beating (as at 1327, where *pileer* correctly renders *estache*). The pillar was associated with the flagellation even by Jerome, who vouched for a relic of it in the Holy Land (Pickering, p. 230). Finally, C may have consulted a MS of the β-branch, as at other points of obscurity (see pp. lxv–lxvii).

2098 **but þat** F3851 *Mais que* 'provided that': τ rendered *Mais* as *but* (so GMO) 'as long as' (*MED but* conj., 5b). CJ, finding this usage ambiguous, emended to *If*.

2108 **fat ... strengthe** following F3867–8 *encraissier ... enforcier*, *fat* and *strengthe* are infinitives.

pouerte F3869 *Pointure* 'anguish' (lit. 'piercing') var. *pourete* MS. *o*.

2110–11 **þe ... purpoynt** F3873–4 *fait est | De pointures le gambeson, | Pour quoi pourpoint bien l'appele on*: play on *pointures | pourpoint* is not so clear in the ME *poynynges | purpoynt*: made by many needle-piercings during its quilting, the doublet is aptly named 'on account of the points' (Leloir, *pourpoint*); the name signifies its manufacture and its protective function.

2116 **an anevelte** F3883 *(une) enclume*: C omitted *an* by haplography. This is one of the occasions when O's witness is important, it alone in the β-branch agreeing with the α-branch.

2117–18 **for to ... endure** in view of F3885–6 *Pour recevoir*, G's reading, echoed in JMO and misread in S, is accepted. CG³'s reading derives from γ's, rationalising the literal translation.

2119 **wered on Ihesus** F3887 *vesti Jhesus*: the function of *on* is unclear; it is either, as F suggests, adv. 'on [his] person' (*OED wear* v¹ c), or indef. pron. 'a certain' (used with *Iesu* by Wycliffe, Tyndale—*OED one* 20).

2120–1 **rihted ... rihtes:** τ transposed F's word-play; see p. lxxxviii.

2125 **forgeden ... him²** F3897–8 *la forgierent ... et monnoierent* 'they forged and minted it [*la raenson*] on his back' var. *le forgierent ... et monnoierent* MS. *A*, which makes it seem that Christ is being forged, although *him* may refer in fact to the ransom. Christ as an anvil originates in Ps. cxxviii 3: *supra dorsum meum fabricaverunt peccatores* (Pickering, pp. 271–2, Pl. 27a): in the *Speculum Humanae Salvationis*, the *Nailing to the Cross* is prefigured by Tubalcain at his forge (Gen. iv 2).

2134–9 **youre ... riht** as at 2120–1, τ transposed F's word-play.

2146–8 **techeth ... riht** the effect of the pilgrim's sarcastic enquiry is ironic: the only carpenters in the *Pilgrimage* are God the Father (1367), and Grace Dieu (963, 969, 1009–10), to whom the irritated pilgrim is speaking. By them he will indeed be cut down to size.

2147 **to wite soothliche** F3935 *A savoir mon* 'for my information' var. *A savoir moult* MS. *M*.

2149 **envyous** F3940 *ennuieus* var. *enuieux* MS. *A*: the correct reading is in doubt in F and ME. If τ saw the var., CS's *envyous* 'irritable' is right (*MED envien* v. 2 and *envious* adj.). But in the other ME readings (*enuiyous* G, *enuyous* JMO) the third letter could be vowel *u* or consonant *v*: if τ's source had *ennuieus*, our reading should be *enuyous* 'annoying' (*MED enuien* under *anoien*, *ennoious* under *anoious*).

2153-4 **Þouh... þee** F3947-8 *Se grief te semble a ce premier, | Ce n'est fors pour toi appointier*: C's omission was due to eyeskip from *rihte þee* in 2153 to *rihte þee* in 2154. Otiose *þerof* may be due to τ's conflation of constructions used with OED *think* v.¹, *think* v.².

2156 **missey... dooth** F3951-2 *mesdie | Ou (qui)... face*: τ probably followed F subjunctive *mesdie*, and then, parallel subjunctive and indicative not being rare in ME (Visser, p. 885), reverted to idiomatic *dooth* for the second verb. Agreement of G(S) and MO suggests that CJ smoothed.

2161-2 **gryndinge of corownement** F 3961-2 *emolument... de couronnement* 'reward of coronation' (I Cor. ix 25; Apoc. ii 10). τ gave the 'etymological' rendering of *emolument* (ultimately from Lat. *emolere* 'to grind out') instead of the developed medieval meaning 'reward, payment'. β read or substituted *grauntynge* (made to *graant* by J).

2165 **þe**¹ F3968 *Les* supports GMOS's reading.

þat¹ **... loueden** F3968 *du pourpoint armes* 'armed with the doublet': τ read *du... aimes* (pl. of pp.) 'characterised by love [of]' (giving 'who loved').

2171-2 **Tribulation... be** see 6442-594.

2184 **a haubergeoun** this jacket of mail (see 2204-5) goes over the pourpoint. The pilgrim does not put it on until 2457: he stands, wearing the pourpoint, to see all the other armour first. The result is the dismay caused by trying to understand and embrace all the virtues at once, instead of being prepared to acquire them slowly.

2189 **purpos** F4009 *propos* 'the power of speech' var. *pourpos* MSS *M*¹*L*.

2192 **who** in view of F4013 *qui*, GJMOS's *ho* 'who' is accepted, with C's normal spelling (he uses *ho* only at 136); however, C's *he* shows that χ had *ho*.

2192-3 **preyseth... bodde** F4014 *ne la prise un bouton*. O's witness is valuable, it alone in the β-branch agreeing with the α-branch. β used *setten* instead of *preysen*, but F's 'bud' idiom is echoed only in CGS, and O's *he setys not þer by a bud* (J and M substituting suitably disparaging comparisons with rushes and beans).

2194 **conquere** F4016 *aquerre* 'acquire' var. *conquere* MSS *oM*.

EXPLANATORY NOTES

2196 **smith** God is pictured as a smith in Ezek. xxii 20-1, Is. i 25, Jer. vi 29. Alanus de Insulis' de velopment of the image probably influenced Guillaume (*PL*, CCX, 453, translated Moffat, p. 43): *Deus . . . tanquam mundi elegans architectus, tanquam aureae fabricae faber aurarius, velut stupendi artificii artifex artificiosus, velut admirandi operis opifex non exterioris instrumenti laborante suffragio, non materiae praejacentis auxilio, non indigentiae stimulantis flagitio, sed solius arbitrariae voluntatis imperio, mundialis regiae admirabilem speciem fabricauit Deus* . . . . Tribulation, bearing God's commission, is also a smith (see n. 2171).

þe light F4021 *l'aube.*

2200 **Force** Tuve, Appendix, lists virtues associated with Fortitude, such as those implied here: patience, prowess, resolution, constancy.

2207 **ryven** om. F4040 *fort* 'strongly'.

2211-13 **þat . . . cruelle** F4049-50 *Que il n'estoit guerre mortel / Ne tourment nul, tant fust cruel* no precedent for *so strong ne*, a rare addition.

2216 **Lady . . . goodliche** F4057 *Dame, je vous pri bonnement*: both C and JMO have *Lady quod I I pray yow*—but though C did consult β, it was usually at points of difficulty. Perhaps τ unwittingly included *quod I*, and it should be accepted, on the assumption that G removed it as otiose after *I . . . seide here*. On the other hand, the phrase is common enough to have been added independently by C and β.

According to F, *goodliche* should modify *pray* (cf. 2263-4, where τ similarly misunderstands the function of *bonnement*).

2116-17 **ye . . . garnement** F4058-9 *ce garnement / Veste* 'you put this garment on [me]'.

2234 **Attemperaunce** is usually bridled rather than helmeted (see Tuve, Appendix and figs. 16, 17) but the effects are similar.

2236 **streyt** F4093 *euilliere estroite*: see p. lvi for J's *strayte olierde*.

2240 **no dart** F4101 *Nul tel dart* 'no dart like that' (i.e. of *murmurynge* or *bakbitinge*).

2241 **harde** F4102 (*fort*) supports GJMOS (C uses *harde* adv. at 1145, 2351).

2244-5 **bi . . . smellinge** F4109 *par [de]sordenee oudeur*. Stürzinger accepted the reading of MSS *TAM¹LMH*: his base MS *t* and some three others have, instead of *desordenee, sordenee [s'ordenée]*. Context allows either: the helmet may prevent an uncontrolled sense of smell from doing any damage, or it may result in a controlled sense of smell, with the same effect. GS's *his ardeyne* suggests that τ saw *s'ordenee oudeur* 'his controlled [as originally ordained] sense of smell' (at 2355 G similarly represents *ordenee* by *ardenee*, annotated by G³ with *ordene*). The editorial emendation assumes that G or his model found *ordene* difficult, and

ÞE LYFE OF ÞE MANHODE

wrote *ardene* under the influence of 'ardent'. Alternatively, χ may have misread an English word (*ardeyne* for *ordene*) or τ may have made a false correction on rereading his own copy without reference to F. (β, no doubt baffled, omitted the word.) I therefore emend to *ordeyne* C's *disordeyned*, which is related to G³'s *disordene*, derived through γ from the alternative reading in F². The corrector from F² did not notice that reading *desordenee* instead of *sordenee* necessitates the cancelling of *his* (*s'*). Indeed, the presence of *his* in all the ME manuscripts is neat evidence that CG³ derive from a MS which made occasional reference to another French MS where the text was difficult, so combining the characteristics of F and F². G³'s nearness to F here is the only evidence in Book 1 that G³ cannot derive from C (see p. lxxvi).

2247–8 **helme ... hedes** Eph. vi 17.

2249 **shulde** F4118 *doit* supports GJMOS's reading.
þe F4118 *(la)* supports GJMOS's reading.

2250–2 **It ... Glotonye** see Tuve, Appendix: Sobriety is part of Temperance in the lists of Macrobius, Guillaume de Conches, Alanus de Insulis.

2256 **double woodshipe** gluttony and bad language: *And for þe mouþ haþ tweie offices, wher-of þat on serueþ to þe swelewyng of mete and drynke, þat oþer serueþ to speche, and þerfore is þis pryncipally departed in two; þat is to seye, in þe synne of glotonye, þat is in mete and drynke, and in þe synne of wikkede tonge, þat is to speke folye* (Francis, p. 46; the French source is 13th-century).

2257–8 **Bi ... goomes** F4133 *Par le gouster les taillans meut* 'by means of the sense of taste she [Gluttony] sets the cutting edges [jaws] in motion': τ took *taillans* as the subject—perhaps his source had a pl. v., or he took *meut* for an abbreviation of *meuuent*. *MED gome* sb. 3c cites this as the earliest example meaning 'jaws'.

2258–9 **Bi ... sleyghtes** F4135 *Par le parler fait les engins* omits the pronoun subject (*elle*) as at *meut* two lines before (see n. 2257–8); τ, having failed to recognise omission of the subject at 2257, finds no subject for *maketh*.

2261 **maisterman:** F4139 *pautonniere* 'whore' is appropriate to Gluttony's gender and to the traditionally sexual connotations of the glutton's delight in swallowing, described in 5558–652, where indeed Gluttony and Lust combine to overthrow the pilgrim. Aquinas, *ST*, 2a2ae, q.143 divides the sense of Touch into Nourishment and Sex. τ seems to have read *pautonnier* 'scoundrel' or 'poor wretch', not noticing that this forced change of gender on Gluttony (see 2774 and note). It is not clear why τ renders this by *maisterman* (GJMO's reading, but if *misterman*, CG³'s reading, is a variant form rather than a different word, no emendation should be made—see Flint and Dobson). Perhaps he loosely meant 'clever operator' (*MED maister man* under *maister* sb. 5a 'master craftsman') or 'monstrous man' (ibid., 5.c) or even 'kind of man' (*MED mister-man* 2, which cites C's reading). He might also, given *mister*'s sense 'need' (*OED mister* sb.¹ 8), mean 'poor wretch', *pautonnier*'s second sense.

2263-4 **þerwith** F4143-4 *te lo bonnement | Que t'en armes soigneusement* 'I honestly advise you to arm yourself in them carefully': τ seems thought *bonnement* and *soigneusement* parallel, modifying *armes*, and so had to supply *and*. At 2216 *bonnement* is again misunderstood.

2269 **Chalyt** F4154 *Chaalis* var. *Challis*: see n. 18.

2270 **Seint William** William de Donjeon, monk of Pontigny, became abbot of Fontaine-Jean and in 1187 of Chaalit. Elected Bishop of Bourges in 1200, he overcame difficulties with the king, with his Chapter and with Albigensian heretics by patience and firmness. He died in 1209 and was canonised in 1218 (Attwater, *William of Bourges*).

2270-3 **þouh ... thirst** *Inter delicatas epulas celebri et sumptuoso apparatu fruentes noverat esurire. inter exquisita vina sitire* (Surio's 'Life of William of Bourges,' Hooff, III, 283; cited Hultman, pp. 110-11).

2272 **ooþere mes ynowe** F4158 *autres mes assez* 'plenty of other courses [or helpings]'. *MED mes* sb.² b cites this *mes* as pl.

2275 **himself atempree** F4165 *Attempres* offers no precedent for *himself*.

2276-80 **Sey ... gladliche** F4167-72 *'Dites' dist (il), 'a cil qui tremble | Qui est en fievre qu'il ne tremble, | Et vous verres, s'il cessera.' | Aussi dist il: 'Certes cil la | Dont vous parles se cesseroit | Mont volentiers, se il pouoit'* 'He used to say "Tell a man who is trembling from fever that he is not trembling, and see if he will stop." He also used to say: "Indeed, he to whom you speak would stop himself very willingly, if he could".' τ omits *Certes*, and the force of F's *ce cesseroit* 'would stop himself' is lost. F closely echoes the story in *Acta Sanctorum*, Jan. 1, p.637 (cited Hultman, p. 111).

2280-1 **armede ... shuldest** τ added *soo* (without precedent in F4174-5 *s'arma | De tel gorgiere et engorge, | Aussi en devras*) to balance *swich*.

2284 **mynged** F4178 *muni* 'equipped': G's *munged*, CS's *mynged*, JMO's *remembrede* (a substituted synonym), are hard to explain. It is as if τ mistook *muni* for the pp. of some verb synonymous with ME *ming* 'remind', used here, or with *mone* 'remember, tell of' (*OED mun* under *mone* v¹); or perhaps he thought it derived from Lat. *monere*. He did not translate *muni* at all at 2439 (F4446), but there he may have omitted what he regarded as otiose after *armed*.

2286-7 **touchinges** F4183-4 *touchiers et atouchements,* / *Palpations*: at 2289-90 τ gives *touchinges* for *atouchemens*, so here omits *touchiers* or *Palpations*.

2287-8 **men ... tastinge** F4185-6 *on puist trouver* / *Par tout le cors sens de taster* 'the sense of touch may be found all over the body' var. ... *sans de taster* MSS *oTAMH*.

2290-1 **it ... ben** F4191-2 *le plus si croit* / *Des gens qu'autre taster ne soit* 'most people think this is the only sense [that matters, because it is experienced all over the body]'. Barthomaeus says: *þe wit of gropinge haþ þis propirte, þat he is in alle þe parties of þe body ... But eueriche of þe oþir wittis haþ certain place, instrument, and tyme i-ordeyned and deputat to his doynge. Among alle þe wittis þis wit is most erþeliche and boistous ... it semiþ more profitable þan oþir wittis* (Trevisa, p. 119). τ perhaps took *le plus* (compar. adj. used as sb.) for a compar. adv., and finding no subject for *croit* took it as a pp.

2291-2 **is ... vnderstonde** the hands stand for the whole sense of touch. F4193-4 *tout generaument* / ... *le taster j'entent* supports GOS's *alle tastinge* (CJM substituted *tastinges* after *alle*). τ may not have written *is ... vnderstonde* for *j'entent*. In view of CG³'s *is* after *generalliche* (derived from γ), he perhaps wrote *alle tastinge generalliche I vnderstonde* or *I alle tastinge ..., I* being corrupted to *is* by χ.

2294 **with ... named** F4998 *des armouriers sont nommes* 'are called among armourers' var. *armeures* MSS *GB*. All the ME MSS are corrupt, with *armures ben armed*. Error in the noun may derive from the F var., from translation or from χ misreading *armurers*. Error in the verb seems to be due to misreading of an English word, implying independent existence of χ, but perhaps τ, particularly if he had written *with armures be named*, rereading his copy without reference to F, falsely corrected *be named* to *ben armed*. The editorial emendation unavoidably results in the use of a pp. found elsewhere in C only at 5334: instead of *namen* C normally uses *clepen*, less often *nempnen*.

2294-5 **þe ... Continence** even by the time of Macrobius' account of Temperance and her train, there existed a 'well-established group of Temperance's manifestations that had become fixed by centuries of repetition': Alanus de Insulis was not the first to make Continence a part of Temperance (Tuve, pp. 65, 66). I have not traced the source of Temperance as the 'third part'. Cicero shows Temperance in three parts, of which the first is *continentia* (Tuve, Appendix).

2299-300 **so ... needen** F4209 *Si ques sans envier .ii. vaut* 'two [gloves] are necessary if you are to be kept from harm' var. *ennuier* MS. *G*; *envier* is in fact *en(n)uier*, from late Lat. *inodiare* (Greimas, *enoier*) 'to harm'. I accept G's *ennuye* because although at 1488 C uses the *an-* form, M's *enmy* is a misreading of an *en-* form,

EXPLANATORY NOTES 429

and at 1941 C uses *ennuye*, for *ennuier* 'annoy [by boring]'. In addition, J's *with outen nuy* may derive from mis-division of *with oute ennoy*.

2302 **couenable** in his errata, Stürzinger emends *convenables* to *avenans*: τ saw the former.

2303 **gaynpayn** F4214 *Gaaignepains*: the relevance to a gauntlet of the name 'bread-winner' is obscure. *MED gain-pain* cites only two examples— this, and one dated 1486. *OED gainpain*[1] 'a sort of gauntlet' cites our text, and then, oddly, Halliwell's *Dictionary*, I, 395. This quotes our MS. S, but glosses by 'the ancient name of the sword used at tournaments' (*OED*'s doubtful sense 2).

2306 **Achimelech** F4219 *Achimelech* vars. *Alchimelech, Achimeleth*. I Kings xxi 1-6. In the *Bible Moralisée* (Bodleian MS. 270[b], ff. 139[v] B7, B8, and 140[r], A1, A2) the priest Ahimelech's giving David and his friend bread on the understanding that they have not consorted with women is explained in terms of the purity required of priests celebrating Mass. Purity of the hands is most relevant in the Eucharistic context of Book 1 (cf. the opening of the Gawain-poet's *Purity*, where sacerdotal cleanliness, literal and metaphorical, heads the types of purity demanded by God).

Because of the easy muddling of *h* and *b*, confusion of *Ahimelech* with *Abimelech* of Gen. xx and Judges ix (an evil man, quite unlike the priest) is common (indeed, χ's form of the name is doubtful). The *Bible Moralisée* itself refers to *abimelec(h)* throughout the passage just cited, and in our text only CG[3] show the correct reading, through their access via γ to F[2].

2309-15 **Seynt... him** PL, CLXXXV, 230-1 and 472-3; Gewande (p. 20) notes Voragine's use of this story.

2310 **naked** om. F4228 *et despoulliee* 'and stripped'.

2312 **ne... assentede** F4232 *Ne de son tast ne se senti* 'nor was he conscious of her touch': τ mistook, or had, *se senti* for *assenti*.

2314 **confused** in view of F4235 *confuse*, GS's *confus* could be accepted.

2325 **Ogiers** F4255 *Ogier*: GS's *ogyers* is accepted against C's *Ogrers* (doubtless due to *i/r* confusion), but with C's habitual use of *i* rather than *y*. Cβ seem not to have recognised the name.

Ogier the Dane, nephew of Charlemagne, had two swords: Curtana and Sauvagine. His deeds are told by Adenet le Roi (see Albert Henry). The origins and Benedictine-assisted development of the stories (which might explain Guillaume's rare mention of romance material) are described in Bédier, pp. 281-316. Ogier's sword is relevant in this context of the Sword of Discipline and Justice: as well as performing deeds of valour, he rebuilt the churches of his country (Barrois, p. x).

2326 **Rowlondes** Roland's battle-deeds with his sword Durendal are told in *La Chanson de Roland* (Whitehead, pp. 28 ff.).

430   ÞE LYFE OF ÞE MANHODE

           Olyueeres Oliver's sword was Hauteclaire (ibid., pp. 40 ff.).
2333-4   **She ... baret** F5269-70 *La pensee fait convertir | A fraude et a barat guerpir* '[the sword] makes the thought change, and give up deception and strife' (var. for *et a barat: et barat* MSS *AM*[1]). τ renders *pensee* freely by *herte*, and takes *A fraude* with *convertir*.
2334-6   **Þe ... chastiseth hem** F4271-4 *La voulente, l'affection, | L'entendement, l'entention, | L'ame et toute sa mesnie | Si adrece et si chastie.* The subject of *adrece* and *chastie* is still *elle* (the sword): 'she [the sword] so puts in order and chastises the will, the emotions, the understanding and the intention, the soul and all her household ...'. τ lost sight of the subject after 2328, and so took the faculties of the soul and the soul itself as subject. The first four nouns name faculties. I have not traced the source of this sequence: 'almost every one of [the Cistercian school's] members composed a treatise ... "On the Soul"' (*NCE*, XIII, 455). Michaud-Quantin examines some major examples in detail, pp. 20-8 dealing with Cistercians. Vacant, I, 971-1016 gives an account of the philosophy of the soul (see especially pp. 973-4).
2337   **drawinge out** F4276 *traire*: perhaps the reading should be *drawinge* (cf. GO) on the assumption that CJMS independently added *out*; but CG might independently omit *out* by eyeskip to the following *of*.
2339   **Seint Beneyt** C's *Beneynt* (which also occurs at 2363) is probably due to the influence of *seynt* in the model. C has *Beneyt* at 68 and 2375.
2339-44   **Seint ... it**[2] I cannot relate either event to Benedict of Nursia, founder of the Benedictine Order, unless the references are general, the king (God, as at 85, 168) dignifying the saint with the Sword of Discipline or Justice (see 2392) when Benedict became a monk. Benedict threw himself into a bramble to cool his lust (*PL*, LXVI, 132), which might be the 'sword of discipline' applied to his body. Perhaps Benedict of Aniane, Abbot, the 'second St Benedict' (d. A.D. 821) is meant. Louis the Pious, successor and son of Charlemagne, made him inspector (*lord of lawes?*) of monasteries in Provence, Languedoc and Gascony, to bring them to conformity in standards. The Abbot was renowned for physical self-discipline (*Acta Sanctorum*, Feb. 12, II, 606-21; *NCE*, II, 280-1).
2345-6   **to his comaundement** F4291 *A li n'a son commandement* 'to him nor to his commandment': τ omits *li n'a*.
2350   **þilke ... þee** F4300 *qui de toi sont dirivez* shows the sense to be 'those who are related to you'.
2354   **baret** F4308 *barat*: the primary meaning in *OED barrat* is 'deception, fraud', in *MED barat* 'conflict, disturbance of the peace', so I gloss by 'disturbance'.
2363   **Beneyt** see n. 2339.

EXPLANATORY NOTES

2365 **wel** has no precedent in F4329.

2372 **perche** F4342 *perche a armer* 'rack for arming [oneself from]'.

2376 **thong** F4349 *renge*: at 2366, 2371 *renge* gave *gerdel*, which seems therefore to be synonymous with thong, meaning a sword-belt round the hips (*girdel/cainture* at 2403, F4399), as opposed to a *baudryk/baudre* at 2403 and 2404, F4399 and F4402), which goes diagonally from the girdle over one shoulder.

2377 **streyne** GJMOS's reading is given C's spelling at 7153, 6236; τ no doubt carried something like G's *streyngne*, misread by C as *strengthe*.

2379-407 **scauberk ... Constaunce** the Scabbard of Humility, Girdle of Perseverance and Buckle of Constancy represent the first three aspects of Fortitude (the Habergeon, 2200): see Tuve, Appendix. Here they modify the severity of the Sword of Discipline (or Justice, 2392).

2382 **hyde it** G's *huded* (S *hyded*) is a form of *hyde it* (*OED it* Aδ).

2383 **dedliche** F4360 *morte* vars. *mortel* MS. *H*, *mortelle* MS. *A*.

2386 **þe ... pharisien** Luke xviii 10-14. F4366 *l'autre pharisien* 'the other, the pharisee' shows that τ om. *l'autre*, and supports GJMOS.

2391 **feebelnesse** F4376 *enfermete* offering no guide, perhaps GS's *feeblesse* should be accepted; 2509 (F4599 *debilite*) shows the same two words, with the same doubt about which should be accepted. Contrast 2526.

2394 **ful ... folk** does not echo the pun in F4382 *plains de vent et gens vanteus*, as Dr Walls noted.

seecheen so C, but perhaps *-een* is a slip for *-en*.

2396-7 **humblinge** om. F4388 *Sans faintise* 'sincerely'.

2398 **thus** F4391 *ainsi* supports GJMOS's reading.

2400 **þou shalt streyne** F4394 *estraindras* supports GJMOS; see n. 2377.

2402 **but ... aboue** F4398 *Se au dessus n'est affermez* 'unless he [the pilgrim] is made secure on top [of the other garments]': *affermez* cannot qualify fem. F4386 *l'espee* 'sword'.

2405 **girt** om. F4403 *et serree* 'and tightened'.

2406 **Þe ... Perseueraunce** Is. xi 5.

2410 **She** F4413, F4415 *La renge* (the *girdel*) is the antecedent.

2412 **oon** F4415 *vestues* 'covered': the girdle holds armour on, or together, so τ could have written *oon* 'together' or *on* 'on'. Perhaps G's *onne* (*on*, in C's spelling) should be accepted, particularly in view of *doon of* following.

2421-2 **of ... entencioun** F4433-4 *de ceste exposition | Pou avoit a m' entencion* 'this explanation was not what I had in mind': τ was too literal.

432   ÞE LYFE OF ÞE MANHODE

2429 **armed** om. F4446 *Ne bien muni* 'nor well equipped' (see n. 2284).

2432 **Prudence** III Kings iii 12-28, iv 29-31; II Paralip. i 10-12.

2434-43 **two ... gold** II Paralip. ix 15-16; III Kings x 16-17.

2435 **targes** om. F4459 *que ... fist* 'which he made'.

2437-9 **whan ... þei weren** III Kings xi 4-13.

2439 **lost** F4468 *perdus et perdues*: τ could not imitate the separate loss of masc. *ecus* and fem. *targes*.

2448 **þe tooþer** C's *þat ooþer*, not in agreement with pl. *armures*, is rejected in favour G's reading (C's spelling) which though in origin a mis-division of *the tooþer* has become capable of going with a pl.

2451 **faste** om. F4491 *et t'en arme bien* 'and arm yourself in it well'.

2459 **þe double gorgere** covers the front of the neck: the mail is double.

2460 **þe helme** would be of the 'bucket' type, roughly cylindrical, very inflexible and constraining. The *viseer* of 2235 is simply an eye-slit.

2461 **gaynpaynes** are *harde out of mesure* (2482) because metal plates are sewn over them, though they are not yet of the elaborate articulated kind (cf. the Canterbury effigy of the Black Prince).

þe swerd F4510 *l'espee*; the long-sword.

2463 **þe targe** F4512 *la targe*: the light shield of the foot-soldier.

2469 **alle** (F4526 *toutes*) a pl. adj. agreeing with 2470 *hem*.

2476 **þat ... so** (F4538-9 *Que semble que estrangler (me) doie / Si m'estraint*): misled by *maistrieth me soo* in 2475, C omits this.

2477 **auale** in view of F4540 *avaler*, G's reading is accepted against C's logical but incorrect *haue* over erasure; τ's *auale* was misunderstood as 'to be of use' by JMOS.

2486 **Souprised** G is accepted as nearer F4557 *Souspris*, but C's *Superysed* could be retained as a var. of the same pp. meaning 'overcome' (*OED, supprise* v.)—*ouercome* is written over it from the now erased gloss in the margin. JMOS show confusion with *suppress*.

2486-8 I Kings xvii 38-9. 'When the pilgrim rests back on the thought that other respectable fighters have declined armor, and fastens upon David, the popular iconographical counter for Fortitude, Guillaume need not say anything overtly about the logic of human self-defences' (Tuve, p. 168).

2490-1 **with ... me** F4564 *du bourdon me passerai* 'I will be content with the staff': τ translated literally. *OED pass* v. ignores this sense.

2497 **þou¹ ... þeron** F4576 *t'en souvient* 'you remember it'; but at 2505 *I bithinke me* is correct for F4562 *il me souvient bien*.

EXPLANATORY NOTES   433

2502   **þat ne is ordeyned** JMOS's all showing *it* would normally
       suggest retention of C's *þat it ne* . . ., but C wrote over erasure,
       following a now erased gloss in the margin, and the abbreviation
       þat suggests that *þat* once filled the space now taken up by *þat
       it*.

2503   **þat, þat armour** F4588 *ce que arme(s)*: GS's literal reading is
       accepted against C's *þat þat þis armo*ur written over erasure in
       obedience to a now erased marginal gloss visible under u.v. as
       þis. Insertion of *þis* caused abbreviation of what was originally
       unabbreviated *þat*.

2507   **þei ... hem** F4595–6 *Que longement pas ne feront, | Quant de
       moi aprises seront* 'they would not do so for long, when I became
       used to them': τ misplaced *longe*, which should modify *shulden
       not*.

       lerned of F4596 *aprises*; τ loses the double sense: armour is
       'taken up', and the virtues it represents are 'understood' by the
       pilgrim.

2509   **feebilnesse** the reading is in doubt: see n. 2391.

2510   **vnlikynge** F4601 *dessemblables*. GJMOS's *on lykynge* is accepted
       against C's *vnliknynge*: *OED like* v.² 'to resemble' is rare
       compared with *liken*, which C probably substituted.

2514   **yrened** F4609 *ferre*: see n. 1884.

2516   **amonested me of hem** F4612 *les amonnestastes* 'advised them'
       var. *les me amonnestastes* MSS M¹GLMH.

2518   **But** om. F4615 *Tout* 'completely'.

2519   **as soone ... armed** f4618 *se tost je ne sui desarmes* 'unless I am
       at once unarmed'; perhaps τ's text had . . . *ke je sui armes*.

2522   **þou art:** F4623 *(tu) fusses* 'you would be' is correctly subj.

2526   **feeblesse** in view of F4630 *flebece* vars. *feblece* MS. *G, feiblece*
       MS. *L, foiblesse* MS. *A*: GS's reading is accepted against C's
       feebilnesse (but see nn. 2509, 2391).

2528   **Þou ... hem** F4633–4 *quant pour toi garder | Ne les pues ...
       porter* 'when you cannot [even] carry them to defend yourself'. τ
       omits *quant ... garder* and begins a new sentence.

2537   **hem. Allas** all the ME MSS have this punctuation, but in
       F4648 *halas* ends a line and may well belong to the previous
       sentence, in which case the reading should be *hem allas.*.

2540–1 **drawe ... goode** the awkward postponement of *and for þi goode*
       echoes the free syntax of F4654–5 *vers celle part | Me traie, quant
       creu de rien | Tu ne m'aras et pour ton bien*, doubtless intended to
       stress *pour ton bien*. Grace asks if the pilgrim expects her to be
       glad to approach him, especially for his benefit, when he has not
       believed a word she said.

2544   **þanne be** F4661 *lors ... sera*: GS's word-order is accepted, but
       C's *be þanne* might be correct; JMO, omitting the phrase, are no

help.
2545   **woundes** om. F4662 *grans*.
2548   **to lerne armes** in view of F4667-8 *d'aprendre* | *Les armes* GMOS's reading is accepted. In C's *to lerne to bere armes*, *to bere* is inserted in obedience to *{to} bere* (with erasure legible under u.v.) in the margin. J similarly has *to lere forto bere armes*. CJ independently modified (or C was contaminated from β) because of the general sense, and *bere* in 2546; cf. n. 2236 on the problem of rendering *aprendre*.
2550   **neede** F4672 *besoing . . . et mestier*: τ avoids repetition.
2551   **softe . . . goth** F4674 *Belement bien loing on va* (Hassell P137?)
2552   **þe mule** F4675 *la vielle* (*uielle* corrected to *mule* in MS. *o*): F contrasts an old lady riding slowly on her pilgrimage, and a reckless man making less speed with more haste. It is interesting that here, as at 2555, τ saw *mule*—supplied in F by MS. *o*'s corrector, and by his illuminator at 2555 (*o* cannot, however, have been τ's only model: see Avril Henry [1984]). Hassell records neither saying.

Seynt James F4677 *Saint Jacques ou a Saint Joce* (vars. *Jose* MS. *o*, *Josse* MS. *A*): no doubt St James of Compostella was as familiar to τ as to Chaucer, but τ omitted *ou a Saint Joce*. Either the repeated *J-* misled him or he did not recognise St Judoc, a priest, younger brother of King Judicael of Brittany. After the latter's abdication he was king for some months. After a pilgrimage to Rome he retired to Villers-Saint-Josse near Saint-Josse-sur-Mer, and died in 668.

2553   **goth** om. F4676 *son chemin* 'on her way' (but translated it at 2555 [F4682]), so improving 2553-4 (*goth roundliche . . . goth sharpliche*).
2554   **maketh him go** F4679 *va* '[he, the man] goes': the subject is *cil* in F4678 (2553 *þilke*).
2555   **mule** see n. 2552.

her wey the reading accepted is GMO's, in which *her* refers back to *þe mule*. C's *his* is a sophistication: perhaps he regarded mules as male or else (since *his* can mean 'its', and mules are sterile) as neuter.

2559-62   **þou . . . for**[2] F4689-95 *premierement regarder | Doiz s'enfance et considerer | Quar enfant adonc et petit | Estoit si com l'Istoire dit; | Les armes aussi d'autre part | Qui pas n'estoient pour poupart, | Ains estoient pour . . .* (var. for *Ains: Mais* MS *A*). G(S) show that τ echoed the clumsy F, in which *s'enfance* and *Les armes* are objects of *regarder | Doiz . . . et considerer*. Cβ tried to begin a new 'sentence' at *also*: CG[3] show that γ, seeing that this left *also . . . cuntre* with no main verb, inserted *considere* before *þe armures*.

2560   **chyldhode** I Kings xvii 33.

EXPLANATORY NOTES 435

2562 **poopet** G's form is preferred to C's *popot*, which may not have been intended: the 2nd *o* has been altered to *a*, and either spelling is irregular (*OED poppet*). J substitutes the more modern form *puppet*, M substitutes a gloss. F4694 *poupart*, a pejorative form based on *poupee*, means in context something like 'weakling'.

2562-3 **þe ... Saul** F4695-6 *le fil Cis,* | *Saul* (var. for *Cis*: *cilz* MS. *A*): 'Saul, son of Cis' (I Kings ix 1-3).

2568 **staloun** F4706 *estalon*: the only occasion on which *-oū-* has not been expanded to *-ioun* in accordance with its modern equivalent in *-ion*, which does not occur until the 16th century.

2568-9 **þat þat ... writen** Aristotle, *Nicomachian Ethics*, x. 5, paras. 8, 9: 'Horse, dog and man have different pleasures; as Heraclitus says "Asses would prefer hay to gold" for hay is more pleasant than gold to asses. So the pleasures of creatures different in kind are themselves different in kind' (cited Wright's 3rd Proof of his edition p. 71, Hultman, p. 75, Bömer n. 4620). Whiting C379 cites only this example of the 'proverb'. The *Ethics* were familiar: Talbot (p. 164) cites a 14th-century *Quaestiones super decem libros Ethicorum Aristotelis* ... in Senlis's mother house (Pontigny MS 274, now Bibl. Auxerre MS. 232). The poet modifies his source, referring to a *young* ass (or horse, F *mulon* and ME *colt* could mean either): see n. 2570.

2570 **But ... sithe** if David had been as old as the Pilgrim, the latter might reasonably follow David's example, dispensing with armour. But David was young at the time: as a man, he fought armed.

2579 **he sleew Golias** I Kings xvii 40-51.

2579 **him** om. F 4728 *diuisoient* | *Et* 'suitable and'.

2595 **biseeche** F4755-6 *requerre* | *Et prier*: τ avoids repetition.

2601 **I ... þee** F4768 *je t'amerrai*, with contracted fut. of *amener* 'bring', supports GOS's *lede* against C's *leue* (? *lene*—*u*/*n* is over erasure).

suich on: in view of F4768 *tel*, perhaps GS's omission of *on* should be accepted, on the assumption that Cβ normalised a literalism.

2602 **shal wel susteyne** F4769 *bien ... soustenra* supports the word-order of GS (echoed in JMO's *schalle wele bere*).

2606-7 **Oonlich ... burdoun** 'I retained only the satchel and staff.'

2608 **Aa** has no precedent in F4781.

2613 **doon of** F4791 *oste et desvestu*: τ avoids repetition.

2618 **alle folk wolden also** F4801 *Touz aussi* supports GMOS's word-order.

2619 **nouht** F4803 *rien* supports GJMOS's reading.

2620 **it is worth** F4803 *vaut* supports GJMO (with C's preferred spelling).

2624 **for to ... ashamed** F4811 *pour moi faire corvee* 'to carry out a task for me' (*corvee* 'exaction of unpaid labour from a vassal'); τ guessed?

2630 **light** in view of F4824 *lumiere* 'vision', GMOS's reading is accepted, with C's preferred spelling.

and bifore om. F4826 *Et par devant*: τ avoids repetition.

2635 **wurþi** F *viguereus*. *OED worthy* a.4 has one example meaning 'powerful' (c. 1300), which may be the meaning here; but since the former meaning is rare, I gloss by 'excellent'.

2639 **þe senewes** F4842 *Les ners*: in view of var. *Tes ners* MS *L*, perhaps JOS's *thy* (*þin* M) should be adopted, assuming that CG read *thi* as *the*.

2641 **armure** om. F4846 *bonnement*.

2643 **all** (F4852 *tout*) neither form nor function is clear. As in F, it might be a sb. so that *of all* means 'in everything', or an adj., giving 'of all [people]'. In the MS the 2nd *l*, ending a line, has a small uncharacteristic horizontal line projecting to the right halfway up the letter as an abbreviation, cancellation or accident. If it is a sb. the reading should perhaps be *al* (more often unambiguously a sb. than *alle*), since C does not use *all* as a sb. elsewhere.

2644-5 **þis ... þee**[1] F4854 *Ceste meschine et amene* has no pers. pron., the object of *amene* (as of *trouve* in the previous line) being *Ceste meschine*. τ may or may not have written *þee*, without precedent in F. JMO or CGS may preserve τ's reading.

2647 **þou shalt see** τ read F4859 *tu merras* 'you shall lead' as *mireras*.

2650-1 **nygh þee** GS's *nygh to þee* may preserve τ's reading, Cβ agreeing by chance.

2652-3 **þis ... shewinge** F4870-1 *ce monstre / Dont vous m'avez fait un monstre*: τ loses F's play on *monstre* 'monster/demonstration'.

2656 **a seruaunt** in F4877 *un vallet* it is clear that the pilgrim expected the help of a youth, not a girl.

2659 **swiche** has no precedent in F4881.

2661 **þis ... Memorie** F4885-6 *Ceste meschine est nommee / Par son (droit) nom et apellee / Memoire* shows that β omitted *et apellee*. I accept G's much marked *thi̠s̠ w̠ẹnche̠ hạṭṭe̠ by her na\a/me ryghte and his* cleped *Memorie* as the more difficult reading (*name ryghte* instead of *ryghte name*) in spite of *his* for *is* (probably a slip, rather than inorganic *h*-, which G does not show elsewhere in Book 1), against CG³(S)'s *Þis wenche is nempned & bi hire rihte name cleped Memorie*. G³ creates confusing marks for gloss, inversion and cancellation in G (there may be two correctors at work, since it is unlikely that one should trouble to insert a second *a* in *name* when marking it for alteration). This is one of

EXPLANATORY NOTES

the occasions when CG³(S) agree against G as a result of inheriting or consulting γ's reading, itself affected by F² (cf. var. *Et par (son) droit nom apellee* MS. *L*).

The reading could be [*hatte*] rather than *hatteth*, since JMO support G in suggesting that τ used this relic of the Middle Voice. C uses *hatte* 13, *hatteth* 16 times (2002, 2114, ?2200, 2250, 2406, 2432, 3140, 4240, 4302, 4449, 4760, 5268, 6290, 6718, 6958, 7185) and in all 16 cases τ apparently had *hatte*. Curiously, C uses *hatteth* invariably (6 times) in Book 4. I do not emend it anywhere. I emend C's *right* (invariably used elsewhere in Book 1 for the v.) to *riht*, the form used in Book 1 for the adj. on all but one occasion, though in Books 2-4 he uses *rihte*.

Memorie is one of the faculties of the pilgrim's own soul (Augustine, *Liber de Spiritu et Anima*, PL, XL, 803: *Dum ergo vivificat corpus, anima est: dum vult, animus est; dum scit, mens est; dum recolit, memoria est*).

2665 **ne hidous** (F4849 *ne hideuse*) is supplied from GJMOS; cf. 2631.

2666 **mugoe** F4898 *murgoe* 'store, source of supply' vars. *mugoe* MS. *H*, *murgoe* MS. *o*, *murgeoe* MS. *L*, *murgoire* MS. *M*. The word (Godefroy *murjoe*, Tobler-Lommatzsch *musgode*) is unrecorded in ME; it occurs in many spellings though not with the final *-s* of G's *mugos* (where *-s*, cramped and superior, ends a line), which G³ marked for a gloss unfortunately missing. βS omitted it. The editorial emendation follows F MS. *H*, most likely to explain G's *mugos*. C's substitution of *ordinaunce* suggests that γ had *mugoe*, misread by G.

2667-70 **Er...kept** F4899-904 *Piec'a fussent a povrete / Les clers de l'Universite, / Se ne gardast leur avoir / Qu'il ont aquis et leur savoir, / Quar peu vaut chose questee, / Se apres l'aquest n'est gardee* 'Clerics in Universities would long since have been in poverty if what [knowledge] they had, and the knowledge they gained, had not been retained, for matter gained is worth little if not retained after the acquisition'. All Stürzinger's MSS read *Se* [or *Sel(le)*] *apres laquest gardee*, but τ either saw the emended construction, or realised that *n'est* would have been easily omitted by confusion with *-uest* at the end of *laquest*. F's odd intransitive use of *gardast* leads τ to supply *hem* as object of *kept*. The poet may have recalled Hugh St Victor's 'Concerning Memory': 'I charge you then, my student, not to rejoice a great deal because you may have read many things, but because you have been able to retain them. Otherwise there is no profit in having read or understood much' (J. Taylor, p. 94).

I assume that C's *havinge or kunnynge*—a close approximation to F *avoir...et savoir*—alone preserves τ's reading, subsequently rationalised or miscopied by βG as *having of kunnynge*.

2675-6 **if ... hem** F4913-15 *se tu li fais gardeer | Ces armes ci, aussi porter | Avec toi elle(s) les vourra* 'if you make her guard these arms she will be willing to carry them with you too'; τ mistook *uourra* 'she will be willing' for *nourra* 'she will nourish', and so failed to see that *porter* was dependent on it, and was obliged to take *porter* as dependent on *fais* and parallel to *garder*.

2684 **eyen** om. F4927-8 *et irrision* 'and derision'.

a seruaunt F4929 *un vallet*: see n. 2656.

2689 **I ... ayensey** F4938 *A voz dis rien ne contredi* 'I do not contradict your statement at all': τ mistook *dis* for 1 per. sg. of *dire*.

2700 **of ... redy** F4961 *De tous poins apointiez fusses*: τ could not echo the play on *poins* 'points, aspects', and *apointiez* 'ready'.

2710 **alonygne** F4978 *esloingnier*: spelling is not regularised here or at 2976 to conform to the scribe's *aloyngn-* form at 3947, 3663, 3946, since the *y* over erasure here, and the scribe's *aloyned* at 5740, suggest that his spelling of the word was genuinely variable. Unfortunately *MED aloinen* v. 3 cites Wright's emendation as sole evidence of an *alongne* form.

2718 **þerfor,** so spelled by C only here, should perhaps be emended to *þerfore* (used 118 times).

2724 **þei shulen be** in view of F5003 *seront*, GJOS's reading is accepted.

2727 **þou do no harm** *no* having apparently dropped out in α, (perhaps because of the similarity between *do* and *no*), it is supplied in accordance with F5007 *tu ne faces mal* and JMO's *na*.

2728 **and** in view of F5009 *et*, G's reading is accepted. CG³MOS have *ne* 'nor'. But perhaps τ used *ne*, in a ME double neg., and G altered it, giving chance agreement with F.

2728-9 **a ... invisible** F5011-12 *une pierre qui la gent. | Quant je veul, invisibles rent* 'a stone which, when I wish it, makes people invisible' vars. for *la, a la* MS. *L*, for *invisibles rent, invisible rent* MS. *H* (the latter rationalised the grammar). τ seems to have seen a combination of the vars: *qui a la gent ... invisible rent*; his awkwardness is not surprising. This is the earliest example under *OED yield* v. 9 with the sense 'make'.

No other mention is made of Grace's *stoon*. Perhaps it puns on the name of Peter (as in John i 42, Matt. xvi 18-19), suggesting that the grace of God works indirectly through the Church founded on Peter's authority (see n. 2737). Various stones are credited with the power to confer invisibility: see Albertus Magnus (Best and Brightman, pp. 26-7); Stith Thompson, D1361.2; Wagnall, *invisibility*; Mackensen, *gyges* especially ii.679).

2730 **me** om. F5013-14 *et me repondrai* 'and conceal myself'.

EXPLANATORY NOTES 439

2733 **þou puttest þee** F5020 *Tu te merras* 'you behave' (fut.): τ or his source confused *merras* with *metras*.

2735-6 **þou ... weyes** F5023-4 *le bon chemin laisseras / Et par mauves chemin iras* (var. for *chemin*², *chemins* MS. *H*); *chemin*¹ is sg., with no var.; *chemin*² may have been pl. (as in the var.) to distinguish the multiplicity of evil ways from the simplicity of the good one. τ's *goode weys* obscures any distinction.

2737 **of ... pyer** F5028 *De la dicte pierre* 'by means of the stone already mentioned': the ME MSS either omit the phrase or are corrupt. GS's readings suggest that τ used the Gallicism *pyer* (though it is not clear why, when at 2729 he translates *pierre* by *stone*—unless *t* wrote *pyer* there too, and χ anglicised). It looks as if *pyer*, not understood by α (who may be τ himself, correcting his fair copy), was read as if it were an abbreviation, becoming respectively *p'eyere, preyer* in G and S (see p. lxxx).

2749 **strok ... arwe** F5052: *Coup de dart et de saete* 'stroke of dart and arrow': τ perhaps saw *coup de dart, de saete*. J's *strakes of dartes and arwes* may be due to his habitual substitution, or independent consultation of a French MS. with the main reading.

2757 **Heere ... book,** which follows 2757, is not numbered as a line in this edition, unlike all the other beginnings and endings to books. It is in red in the MS.

2761 **yow** om. otiose F5071 *et reciter*.

2764-5 **bar ... me** F5080 *apres moi les apertoit* 'brought them near me': ? τ saw var. *portoit* MS. *T*.

2768 **miht** om. otiose F5088 *et si remis* 'and so enfeebled'.

2772 **cherl** Hultman, p. 127 compares *Rude Entendement* to *Dangier* in *Le Roman de la Rose*, 2837, 3168.

2773 **crabbe tree:** F5097 *cornoullier* means 'dogwood' or 'cornelian cherry' (*cornus mas*); Yvain's rough adversaries at Pesme Avanture also carry crooked clubs of this wood (*Yvain*, lines 5508-9: Chrétien de Troyes, p. 168). It bears appropriately sour berries rarely produced in Britain but resembling the fruit of *crabbe tree*, which can mean 'crab-apple' (*malus sylvestris*). But the staff Obstinacy (2847) may be of *crabbe tree* only by association with *crabbed* 'ill-tempered' (derived in fact from *crabbe* the crustacean).

2774 **misterman:** F5098 *pautonnier* 'tramp, hanger-on, ragamuffin' has no variants, in contrast to 2261.

2776-7 **with ... lette** (F5105 *a moi l'ara* 'he'll get it [a blow] from me' var. *laira* MS. *T* 'he will pass') probably means 'he will delay with me' (*MED letten* v. 1), but the F var. could mean that the sense is 'he will pass by in my company' (*MED leten* v. 4).

2786 **hath wold ordeyne** F5124 *a voulu ... ordener*. I assume that G's *wull ordeinge* is literal, representing an unrecorded pp. followed by inf. C's habitual pp. *wold* is used. A similar construction appears in 6669 *Þou hast alwey wold ... medle*. See

2884, 3749.

2787-8 **þe kyng ... burdoun** Matt. x 9-10. Literal prohibition of possessions, including satchel and staff, is presented as a prohibition of Faith and Hope: Reason's function in the subsequent argument is to show that these theological virtues, incomprehensible to an untrained understanding (*Rude Entendement*), are not irrational.

2788 **ne ne** only GS have this but it more likely that *ne* dropped out in error than that it was added; F5128 *Et que bourdon ne maniast* has var. *Ne que ...* MS. *L*.

handelede should perhaps be *[handel]* (after JMO), retaining F's subj.

2791 **hast ... hardi** follows F5134 *As este ouse et hardi* var. *As tu osei estre hardi.*

2809 **repere ... mowere** i.e. solitary worker.

2819 **sithe ... him** G's omission of preceding *and* is accepted, since there is no *et* in F5187 *Puis il dist* (but see var. *Et li dist* MSS *TA*).

2833 **grummede** *MED grummen* records only this and 3078 *grummynge*.

2841 **shrewede ... daungerous** F5227-8 have four adjectives: τ om. either *mal savoureus* 'smelly', or *lourt* 'ugly'.

2844 **vnscrippe** *OED* (under *vnscrew*) records only this example.

2849 **yiven you nouht** perhaps G³'s cancellation of *nouht* (a cancellation echoed in S) should be accepted, since there is *nouht* having no precedent in F 5244 *Te donnon et commandement*—but it looks as if τ wrote *nouht*, somehow misreading *-non et*. Cf. 6563.

2861 **Seint Germeyn** St Germanus, Bishop of Paris c. 496 (cf. St-Germain-des-Pres, Paris)?

2863 **take** (F5270 *faire*) should perhaps be *[make]*, assuming that χ misread τ; but t/m confusion is uncommon.

2864 **Symeon** F5271 *Symon* may refer to the Apostle, but in the absence of any obvious reasons for the exchange of ejaculations using the names of SS Germain, Simon and Benedict (2861-6) it is hard to be certain: the reference might be to St Simon Stock (c. A.D. 1165-1265), General of the Carmelites.

2867 **quod he** F5278 *dist*: var. *dist il* MSS *TH*.

2872 **resoun** a miller's measure: that the object was associated with misuse is apparently suggested only by this text (see 5109), but see Whiting M560-1 on thieving millers. This long distinction between Reason's name and nature, in an argument where she effortlessly displays her intellectual superiority over *Rude Entendement*, may remind us of 793-814, where she was herself baffled by the Transubstantiation effected by Wisdom. Reason's

EXPLANATORY NOTES

limitations and powers are thus defined in these passages. It is also appropriate that the name of Reason, who preached on Moderation at 455, should be used of an actual measure.

2873 **þerfore** F5290 *Ainz* 'rather', 'on the other hand': var. *Ainsi* MS. *A*.

2878 **make** subj. 'might make', the opening clause having been felt to suggest only possibility.

2879 **make** see n. 2878.

2884 **hath wold** F5311 *Sest voulu*; again I assume that G's *wull* Is an unrecorded pp., and use C's form (see 2786, 3749).

2887 **Þat ... part** F5315 *Dieux i ait part*. The ME is an ejaculation, such as 'God help us'; cf. Chaucer, *Shipman's Tale*, 1. 215: *The devel haue part on ...* 'the devil take ...'. MED *haven* 4a(h) suggests that *haue part* is 'have [anything] to do with.'

part om. F5316 *Me retournez vous le billart?* an idiom from the game of billiards which appears to mean something like 'are you cheating?' or perhaps ' ... putting the ball in my court?'

2888 **kneewe ... mylk** F5319 *mouche en lait ne connoissioe* (Hassell, M218) 'missed the obvious'.

2896 **þine** perhaps G³JMO's *þi* should be accepted.

fallaces F5334 *vos fanfelues rimees* 'your rhymed claptrap'.

2899 **lerned** om. F5340 *et qu'en savez* 'and you have learned from it'.

2901 **and** (no *et* in F5343) should perhaps be omitted: I accept G³S.

if ... bely F5343 *Se pance plus grant eussies* 'If you had thought more carefully': τ read *pance* as *pauce*.

2903 **wite it wel** F5346 *sachies*: perhaps *it* should be omitted.

2919-20 **þou¹ ... nempned** '[by being illogical,] your argument shows more clearly than any logical argument could, that you are rightly called Untutored Understanding'.

2925 **and¹** (F5389 *et*), retained though absent in G, should perhaps be omitted, as having been included by other scribes only for clarity.

2949 **to ... thinken** F5436 *Ou tendent tout bon pelerin*: τ read as *Qu'entendent ...?*

2960 **wherof ... herd** τ perhaps read F5457 *Dont tu as* 'about which you have been silent' as *Dont cu as* 'about which you know'.

2961 **Hath ... lakked** 'has anything been lacking to you?': Luke xxii 35-7.

2966 **was defended** F5468 *Aus sains apostres deffendu* 'the holy apostles were forbidden'.

2969 **þat was ... wey** Christ is the destination of the Pilgrim, who needs Faith and Hope, which are superfluous in the presence of Christ (of the Theological Virtues, only Charity exists in heaven).

2973 **a scrippe þerwith** F5480 *s'escherpe avec* 'make himself a satchel

ÞE LYFE OF ÞE MANHODE

of it': τ mistook the v. for a sb.

2979 **Pilgrimes ... ayen** F5495 *Pelerins vous refaurra estre* (*Pelerins* is probably sg.).

2981-2 **ye ... fynde** F5499-500 *vous ne trouveres / Nul*. Confusion was caused by χ's use of *nouht* rather than *noon*. G replaced by *fynde not*, but G³ corrected, reinserting *nowght* before the v., and subpuncting *not*. JMO also took the pron. for a negative, but moved it to modify *shal*.

2984 **it** F5505 *tout* 'all this'.

2988 **it**¹,² F5511-12 *les* (both staff and satchel).

2991 **walkere** τ read F5517 *paisant* 'peasant' as *passant*; the error was glossed *churl* in JMO's model, but M rejected the gloss.

2994 **ordinaunce** in view of F5525 *ordenance*, JMO's sg. is accepted against CGS's pl.

3005 **amase** F5543 *enfantosmer*.

3010 **bigilouresse** om. F5554 *et enveloperresse* 'and a tier-into-knots'. *MED* records only this example.

3011 **thre verres** (F5555 *.iii. neres* (? 'nuts') var. *veires* MS. *B*); the ME image is perhaps of cheap glasses as opposed to silver goblets.

3012 **seeche** τ mistook F5558 *crerai* 'believe' for *querre*.

3019 **dred** F5570 *redoute et cremus*: τ avoids tautology.

3022 **frendes** τ read F5574 *avis* 'opinion' as *amis*.

3023-4 **more ... knyf** Whiting, G188.

3027 **rudeliche** F5586 *Grossement a tout le hauton* 'unwinnowed, with all the bran left in'.

3033 **it** perhaps CG³'s *him* should be adopted, but I assume that τ wrote *it* referring to *wight* in 3032, then α corrected, and β omitted, the unEnglish impersonal pron.

3037-8 **Nabal and Pharao** I Kings xxv 2-39 and Exod. vii 1 - xiv 31; *Rude Entendement* is like Nabal impervious to courtesy, and like Pharaoh unmoved by demonstrations of power.

3048 **ne wolt þou** G's reading is essentially accepted, as slightly nearer to F5625-6 *weilliez / Et ne veullies*, with C's habitual *wolt þou* rather than *wult(e)*. Perhaps C's *wolt þou not* should be retained.

3050 **cite ... jugement:** if this refers to an early form of jury, the literal sense is that Reason will take Rude Entendement to Court for ignoring the law; the Royal Justice would attend the Royal Action (for the wrongful retention of goods?). The allegorical sense is that he who will not abandon the 'blunt instrument' of untaught reason in matters of faith will be accused at the Last Judgement.

3056 **Salamon** Prov. xxvi 4.

EXPLANATORY NOTES   443

3057 **suinge** 'afterwards': Prov. xxvi 5.

3065 **ayemaunt** is rare: *MED aimant* cites only two examples, from
      1400. τ om. F5658 *Plus dur qu'acier* 'harder than steel'.

3072 **whateuere it were** F5672 MSS have *Saucun convoi* 'some
      escort'. The ME is mysterious. Could a scribal note ('something
      or other') have be come part of the text (cf. *vacat* in CS's text at
      6491)?

3083 **not** om. F5693 *porter | Ne* 'carry, nor'.

3096 **to thikke** see 2139.

3105 **arraye** F5736 *mainbournir* 'superintend': ? τ saw var. *maintenir*
      MSS *HyP*.

3111 **Þow norishest** preceded in F5748 by *Tu doiz savoir* 'you ought
      to know that'.

3113 **delitous** I accept GS's more difficult reading, since F5752
      delicieuse has var. *deliteuse* MS. *M*: but perhaps the reading
      should be *delicious*.

3116 **wantounliche ... him** F5757 *Au lignolet le veus chaucier* 'you
      want to shoe him with laces' (provide him with extravagant
      shoes?).

3118 **girdelles** F5761 *greille couroie ferree* 'grey girdles studded with
      iron'.

      purses F5762 *bourse pinpelotee* 'a decorated purse' (of a fop).

3119 **aray** F5765 *espigacier* 'perfume' or 'make shiny'.

3122 **kembest** om. F5771-2 *et le blondis | Et aplanies* 'and bleach and
      smooth him'.

3126 **þat** (F5779 *que*) appears to mean 'since', but *OED that* rel. pron.
      7c records only one such (13th-century) example. Perhaps the
      reading should be *[sithen] þat*, following JMO, though this looks
      like rationalisation from β.

      bigonne (as in *MED biginnen* 5b, a 1425 entry) has no precedent
      in C, which has no other pa. t. 2 sg. of *biginnen*; C's normal form
      of pa. t. 3 sg. is *bigan*. Perhaps the reading should simply be
      [bigunne], assuming that C's *biginne* is due to accidental omission
      of a minim.

3128-9 **albeit ... him** F5783-4 *comment qu'ainsi a son gre | L'aies servi*
      'albeit you have thus served him at his pleasure'.

3132 **ne to** perhaps G's omission of *to* should be accepted.

3145 **deyngne to preyse** F5812 *prisast ne contredaignast* 'praise or
      show respect for'.

3146 **buryelles** τ read F5814 *Un similacre* 'an image' or 'a counterfeit'
      as *un sepulcre*. G (like JOS) has the incorrect form *buryell*, as if
      buryelles were pl. (as does C at 4293).

      a restinge for a coluer F5815-16 *Une estatue de limon, | Un
      espouentail a coulon* 'an image made of dirt, a scarecrow'. τ seems

3150 **an herte** F5823 *Un ver* 'a worm': var. *Un cuer* MS. *o*.
3171 **chastiseresse** *MED* records only this example.
3172 **sesoun** F5862 *saison*: var. *raison* MS. *M*. Only C has *resoun*, by simple *s*/*r* confusion or by the influence of a second French MS with the var.
3172-3 **Perfore ... bete him** F5863 *Se li bailles, si le batra*: var. *Si ...* MS. *H*; *Se le li bailles, elle batra* MS. *L*. τ seems to have seen a combination of the variants.
3174 **forthward** should perhaps be emended to the other MSS's *forward*.
3176 **lede** I accept GS's reading since it is less obvious than CJMO's use of an object (*þee*/*hym*), and F5870 *pour li* does have var. *pour* MS. *P*.
3177 **to þe hauene:** F5870 *aport* 'dowry' or 'estate' gives the overall sense: '[it (the body) has been given to you] to bring you a share of life and salvation'. τ understood *a port*.

saluacioun om. F5872 *Et pour li faire outre passer* 'and to make it [the body? the life?] go to the other world'.
3193 **þe** C's *þis* is rejected in favour of the other MSS's *þe* and in spite of F5902 *cest*: there is var. *ce* (easily read as *le*) in MSS. *oTABM¹PH*.
3203 **is** F5922 *estre seut* 'usually is'.
3206 **tweyne willes** Rom. vii 21-4.
3209 **not** om. F5932 *Si me dites donc qui je suy* which repeats the sense of F5930 (3208 *þat ye sey me who am I*).
3212 **who is** F5938 *Qu'estre* shows that JMO's *to be* is 'right'. It is, however, probably the result of correction from F³, for CGS's reading is not a rationalisation. τ's error is therefore retained.
3217 **to** should perhaps be omitted, following G.

is F5946 *Et*: var. *Est* MSS. *AlLM*.
3217-18 **Þow ... figure** Gen. i 27, also Wis. ii 23. See n. 3327.
3219 **þee** om. F5949 *et te crea* 'and created you'.
3223 **but ... nothing** 'as long as you have not forfeited [grace by sin] at all'.
3235-7 **God ... ensaumple** after directly creating Adam and Eve, God allowed man to initiate the creation of bodies, but retained responsibility for creation of souls: Aquinas, *Summa Contra Gentiles*, II, caps. 83-7 (see Aquinas, *Liber de Veritate*).
3250 **Dalida** F6009 *Dalila* var. *Dalida* MSS *oTAaBM¹GLMPgycH*. Judges xvi 4-21.
3262 **fleen ... eres** F6032 *puces' es oreilles* 'fleas in my ears' (Whiting, F259): confusion or the reception of unwelcome information indicated by a shaking of the head (*pace MED fle* b).

3268 **for my loue** F6043 *par fine amour*. τ read *fine* as ME *mine*, or perhaps he rationalised Reason's apparently inappropriate oath.

3284 **swiche** τ misread F6075 *iex* 'eyes' as *tex*.

3286 **þese**[1,2] F6081 *ses* 'its' var. *ces* MSS *ABM¹LH*.

3289 **Tobye** Tob. ii 10-18, iv 1-23.

3290 **body** G³'s marginalium *Jo* refers to Job in Tob. ii 12-15.

3310-13 **Þe ... difference** the relationship between the user and what he uses is employed to explain the relationship between body and soul in Plato (Lamb, *Alcibiades*, 129E, 130C); Aquinas objects to Plato's alleged contention (*Summa Contra Gentiles*, II, ch. 57, in Aquinas, *Liber de Veritate*). See n. 3316.

3312 **Lady** All the MSS add *quod she*, giving *or gouerned þee in any wyse. Is it þus?' quod she. 'Lady,' quod I, 'ye.' 'Quod she: 'But this in difference ...'* I omit *quod she*, assuming it to have been added by χ, since there is no precedent in F6130-3: '*Ou que de rien te gouvernast.*' | '*Est il ainsi, dame?' dis je.* | '*Ouil voir,' dist elle, 'mais ce | En difference ...*' (punctuation mine).

3315 **bi accident** is a technical phrase in philosophy (see Glossary).

him F6137 *La* var. *Le* MS. *M¹*. The pron. should be fem., referring to the soul (as Dr Walls noted).

3316 **is entendaunt** τ misread F6138 *et rendant* 'and giving it back' as *entendant*. The whole sentence should mean 'The soul supports the body by nature, but the body contains the soul in a less fundamental way, in taking its power from the soul, and in giving it back'. This may be a highly condensed reference to Aquinas's alternative to Plato's account of the distinct being possessed by both body and soul (see n. 3310-13). Aquinas regards the two as making a single being, and his analogy is with the relationship between mover and moved.

3318-19 **Þe ... leedeth** F6143-5 *Le gouverneur qui dedens est | La maine et mene y est | Si maine* 'the controller who is inside it leads it, and is led—yet he leads ...'. Comparison of a soul in a body to a sailor (not specifically a steersman) in a ship is in Aristotle, *De Anima*, 413a (Ross, Vol. III), questioned by Aquinas (who attributes it to Plato, op. cit. in n. 3310-13).

3320 **withinne** has no precedent in F6145.

3323 **it:** F6151 *la* correctly makes the soul fem.

his wille F6151 *son talent*: τ was misled by *son* 'her' (the soul's).

3327 The Pilgrim follows the advice of Augustine (*PL*, XXXV, 1588-9): 'Recognise in yourself something within, within yourself. Leave aside your clothing and flesh; descend into yourself, go into your secret room, your mind ... for not in the body but in the mind was man made in the image of God. In his own likeness let us seek God'. Reason assists the Pilgrim since man is the image of God by virtue of his intellect (Augustine, *PL*, XXXIV,

159). The ways in which man is in God's image are summarised by Aquinas, *ST*, 1a, q.93. On Aquinas' concept see Mondin, ch. 5.

3328-36 **If ... litel** this long passage lacks a main clause in F6162-78 too.

3333 **ye ne seyn** F6172 *vous ne me dites*: τ perhaps omitted 'me' by eyeskip.

3338 **Obstacle** Augustine, *PL*, XXXV, 1395 (the soul blinded by the body).

3342-3 **trusse ... bak** F6189-90 *li retrousser / Te refaurra et rendosser* 'it will be necessary (to you) to truss him on again and once more put (him) on your back'. I assume that G's *thou schall moste* 'you will have to' reflects τ's rendering of the 3 per. sg. fut. ind. (cf. Gower, *Confessio Amantis* 2/1670 *it shal ... mow*, and 4/38 *Thou schalt mowe*), and that CG³ rationalise.

3350 **contracte** F6203 *le contract*; in both languages the word, though primarily a sb. ('burden one has to carry', a sense recorded by *MED contract* 3 only here), has overtones of the substantival adj. 'paralysed, helpless one': see *contract*, adj., in 3148, 5335.

3365 **a stike** (F6234 *un tronc* 'a log' or 'a tree-stump') is based on G's subpuncted *stykie*, the spelling being based on C's *stiked, stiketh* (70, 1904, 2058, 2060) rather than *stikke* at 5923, which is in the *A.B.C.*, where the scribe's spelling departs from his norm. MO's *a straw* suggests that δ (if not β, but J's *strare* is odd) substituted; it is not possible so easily to explain CG³S's *a blast of wynde*.

3366 **in** should perhaps be omitted as in JMO: F6234 offers no precedent.

3384 **naked** F6266 *mu* 'silent': var. *nu* MSS *TALH*. Both *blynd* and *naked* may qualify *þou* in 3383 rather than *contracte*.

þi dedes τ misunderstood F6267 *son faiz* 'his burden'.

3384-5 **wele ... parte** follows the ambiguous F6268 *bien vourra au bien partir*, probably: 'he will want to divide the profit (when it comes to the reward)'. Confusion was caused by *bien*¹, which may be adv. or sb. If it is adv., the reading should be *[wel] he ...*; but the sb. is suggested by G's repetition of *weelle* 'wealth' for *bien*¹ and *bien*², and by C³'s two corrections over erasure to *welþe*. C's *wele* 'wealth' (never used by C for *wel* 'well'), is therefore reinstated.

3390 **oo ... seye:** F6277 *o adire* which neither makes sense nor rhymes with *absconse* in the next line. Perhaps τ thought it meant 'to put it in one [i.e. briefly]', or translated literally without comprehension.

shadewed F6278 *mucie, tout absconse*: τ avoids repetition.

3395 **shulde** the other MSS's reading is accepted against C's *wolde*; the spelling is C's normal form (though he uses *sholdest* at 5708).

EXPLANATORY NOTES

3397 **Þou what** perhaps should read *þou, what* (as if *Allas ... þou* meant 'poor you, alas': but cf. 226 *Þou what seiste*, and *OED thou* 1b, used 'in reproach or contempt'.

3404 **egret** F6304 *grues* 'crane'.

3409 **lost** perhaps G's *ilost* should be accepted.

3411 **flowen** τ read F6316 *enfoui* 'buried' as *enfui*.

3416 **writen** Wis. ix 15.

3418 **am I** should perhaps be left out, but I accept G³'s marginal insertion, following F6331 *sui je*, and assuming a similar easily missed insertion in τ, omitted by χ.

3423 **Eche ... dung-hep** F6351 *Chascun est fort sur son fumier*; Hassell, F188; Whiting, C350.

3433 **in oÞer places** F6357 *autre part* 'on the other hand'.

3436 **faitourye:** F6362 *fetardie* 'idleness, inactivity' but *MED faiterye* 'deception, imposture, fraud (especially as practised by beggars or vagabonds)' does not record this sense, so perhaps 'idleness (such as is common in work-shy beggars)'. Reason wants to avoid making the Dreamer feel helpless to the point of inactivity.

3440 **goode** perhaps GMOS (*wel* in C's form) should be accepted.

3444 **adaunted** om. F6378 *et soupeditez* 'and trodden down'.

3450-2 **I² ... oon:** F6391-2 *Je cuidoie que moy et li | Fussons un* shows that the sense is 'I had thought myself and it were the same'.

3459 **suffre** F6408 *laisse*: if CJS's correct subj. is a rationalisation, GMO's *suffreth* should be accepted.

3461 **slugged** GS's reading is accepted: the spelling is that at 3447.

3464 **good** F6416 *point* 'time'.

3464-6 **whan ... þee¹** F6418-20 is differently constructed, giving the sense 'when it is time to flatter you, and then when you are not aware of what is going on, you will find yourself deceived'.

3465-6 **and ... disceyued** since it has JMO's support, G's cancelled reading is accepted, τ having probably misread F6419-20 *Et lors quant garde d'en dourras | Deceu* by taking *quant* as *grant* (giving *gret keepe*) then added *butt* to clarify the resulting sense. G³'s notation is complex: he subpuncted words to be omitted, put crosses over those to be replaced, forgot to put a cross over *thanne* and misplaced the caret in the text for his marginal correction (f. 47ʳ). G³ (and so CS) reflect F more accurately, but as a result of correction from F².

3470 **tool** F6428 *les oustis* 'tools'.

3478 **goodes** GMOS's reading, the *difficilior lectio*, is accepted— perhaps erroneously, in view of F6442 *le bien*.

3480-3 **where ... weren** a rare example of a large omission in α, resulting from eyeskip from 3480 *with me* to 3483 *with me*. Following F6447-51, MO's reading is accepted against J.

3482 **enemy** I assume that τ misread F6448 *ennuy* 'hindrance', but perhaps the reading should be *ennuy*, as if α misread the ME.
paas F6450 *les . . . pas* 'the . . . paths'.

3488 **I . . . þee** the clause, supported by F6461 *Je iray*, appears only in G, where it is subpuncted as if mistaken for dittography.

3499 **thankinge** F6483-4 *regraciant . . . et merciant*: τ avoids repetition.

3507-8 **þilke . . . despyte** F6501-2 *Qui onques nul jour ne me vit / Me fera asses plus despit* 'it seems to me that someone not seeing me at all will do me greater harm'. Since the pilgrim expects trouble from his own body, he may expect worse from strangers. The sense of the ME is that the pilgrim has little more to fear from unseen enemies when he has a 'friend' like his body: either τ misunderstood F, or his *not* is due to his having read *Ne* for *Me*.

3510 **wey fourchede** Prov. ii 13-16 compares life's choices to paths, but their comparison with a letter *Y*, the left path representing vice and the right virtue is, according to Servius, Pythagorean (Hill, p. xxx n. 1, where other classical treatments of the image are listed).

3511 **þat . . . ooþer** F6508 *ne dessemblassent / l'un de l'autre* 'nor separated one from the other'.

3513 **bushes** F6512 *bous* 'bush' is the majority reading. Hultman, p. 129, compares the thorny hedge with the opiny obstacles which hinder the Lover in *Le Roman de la Rose*, 1805-14.

3514 **bushes** F6514 *Bos* 'woods, trees'.

3519 **vnder hire spayere** F6524 *dessouz s'aisselle* 'under her armpit'. Prov. xxvi 15: 'The slothful hideth his hand under his armpit'.

3521 **turnede** om. F6528 *et retournoit* 'and turned (it) again'.

3532 **bettere** om. F6550 *Je voy cy deus devant mes iex* 'I see two here before my eyes'.

3536 **Come . . . for:** F6557-8 *Vien t'en . . . a moy par ci, Quar . . .* and C's punctuation show that C took *here for* as adv. meaning 'for this reason', and so wrote *Heerefore*, beginning a sentence, and using the final *-e*. See n. 3546.

3539 **biyounde see:** F6562 *d'outre mer* (applied to crusading areas of French interest) suggests the Holy Land, thus associating the pilgrim's life-journey with the recovery of a lost heritage (heaven).

3546 **fore** only here, in 1140 occurrences, does C deviate from *for*, to which, perhaps, emendation should be made.

3550-1 **þe . . . of** (F6583-4 *le mestier / Qui povres est a mieux mestier*) loses the play on *mestier* 'craft/necessary' (noted by Dr Walls).

3556 **idel** F6594 *Huiseuse* 'an idle person'.

3561 **made it ayen** in view of F6604 *refaisoye* perhaps G's *made ayen* should be adopted; I accept CJMOS, which may be a

EXPLANATORY NOTES

rationalisation.

3562 **to þi rihtes** could read *to þi riht*, following F6606 *a ton droit*.

3564 **as me thinketh** om. F6611 *Et comment te pourroye amer?* 'and how could I love you?'

3566 **folye and cokardye** om. one of the three nouns in F6615-16 *sotie, | Et nicete et musardie*, then om. F6617-18 *Qui prises mieux ceus qui paine ont | Que ne fais ceus qui aise sont* 'you who value more those who take trouble, than you do those who are idle'.

3574 **countenaunce** F6632 *acointance* 'acquaintance'.

3576 **foorbushed** om. F6636 *Et acier luisant et burny* 'and shining, burnished steel'.

3579 **ouercome** F6642 *confus* 'confused': var. *vaincus* MS. *L*.

3586 **filour** should perhaps read *a filour*, following F6656 *un limeur*, but I accept GO, assuming rationalisation in CM(S).

3599 **Ocupacioun** Ecclus. xl 1 : *Occupatio magna creata est omnibus hominibus*.

3606 **wey** F6692 *chemin et par sa voie*': τ avoids repetition.

3620 **wode** F6718 *bos* 'bush': var. *bois* MSS *AH*.

3622 **ne is** G's elliptical reading is accepted: CJMOS's forms of *þat ne is* are probably due to rationalisation in Cβ.

3632 **God looke** F6740 *Diex gart* 'God protect you': var. *Dieu te gart* MSS *AM*. Either τ read the var. as *Dieu regart* or his ejaculation is analogous to the idiom *God you se* 'God protect you' (*MED God* 10a).

3633 **do** GJMO's pres. subj. is accepted against CG³'s normalisation.

3640 **organes** the MS has *orgāns*: I have expanded to C's spelling at 6837, 6981 (see also 4138, 6987).

3642 **pleyeres ... bal:** F6759 *baleurs* 'dancers'.
of iogelours F6760 *de bastiaus et de jugleurs* 'of tumblers and of jugglers'.

3643 **merelles** (om. F6763 *d'entregeterie* '[of] juggling'): Nine Men's Morris (Fivepenny Morris) was played by two, with counters, usually on a lined board; on the continent, *merelles* could mean 'hopscotch'.

3644 **museryes** F6764 *muserie*: *MED* records only this example.

3659 **þee¹** om. F6792 *et n'en ment* 'and don't lie about it'.

3675-6 **pilgrime ... now** F6824-5 *pelerin | Qui autre foys i est venu* 'pilgrim who has come here before'.

3681 **many ... passed** if *þer* means 'there, at that place', C's *þ* would be expanded to *þere* (see n. 27-8). F6835 *plusier ont ... passe* offering no precedent, I give the unemphasised form *þer*: 'there are many who have passed'.

3685 **heere** F6842 *jadis* 'before'.

3686 **tender sister** τ misread F6846 *tendre sevree* ('gentle separation' because Idleness imperceptibly severs the soul from God?).

strike 'stroke', but in view of F6847 *enformer* 'put on', perhaps 'put on [by stroking down the fingers of a glove]'. For the immoral connotations of gloves as invitations to the *olde daunce* of lust in, e.g., *Le Roman de la Rose*, see Fleming (1969), pp. 84–6.

3688 **mirour** the image of Peresce owes something to other bearers of comb and mirror: the Siren-Mermaid, Luxuria, and above all to Oiseuse in *Le Roman de la Rose* (Fleming [1969], p. 76; Hultman, p. 130).

3689 **vanitees**: F6852 *elenches* refers to Aristotle *De Sophisticis Elenchis*, on specious argument (trans. W. Pickard-Cambridge in Vol. I of Ross).

3696 **wormes... hondes** 'handworms' or itchmites (scabies), implying both inactivity and uncleanliness.

3701 **wey** F6873 *chemin et a voie*: τ avoids repetition.

3704-5 **I...passe** F6881-2 *par la haye lourdement | Le passeroie et asprement* 'I would make him pass through the hedge, firmly and sharply'.

3705 **Soone ynowh** τ misread F6883 *A ses couz* 'with his elbows' as *Asses tost*.

3706 **bipleyne** *MED bipleinen* records only this example.

3720 **berkinge** τ misread F6911 *la baveuse* 'foaming' or 'raving' as *l'aboyeuse*.

3722 **to** F6914 *droit a* 'straight to'.

3724 **stepdame** i.e. enemy, as in traditional stepmothers (*OED stepdame* b; Whiting, I6, especially entries for *c*. 1450, 1483, 1509). St Bernard, *PL*, CLXXXII, 756: *Fugienda proinde otiositas, mater nugarum, noverca virtutum*, and *PL*, CLXXXIV, 1273.

3741 **who...hegge** F6951-2 *que fait ci | La haie* 'what this hedge does': τ shows *que/qui* confusion.

3749 **hath wold bitraye** F6967 *a voulu trahir*: see 2786, 2884.

3771 **it is** perhaps G's *is it* should be accepted, C(S)β having regularised.

3773 **be** F7010 *fait*: τ may have seen the subj. var. *face* MS. *A*.

3781 **nygh...market** 'about to come off badly' or 'about to see my plans fail' (? *OED market* 1b).

3785-6 **He...wolde** F7031-2 *Fol est qui ne fait quant puet,| Quar il ne fait pas quant il veut* (Hassell, F13).

3788 **misfel**, suggested by G's *mys full* and M's *mysse fell* (J *myssauenture felle*), has no precedent in C, which has *misbifel* at 1453,

EXPLANATORY NOTES

5496, 6332.

3788 **As ... musinge** having wandered about unoccupied, looking vaguely about, the pilgrim is suddenly seized by sloth, getting tangled in a bird-trap just as he seeks Occupation's path. As Wenzel (p. 124) observes 'the genetic and functional relation between [Idleness and Sloth] is clear'. Bird-traps (nets slung between trees, and cords stretched between pegs in the ground) are illustrated in a *Pèlerinage de la vie*: British Library, MS. Cotton Tiberius A7, ff. 51^r,^{v}, 57^r. Hultman, p. 131 compares Cupid's snares, *Le Roman de la Rose*, 1596.

3796 **Sampson** see 3249-50, where the Pilgrim is Sampson, his body Delilah.

3800-1 **foul ... salwh** F7061 *Orde et noire et ville et sale*: τ adds 'old', perhaps incorporating a gloss, for *ville* has var. *vielle* MS. *H*. CS's *and salwh* could be accepted as nearer F, but looks like normalisation.

3804 **bounden** F7068 *liess ... et enfardelees* 'bound and bundled'.

3805 **for** om. F7071 *ai veu* 'I have seen (that)'.

3805-6 **to ... trusses** trip ropes were stretched across wolves' runs, and otter nets were hung across rivers (Gaston Phoebus, pp. 52 and 60 respectively). Manufacture of varied nets is illustrated ibid., p. 100.

3824 **Þou** F7104 *qui* 'you who': τ's syntax differs.

3826 **if ... me** F7108 *se cheu n'i estoies* 'if you had not fallen into them': it is remarkable that in MS. *o* the illuminator changed this to *se eschappe mest*, a var. not recorded elsewhere. This suggests that here τ was reading *o* or a MS. closely related to it.

3833-4 **þat**[1] **... swyn** F7120-4 *Qui li amaine par cordiaus, / Aussi com se fussent porciaus, / Les pelerins que arrester / Je puis par les piez et lier* 'who leads to him [the devil], by cords as if they were pigs, the pilgrims whom I can catch by the feet and bind'. τ's *it* in 3834 may be due to a *fussent* so abbreviated that it looked like *fust*—a sg. he would have expected if he had mistaken F7120 *li* for a direct object. 'Attraction' in the relative clause gives l*ede* agreeing not with *þat* but with *I*, the first subject (Jespersen, Pt. VII 4. 5[5]).

3840-1 **þat ly ... þat make** see n. 3833-4, last sentence.

3842 **to ley ... cradel** F7139 *pour eus bercier* 'to rock them in a cradle'.

3844 **gouernour** cf. 3316-26.

3850 **rise** om. F7156 *Et cauquetrepes sans semer* 'and thistles, without sowing them': even French scribes found the noun difficult.

3862 **alle thinge** C's favoured form is *thing*, except in the phrase *alle thinge*, which in four out of six occurrences (172, 3852-3, 3934, 6872) carries the final -*e*.

3863 **Annoye of Lyf** *Accidie*, lack of interest in living, which, when not identified with Sloth, is the desperate outcome of it.

3865 **dullede** om. F7186 *et aplommai* 'and coshed'.

Helye Elias despaired, and longed to die (III Kings xix 1-7).

3866 **þe hye honged** F7187 *le haut pendu*; the hovering angel who twice fed and encouraged the prophet 'Arise, and eat', adding on the second occasion: 'for thou has yet a great way to go'. There may be covert reference to Christ Crucified.

3870 **two or thre** F7196 *.III.*: perhaps τ wrote *two othere* 'two others', subsequent scribes mistaking *othere* for 'or', so adding *thre*.

3875 **Cleeruaus ... synewes** F7203-4 plays on words: *Clervaus / Ains furent faites a Nervaus*: τ mistook *Nervaus* for *nerveurs* 'sinews, thongs'. *Nervaus* is apparently an invented place-name, but Cottineaux, II, 2051 records a Nervieux Priory in the diocese of Lyons, given to Cluny in 1203—could there be a pun? (The Pilgrim is given the choice of Cluny or Citeaux at 6751.) Contrast between *Cler-* (light) and *Ner-* (dark) accounts for the cords being *al black*. The point of the word-play is not apparent until 7005: the pilgrim, having become a religious, finds his feet and hands bound not by Sloth but by Obedience: stillness is not the same as sloth.

3877 **Weryness and Letargie** could be two names rather than one.

3878 **sownere** F7216 *pasmee* 'swooner'; *OED sowner* cites only this example.

softe om. F7212 *Et tresalees et blesmies* 'and overblown and faded'.

3888 **Judas** Matt. xxvii 5.

3889 **helle** om. F7234 *Qui plus que arrement est ner* 'who is blacker than ink'.

3891 **aboute** F7237 *aval* 'down into'.

3892 **to**[1] om. in G(S): perhaps their reading should be accepted.

3894 **euele sorwe** F7242 *male semaine* 'a bad time' (lit. 'a bad week').

3895 **wynd ... north** an evil wind, from the devil's quarter (Jer. i 14): contrast the wind of the Spirit, blowing soul-ships to haven (6749).

3907 **oynement** has not been mentioned in connection with the satchel before (1835-66, 1890-997). The only oils discussed have been the general 'oil of mercy' described by Reason at 317-37, or the oils used in Baptism, Confirmation and Extreme Unction (see nn. 275-6, 289-303). Here *oynement* may refer to the healing Eucharist (*þat þe kyng maketh*) which was indeed put in the Pilgrim's satchel (though not by Grace Dieu) at 2707-8. However, at 4827-30 the Pilgrim, subject to four of the seven sins, dare not touch this bread that he carries '*as longe as I am on*

EXPLANATORY NOTES 453

þis half in þe wronge wey' (then as now in unconfessed mortal sin). The ointment may simply be comfort found in Faith—the *vitaile* of 1892 being distinct from the *bred*.

3912 **olde** F7273 *vielle estrie* 'old witch'.

3922 **drawestere and hangestere** the textual variants show that the feminine gender of the executioner in F is retained only in GS's reading, here adopted. *MED* omits *drawestere*, and for *hangestere* cites only 5115.

3926 **gripede** om. F7297 *et pris* 'and held'.

3927 **dressede me** F7300 *me redrecai* 'got up again'.

3929 **slepy** om. F7302 *de moi suir* 'in following me'.

3930 **vnenpeched** *OED unimpeached* records only this example of 'unhindered'.

3939 **Þat ooþer** F7325 *Les autres*: F, and *hem* in 3942, require a pl.

3944 **rekeuer** F7334 *retourner*, and grammar, require that GMS be accepted.

3955 **an horn** F7357 *un cornet* 'a little [musical] horn', distinguished from F7355 *une corne*, the horn projecting from her forehead: CG³S clarify by adding *to blowe with*, which GJMO show was not in τ.

3956 **baudryk** F7358 *escherpe* 'pilgrim's satchel'. *MED bauderik* does not record this sense (but see n. 4716).

3957 **arayed** F7359-60 *atournee/ . . . et afublee* 'arayed and dressed'.

3980 **leedeth** F7403-4 *maine/ . . . et pourmaine*: τ avoids repetition.

3992 **noon so old** behind Man's fall lies the fall of Lucifer, due to Pride.

3997 **disclosed** the earliest example *MED* gives with the sense 'hatched'.

3999 **falle doun** om. F7441 *du haut ni jus* 'from top to bottom'.

4002 **salt** τ misread F7447 *sale* 'ugly' as *sal*.
werse F7448 *plus . . . lait* 'uglier'.

4008-13 **a . . . clymbe** the devil's envy and pride gave him the desire to afflict man, who was to fill the place left in heaven by the fall of the angels (Augustine, *PL*, XXXVI, 709; Aquinas, *ST*, Ia, q.98. a.2).

4014-15 **so . . . swelle** F7471-2 *Si (le) souflai en sa pensee / Et (si) li fis sa pance enflee*: as Dr Walls noted, τ loses the pun on *pensee/pance* 'thought/paunch' weakening the link between physical and spiritual hunger.

4017 **as . . . wisdom** F7475-6 *Ausi com Dieu son souverain / De science seroit tout plain* suggests that GMO reveal τ's reading; G³'s *konnynge* (echoed in C) represents F *science* more accurately than does *wisdom*, but is probably from F².

Be is a form of, and should perhaps be emended to, *bi*: this is the only occasion (in over 490) on which C so uses *be*.

4018 **from al to al** *MED al* sb. 5c cites only this example of 'utterly'.

4019 **straunged þertoo** ? 'banished from there'—but the construction with *þertoo* is not in *OED strange* v., so perhaps 'made strangers to it'.

4021 **tweyne chyldhodes** i.e. in heaven and on earth.

4026 **þat oon** F7489-94 show that the sense is '[I make] one . . .'.

despise F7494 *envair* 'invade': var. *en vier* MS. *L*.

4027 **condyeresse** *MED* records examples only here and at 6745 (*conduyeresse*).

4028 **stoures** F7497 *estours*; I assume that this is OF/ME 'battle', but it may be OF 'stores, equipment', in which case, being not part of *OED stour* sb., but of *store* sb., it merits a separate Glossary entry.

in F7497 *et*: var. *es* MS. *o*.

4029 **helmes** om. F7500 *Timbres* 'timbrels', perhaps because τ was puzzled by the mention of instruments among garments—but percussion instruments often mark the progress of important persons.

4031 **queyntisinges** *OED quaintise* records only this example.

neewed F7503 *Nouveletez* 'novelties': var. *Nouuelles*.

me om. F7504 *Plus en fais assez que li roi* 'I make a lot more of these than the king'.

4033 **crestes** om. F7508 *A marmouses cocus locus* 'with oblong, shaggy (?)': the meaning of *marmouses* is unknown.

4033-4 **streyte . . . sides** F7509 *Estroites cotes par les flans | Manches a penonchaus pendans* 'jackets with tight sides and hanging sleeves'.

4034 **surcotes rede sleeves** F7511 *surcot rouge manche* var. pl. MSS *LTG*.

4038 **tweyne or thre** F7518 ·III·: see n. 3870.

4040 **blynde** F7522 *Borgne* 'one-eyed'.

4043 **paringall** F7528 *onnis* 'equal' supports GJMOS's reading.

4048 **vndertakere** F7537 *repreneur*; *OED* records only this example (see also 5442), reading F as *repreueur*.

4061 **cristened** F7562 *crestiens* 'Christian'.

4064 **fame** F7569 *faute* 'fault' var. *fame* MS. *o*.

4071 **tale** F7582 *trueil* '[screw of the] press'. The image may be of the press lifted, perhaps relating to 4083-5, where Pride cannot bear to be *empressed* (crowded). Perhaps τ, puzzled, substituted *tale* (*OED Tail* sb.[4] 2), referring to the handle of the spear just mentioned.

4075 **Boloyne-þe-Grace** (F7588 *Bouloigne la crasse* var. *Bouloigne la grasse* MSS *TAA*[1]*L*) Hassell, B129. Bologna (University?),

EXPLANATORY NOTES 455

known from the 13th century as 'la grassa' because of its opulence (Battaglia, *grasso* 4).

4079 **hoppeth** F7597 *halete* 'pants' var. *balete* 'dances' MS. *o*.

4081 **maken me place** F7601 *Place me faut* 'I have to have a place'; τ read *Place me fant*.

4089 **þe¹ ... liyoun** F7614 *roe de paon* is Stürzinger's preferred reading in the light of F7771-2 (see 4171-3) but most MSS (*toTaBM¹GLMg*) have *roe de lion*. *Roe* 'circle' can be used of any round object: in F7771-2 it refers to the peacock's spread tail; here it seems to refer to a supercilious expression.

spaulinge F7615 *espauliant* 'moving up and down (as I walk)'; *OED* records only this example.

4090 **ioyntes stiryinge** F7617 *jointes jontoier*: τ loses the word-play suggesting exaggerated movement.

4092-3 **Of ... scaffold** F7621 *D'autri bien vuel faire eschaufaut* 'I love to use other people as scaffolding': τ mistook adv. *bien* for sb.

4093 **ape** om. F7623 *En moi n'a que vent, et fumee* 'there is nothing in me but wind and bad air'.

4098-100 The variants are too complex to convey clearly in textual apparatus. F7631-7 have *Les defautes d'autri voi bien,| Mes de leur bien je ne voi rien; | Et pour ce sui (je) moquerresse | (De) touz et escharnisserresse, | Nulle telle a Chastiau Landon | Pour denier ne trouveroit on. | Anciennement couronnee ....* That χ carried the equivalent of this is clear: 4098-9 *but ... therfore* is omitted only by C; 4099 *I ... folk* is in CG³; 4099-100 *such ... peny* survives in part in G (*laudoun for no peny*), in O, and in modified form in M, who at this stage often modifies freely. These last two lines are a rare example of reliance on MO (though I accept neither in its entirety).

4100 **Castell Landoun** F7635 *Chastiau Landon*: a place, in Dept. Seine et Marne, apparently associated with mockery (Tobler, *chastel*; Godefroy, *chastel Landon*).

4101 **ysaie** Is. xxviii 1: 'Woe to the crown of pride.'

4107 **horn of vnicorn** The Bestiary interprets the unicorn's horn as 'wrath' (McCulloch, pp. 179-80), and in *Ancrene Wisse*, Bk. IV (Tolkien, p. 104), Wrath is a unicorn.

biscorn the bicorne is a fabulous two-horned beast which eats patient husbands: see 'Bycorne and Chychevache' in Lydgate (1934), p. 433, and Robinson, p. 712, n. 1188. The sense may simply be that the unicorn is more cruel than any ordinary two-horned beast; Tobler cites only F (and Godefroy, I, 645: *faire a bicorne* may mean 'to mock').

4110 **mihte** F7655 *peust* supports the subj., but perhaps the reading should be *may*, as G's *my* could be an error for *may*, which is also in JMO.

4111 **made** F7658 *faisoit*; the reading should perhaps be *make*, following GJMO (*helpe* might be pr. or pa. subj.).

4112 **swerdes** om. F7660 *et aus fauchons* 'and to sabres'.

4114-15 **and ... bole** (F7665-6 *Et plus crueusement en fier | Que un tor tressauvaige et fier* 'and am more vicious in striking than a completely wild and fierce bull') is in JMO only, omitted in α by eyeskip from 4114-15 *and more cruelliche* to the same in 4117; *bole* is an editorial emendation of their *bore*, assuming that β or χ mistook *l* for *r*.

4116-18 **þilke ... ooþere** follows the word order of MO rather than G³ because it explains the eyeskip in 4114. The virtuous are particularly prone to arrogance, and the previous two sentences also imply that all violence (perhaps all sin) has its roots in arrogance, the horn which first opens wounds to receive worse weapons.

4122 **folk** χ probably misread F7677 *folz* 'fools'.

blacked om. F7677-8 *et touz salis* 'and dirtied all over'.

4124 **Nabugodonosor** Dan. iv 27. The whole of Dan. iv shows the humbling of pride. The image of windfalls which follows may have been suggested by the doomed tree (representing Nabuchodonosor) in Daniel's dream, but in context it recalls the familiar image of the Tree of Virtues, e.g. in the 13th-century Lorens d'Orleans' *Somme le roi* (the ME version is the *Book of the Vices and Virtues*, pp. 10-97).

4133-46 Aesop's fable 'The Fox and the Crow' is told by Marie de France but she is not quoted here.

4135 **so ... song** F7702-3 *se Diex te gart, | Que me dies une chancon*; τ was literal 'if God keeps you so that you may sing me a song'.

4137-8 **symphanye** may refer to several kinds of musical instrument, such as the hurdy-gurdy, which together with *organe* and *sautree* is described and illustrated in Munrow, pp. 15-16, 16-17, 23-4.

sautree the psaltery is a stringed instrument like a harp but with the sounding board behind and parallel with the strings (n. 4137-8).

4150 **I drawe for oon** F7730 *(je) traie pour une* may refer to putting an opponent in a game at a disadvantage: *traire* is used with *merelle* (a gaming piece) as in *mes traire la merelle* 'to have bad luck'.

4154 **dunge** τ read F7738 *fumee* 'smoke' as *fumie*.

4157 **shalmuses** the shawm is an instrument of the oboe class, with a double reed enclosed in the mouthpiece: see Munrow, pp. 8-9.

often as Dr Walls noted, τ read F7743 *sonner* 'produce sound' as *souvent*: G cancelled, and C(S) omitted the meaningless *often*.

4158-9 **I ... þilke** F7747-8 *De ce souflet (je) soufle l'astre | A cil* 'with

EXPLANATORY NOTES

these bellows I blow on the hearth belonging to him'. Pride fans the cooking-fire of those making their soul into a titbit for the devil (cf. 4107).

4161-2 **whoso...fanne it** F7751-2 *qui lumiere a en son sain, | De ce souflet je li estain* 'if anyone has a light in his heart, I extinguish it with these bellows'. τ thought the clause developed the imagery of 4158-9. The idea of flame not fanned but blown out is followed by that of winnowing: blasts of Pride extinguish the love of God, and disperse and destroy the useless products of a sinful soul. S's *wane* 'diminish' instead of *fanne* is no doubt intelligent substitution, but perhaps τ did write *uane* (for *wane*), χ taking it for a form of *fanne*.

4172 **araye** F7771 *roer* 'spread [my] tail'.

4172-3 **to...confusion** spreading of the tail is on one level an exaggerated gesture of mock-modesty, designed to attract attention; however, *confusioun* may mean not only 'confusion' but also 'private parts' (*Thesaurus Lingvae Latinae, confusio*, 5—cf. *mulier est hominis confusio* in the *Nun's Priest's Tale*), and The Bestiary describes how the bird reveals its rear-end by the gesture of which it is so proud, making itself an object of ridicule, and resembling a vain prelate (Pseudo Hugh St Victor, *PL*, CLXXVII, 53).

4174 **Argus** the 'eyes of Argus' placed by Juno in the peacock's tail, commonly implying watchful jealousy, here signify a show of intellect: cf. the *Pilgrimage* Second Recension (Lydgate, p. 167, lines 6355-61).

4174-5 **beter...jugements** F7777 *Miex croi et a leur jugement* is odd: should *croi et* be *croirent*, giving 'they prefer to trust their judgement'? Pride's display convinces the gullible that her intellect is great and her opinion sound, when in fact her 'eyes' focus only on herself.

4190 **tournements** F7805 *cornemens* 'trumpet blowing'. Since there is no record of ME *cornements* in this sense I assume that τ read *c* as *t*.

4206-7 **þat...fool** F7836 *Qui du cornet est dit cornart*: as Dr Walls noted, τ loses the pun on *cornet* 'horn' and *cornart* 'fool'.

4208 **but of him** τ read F7839 *Fors que li* 'except himself' as *Fors de li* (see 4210 *of himself* for F7842 *fors de li*).

4212 **recoupeth** *OED recoup* cites only this example of 'interrupt'.

4213 **fooles** F7848 *foles* 'foolish' (qualifying *paroles* 'words').

4216 **clout...colour** (F7852-4 *clut | Que qui li diroit que pas n'est | De tel couleur*): the Glossary gives *clout* an entry separate from *cloþes*, as if *clout* were from OE *clūt* 'rag': the arrogant man 'weaves' a false argument—a rag, rather than a piece of sound cloth. But both words may be from *MED cloth* (OE *claþ*), where sense 7 'cloth of a different colour' means 'a case altogether

ÞE LYFE OF ÞE MANHODE

different' (Whiting, C305 but not in Hassell).

4217 **poudre** τ read F7856 *foudre* 'lightning' as *poudre*.

4219 **and**[2] om. F7861 *Loer* 'to praise'.

4220 **vertues and penaunces** F7861 sg. Stürzinger may be right in giving *pense* 'thought' for *penaunces*, but τ saw var. *pance* MSS *toTBM*[1]*GMH*.

4229 **Rolandes** see n. 2326; Roland's triple sounding of his ivory horn Olifant at his imminent defeat showed both his courage and his humility. Pride's horn sounds only for sham successes, and on one level is simply a fart (4181-5).

4230 **þe ... oxe** by which a tame beast is led (Whiting, O88 'to lead the ox by the horn'; Hassell, B116, B118).

4230-1 **longe ... neewe** F7880 *lonc temps a qu'il ne fu neuf* 'it is a long time since it was new'; τ literally rendered F's pleonastic *ne*, having understood 'it was not-new a long time ago' (i.e. it was new even longer ago).

4233 **By it** om. F7885 *tous temps* 'all the time'.

4237 **to go** perhaps GO's *go* should be accepted.

4241 **took on him** F7899 *se chauca* 'put on his feet'.

4245-7 **þe ... a spore** eating the apple turns the spur Disobedience into a barbed, baited hook in Adam's mouth. Perhaps the image plays on a common one which is its antithesis—the Cross as a hook to catch the devil, as in *The Golden Legend*: 'Jesu Christ hath hid the hook of his divinity under the meat of our humanity, and the fiend would take the meat of the flesh and was taken with the hook of the Godhead ... He laid out his bait to our deceiver and adversary; he hath set forth his cross' (Voragine, I, 79); see Rabanus Maurus, *PL*, CXI, 240.

4247-8 **in ... it** 'it is a pity he had a horse at all if he had to wear this spur to ride it'.

4248-9 **þe ... foormed** F7915-16 *li destrier este | Qui de sa destre estoit forme*; τ lost the word-play on *destrier/destre* which underlines the fact that Eve, made from Adam's rib, is regarded as Adam's horse.

4251 **Pharao** cf. 3037 where *Rude Entendement* is compared to Pharaoh (at 4270 we find that Pride's staff Obstinacy is *Rude Entendement*'s).

4252-3 **þe souereyn ... hond** F7921-2 *le roi souverain | De sa poste et de sa main | Le pueple Israel vout oster*: τ translated *De sa pouste* twice, either carelessly or (as Dr Walls thinks) having first thought that *De sa poste* referred to God's power, not Pharaoh's, then realised his mistake and given the correct meaning.

4256 **spored** F7929-30 *talonne | Et longuement esperonne*: τ avoids repetition.

4259 **he ... poynt** (Hassell, A51; Whiting, P377) a fool 'kicks against

EXPLANATORY NOTES

the pricks'.

4267 **resoun** ? *Resoun*: perhaps this is (as at 4271) personification.

4273 **Saul** I Kings xv 1-33: Saul, commanded by God to kill even his enemies' cattle and sheep, disobediently retained them, not to deprive God of the best of the booty, but to sacrifice it publicly later, with an eye to his own popularity.

4276 **knorred** *MED* records only this example.

In . . . Egipte perhaps because of Pharaoh's twelve-fold obstinacy during the plagues (already referred to at 3038), or because *Per Ægyptam vitam nostram ignorantiae tenebris involutam. Ægyptam enim tenebrae interpretatur* (Pseudo Hugh St Victor, *PL*, CLXXVII, 29).

4284 **tye too** F7984 *metre et atachier*: τ avoids repetition.

4289 **arayed** F7993-4 *paree | . . . et afublee*: τ avoids repetition.

4293 **peynture** the original effect of richly coloured tombs rarely survives, but see, e.g., the Bronscombe tomb effigy in Exeter Cathedral, bearing elaborate all-over colour from *c*. 1291.

4298 **hat** F8010 *chapel leveis* 'hat that goes up and down' (because the conjuror constantly moves it about?).

4302 **Blow** F8018 *soufle*: ? 'pshaw!' or a ruder, raspberry sound: *soufle* can mean 'fart'.

ostrich The Bestiary describes the bird's flightlessness (McCulloch, pp. 146-7).

4319 **sanctificatur** apparently a prayer made in ostentatious humility under abuse, perhaps echoing I Tim. iv 5: *sanctificatur enim per verbum Dei et orationem* (if not an error for the *Pater Noster*'s *sanctificetur [nomen tuum]*).

Renard the story is in the 12th-century Branch III of the Renart cycle (Martin, pp. 131ff).

4324 **ooþere . . . do** F8064 *(Autri) mestier con ne [pas] scet faire* 'the crafts of others, which one does not know how to do' suggests that τ read *Autre* for *Autri*: the sense (ignoring Stürzinger's intrusive *pas*) is then 'crafts other than those one knows'.

4327 **livede** τ read F8070 *jeunant (iunant)* 'fasting' as *vivant*.

4329 **Þe ape** the story, common in French literature from the 12th century, is told by the 16th-century Bonaventure Des Périers (Des Périers, pp. 97-9). A cobbler's work was repeatedly ruined by a monkey which watched his every action then ineptly imitated it whenever the man left his workshop. Finally the cobbler, knowing the monkey to be watching, furiously mimed the cutting of his own throat. The monkey killed itself.

4334 **to his aray** τ read F8083 *a son tour* 'in turn' as *a son atour*, or anticipated it at the end of F8084 (see 4380).

4335 **wurþi** τ read F8085 *viguereuse* 'active' as *dignereuse*.

4336 **vsed** F8089 *vestus et afublez*: τ avoids repetition.

4342 **Oolde** (F8099 *Vielle*): if C has O olde rather than one badly-spaced word, the reading should be *Olde* (C's spelling without exception elsewhere) since there is no precedent for *O*.

4350 **doinge ... fetheren** Flattery appears to behave like Fortune, who 'plucks the proud of their fine feathers' (Whiting, F104): i.e. she strips the proud of virtues (see n. 57–63).

4352 **Placebo** 'I will please [the Lord]' (Ps. cxiv 9): the usual name for the Vespers of the Dead with which the Office used to open, and a commonplace for Flattery (Hassell, P188; Whiting, P248).

4357 **sore** F8124 *teigneuse* 'ringwormy'.

oynture *OED ointure* cites only this text.

4358 **a ... cryeth** Hassell, R83; Whiting, W207.

4362 **desceyue ... floyte** F8134 *les decoif au flajol* (lit. 'deceive them with the flute') 'flatter them'.

mere mayden see n. 6399 and line 6437: Flattery is associated with Worldly Pleasure, both being mermaids.

4362-3 **I ... make** see n. 7077.

4363 **þat**[1] om. F8136 *par mon doucement chanter* 'by my sweet singing'.

4364-5 **Tresouns cosyn** Treachery (Treason) enters at 4392, riding on Envy, (and appears at 5303 as the sixth, many-named hand of Avarice).

4368 **brestes** Flattery is thus a horrible parody of Mercy, who at 7182-7 suckles the dying pilgrim.

4375 **vnicorn** for the capturing of a unicorn's attention in a mirror held by a virgin see Einhorn, pp. 179-80, Abb. 77, 101-3. Here, the image is a parody of Incarnation, often represented by the unicorn (Christ at his Conception) laying its head in the lap of the virgin (Mary). These images depend on the tradition of the Unicorn of Pride (Einhorn, Abb. 54): the proud unicorn shows God's humility in submitting to Incarnation.

4379 **eche ... wundre** F8167 *Chascun hurteroit* 'she [Pride] would blunder against everyone' or, in context, 'stick the horn into everyone': unless flattered, Pride is dangerous; *hurteroit* may carry obscene connotations: the horned Pride, who *for loue ... wolde nothing do*, perhaps violates its victims, in contrast to the Christ-unicorn, who submits in love. τ mistook *Chascun* for the subject, and did not quite understand *hurteroit*.

4380 **in hire manere** F8167 *a son tour* 'in turn': see 4334.

4383 **Resonance** (F8173 *resonance*) is a rare example of acceptance of JMO—against CGS's *resouenance* 'remembering' (the only example cited by *OED* under *resouvenance*): *Resonance* echoes F, and is required by the context (see *Ecco* in 4390).

4384-5 **Þou ... sooth** F8176-7 *Vous dites bien / Vous dites voir*': τ avoids repetition.

EXPLANATORY NOTES 461

4390 **folage** Echo *of þe hye wode* is a nymph of mountains or woods. Able only to repeat the end of what she heard, she spoke to Narcissus (self-love)—in a wood, hence the play in F8188 *folage* on *folie/foliage*, retained by τ (though *MED* does not record *folage*). Despised by Narcissus, Echo pined away until only her voice remained. Flattery, also loving self-love, is similarly insubstantial.

4408 **bitwixe hire teeth** i.e. like a tongue, as we learn at 4607.

4417 **hidouschipe** *MED* records only this example.

4420 **Deth** ? *deth*; it is hard to know when death is personified, apart from 4438, 4440, and 7037ff (7172 excepted).

4420-1 **which ... hire** see n. 4008.

4424 **Joseph** Gen. xxxvii 1-34.

4427 **which ... with** 'by means of which I live'.

4430 **Ooþeres ... me** F8263 *Autri mesaise mapastelle* 'the suffering of others attracts me' in most MSS; perhaps τ saw var. *ioie me apastelle* MS. *o*, and corrected so that the joy of others annoys Envy.

4433 **lene** om. F8269 *et dehaslee* 'and wasted'.

4435 **leches** F8274 *sansue* 'a leech' (lit. 'bloodsucker').

4441 **him** τ forgot that Death is f. in both grammar (*la mort*) and allegory.

4443 **beste serpentine** see 4675.

4450 **Saul** I Kings xviii 5-11: Saul threw a spear at David. In *Speculum Humanae Salvationis* the scene prefigures the Betrayal.

4453 **perced** om. F8308 *et fondu* 'and split open'.

4455 **Longis** G's form, common in French, is accepted against the commoner ME *Longi(n)us* because it echoes F8312. The soldier of John xix 34, who opened Christ's side with a spear, gave rise to the legend of Longinus, named in the 4th-century *Acts of Pilate* (Hennecke, I, 449-70) and in 6th-century art (Schiller, II, figs. 327-8). Christ's blood ran down the spear and restored Longinus' sight: the image of Envy's destructive cruelty thus contains its own antithesis, the healing mercy of God.

4459 **lookinge** om. the cryptic F8320 *Sans laissier disme ne champart* 'without leaving a rent or a tithe' ('scot-free', no mark being left?).

baselique G's reading is accepted in view of F8321 *basilique*. The basilisk, hatched by a snake from a cock's egg, could kill by glance or breath. The common confusion of basilisk and cockatrice is clearly presented by Robin, pp. 86-91 (and Appendix); Rowland, pp. 28-9 also gives a clear account of both.

4489 **wacches** F8378 *espouentaus* 'scarecrows'. *OED watch* does not record this sense, which is perhaps an extension of sense 10 'guardian'.

þe thikke F8379 *la pesiere* 'pea-field': τ read an abbreviated form as *l'espe?*.

4490 **pathes** F8380 *chaneviere* 'hemp-field'.

4497 **oþer** is C's normal spelling of conj. 'or': in C's *ooþer thing, ooþer* has the adj. form.

4497-8 **þat . . . bihynde** *Scorpioni non est in facie quod formides, sed pungit in cauda* (St Bernard, *PL*, CLXXXIII, 1197).

4503 **Amason** F8405 *Amasam* var. *amasen* MS. *o, amason* MS. *L*. II Kings xx 4-13: Joab, jealous of Amasa's friendship with King David, greeted Amasa with apparent affection, but as he kissed him, stabbed him to death. In *Speculum Humanae Salvationis* this prefigures the Betrayal.

Abner II Kings iii 23-33: Joab murdered Abner, ostensibly for having killed his brother, but also in jealousy of the king's affection: the murder was similar to the murder of Amasa in that Joab spoke courteously to his victim as he stabbed him.

4504 **solde** is an editorial emendation in the light of F8408 *vendi*: perhaps χ read *solde* as some form of *slohe* or *slowe*, or (as Dr Walls suggests) τ accidentally repeated *slowh* from 4503.

4505 **Triphon** (I Machab. xii 39 - xiii 23): like Joab, Tryphon greeted his victim Jonathan with courtesy, offering hospitality in the city where he then had him killed. In *Biblia Pauperum* sig. .a., this and the murder of Abner are types of the Betrayal.

4505-6 **ben . . . haue hem**[1] 'who were anxious to have them'.

4509 **darst not smyte** F8416 *ferir voudras* 'you want to strike'.

4515 **duk . . . baroun** F8427 *conte ne baron* var. *duc conte ne baron* MS. *o*.

4521 **he wente** F8436 *issi* might also mean 'I went', giving better sense.

4524-5 **lawhe . . . mouth** F8444 *Et de rire du bout du dent* 'and (I know how) to smile until the roots of my teeth show': τ mistook *bout* for *bouche*?

4525 **I can wel** in view of F8445 *Bien sai*, G's subpuncted reading, supported by JMO, is accepted.

4533 **wilow** om. F8462-4 *La planche au besoing rompue, | Un planchier dont sont les corbiaus | Rompus et cheus les soliaus* 'a plank which is broken when needed; a floor with broken joists and fallen supports'. French MS. *M* also omits these lines.

4535 **fro . . . him** F8468 *de moi ne se peut garder*: Hassell, T73.

4539 **Tresoun** F8475 *Trahison* 'Treachery', not just betrayal of a ruler.

4542 **neiþer . . . king** F8481 *ne roc ne roi*: Hassell, R58.

4547 **þe ooþere** F8491 *les autres clers* 'the other clerks': var. *les trois clers* MS. *H*. The story in which St Nicholas Bishop of Myra

EXPLANATORY NOTES 463

restores life to three youths who had been chopped up and pickled, suggests that the F var. is correct. However, GMO suggest that τ saw *les autres* (doubtless knowledge of the story led CS to mention *thre*). Perhaps the reading should be *oopere [clercs]*, assuming that τ accidentally omitted the sb. The story is in *The Golden Legend*, and in Baring-Gould, December, p. 67; Réau, III, ii, 984 lists appearances in art (including 13th-century glass at Tours and Bourges, whose St Nicholas window is in Cahier and Martin, Pl. XII); see also York Minster's 13th-century Chapter House glass.

4568 **þi skin ... body** F8528 *la pel du dos* 'the skin off (your) back'. Editorial emendation of *þe soule out of* is based on F and the assumption that τ translated *dos* freely, χ then reading *skin* as *soul(e)*.

4571 **strangeled** F8535 *estranglees* 'gobbled up': *OED Strangle* v. 2c suggests only the unspecific action of wild beasts upon victims.

þe folde F8534 *tai* 'mud' or 'swamp'.

4572 **rounged his chekes** F8536 *ses guernon fourbis* 'cleaned his chops (by eating a lot)'.

þe raven Gen. viii 6-7: the raven which did not return to the ark traditionally appears eating carrion—e.g. the *Holkham Bible Picture Book* (Hassall, f. 8).

4607 **Mi ... spere** F8603 *Mon glaive ma langue j'apel*: Hassall, L11; Whiting, T395.

4608 **whiche ... cruelle** F8604 *qui est cruel*. In view of G's subpuncted reading, supported by MS and to some extent by JO, I assume that τ mistook *est* for *fait*.

4621 **tresoure** F8629 *grant tresor*. As at 6527 tresour, -ur is indicated by an unambiguous abbreviation mark, though C's normal form is *tresor*.

4622 **good ... richesse** Whiting, N10, N121 (derived from Prov. xxii 1: hence *Salomon* in 4623).

4631-2 **þe ... now** F8648 *Ja je t'en ai dit nouvelle* 'I have only just told it to you': τ read *nouvelle* as *nouvelte*.

4637 **Johan** probably the Apostle, the disciple 'whom Jesus loved' (John xiii 23), perhaps in the light of John xxi 20-4; but the reference in 4644, apparently to postumous defamation, is obscure.

4639 **shadwe** om. F8662 *et abri* 'and shelter'.

4651 **Haue I hors** the pilgrim has not been aware of a horse until now. Cf. 'To know not whether one is on horseback or foot' to imply confusion (Whiting, H542)?

4656 **Þou what** (F8695 *Comment* 'What?') conceals an editorial emendation. χ apparently had *Þou what hattest þou*, but in view of F I assume that χ misunderstood τ's exclamation (see n. 3397

464   ÞE LYFE OF ÞE MANHODE

for *Þou*). Alternatively, F8820 *Comment as non* 'What is your name?', caught τ's eye, giving *Þou what hattest þou?* In this case, the reading should be simply *What?*.

4659-70 **on ... witnesses** (F8701-20): 4669-70 suggest a pun on *beren witnesses* 'carry witnesses/bear witness' (F *portent tesmoignages*): the horse's four feet enable it to bear a rider, and are four qualities required in a witness in a court of law; but though Roman Law required a legal witness to be without criminal record, free and sane, legitimacy was required only for religious 'witness'—for certain ecclesiastical offices (*NCE*, VIII, 618). This allegorical horse may be compared with one in the mid-14th-century *Concordantia Caritatis* (described in *RDK*). At the end, in a section thought to be Ulrich of Lilienfeld's own invention (Tietze, p. 32), several images recall our text. A woman holding allegorical armour (the helmet of Charity, Lance of Perseverance, etc.) stands by a knight (*anima*) mounted on a horse (*caro*) whose four legs are Justice, Humility, Fortitude, Prudence.

4665 **but ... fame** F8711 *Qui sente diffamation* 'that smacks of ill repute': τ seems to have read *Qui* as *Que* (for *Ne que*), misconstrued *sente* as *holi*, and then expected a word meaning 'fame'.

4674 **quod she** is otiose; *Detraccioun* still speaks: her sister answers at 4686.

4675 **Israel of Daan** Gen. xlix 16-17: Israel (Jacob) prophesying the deeds of his sons in the 'Blessings of Jacob'.

Fiat ... via in large lower-case letters in C, is from Gen. xlix 17: 'Let Dan be a snake in the way, a serpent in the path, that biteth the horse's heels that his rider may fall backward'. The serpent is commonly Antichrist, the horse the world, and the rider the worldly man who falls backwards (4685) off his stricken horse because he is without awareness or repentance (the penitent falls prostrate): see Ambrose, *PL*, XIV, 717-18; Paul, *PL*, XX, 725; Rufinus, *PL*, XXI, 321-4; Isidore, *PL*, LXXXIII, 107.

4676 **Cerastes þe hornede** the Horned Viper is distinct from *coluber*, to which Dan is compared (*Speculum Naturale*, bk. 20, ch. 27-8 [Vincent de Beauvais, f. 248^v].) Rabanus Maurus, *PL*, CVII, 661-2 (largely repeating Bede, *PL*, XCI, 280-1) explains: whereas *coluber* lies in wait on the world's wide *via* where there is room to stray, *cerastes* waits *in semita*—on the narrow path—attacking from the rear when the horse has passed. The text seems to conflate both serpents.

4683-4 **Thinges ... so** F8747 *Les ongles insensibles sont* 'hooves are without feeling'. τ read *sont* as *font* (and abbreviated *ongles* as *objets*?).

4684 **He ... apperceyue** F8748 *Nullement ne s'apercevront* 'they (the hooves) do not feel at all'.

EXPLANATORY NOTES 465

4688   **exposed** F8755-6 *expose . . . et glose* 'expounded and explained'. τ avoids repetition. The ME word is rare in this sense: *OED Expose* 8b cites only Caxton; *MED* omits it.

   Jacob i.e. in Gen. xlix 16-17 (see n. 4675); perhaps with a glance at Ps. lxxv 7.

4691   **þe hors** F8761 *Mon cheval* 'my horse'.

4693-4   **dragownes kynde** F8765 *lignage a serpent* 'serpent-kind'. τ's use of *dragownes* disguises the reference back to the *coluber* in 4675.

4699-700   **on^1 . . . daggere** cf. Treason's murders of Abner and Amasa (4503).

4700   **in . . . knyf** in view of F8776-7 *u ventre me boutoit | Son coutel*, perhaps G's omission of *with* should be accepted, assuming other scribes' rationalisation.

4701   **Þe . . . staf** Pride, whose staff is described at 4263. By 4710 the Pilgrim is under simultaneous attack from the first three sins, mentioned in reverse order: Envy, Pride, Sloth.

4716   **baudrike** F8808 *escherpe* 'satchel' (see 3956).

4717   **greye** F8809 *bis* '?'.

4728-30   **I am . . . vertu** τ lost the word-play in F8829-32: *(Je) suis la vielle hericiee | (La) mal pigniee et mal herciee | La fille au hericon heru | Qui se herice pour vertu* 'I am the old bristly one, the disheveled and ill-combed, the daughter of the unkempt hedgehog, which to make itself strong rolls itself into a spiky ball'—and he did not translate *heru* 'bristly'. τ's *tressed* in 4729 is explained by F8830 *herciee* 'combed' having var. *treciee* MS. *o*.

4728   **angry** τ read a form of F8829 *hericiee*, 'spiky', as *iriee*.

4732-52   **Vengeaunce . . . shadewed** the most corrupt passage in the book: perhaps τ's source, or τ, was damaged in this area.

4734   **in . . . . halwen** F8839-40 *en atentant | Contre Dieu et sa main brisant* 'offending against God and his destroying hand': active anger infringes God's right to vengeance (Deut. xxxii 35: 'Revenge is mine, and I will repay'). τ's errors are puzzling: he seems to have miscontrued *atentant* as *kindeling* (if it was abbreviated to *ate^{n}tant* he may have read it as *aticant (acicant)*. He also read *main brisant* as *(?) sants* '(?) saints'.

4737   **ryght bisy** F8846 *desdaigneuse* 'disdainful' var. *soingneuse* MS. *o*.

4738   **þan** om. F8847 *gletonnier* 'burdock' (which is covered in burrs).

4739   **a . . . subtile** F8850 *haie fort, s'estoit soutil* 'a strong hedge, if he [the gardener] were clever'.

4741   **Noli Me Tangere** is in large lower-case letters in C. Anger is unapproachable; compare two later examples: *Mankind*'s 'I xall spare Master Woode of Fullburn; He ys a noli me tangere'

(Eccles, p. 170) and *Mirour de l'Omme* line 1518, where Arrogance is 'Le mal *Noli me tangere*' (J. Gower, p. 21). The specific reference may be to a plant such as Touch Me Not (*Impatiens noli-tangere*), the Balsam which bears this name because if touched it shoots out seeds (see 4741–2); but it is not prickly, as 4740 suggests, and I have not found it bearing this name so early.

þat haue ... ve In F8854 *Qui ai tantost carmeen ve* the last three words are presumably for *carmen in ve* (*ve* for *vae*) 'song in woe': Anger makes, or causes, an outcry (Whiting, S467, S469, 'To sing of woe' etc.). The space left by G, and JMO's readings show that τ carried the Latin, oddly rendered *sorwe in weylinge* by CG³ (was a gloss *songe in weylinge* misread at some stage?). In Ezek. ii 1 - iii 3 the prophet dreams that God, provoked to anger, gives him a book (interpreted as Prophecy) to eat, in which is written *carmen et vae* 'song and woe' (which Lydgate's translation [p. 420] shows is the reading in F Second Recension— in which case the First Recension *en* may be an error): but the relevance is unclear, unless as in St John Chrysostom (*PG*, L, 460) *carmen et vae* refers to the reproaching of sins, and lamentation for the Church, which was the prophet's function. The Latin phrases were obscure to Shirley, who omitted both.

4741–2   **with ... enchesoun** F8855 *Mue a petite achoison* 'moved by something trivial' var. *en petit achoison* MS. *o*

make ... poynt F8856–7 Et *fait un saut, quant d'aguillon* / *Sui pointe* 'and jump away when I am pricked': Anger is easily offended. Did τ read *saut quant* as *lancement*, giving his *cast*, and read *Sui* as *sur*, giving his *upon*? He seems to have thought that Anger describes how like Balsam or like a hedgehog she hurts people who touch her, whereas she describes her own reaction to the least sharpness.

4744   **howlinge cattes** F8859 *chauhuans* 'screech owls' (nocturnal birds, so blind at noon): Anger makes men oblivious of everything but rage. Either he saw *chats huans* or τ made a howler in more ways than one.

4746   **greynes** F8864 *aigruns* 'sour fruit': var. *grains* MS. *o*.

4748–9   If τ had the reading of French MS. *o* in front of him, the dots should be omitted, for MS. *o* omits F8867–9. F8867–70 run: *Je fas ou firmament de l'omme,* / *Qui microcosme ou petit monde* / *Est apele, lever les vens*: 'In the firmament of man, who is called 'microcosm' or 'little world', [like the weather-controlling stars] I make the winds rise ...'. Anger upsets man's 'climate'. I indicate omission, however, because G left a gap which he may have copied from τ, who could have been puzzled by the imagery. The image is a modification of the standard 'microcosm' conveniently illustrated in Seznec, pp. 65–8, where man is at the mercy of the stars in the firmament encircling him, and

EXPLANATORY NOTES

himself echoes celestial structure (ibid., p. 65, n. 104).

4749 **in** τ read F8869 *ou* as *en*.
reise CJMO regularised to *I reise*.

4751 **resoun** ? *Resoun*.

4755 **coles** τ read F8877 *chardon* 'thistle' as *charbon*. Anger continues to use botanical similes here and in *wurmode*.

4756 **kyndlinge** is an editorial emendation on the assumption that χ read *kỹdlīg* (F8879 *ramnus* 'brand') as *hydinge*.

4761 **Chidinge** om. F8889-90 *Ce sont li caillous dont souvent* / *S'entrefierent la sote gent* 'these are the flints with which stupid people often strike each other'.

4763 **Salomon** III Kings iii 16-28: there may be irony in the use of this, a type of the last judgement (*Biblia Pauperum*, sig. .r.).

4766 **anevelte** at 2091-126 an anvil was fixed on the doublet or purpoint of Patience (Anger's opposite): indeed it was equated (2122) with Christ crucified. As at 4763, the allegory works two ways at once.

4778 **I haue maad** F8910 *a fait* 'she has made': var. *ai fait* MS. *L*.

4779-80 **bi ... vnite** F8922-4 *Par qui' est desjointe et sciee* / *L'union de fraternite* / *Et l'aliance d'unite* is best but not accurately rendered by G³'s *by whech disioygnte {i}s saawe the onhede of brotherhede and the trouthe of oonheede* (though faithfulness to F requires *by whech disioygnte and ysaawe is the onhede of brotherhede and the trouth of vnyte*. Perhaps this was the construction intended by τ, as suggested by G's *by whom disioygnte* followed by subpuncted *and*—a construction he did not complete, so that he had to add *is saawen* after *vnyte*.

4781 **In ... figure** as in 4763, 4766, the image works in two ways: Jacob and Esau are the standard *figure* (by contrast, since Jacob succumbed) of Christ's victory in the Temptation (*Biblia Pauperum*, sig. k).

4782 **and**³ F8928 *de* 'from'.

4784-9 **I¹ ... meward** is a perfect image of Wrath's self-destructiveness: being unforgiving, she invites the treatment she gives to others.

4791 **pit** in the sawing of trees laid across a pit mouth, the sawyer in the pit, the junior man's place, brings down sawdust on his own head.

4796 **Barabas** Matt. xxvii 15-26: the image recalls its opposite, Barabbas' release heralding the Crucifixion.

4801 **beste** F8961 *Beste sauvage* 'wild beast'.

4805-6 **with¹ ... lyfe** F8971-2 *Ou le fauchon je te caindrai* / *Ou je ta vie en faucherai* 'Either I will gird you with the scythe or I will mow down your life with it': τ read *Ou ja ta vie*. Uncontrolled Anger's last action is murder: the Pilgrim is to become a murderer, his life then being forfeit?

4808 **Sey me whi** F8976 *Di moi, pour quoi* is clear and without variant, so I (perhaps erroneously) make an editorial emendation on the assumption that τ's *whi* was read as *saymi*: *wh* can look very like *say*. CG³S's *now* looks like an insertion to soften the repeated *Sey me*: as it has no precedent in F, I omit it.

4809 **swich** τ **read** F8977 *Tes* 'your' as *Tels*.
wolt not of τ read F8977 *tu ne vez* 'you will put on' as *tu ne veuz*.

4825 **bifore** om. F9007-8 *Desarmes remains com devant | Las et afflit et recreant* 'I remained unarmed as before: weary, afflicted, recreant'.

4830-1 **I² ... bred** 'I am starving right by the bread': the Pilgrim cannot receive Communion while in mortal sin.

4836 **rounginge on my brydel** 'chafing at my bit' is metaphorical (Whiting, B533): the Pilgrim has not put on any allegorical bridle. Appropriately, after his subjection to Anger he registers impatience, either at his own cowardly refusal of Memory's offer of the armour of Virtue, or at his inability to receive Communion.

4839 **al** τ read F9034 *tost* 'soon' as *tot*.

4850 **eche maketh** F9054 *Chascun a* 'each has' var. *Fait chascun* MS. *o*.

4860 **Daniel** the Pilgrim refers to notable nightmare visions. Most relevant of those in Daniel (ii 31-45, iv 2-31, vii 1-28, viii 1-27, x 5-9, xiv 2-26) are the first two. Nebuchadonosor's vision of a conglomerate idol broken by an unquarried stone which becomes a mountain is appropriate to Avarice's composite appearance (and the stone is an ancient prophecy of the Incarnation [*Biblia Pauperum*, sig. b]); his vision of a felled tree (its fruiting branches perhaps suggesting Avarice's six full hands and two stumps—see n. 4868) foretold his humiliation and penance.

Ezechiel Ezech. i 4-28 or viii-x, xxxvii 1-8, xl, xlvii.

4861 **Apocalipsis** the Apocalypse contains many horrible dream images: perhaps xii 3-4, the seven-headed dragon threatening the woman interpreted as the Church or the Virgin, is intended—or xiv. 11-18.

4864 **leþer** τ read F9076 *churriaus* 'patches' as *cuiriees*.

4868 **foule defaced** om. F9083 *et sursemee* 'and spotted'.

4868-70 **Sixe ... manere** Avarice has six hands plus two stumps. Those with claws griffin-claws are Hands 1 and 2. Hand 3 carries a file and scales, Hand 4 a dish and bag, Hand 5 a crook, while Hand 6 moves between her wounded hip and her mouth.

4875-6 **which ... downward** idolatry stops Avarice lifting her eyes to heaven.

EXPLANATORY NOTES

4882 **þese busshes** F9112 sg.

4893 **To...þee** (F9131 *A li faut que te soumetes* 'to him [it] is necessary [that] you submit') follows G; CMOS regularise in different ways.

4894 **shamefulliche...þee** G echoes τ's awkward rendering of F9133-4 *Et puis apres honteusement / Mourir te ferai et vilment*: *shamefulliche* should modify *dye* not *make*.

4900 **I...me** F9144 *je m'afolle* 'I make myself mad': did τ read as *je me mette*?

4910-11 **þe sorwe...sorwe** F9163-4 *le ve de pleur / Et la heu plain de douleur*. In view of 4927 and 4929, perhaps τ retained *ve* and *heu*, χ substituting *sorwe* and *weylinge*.

4915 **biholde** in view of F9170 *regarder*: C(J)'s substituted phrase is rejected for the inf.

4916 **chekeer:** F9172 *eschequier* is 'court-house' or 'Exchequer', so there is a pun on *eschecs* 'chess' (noted by Locock, pp. 685-6, 463/17269-71 and Hill, p. xxxv). In Jacobus de Cessolis' late 13th-century social allegorization of chess (sigs. 48-95), the 4th pawn is avarice.

4917-18 **ledden gret estaate** F9176 *en menoient grant desroi* 'who carried on in great disorder': τ read *desroi* as *d'estat*?

4927 **ve** om. F9195 *que (me) disoies* 'of which you spoke to me' (at 4910-12): τ avoids repetition of the clause, whose parallel in 4928 he does translate.

ve...heu F9195-6 *le ve...Et le heu*. τ retained the Latin words here (cf. 4910-11): not only do they appear in JMO, but G left spaces in place of them, which G³ filled with faint *ve* and *heu* respectively, in accordance with *ve* in the right margin, where the tight binding probably conceals *heu* also. See n. 4929.

4929 **heu and ve** F9198 *heu et ve*. JMO show the Latin, and G leaves spaces filled faintly by G³ with *heu* and *ve* respectively; this annotator's hand is very early, appearing also in *heu* under rubrication on f. 67ᵛ.

4938 **bineme** om. F9214 *et pour haper* 'and grab'.

4947-9 **whan...it** F9232-5 *Qui le baston dont soustenu / Est le moustier et gouverne / Et du quel il est honnoure, / Baille...* 'who gives the staff, with which his church is sustained and governed, and by which he is honoured...'. τ took *le baston* as the subject (which would have been *li bastons*), rather than object.

4948 **susteyned** should perhaps be *susteyned with*, following G.

4953 **tool** τ read F9243 *oustis* 'tools' as *oustil*.

4954 **His...burdoun** F9245 *Sa croce et (son)) pouoir* 'his cross and his power'. Either τ added *to his burdoun* to show that the cross was on the crosier, then ignored *et (son) pouoir*, or he misread the latter as *a son bourdon* or *a son baston*.

ÞE LYFE OF ÞE MANHODE

4956 **Jeremie** Lam. i 1-10; verse 1 is quoted in 4959-60: 'How is the mistress of the Gentiles become as a widow: the princes of provinces made tributary!'

wepte: for F9248-9 *ploura | Quar quant* suggests this syntax.

4970 **þat... thre** F9276 *en son double trois* 'in his double three'. Jer. vi 5-6, which refers to the undermining of Jerusalem (the Church), and vi 13: 'for the least of them, even to the greatest, are given to covetousness'. See also Jer. xxiii's attack on corrupt governors?

4983 **Apemendeles... lawheth** F9302-3 *Apemen, de les qui s'est mis | Le roi qui rit* 'Apame, next to whom the king who smiled put himself'? τ mistook the awkward *Apemen de les* for a proper noun. Apame, daughter of Bartacus, was concubine to Darius I, who sat her next to him. She made him a willing fool by putting his crown on her head. In the *Speculum Humanae Salvationis* it is a Type of the *Crowning with Thorns*. *Apemen filiam Bezachis* is described in III Esdras iv 29 (in the Vulgate, where it is often in the Appendix, since Jerome rejected it as uncanonical: it is 1 Esdras iv 29 in the *New English Bible* Apocrypha. For the complex history of Esdras see *ODCC*.) The story is also in Josephus, lib. 11, cap. 4. Ambrose, *PL*, XVI, 1132-3, associates it with avarice, illustrating the fate of those enslaved by buying and selling, who buy themselves women by whom they are then subjugated.

4987 **secunde:** F9308 *secont* is no doubt due to corruption from *iii* to *ii*.

5003 **þere in view of** F9339 *la*, C's *þ'* is expanded to *þere* rather than the indicated *þer* (see n. 27-8).

5015-16 **derke helle** F9360 *l'infernal pal* 'the infernal marsh'.

5017 **vsereres** F9363 *Chaours*: Cahors in the Garonne, or Caorso in Lombardy, legendary for its practice of usury (Greimas, *caorsin*): an influx of Lombardy bankers gave Cahors a similar reputation. Cf. Hassell, L78: 'usurier comme un Lombard', and *MED caversin* n., which unaccountably places Cahors in Languedoc.

vserere: F9364 *Chaoursine* 'an inhabitant of Chaours (a usurer)'.

5020 **I am cleped** F9369 *sui nommee*. G's subpuncted reading is accepted: it shows that α eyeskipped from 5019 *Auarice* to *Auarice* in 5020: G³ cancelled the then redundant *I am cleped*.

for... miche F9370 *Pour (ma) substance trop gardee* 'on account of my too carefully retained goods': τ read *garde* 'I keep'. Distinction between covetousness and avarice, not always made (e.g. Zeno, *PL*, XI, 329; Haymo, *PL*, CXVII, 796), is found in Augustine (*PL*, XXXVIII, 628) and Peter Damian (*PL*, CXLV, 534).

5022-3 **I... myn** F9376 *faire bien | Onques ne m'endurai du mien* 'I will

EXPLANATORY NOTES

not ever endure anything of mine doing good'. τ read *ne m'endurai* as *ne en durrai*.

5027 **hound** Aesop's fable *The Dog in the Manger*.

5045 **ape clogged** Rowland, p. 11, cites Pliny's account of catching apes by using weighted boots. Bartholomaeus, Bk VIII *de simea* (Trevisa, pp. 1246-7) describes catching apes as they try to put on boots.

5052 **handes** F9427 *.vi. mains* 'six hands'.

5056 **Rapyne** is among the offspring of Avarice (e.g. in *PL*, LXXXIX, 1277).

5059 **she** F9441 *elle*: τ has made Rapine masc. thus far, perhaps misled by F9435 *Rapine est qui gentil fait* (though MS. *A* does show var. *gentile*); henceforth τ makes Rapine fem.

5060 **drede ... forsake** F9442-3 *ne me doit | Chose que veulle refuser* 'I should not be refused what I want': var. *ne me doit | Chose que il veulle refuser* MS. *o*.   τ read *doit* in the variant as *dout*, giving *drede*.

5061 **hool it is** F9444 *s'ainsic est* 'if it is so,' τ read the var. *sains est* (MS. *o*) not noticing that masc. *sains* cannot agree with fem. *main*.

5064 **puttok** F9449 *huat* 'red kite': n. 1706.

5069 **his lust** F9458 *son talent*: τ forgot that a French pron. agrees with the sb., not the possessor. Noticing that Rapine had recently been fem., C(S) wrote *she*.

5070 **it ... breketh** F9460 *j'esrache et ront* 'I tear out and break' var. *esrache et ront* 'it tears out and breaks' MSS *AH*. τ probably saw the var., β regularising to *I arace and breketh*, but perhaps JMO's reading should be accepted.

5073 **souketh it** om. F9466 *(Et) eviscere* 'and disembowels'.

5074 **skorcheresse** *OED scorcheresse* cites only this example.

baconresse F9468 *bacon(ne)resse*: *MED baconresse* cites only one example—CG's *bacouresse* being an error for *baconresse*.

5075 **þe ... skyn** F9469 *le poil souz le cuir* 'the skin to the root of the hairs': Rapine does not merely fleece people, she almost flays them. τ read *poil* as *pous*.

5078 **lyflode** F9475 *vie* 'life'.

5078-9 **to pulle** F9477 *cerchier* 'to seek out': var. *errachier* MS. *A*.

5084 **with which** F9485-8 *dont repostement | Je sache a moi or et argent, | Dont les biens d'autri trai a moi | Repostement et en recoi* 'with which secretly I seize gold and silver for myself—with which ...'. τ eye-skipped from F9485 *dont* to F9487 *Dont*.

5086 **þe[1] ... kitte** thieves are hanged or have their ears cut off.

5086-7 **Coupe ... Larescyne** F9491-2 *Coupe Bourse est apellee | Et Larrecin*. G's reading is accepted: τ retained French, Europe's legal language.

5094 **accrocheres** is the only example cited by *MED* (but see Glossary).

5097 **hole makere** G's reading is accepted against CS's *vnmakere*, in the light of F (see Variants), and MO's corruption *ill maker*.

5098 **vnhelere** 'one who strips the roof off a house' (*pace OED*).

5101 **pens** om. F9517 *Une Poitevinerresse* 'one who deceitfully pockets another's money' (Tobler) or 'one who counterfeits the money called Poitevine' (Godefroy). τ was understandably baffled.

5103 **Þilke is** F9523 *s'ell'* 'if she is' var. *celle est* MSS *oALM*[1]. τ saw the var., so began a new sentence.

5104 **residue ... testat** F9524 *restat* 'residue' var. *testat* MS. *L*. Was τ's F glossed, so that he incorporated both readings?

5107–8 **Þat ... folk** F9531 *Gent qui servent* 'people who serve' var. *Ceus qui serrent* MS. *P*[2], in which τ may have read *Gent* as *Ceus*.

5109 **resoun** see n. 2872.

without F9534 *Sans point* 'without at all'. In view of F I accept CG[3]S, but perhaps the reading should be GJMO's *with*, τ suggesting not that millers fill their measures unreasonably, but that they fill them deceptively by pretending to be accurate and reasonable.

5111 **þe hand selfe** F9538 *La main me[e]sme*. G's echo of F's order is accepted, assuming that other scribes regularised to *selfe hand*.

5116 **tolde me** (at 3888).

5122 **him** om. F9556 *haut* 'high', missing in var. MS. *o*.

5124 **þat ... hire** F9560 *a li pas n'apartenoit* might mean 'that's not her job' or 'that (body) does not belong to her'. Sloth would be disinclined to haul up a heavy body by herself, but it is Avarice's very nature to 'weigh' things in that manner. They both put the knot round Judas' neck because Avarice motivated his betrayal of Christ, and Sloth (whose ultimate manifestation is Despair) his suicide.

5125 **leue** might be emended to *leeue*, the spelling used elsewhere (with one exception) for 'believe' (see n. 1344).

5126 **she ... rerewarde** F9564 *elle fait l'arriere garde*: see 5083.

5133 **to brode** renders *couver* in F9574–6 *elle met cure / D'arain et fer metree couver / Pour autre pondre et engendrer* 'she busily sets brass and iron to multiply, in order to breed and engender more'. GJMO's *breede* could be accepted: *OED brood* v. 8 'Breed (interest)' is unrecorded before 1678; *MED broden* v. 2 omits this sense, and *breden* v. 3 this form, citing this phrase under *brod* sb. 2.3a 'unhatched young', giving the similar sense 'to put [metals] to work multiplying', but as the only record of *sette to brod*, rather than *sette on brod*. However, F, and the fact that the incubation metaphor has not been used of this money, suggest

EXPLANATORY NOTES 473

that *brod* is a verb.

5133-4 **to² ... pondre** *pondre* is a problem. *OED* gives it as the sole example of a v. meaning, like F, 'to breed'. If this is so, *ooþer* should be emended to [*oþer*] ('or'), the spelling of the conj. in CG. In fact, CG's *ooþer* ('other') shows that they took *pondre* as a sb., and retained the French form of a puzzling word (cf. *mugoe*, *pyer*).

5137 **conuerte into paresis** F9582-3 *tournois ... Fait convertir en parisis* 'turns coins minted in Tours into coins minted in Paris' (she turns it into better currency: Paris money was worth 25 per cent more).

5138-40 **She ... hem** F9585-8 *Vaches qui ne pueent mourir | Fait et forge sans coup ferir, | Et par leur longuement durer | Vaches de fer les fait nommer* 'she makes, and without striking a blow forges cattle [horned beasts?] that cannot die, and since they last so long, she causes them to be called Iron Kine'. τ lost the word-play on *ferir/fer*. The meaning is in doubt. Though not in Lafaurie, where *paresis* are extensively illustrated, the coinage referred to in 5137 may have had 'horns' of some kind (Tobler, *parisis*: *Parisis cornus si valoient | Deux parisis* 'horned *paresis* are thus worth two [ordinary] *paresis*'); Trojanowsk, p. 214 (referring to a period at least 130 years after our poem) observes tantalisingly that sources mention counterfeiting *écu à 'la vache*'; but the money-making process here (*withoute smitinge of strok*) is not forgery, which is Hand 2's skill (5100). Since not even low value coinage was iron, perhaps *yren* is used loosely (as 4866, 5133 imply), or *Kyne of Yren* refers to a promissory token given by the borrower, and hard to redeem because of accumulating interest. The reference is clearly to making money by market manipulation, so it may simply mean that such money breeds like cattle, providing permanent ('iron') income. I am grateful to Dr Michael Metcalf for advice on this coinage.

5140-1 **corn** F9589/91 *avaine* 'oats'.

5144 **ooþere** F9596 *L'autri* 'that of others' (their substance, cf. 5143).

5145-6 **þat ... go** F9598 *Que tout au paraler n'usast* 'that is not used up by the movement [of the file]' var. *Que tout a parler n'usast* MS. A. τ read *n'usast* as *n'alast*? It is harder to explain *to vsure*: did he misread the nonsensical var. *p^{ar}ler* as *vsur^e*?

5153 **balaunce** Lev. xxv 14-37 deals with the legitimate variation in the price of perishables according to their age. Mosaic law permits collection of interest, but not Usury (Ps. xv 4; II Esdras v 7). The long discussion (5135-210) of charging for wood standing or felled may reflect a local monastic preoccupation (Ermenonville forest surrounds Chaalit).

5156-7 **Grace ... shyne** F9617-19 *Grace de Dieu jadis assist | Entour le zodiaque et mist | Le soleil pour luire* .... If MOS echo a more literal syntax in τ, the reading should be *Grace Dieu sumtime* *aboute þe zodiac sette þe sunne to shyne.*

5157 **sette** F9617-18 *assist* . . . *et mist*: τ avoids repetition.

5163 **approprede** F9629-30 *apropriai* / . . . *et usurpai*. τ avoids repetition.

5166 **vtaues** F9636 *vtanes* 'periods of eight days'. There is also an OF *vtaues* 'periods of eight days beginning with a religious festival', but the context *(par) semaines, / Par uitaines et (par) quinsaines* shows that the former, less specific word is intended. I assume that τ read *vtaues* (*vtawes* in G); the reduced form of this pl., used even when the sense is sg., appears in MO's *vtas*: I reject CJ's *vtases* (perhaps unnecessarily), as a pl. formed as if *vtas* were sg.

5167 **pound** F9638 *livre* 'pound's-worth of time': a sense not in *OED*.

pens F9638 *deniers*: a denier was one-twelfth of a sou, so in this the coins were equivalent to pence and shillings.

5168 **ten** om. F9640 *Et la semaine .v. ou .vi.* 'and the week for five or six'.

5181 **þilke** C punctuates after, and G before, this word: the syntax is ambiguous.

5187-8 **sellen . . . stokkes** F9677-8 *les bos / Pou vendent mes sur les estos* '[they] seldom well the growing wood for less'; τ read *mais* for *mes*, giving almost the opposite sense.

5196 **kitte:** F9692 *debite* 'cut up for selling' is more specific. Tobler cites only this example.

5200 **hem²** om. F9702 *et cherpenter* 'and cut [them] up': τ avoids repetition.

5203-5 **if . . . trowe** F6709-11 would also allow *If . . ., I trowe . . .* .

5213-14 **This . . . clepe it** F9725-8 *Ceste main (ci) Coquinerie / Nommee est, (et) Truanderie. / Hoguinenlo par non la claim / Et qui apelle Mengu pain.* MS. *o* omits *(et)*, giving τ's reading, except that τ om. the obscure *Hoguinenlo. Coquinerie* 'knavery' and *Maungepayn* 'breadeater' are recorded by *MED* only here.

5224 **cloutes** F9745 *rives*. Tobler cites only this, as 'welts of shoes'.

pauteneers F9746 *pautonnieres* 'bags, purses' (but only 1419 in Godefroy).

bagges F9746 *saches*. Tobler cites only this example, seeing in it a reference to mendicant monks of the Ordre du Sac.

bribes F9747 *la penthecouste*: Tobler gives '?'.

5237 **glooven** F9771 *desganter* 'unglove' var. *enganter* MS. P².

5239 **in askinge** F9774-5 *(l')estendent / En demandant* 'they extend it to beg'.

5240 **a loyne** F9777 *Unes longes* 'a pair of falconer's thongs'. τ did not recognise the pl. indefinite article.

5243 **russet** F9284 *blanchet* 'white cloth' (of the Benedictines): *russet*

EXPLANATORY NOTES

could be neutral in colour. J's additional outburst suggests that such demands on English abbeys were frequent.

5245 **I preye yow** has no precedent in F9786.

5246 **twey** om. F9789 *bonnes* 'good'.

5247 **from ... hand**[2] F9791 *de ma main* 'by means of my hand' var. *de main a main* MS. *o*.

5248 **hemself** om. F9792 *Et (ain)si de l'autri se vivent* 'and in this way they live on others', no doubt by eyeskip: four F lines end in *-ent*.

putte ... hand in view of F9806 *leur met ma main*, I accept G's *hem*: τ or his source neglected *ma* before *main*.

5256 **I shame hem** F9808 *Je leur flavelle* 'I sound my leper's clapper at them'.

5260 **as ... me** 'I've had enough of this one'.

5262 **Simon Magus,** after whom the sin of Simony is named, tried to buy spiritual power (Acts viii 18); see *ODCC Simony*.

Giesy this servant of Eliseus took by deceit the money which his master had refused for curing a leper. In punishment for dishonesty and Simony (the selling or buying of spiritual gifts) he was struck with leprosy (IV Kings v).

5263-4 **þe ... Simon** 'Simon gave her [the hand] the hook'.

5265 **.S. it is** in view of F9826 *'s' est*, MO's reading (supported by J) is accepted.

5268 **crochet ... Simon** F9831 *ce crochet et ce Simon* is Stürzinger's reading, which the ME suggests is correct: the F MSS have, with one exception, *ceste croce et ce Simon*, where *et* seems to have led to the loss of *-t* at the end of *croc(h)et*. F, and G's curious *this crochet esce Simon*, suggest that τ wrote *et ce*, momentarily lapsing into French, which was then misread by χ as *esce* (for *esche* 'ask'?). Cβ not unnaturally thought the word was a form of *.s..*

5269-70 **þat ... theeves** F9833-6 *qui entroduit | En la meson de Jhesucrist | Par fausses breches et pertuis | Les larrons* 'that introduces thieves into the house of Jesus Christ by evil breakings-in and holes'. τ somehow read *ent^{r}oduit* as *entre*, so om. F9836 *sans entrer par l'uis* 'without entering by the door'?

5276 **disencresen** τ read F9846 *descrochent* '(they) unseat by means of a hook' as *descro(i)strent*.

5294 **resoun** ? *Resoun*.

5299 **were** F9891 *nasse* 'net'; the clause following suggests shows that in F the image is of a funnel-shaped trawl. Either the ME word is an earlier example of this sense than is recorded by *OED weir* sb. 2b only from 1611, or τ substituted an English idiom, and it is *OED weir* sb. 1a, 'fish-weir', as in Chaucer, *Parlement of Foules*, 1. 138.

5307 **Tricot** *OED* records only this example.

5318 **I ... it** τ read F9926 *le truis* 'you will find it' as *je le uis*.

5319 **Prouerbe** F9926 *Prouerbes* (Prov. xi 1, xx 10) var. *prouerbe* MSS *oG*.

stenderesse F9927 *(es)tenderesse* supports G(JO)'s reading against C's *steynoresse* (see n. 6241). *OED* omits the word.

5324-5 **Manye ... harmes** F9937 *Mont fair ceste main ci de maus*. I accept G's literal rendering.

5327 **gerdeles** τ read F9942 *saintuaires* 'reliquaries' as *saintures*.

swiche ... thinges τ read F9942-3 *faintis / Porte* 'carries wicked [? counterfeit] things' as *lautres / Sorte^s*, and supplied *swiche*?

5332 **in ... maad** F9950-1 offer no precedent.

5333 **it ... swet** F9952 *dite sueur/ Soit* 'it may be called sweat': τ read *sueur* as inf. *suer*.

5334 **named** F9954 *renomme* 'renowned': τ read *nomme*.

miracles om. F9955-6 *Et a fin que plus couloure / Soit le miracle et renomme* 'so that the miracle might be more colourful and famous'.

5335 **embosed** probably 'hunchbacked' (*MED embocen* v. ppl.) but in view of F9959 *boisteus* 'lame', possibly 'exhausted [as if over-hunted]' (*MED embosen* v.).

5336 **dowm** om. F9960 *ou contrefais* 'or phoney'.

5338-9 **And ... hol** F9965-7 *(Et) adonc de ma main les lieve / Et touz garis en heure brieve / (Les) moustre* var. *Et adonc tous garis les lieve / Et de ma main en brieue heure / (Les) moustre* MS. *o*.

5341 **nouht** om. F9971 *Il le reputent (a) miracle* 'they attribute it to a miracle'.

5350 **mouth** F9986 *hanche* 'haunch' var. *bouche* 'mouth' MSS *BM*, *bouche* corrected to *hanche* MS. *t*. That F should read *bouche* is suggested by the logic of Avarice's 6th hand alternately touching her damaged leg and diseased tongue: an image evoking the unsavoury activities of corruption, restless in crippled self-absorption. This Hand (best thought of as FRAUD, though it has many names, such as *Treccherie* and *Baret*) is clearly associated with THE LIE (*Mensonge*, the Mouth), with LYING (*Menterye*, the Spavin or sore, bony malformation on the Haunch) and with PERJURY (*Periurement*, the diseased tongue, which at 5832 lolls out for dishonest lawyer's fees). With the hand's help, the sore on the leg nourishes (infects) the mouth and tongue (5354-6): aided by treachery and conflict (5351-2), the habit of lying produces lies in general, and in particular perversion of justice.

But why should Lying be a diseased leg? Explanation occurs only at 5363-71: Avarice, fleeing from the labour and poverty

EXPLANATORY NOTES 477

endured by Truth and Equity (who were on the 'right path'), was lamed in rough ground. She fell victim to the 'easy way out', Lying (the sore spavin), which rendered her still more incapable of honest activity (the pilgrim path).

Mensonge (F9986 *Mensonge*) *MED mensoige* records only this example, in C's unemended form. G's reading, nearer F, is accepted here and at 5356.

5354 **Menterye**[1,2] *MED* records only these examples.

5368-9 **molle hill** Did τ read F10,023 *mote* 'clod of earth' as *mole*, as if *mole* were ME?

5371 **virly** *OED* records only this example.

5373 **it is necessarie** Avarice's deformed hip rouses sympathy in almsgivers.

5379 **goth ... me** F10,043 *Dedens moi naist* 'within me is born' var. *De moy naist* MS. *o*.

so stinkinge F10,043 *Si grant chaut* 'such great heat': τ read *si grant puant*.

5380 **Of** F10,045 *et* var. *de* MS. *o*.

5386 **whan ... haue** F10,056 *Mes quant veu le stille ai* 'but when I have seen the proceedings'. τ saw *veul* 'I will' for *veu*, and misconstrued *stille* ('when I want to, I use the appropriate style'?).

hippe (F10,057 *clopine*): *MED* 'limp, hobble', but in the context of τ's preceding error, it may well mean 'omit some of the true facts' (cf. *MED hippinge*).

5390 **enclineth his tunge** a vertical metal tongue attached to the centre of a balance's horizontal beam, and projecting *downwards*, indicates (by deviation from the vertical support) which of the two scales is depressed. I am indebted to Dr D. Vaughan of the Science Museum for tracing a drawing of such a balance by Dürer (in the Kupferstich kabinet, Berlin-Dahlem 12), which though late 15th-century, resembles earlier models. The image reappears in the *Soul*; as Caxton says: 'Pledoures in worldly courtes hauen tongues lyke to the languet of the balaunce that draweth him alwey to the more peysaunt party / that better wyl rewarden' (*Guillaume de Deguileville*, f. viii[v]).

5402 **riht** om. F10,087 *et droit en tort* 'and right into wrong': τ avoids repetition.

5403 **sum siluer** τ read F10,089 *autri argent* 'others' silver' or 'someone else's silver' as *aucun argent*.

5407 **I haue** F10,097 *a* 'it has' var. *ay* MS. *M*. An *M*-type MS appears more often now as one of the possible sources, at least until 5500.

5408 **I shal** F10,099 *sera* 'it shall' var. *seray* MS. *M*.

5409 **or** F10,100 *et*.

5410 **is ... Nature**[1] F10,102 *n'est mie d'on* 'is not at all human'. τ read *Nature* at the start of F10,103 twice, or it was a gloss or catchword in his source.

5419-20 **þat ... ooþere** F10,120 *qui se doivent limiter | Selonc droite riule et riuler* 'who should control and rule themselves according to the true law'.

5421 **rules bowchede** F10,122 *la riule ... bocue* puns on rule 'law/ straight-edge': lit. 'a humpy straight-edge'.

5423-4 **þe ... heuene** F10,126 *La porte ecus* 'the narrow gate' (Matt. vii 13); the camel is from Matt. xix 24.

5424 **Whan ... world** F10,128 *Quant u monde est entre nuz* 'when he entered the world naked' (var. *Quant homme u monde est entre nuz* 'when man entered the world naked' MSS. *TALH*) does not begin a sentence.

5429 **or** F10,136 *et* var. *ou* MS. *M*.

professioun om. F10,137-8 *Et par postis qui est estroit, | Se puis aprez boce se fait* 'and by the narrow gate, and if then he later makes himself a hump'. τ was confused by similarity between F10,137 and F10,129 *Par le postis qui est estroit?*

5435 **shende** F10,149 *esmerder* 'frighten into losing control of the bowels'.

5439 **ben comen into** F10,158 *en ... sont reclus* 'had recourse to' var. *en ... sont venus* MS. *o*.

5440 **many ooþere** F10,160 *plus que* 'more than' var. *pluseurs* MS. *o*.

5442 **redressere** F10,163 *adreceur*: *OED redresser* cites this as the earliest example of 'one who redresses or rectifies (especially a wrong)'; the context, however, suggests a guide.

5443 **of my bouchede** 'among my hunch-backs': C's *me bouched* ('made hunch-backed by me') is rejected.

5444 **hem** τ read F10,165 *le* as *les*.

5445 **ydole** Lev. xxvi 1.

5453 **wormes:** F10,186 *les mulos* are normally 'field-mice', but these do not live *in eerþe*, so *mulos* here perhaps has the rare sense 'moles' (Tobler, *mulot*).

5455 **waite þe moldewerp** the mole signified the worldly man (*MED moldewerpe* b); in addition, *OED mole* 8 gives *mole-catcher* as a (17th-century) term of contempt.

5458-9 **haunteth me** τ read F10,196 *m'ahaite* 'he pleases me' as *me hante*.

5462 **Laurence** (d. 258) is mentioned in the Canon of the Mass among early Roman martyrs. Legend of the 4th century describes how the saint was allegedly roasted on a gridiron for refusing to surrender Church treasure to the prefect of Rome, giving it instead to the poor, whom he then presented as the 'Church's

EXPLANATORY NOTES

treasure'.

5464 **þat** om. F10,205 *pour li* 'for his sake' (*For him* later in 5464 was enough?).

waxe τ read F10,205 *sui* 'I am' as *fu*(*s*).

5465 **I ... seest** F10,207 *a mains gieux deveez* 'I have been led astray by many a game' var. *a mains gieux ce veez* 'by many a game you see' MS. *o*: τ read the var. *a* as *ai*?

5473 **lowe** has no precedent in F10,222.

5474 **þe man** F10,224 *.i. hom* 'one man' var. *hom* MS. *M*. I accept JM's reading, assuming that τ saw the var.; but possibly τ wrote *.i.*, misread as *þi* by χ.

5484–5 **a ... perced** F10,243 *un ort sac ou fons percie* 'a foul bag pierced at the bottom' (the stomach, evacuating through the bowel).

5485 **it** om. F10,244 *enbouchie* 'put in through the mouth'.

5486 **tonell** 'cask' (in view of n. 5484–5, the bladder?). Gluttony has two 'stomachs' (5611–19), one for food and one for drink.

5488 **George ... throte** F10,249–50 *George | Que(lle) me prendroit par la gorge*. St George is chosen for word-play on *George/gorge*, lost by τ.

5490 **visage** om. F10,253 *painture* 'painted'.

5495 **Bi þe eye** Hultman, p. 133 draws attention to the ironic echo of the Lover's subjection to Love in *Le Roman de la Rose*, 1702.

5496 **wherfore michel** τ read *Dont grandement* for F10,266 *Mont grandement* 'Much severely'.

5500–1 **þe² ... honge** F10,274 *Le fol ne croit, devant qu'il prent* (Hassell, F152) 'the fool does not think before taking (what he wants)': the pilgrim was too quick to opt for removing the armour of virtue (2464ff). τ saw var. *Que foulz ne doubte tant qu'il prent* 'the fool does not hesitate as long as he takes (?)' MS. *M*, and read *pent* 'he is hanged' for *prent*, giving the sense 'the fool will not stop [to think] until he is hanged' (cf. Whiting, F405, F416).

5505 **a def note** 'an empty nut' (Whiting, N188, N195); F10,283 *un hututu*: Tobler cites only this example, meaning 'a pile of wood-shavings'.

5514 **þe ... perced** F10,294–5 *le sac lait | Percie u fons* 'the ugly bag pierced at the bottom', with a pun on *fons* 'base/buttock'.

5516 **Epicurie** Epicureans, after the philosopher of *c*. 300 B.C., who believed that the highest good was pleasure (which, however, he identified with the practice of virtue). The form may derive from Lat. *Epicuri* for *Epicurii* or *Epicurei* (*OED*, *epicure*, *epicury*).

5518 **It ... folk** see *MED hit* pron. 4e for pl. *it*.

5530 **Castrimargie** F10,331 *Castrimargie*: a form of *Gastrimargie* 'Voraciousness' (*MED castrimargie* cites only this example and Lydgate's equivalent). See Cassian, *De Spiritu Gastrimargiae*

(*PL*, XLIX, 202-66).

5533 **lopyns** (F10,335 *lopins*) *MED* records this only here and at 5565.

5534 **too** om. F10,337 *Puis qu'en mon sac les ai plungies* 'since I have plunged them into my bag'.

5536 **Left** F10,342 *laisse* 'I leave'.

5538 **abhominable** om. F10,346 *(Et) laide* 'and ugly'.

5541-2 **þat ... michel** F10,351 *Trop mengus et Trop gloutoie*, 'I ate too much and gulped too much': τ misunderstood the tenses, and hedged his bets in translating *gloutoie* two ways.

5544 **Beel** Baal, the tutelary god of Babylon. Jer. li 44, Dan. xiv 2-27 describe Baal's subjugation and destruction: the image is two-edged.

5548 **I putte it** F10,363 *se boute* 'it puts itself' var. *le boute* MSS *oTL*.

5548-9 **in ... wite** F10,364-5 *En flairier s'entente est toute | Pour savoir* 'it concentrates on smelling, to know' var. *En flairier mais mentente toute | Pour savoir* MS. *o*.

5550 **þou fille** F10,370 *Tu feis* 'you filled' var. *Tu fais* MS. *o*.

5551, 5552 **gret** F10,370 and 10,373 *gros* 'rough' or 'coarse'.

5554 **rudesse** F10,375 *avidite* 'avidity' var. *la rudite* MSS *ABGM*; MS. *o*'s *la widite* 'emptiness' might have been read as *rudite* too. JMO's *ruydeste* suggests this acceptance of G's reading (a form without precedent in C) against CS's *rudenesse*.

5556 **guste** F10,380 *gouste*: a rare example of CG³ being accepted (in the light of F, and of *guste* being echoed in 5558) against GJMO, whose *savouringe* is probably the result of Gβ accepting a gloss in χ. *MED* records this word only in this text (5558, 5567, 5568; *gusten* 5568).

5560 **bouchinge** F 10,385 *embouchment* is the mouth of the bag (Gluttony's belly), the tasting or mouthing of morsels, and the bulging of mouth and throat enjoyed during swallowing (see 5562-5, and *bouche(d)* as used between 5415 and 5444). *MED* cites only this example, with the first two senses.

5561 **towchinges,** in view of F10,386 *atouchement*, should perhaps be *towchinge* (after JMO).

twey F10,387 *iii* var. *ii* MS. *o*. That the var. is correct is suggested by *Voluptas gutturis, quae tanti hodie aestimatur, vix duorum obtinet latitudinem digitorum* (St Bernard, *PL*, CLXXXII, 842).

5563 **heroun** F10,390 *grue* 'crane'. The crane was once quite common in Britain, but if τ knew the difference between crane and heron, he may have substituted the more familiar bird.

5564 **sweete** F10,392 *cras* 'fat'.

5564-6 **þat ... neuere:** F10,393-5 *Que de lopins fust bien froie, | Fussent*

EXPLANATORY NOTES 481

a cheval ou a pie, | Ne me chauroit perhaps means 'that it should be well caressed by morsels, whether they were on horseback or on foot. I do not care ...'. Are mere scraps of food suddenly seen as entire persons, occasionally with their horses too, eaten by Gluttony—cf. 3972, where pilgrims are 'on horse or on foot'? τ's *I were* (and his syntax) may be explained by *Fussent* var. *Feuse* MS. *o, Fusse* MS. *L*.

5570 **eiþer ... brod** F10,402 *ne li lonc nez* 'or the long nose' var. *ne lonc ne les*.

5576 **hath touched** F10,413 *atouche* 'it touches' var. *a touchie* MSS *To*.

5577 **touchede** F10,415 *retouchoit* 'touched again'.

5578 **I wole** F10,417 *veut* 'it will': τ read *veus*.

5579 **stintinge** om. F10,418 *aussi com li gout* 'as often as it pleases'.

5582 **wichche** F10,423 *sauciere* 'kitchen servant': τ read *sorciere*.

5582 **seith and telleth** F10,425 *a tost dit et raconte* 'has at once said and recounted': τ read *tost* as *tout*, so construed *a* as 'to'.

5583 **Maleschique** F10,427 *Male clique* '? Bad Door-bolt (Blabbermouth)'; var. *Male chique* MS *o* (?). Gamillscheg *chique* gives 'marble', as in the game: the sense escapes me. One expects something suggesting foul language, a product of Gluttony (as in *The Pardoner's Tale*).

Malevoysigne also a derogatory nickname: 'Bad Neighbour', alluding to malicious gossip (*voisin* 'neighbour'), or perhaps something like 'Old Malmsey', for someone with a loose, drunken tongue (*MED malvesi(e)* 'a sweet wine originally from Napoli di Malvasia in Greece').

5586 **filled hire with** F10,432 *a essaie* 'has tried'.

5588 **What ... seide** F10,435 *Qu'est elle donc, a elle dit* ' "What is she then?" She said:', so perhaps the reading should be *What is she þanne?" She seide:*. Judging by G's punctuation, τ thought *donc* modified *dit*, but possibly τ followed F, χ ignoring his punctuation.

5592 **aualeth** *MED avalen* 2c, misled by the corruption *fonelle*, wrongly cites *The fonelle ... aualeth and tunneth the wine* as the only example of *avalen* 'to make flow down'.

5599 **Oure Lady** has no precedent in F10,456.

5603-4 **I ... out** F10,465-6 *De elles je me moqueroie | Et chacier hors (je) les feroie* 'I would hold them in scorn, and would have them driven out'.

5606-7 **and ... eyen** F10,471 begins a sentence: *Les iex esrooulle* 'I roll my eyes'.

5607-8 **It ... bicome** F10,472-4 *Pour nient n'ai mie com butor | Deux ventres, quar butordement | Parle a la gent et lourdement* 'not for nothing do I have two stomachs like a pelican/bittern, for I speak to people rudely, like a bittern/pelican'. var. *quar butor deuient / Et bien souuent ceci auient* MS. *o* 'for he becomes a bittern/pelican and this happens very often' explains τ's reading, except that he misread *deuient* as *deuien* 'I become'.

Two birds are conflated, the bittern commonly, the pelican rarely being called *butor* (*MED* misleadingly cites this example only under *bitour* 1 'bittern'; *bito(u)r* 2 cites two 15th-century examples meaning pelican, Lat. *onocrotalus*). The pelican has 'two stomachs', its habit of storing fish in its bill-membrane giving it a reputation for gluttony: *turpe ravennatis guttur Onocrotali* (Martial, XI, Ep. 21/10). The bittern has the ugly, booming voice. Trevisa's translation of the 13th-century Bartholomaeus Anglicus, *De Proprietatibus Rerum* (Trevisa, I, pp. 635-66) describes *onocrocalus* and *pellicanus* in order, the former clearly showing qualities of both: as *mirdrommel* (bittern) it points its beak up to camouflage itself, but it also has *twey wombes*, the first (distinguished from the crop) a beak-membrane. Gluttony's pelican greed may be a calculated contrast with the familiar Bestiary 'Pelican in her Piety', who fed her children with her blood, as Christ nourished man (Trevisa, ibid.).

5610 **þat**[2] ... **heere** F10,477 *qui m'ensuit* var. *qui ci me suit* MS. *o*.

5611 **Yueresce** (F10,478 *Ivrece* 'Drunkenness') *OED* cites only this example.

5612 **stinte etinge** F10,481 *a beu* 'has drunk'. τ obscures the point: drink stimulates appetite.

5614 **drinke**[1] F10,485 *mengut* 'has eaten'.

5615 **I reuye it** F10,486 *je le renvi* 'I'll top that' (of a raised stake at dice). *OED revie* v. 'return an invitation' cites only this example.

5620 **reuelle** om. F10,496 *et repesner* 'and jib' (like a horse): Gluttony makes Lust ungovernable.

5620-1 **most/lest/most:** F10,497 *plus/mains/plus* are comparatives.

5632-3 **In ... is** F10,518 *A toi en est* 'It's up to you!'.

5643 **Þe aungeles** F10,541 *Li angre* 'the angel' var. *Li anges* MS. *M*: var. *Les angels* MS. *H*. The story of angels who stop their noses at a youth because his sins are more offensive than the stench of a corpse at which he is stopping *his* nose, is in Jacques de Vitry's *Exempla* (e.g. London, British Library, MS. Harley 463, f. 7: Crane, p. 48, no. 104, and p. 178); it derives from the *Vitae Patrum* (see n. 6325 for use of the same kind of material).

5650 **any come** F10,554 *vient* 'she should come'.

5651 **of oon** F10,555 *Dina*: the virgin Dina was ravished as soon as she left her house (Gen. xxxiv 1-2). τ saw var. *dune* MS. *o*. In the *Bible Moralisée* Dina signifies the contemplative attracted and corrupted by worldly things (Oxford, Bodleian Library, MS. Bodley 270b, f. 21ᵛ, Bl, B2). She was familiar enough to be recognised in a historical sequence *bas de page* in the Exeter

EXPLANATORY NOTES

Bohun Psalter (Oxford, Exeter College, MS. 47, f. 33ᵛ).
he should be *she* but τ was not to know that (see above).

5657 **stinkinge** F10,566 *pueur intolerable* 'unbearable smell'.

5658 **lace** F10,569 *laissier* 'leave': τ read *lassier*. Chastity would rather exchange her worldly clothes for a religious habit than associate with Lechery. Cf. *Le Roman de la Rose*, 4215 (Hultman, p. 134).

5661 **white ... blake** see n. 72.

5675-6 **vnder myn hood** has no precedent in F10,599.

5677 **queyntrelle** *OED* cites only this example.

5681 **of ooþer siht** F10,609 *d'estre veue* 'to be seen': τ read *d'autri veue*.

5681-2 **sihte ... go** F10,609-11 also allows *sihte in place þer no sighte is. I go ....*

5688 **wunderful** F10,621 *mauves* 'ill-behaved': τ read *merueil*.

5690 **Euele Wil** F10,625 *ma voulente* 'My Will': τ read *ma(le)voulente*.

5691 **bidunge hire** F10,628 *le bourbier* 'the excrement': τ read *se bourbier*.

figured ... swyn the 'horse' is in fact a pig (5636): Lechery is subject to fantasy and delusion.

5694-5 **and² ... foulere** F10,635-6 *Par li ainsi in abstracto / Laide sui, mes in concreto / Encor je sui* 'so I am foul in the abstract, but in reality I am still more foul'. There are several problems:

1. 5694 *and he also* suggests that τ saw *Et li aussi* (cf. var. *Et par ainsi* MS. *L*).

2. that τ wrote *abstracto* is suggested by F, by G's space (often left for Latin) and by G³'s *stoppaile* (? *storpaile*, as in CS) 'bung' or 'obstruction': χ misread *abstracto* as *obstructō* (*obstruc*tion). β omitted the difficult phrase.

3. that χ misread τ's *conc'to* (*concreto*)—or *concᵉ'to* (*concreto*)— as *cou'to* (*couerto*) is suggested by F, by G's space, G³JMO's *cou'te* (*couerte*), and G³CS's *hudles*. The first G³ reading may be *conc'to* (*concreto*), but the basic argument remains the same.

5698 **Fardrye** (F10,641 *Farderie*) *MED* cites only this and Lydgate's equivalent.

5700-1 **pryue chaumbre** means in itself only 'private room'; the context, and 3157, show that 'latrine' is meant. Public conveniences existed: Conway's late 13th-century town walls have twelve (*An Inventory of Ancient Monuments in Caernarvonshire*, p. 56 and pl. 57). Lechery also refers by implication to the services of a whore: *make ... filthe* may refer to illicit sexual activity.

5710-14 **þat ... þee** F10,665-70 '*Li .i.*', *dist elle*, '*a non raptus / L'autre struprum, l'autre incestus, / L'autre est dit adulterium / Et l'autre fornicacion. De l'autre qui n'est a dire / Te puet il (bien) a tant souffire*' (my punctuation). τ altered the construction, so that the

Pilgrim is to be satisfied by this brief account of all the sins, not just by veiled reference to *þat ooþer*.

5713 **þat ooþer** unnatural vice; Aquinas, *ST*, 2a2ae, q.154. a.1 lists all six species, adding this to the five in John Gratian's 12th-century *Decretum* (*PL*, CLXXXVII, 1699, but at 1499 and 1545 Gratian discusses sodomy and bestiality). Gratian 1698 offers a neat distinction between *raptus* and *stuprum*: *qui raptu potitur stupro fruitur*.

5717 **vnthrifty feture** 'deformed shape' loses the word-play of F10,675-6 *faiture* / *Contrefaite* 'ill-made making'.

5719 **tigre** (F10,680 *Tigris*) Whiting T288 (Lydgate) refers to the tiger's speed; Isidore (*PL*, LXXXII, 434) says it is so-called after the swiftest of rivers. The form of F (and Hassell's silence) may mean that the Bestiary's fabulous beast is intended, if not the river.

5735 **me** F10,708 *te*.

be om. F10,709-10 *avortez* / ... *et* 'aborted and'.

5737 **freend** om. F10,713 *par ta folie* 'by your stupid behaviour'.

5738 **þe** F10,717 *ta* var. *la* MSS GL.

thorny: F10,717 *espineuse*, so G's *horny* is rejected (*MED horni* not giving 'spiny'); JM's omission of the word and O's substitution of *egre* ('sharp', not recorded in *MED* of plants) suggest that τ wrote *horny* by attraction of *hedge*, C(S) intelligently substituting.

5742 **He** is the first of three exclamations (see 5748, 5751) each recalling a time in the Pilgrim's dream earlier than the last: his arming (2453), Communion (2705), and first sight of New Jerusalem (19).

5751 **He** F10,741 *Hee* 'Ah!'. In view of F, O's *the*, CS's *Oo þou* and JM's omission of the word I assume that τ's *He* was read as *Þe* or rejected.

5755-6 **soo ... seene** has no precedent in F10,750. Perhaps this rare addition (an echo of the Saviour's wounds?) was a heartfelt marginalium in τ or χ, and should be rejected.

5768 **crept ... doun** F10,774 *croupi et geu jus* 'crept about and lain down'.

5768-9 **Þou ... craft** F10,775 *n'as d'espreueve mais mestier* 'you no longer need any proof': τ read *mais* as *mal*, and miscontrued *mestier*?

5783 **sweete** om. F10,802 *debonnaires*.

5784-5 **yit ... forsaken me:** in view of F10,804-5 *encor(e) m'ame* / *N'as pas de touz poins oubliee* 'you have not yet utterly abandoned my soul' JMO's *yit* is accepted, assuming that α or G read it as *yif*. τ read *m'ame* as *m'aime*, then had to add *me* after *forsaken*.

5790 **it** F10,815 *m'* 'myself'.

EXPLANATORY NOTES

5791 **foryiveth** F10,817 *aide* 'help' var. *pardonne* MS. *o*.

5797 **awmeneer** om. F10,828 *De moy* 'of me'.

5802 **to ... lady** F10,838 *de toi despenser est dame* 'is the lady who distributes you' is the reading of MSS *tTAG* and others unspecified (*dispenser* MS. *L*, *desparere* MS. *o*). Mary is responsible, as *mediatrix*, for distributing Grace. GMO echo τ's literal *to ordeyne*.

5805 **þin ... hire**[1] F10,843 *aces a li* 'access to her' var. *ton cuer a li* MSS. *LM*[1] (*M*[1]'s *aces a li* cancelled and replaced by *ton cue a li* by the scribe).

5810 **charbuncle** see 1878, 2019 and n. 122.

5815 **to my,** without precedent in F10,863 *mon*, is retained because it is in CGS, and M's *so* may be a misreading of it; τ misconstrued *mon* as oblique case?

5823 **olde hondes** F10,876 *mains des vielles* 'hands of old women'.

5828 **redde** τ read F10,884 *vi* 'saw' as *li*.

5831 **A.B.C.** Chaucer's *A.B.C.* follows. The familiar line numbers are included. For a text in the light of all sixteen manuscripts of the *A.B.C.* we await the *Chaucer Variorum* edition; however, the *Pilgrimage* MSS form (with the miscellany London, British Museum MS. Add. 36983), the whole β-group, of more authority than the α-group. For the marginal attribution to Chaucer in S (f.97[a]), hitherto regarded as Shirley's, see Variants at 5834.

The poem replaces a twelve-line four-accent stanza (*aabaabbbabba*) by one with eight lines and five accents (*ababbcbc*). In most stanzas 'literal translation gives way to paraphrase, paraphrase to original composition' (Geissman, p. 216). This means total departure from the hitherto literal rendering, so no attempt is made to record every deviation from F (in Skeat [1896] pp. xlviii–lv).

Doyle and Pace give an account of the α-group MSS. Clemen, pp. 175–9 gives a brief account of Chaucer's originality. Reiss's controversial analysis of sound patterns, especially stress reversal, is attacked by Robbins in Rowland (1968), p. 328, in turn dismissed by Zbozny, p. 139, in his study of its scansion. Chesterton, pp. 119–12 gives religious, and Crampton rare literary appreciation.

5834 **Almighty** JS have alphabet letters in the margins (J's in red). J's at first bear no relationship to the stanzas, going A–Z (minus J, U, W) by quatrains, then leaving a quatrain unlettered before beginning again at N and correctly relating to stanzas until Z (minus U, W). On the importance of the poem's initial letters see Pace (1979).

5837 **of ... floure** is not in F; cf. Chaucer, *The Legend of Good Women*, F Text, 1. 53 (Robinson, p. 483).

5840 **of** *Haue mercy of*, usually rejected, is normal (*MED merci* 3.b).

ÞE LYFE OF ÞE MANHODE

5847 **Hauen of refute** relates to 5849. It is not in F: cf. Chaucer, *The Man of Law's Tale*, 852.

5848 **theeves sevene** the Seven Deadly Sins.

5849 **ship** is not in F. The image of return from the wrong path to one with a 'door of salvation' is replaced by ship and haven, recalling 3316–25, where Reason compared the Pilgrim's body and soul to a ship and its controller, bound for *hauene after þe deth*.

5853 **take ... accioun** 'brought an action against me': the stanza begins a legal image (still more elaborate in F) extending to 5897 and reappearing at 5919, 5935, 5943, 5976, 5991. This foreshadows the case against the Pilgrim at the Judgement in the *Soul* (Guillaume de Deguileville, ff. ii–xxx).

5854 **Of ... desperacioun** 'founded upon rigid justice and the fact that I am on the point of despair'. The Pilgrim narrowly avoided the final, fatal sin of Despair which often follows subjection to the sins: Sloth threatened him with the noose (Desperation) at 3920, 3936.

5855 **susteene** 'sustain the plea' (Skeat).

5857 **queene** CS's rejected *heuene queene* destroys functional stress on *you*.

5858 I am not convinced by Klinefelter's claim that this stanza refers to the Four Daughters of God, though three of them do appear in *the Soul* (Guillaume de Deguileville, ff. xvii^r–xxix^v).

misericorde begins word-play (still more elaborate in F) on the *corde* of a *bowe*: see 7173 (and n.) where the image is developed; the bow is on one level the rainbow common in depictions of the Last Judgement—5870's *Hye Iustyse*: see nn. 7173, 7174, and Ps. vii 13.

5869–70 **But ... Iustyse** could be punctuated *But merci, ladi ... Iustyse*, but I assume that the immediate appeal is for present, not future help (Mary does not intercede in person at his Judgement trial in the *Soul*, though the effect of her intercession is relayed by Prayer).

5871 **litel** CS's *litel fruit*, commonly accepted by editors, is a destructive smoothing: the rhythm (*Só lítel*) stresses emptiness in the absence of grace.

5872 **correcte vice** is a new editorial emendation. F is no guide. GJO show that, as pointed out by Severs (1949), χ had some form of *correcte me*, in spite of its not rhyming with *iustyse* in 5870. Severs, however, justified the resulting irregular rhyme-scheme by the precedent of Chaucer's *The Former Age*. I suggest that the stanza is in fact regular: that τ wrote *correcte uice* ('overrule sin' or 'eradicate sin'), misread as *correcte mee* by χ— *uice* and *mee* are easily confused. The pilgrim appeals not for correction of himself, but for suppression of his sins—their

EXPLANATORY NOTES

overruling in the court to which at 5851-3 they summoned him (see n. 5853). He appeals not for discipline but for grace: see Avril Henry, 'Chaucer's *A.B.C.*: Line 39 and the Irregular Stanza Again'.

5873 **confounde** G adds a 9th line to the stanza: *Eeuere to ha\a/ue ther by helle grownde* ('To be, as a result, at the bottom of hell for ever'), giving *ababbcacc*. This is a rare example of a unique G reading being rejected, although G is not given to addition. The line is at the bottom of f. 82^r, but it is the scribe's, and shows no sign of being an afterthought. Was it a marginalium in χ? If Chaucer wrote it, he intended a stanza more irregular than has ever been suggested in connection with 5872 (*A.B.C.* 1. 39). I assume that G, disturbed by the irregularity produced by *correcte mee* in 5872, unaccountably produced greater irregularity than he sought to remedy.

5874 **Fleeinge ... flee** F10,953 *Fuiant m'en vieng*: the repetition is Chaucer's. Both *fleeinge* and *flee* may derive either from *MED flen* 'flee' or *flien* 'hasten (as if on wings)'. 'Fleeing I flee' may be repetition to suggest panic; 'As if on wings, I flee' may be word-play—and so on, through the other permutations. Ambiguities (of less consequence than this) occur in *flee* at 4225, 4490, 5719.

5883 **bitter** puns on Maria, who is not *Mara* 'bitterness' (Exod. xv 23).

5892 **with ... bille** Christ gave a bill of acquittance in his own blood (i.e. he paid the debt owing to him). The image suggests a Charter of Christ: the Crucifixion seals the document giving man his eternal inheritance, Christ's body being the parchment, etc. (see n. 1339).

5906 **Kalendeeres enlumyned** this image is not very clear. F11,001-3 means 'Calendars are illuminated, and other books are authenticated, when your name illumines them': probably an allusion to rubrication of feasts of the Virgin throughout the year in MS calendars (for medieval calendar structure see Boyd, pp. 9-25). The image may find full expression in the *Soul*'s Calendar of Heaven, Book 5, ch. 6 (*Guillaume de Deguileville*, ff. lxxxxv-lxxxxix). Chaucer may simply mean that those who travel by the light of the Virgin are shining guides to us (*MED calendar* 3, rather than 2a): the *carboncle* on the Pilgrim's staff, which lights his way, represents her.

5914 **sorwe** Chaucer's source perhaps read *douleur*, which is better sense than the accepted *douceur* (Koch).

5918-19 **he ... deere** 'that on his battleground of evil he has overcome those whom you both bought at such expense'.

5920 **substaunce** as the mother of Christ, Mary is the source of our redeemed existence.

5922 **Moises** Exod. iii 2; cf. Prologue to *The Prioress' Tale*: *O mooder*

Mayde! o mayde mooder free! | O bussh unbrent, brennynge in Moises syght!; the Burning Bush is an ancient Type of the Virginity of Mary unconsumed by the 'fire' of the Holy Spirit at the Annunciation and intact even at the Nativity (Biblia Pauperum, sig. b). The analogy is in the Office for the Circumcision and of the Virgin: it appears as early as the 4th-century Chrysostom (PG, L, 794-95); and in the 9th-century Rabanus Maurus (PL, CXl, 513) by which time art sometimes showed Virgin and Child in the bush's flames; the associations are commonplace by the 13th century (Schiller, I, p. 71).

5933 **We ... glee** F11,042 *N'avons autre tirelire* 'we have no other place in which to secure what we possess' (see 5940); Chaucer took *tirelire* (lit. 'money-box') for *tirelire* 'warble'—cf. 'tirralirra' (Skeat).

5939 **rest** in view of F11,050 *repos*, JMO's reading is accepted, though this means rejecting CGS's *lust*, usually accepted by editors. I assume an obvious scribal error in α. The spelling could be *reste*, C's spelling elsewhere, even at 5847 (in the *A.B.C.*, where he often departs from his norm).

5942 **ancille** Luke i 38.

5943 **oure ... beede** 'to offer a petition on our behalf' (Skeat); cf. 5892.

5946 **Purpos ... enquere** the pilgrim in anguish finds time to recognise but not grapple with the mystery of Mary's unique qualities; see *NCE*, I, 564 for doctrinal questions raised by the Annunciation, and X, 22 on 'why should God choose to have a mother?'.

5948 **Gabrielles vois** Luke i 27-37.

5949 **to werre** F11,065 *pour guerre* 'by way of attack' (Skeat), but according to *OED war* v.[1] 'to wage war on us': the former is probably correct, in view of 3648 *to werrye*, F6772 *guerroier*.

5965 **it is** *is his* (Robinson), *hit his* 'strikes his' in Koch, emending—perhaps correctly—in view of F11,088 *Son chastoy si fiert a hie* 'his punishment strikes so hard (?)'; but *hidous* adv. is rare, and the unemended reading may suggest the Pilgrim's fearful reluctance to mention his possible fate 'It is so horrifying—just payment [for sins]'. F goes on: *Rien n'ataint que tout n'esmie, | Quant il veut penre vengement. | Mere ....*

rihtful F11,088 is no guide. Perhaps JMO should be accepted, the reading in C's spelling then presumably (it is without precedent in C) being *rewful*.

5974 **þis world** F11,106 *monde* var. *cest monde* MS. *M*.

5982-3 **thornes ... yore** Gen. iii 17-18: after God's warning to the serpent ('she shall crush thy head'), long interpreted as a reference to the Virgin (*Biblia Pauperum*, sig. a), comes his 'cursed is the earth in thy work ... Thorns and thistles shall it bring forth to thee.' The Pilgrim is poisoned by the Seven Sins'

EXPLANATORY NOTES

weapons, which derive their power from the serpent's venom.

5987 **Ledest** I reject the usual *And ledest*, accepting G's reading (supported by JMO's *Led*), and assuming that C (and S, which at this stage is its derivative) smooth a subj. 2 sg. 'may you lead'. Inserting *And* merely destroys effective emphasis on the wish that the Virgin might be our guide, and does not improve the metre, which often shows such initial stress (see Zbozny, in n. 5831 above).

5992 **þi bench** the court bench at which the Virgin sits as one of the King of Heaven's councillors—as distinct from the King's Bench over which the King alone presides.

5994 **Xpc** (from the Greek letters χρς for *CHR*istu*S*, to which one cannot transcribe without breaking the 'A.B.C.' sequence) looks objective, governed by *thanke* in 6001 (Skeat): but the thanks may be offered either to Christ or to the Virgin as *socour of al mankynde*, and it is more likely that the poet's address to her remains unbroken, giving the vivid sense: '(For) Christ that . . . I thank you'.

5996 **suffred** 'All MSS. insert *suff(e)red*, apparently repeated from l. 162' (Robinson, who like Skeat omits it, as obstructing the metre: but one smooths the metre of this poem at great risk to its metrical daring).

Longius see n. 4455; not in F.

pighte the common emendation to *prighte* is unnecessary: the lance-thrust is felt as a blow.

6002 **Ysaac** The Sacrifice of Isaac (Gen. xxii 1–18) is an ancient Type of the Crucifixion (e.g. 2nd-century Melito, *PG*, V, 1218); like the Burning Bush of 5922, it appears in the *Biblia Pauperum* (sigs. .e., .f.).

6005 **as a lamb** Is. lxiii 7; John i 29.

6010 **Zacharie** Zach. xiii 1 is normally interpreted as a reference to the availability of God's grace, or, as in the *Biblia Pauperum* (sig. i), to the Baptism of Christ: it is the *closed* well (*fons signatus*) of the Song of Songs which is commonly interpreted as the Virgin, e.g. in Ludolphus Saxoniensis (see Ludolphe, I, p. 29). Haymo, however, observes that the *fons patens* of Zacharias is *largissima Dei misericordia, patens domui David, id est universae ecclesiae*, and a rare extension of this image to the Virgin is in the late 12th-century Cistercian Abbot Adam of Perseigne (*PL*, CCXI, 739): *Fons est Maria patens et accessibilis ex profusione et facilitate misericordiae* (*fons patens* is in the Vulgate only in Zacharias, though he is not mentioned). Chaucer's 'open well' (F *Fontannie*) may echo the ME Bible: according to Forshall and Madden the later version of the 'Wycliffe' Bible has *an open welle* (the earlier has *a welle opnynge*).

6017 **to merci able,** 'fit for mercy', not only puns on 6015's *merciable*,

490   ÞE LYFE OF ÞE MANHODE

but also echoes the poem's opening line, itself of Chaucer's composition (Zbozny, pp. 128-9).

6018 **Explicit** Chaucer ignored the last two stanzas, beginning *Ethiques* and *Contre* respectively to give the '*ET Cetera*' (ampersand) often ending alphabets (Skeat [1899], who prints the French stanzas on p. 60).

6020 **to** F11,195 *De* var. *A* MSS *AA¹L*.

6026 **he** refers to the *charboncle* (masc. in F). C (followed by S) corrected by erasure to *she*, thinking the reference was to the Virgin symbolised by the *charboncle*.

6027-8 **þei ... hurt** F11,210 *a mort soient navres* 'are fatally wounded'.

6029 **ye ... aboute** F11,213-14 *qu'a tous despensee / Soies et (a) tous aumosnee* 'that you are distributed to everyone, and given to all as alms.'

6040 **to here confusion** F11,233 *a sa confusion* 'in confusion'.

6056-7 **and ... himself** F11,264-5 *et son eul devers li / Li fais convertir et tourner* 'and I make him alter the direction of his eye and turn it on himself': var. *de son eul ...* may explain *and with his eye*.

6057-8 **for ... dedes** F11,266 *Pour soi, quel s'est fait, regarder* 'to see how he himself is made' var. *Pour soi quel s'est faiz regarder* MS. *M*.

6060 **teres** om. F11,270 *et degouter* 'and drip'.

6065 **in þe herte** F11,280 *aucun* 'any' var. *au cuer* MS, *o*.

6067 **Magdaleyne** Luke vii 37-8: the 'woman that was ... a sinner' who wept on Christ's feet was traditionally identified with Mary Magdalene of Luke vii 2, Mark xv 40, xvi 1, Matt. xxviii 9.

Peeter Matt. xxvi 69-75.

6068 **Egipcian Marie** a 5th-century penitent once an infamous actress and courtesan: Deguileville may have known her life by the 13th-century Rutebuef (*ODCC* 'Mary of Egypt').

6070 **þou seye hire** F11,290 *la veis* 'I saw her' var. *tu la veis* MS. *o*.

6079 **was ... half ful** F11306 *n'estoit pas plain a demi* 'was not half full': as Dr Walls noted, τ did not realise, until he translated *plain*, that *a demi* modified it.

6082 **in hire hand** has no precedent in F11,311.

6084 **Moiseses** Moses striking water from the rock in the desert (Exod. xvii 1-6) is a Type of the Crucifixion in the *Biblia Pauperum* (sig. .f.), for according to Augustine (*PL*, XXXV, 1513) the sacraments flowed from Christ's side as the water from the rock (I Cor. x 3-4). Here, the image of Penance recalls the cleansing water of Baptism, already associated with Christ's blood (see n. 273-5). In the *Bible Moralisée* (Oxford, Bodleian Library, MS 270b, f. 50, C1, C2) Moses is a prelate, his rod the Cross (Augustine, *PL*, XXXIX, 1553-4), the rock Christ, the action the Crucifixion, the water Faith.

EXPLANATORY NOTES

6084-5 **with ... Soone** F11,317 *dont u desert feri | La roche et* 'with which he struck the rock in the desert and'. Perhaps *Soone* is explained by τ's eye having been caught by F11,321-2 *feri | La roche, tost*.

6092 **in** F11,331 *ens*: perhaps CJ(S)'s *þerinne* should be accepted instead of GMO's reading, as *þer* may easily be lost after *þe*.

6093 **for þee** has no precedent in F11,332.

6097 **David** II Kings xii 13-22: the penance of David is a Type of the Repentance of 'Magdalene' in the *Biblia Pauperum* (sig. n).

6101 **I hadde** F11,346 *t'eusses* 'you had' var. *teusse* MSS *TAM¹LH*.

6105 **desired** F11,354 *desirree* may be word-play on 'desired: (see 5793-4) and 'gone away from': the pilgrim showed both reactions to the hedge.

6118 **allas²** F11,377 *chetif has las* 'wretch, alas': τ avoids repetition.

6122-3 **and ... me** τ read F11,386 *et (ma) voie* 'and my path' as *et me con voie*?

6131 **iorney** F11,465 *journee* perhaps plays on 'journey/day's worth'.

6145 **swommen** F11,424 *nooient* 'were drowning' var. *noioient* MS. *T*.

6168 **blisseth yow** 'Cross yourself' (because the Devil is to be described).

6171 **I bithinke me** F11,474 *il l'en souvient* 'it [the soul] remembers' var. *m'en souvient* MSS *ALMH*.

6172 **so foule** has no precedent in F11,475-6.

6174 **peynted ... figured** the original F MS must, like MSS *toAHTM¹*, have had an illustration here (near F11,482). Neither of the illustrated English MSS (MO) has.

6178 **handes** MS. *o* has not *mains* but *dens* 'teeth': though τ largely used an *o*-type MS, he did not use *o* alone.

6189 **thwartouer** F11,508 *de travers*; according to *OED* this modifies *ran*, but it is clear from 6210-2 *purblynd eyen and thwartouer* that it modifies *biheeld*, and so means something like 'crookedly' (see n. 6190).

6190 **purblynd** F11,508 *borgne* 'one-eyed'.

6194 **Heresye** is interestingly placed in the allegory. She is parallel to but in contrast with *Rude Entendement* who, at the beginning of Book 2, was innocent of any learning, and interpreted Scripture literally (requiring, however, a great deal of highly skilled argument from Reason). Heresy, the educated man's temptation, simply rejects Scripture. Significantly easier to defeat than the terrible personal sins which the Pilgrim has already survived (as Red Crosse defeats Errour with comparative ease in *The Faerie Queene*), she is also easily despatched as the first serious attacker after his penance.

6204 **and** F11,534 *ou* 'or' var. *et* MSS *oTALMH*.

6210 **Templeres** the Templars were arrested in 1307, and in 1308 127 charges were laid against them in 'a deliberate and successful attempt to vilify them and ruin their reputation' (Barber, p. 192). These Barber lists (pp. 178-92, with a complete list on pp. 248-52) under seven heads, the third, 'disbelief in the sacraments, and omission of the Consecration from Mass' being associated with the Cathar heresy. I am grateful to Professor Christopher Holdsworth for this reference.

6212 **stirede ayens** F11,549 *esmu plait contre* 'raised a plea against'.

Augustyn M's marginal *Augustine d{ . . . . .}* perhaps mentioned *De Haeresibus* (*PL*, XLII, 21-50), but Augustine's writings against heresy are legion (*ODCC*, pp. 109-10).

6225-6 **doon . . . awey** F11,572 *aucune chose en ostast* 'take something out of it'.

6233 **al** F11,588 *ja* 'already'.

6234 **also** F11,590 *ja* 'already'.

6241 **stended** (F11,600 *tendu*) cf. 6302, 6305, *stenderesse* at 5319, has no precedent in C, whose *stented* should possibly be retained. F and the ME variants suggest, however, that τ used *stend-*.

6244 **and seyde** has no precedent in F11,606.

6255 **ben weenged** F11,626 *elles se font* 'makes themselves wings': virtues are acquired by effort (see n. 57-63).

6256 **keepen** F11,629 *quierent* 'seek'. Did τ write *seeken*, misread by χ?

6260-1 **þei . . . upriht** F11,636 *drois noent et vont* 'they swim and go straight on'.

6262 **Ortigometra** from the Greek meaning 'mother of quails': *Ortyga* means 'quail', a migrating flock of which was, according to The Bestiary (McCulloch, p. 160), led not by one of their kind but by a rail; the bird shares with man the 'falling sickness'—perhaps significant in the allegory here—but use of a wing as a sail is not mentioned. According to Locock, p. 689 and White, p. 148, the landrail or corncrake (*crex crex*) is meant: but the water rail (*rallus aquaticus*) is more likely, as it flies weakly. Like the bird, a virtuous man is equipped perfectly neither for flight (to heaven) nor water-life (the world), its wings (feathered with virtues, see n. 57-63) being rudimentary. Thus when forced to the water it uses its wings as best it can. The Pseudo St Victor (Hugues de Fouilloy, says Glorieux) explains: *Coturnix/Ortygometra* is the soul that for love of its neighbour crosses the sea of the world to the love of God, through the storms and winds of temptation (*PL*, CLXXVII, 49-50).

6271 **michel beloued** τ read F11,655 *mondaine* 'worldly' as *mout aime*.

EXPLANATORY NOTES   493

6273   **needes** F11,659 *negoces* 'matters'.

6278   **kyn** in view of F11,668 *paremens* 'outward show', GJMO's reading is accepted, assuming that τ read *p'emēs* (*paremens*) as *p'enes* (*parenes*) 'parents, family'.

6280   **blyndfelled ... fooles** either literally follows F11,672-3 *bendiaus se font | Les fols* 'the fools blindfold themselves', or means 'they blindfold themselves, the fools'.

6282   **Pistel ... Magdaleyne** the Epistle for the Feast of Mary Magdalene contains Cant. viii 7: 'Many waters cannot quench charity, neither can the floods drown it: if a man should give all the substance of his house for love, he shall despise it [his wealth] as nothing'. The verse is doubly relevant: the world's goods are valueless, and the waters of the world (the sea, here) are essentially powerless.

6292-3 **with**[1] **... temptacioun** F11,693 *Sa ligne est sa temptation* 'his line is his temptation': τ saw *et* for *est*, so supplied *with* twice. In view of F, GM's sg. *temptacioun* is accepted against the pl.

6298   **not** om. F11,703 *touz* 'everyone'.

6300   **for ... fetheren** F11,707 *pour chacier penneaus* '(?) for hunting': net or basket traps?

       for[2] **... fleeinge** F11,708 *rois volans pour les oisiaus* 'cast-nets for birds': τ thought *volans* qualifed *oisiaus*.

6302   **stended** see n. 6241.

6312-13 **stercheth ... reedes** F11,729-30 *endruist ses verveus | Et ses penniaus et ses raiseus* 'strengthens his nets, and his [?] and his fishing nets'. τ presumably misread *ses penniaus* as *les* [?], *et* as *en*, and saw not *raiseus* but var. *roseulz* 'reeds' (MS. *M*).

6305   **stended** see n. 6241.

6317   **Jerome** Bömer, and Hultman, cite *PL* XXVI, 512 in error. The poet may have conflated two Jerome passages. *PL*, XXVI, 544 asserts that the power of the devil is not in himself but in our will. *PL*, XXIV, 1195 (XXIV being at the end of XXIII, the columns being consecutively numbered through both) describes the devil's nets: we 'walk in the midst of snares, passing beneath threatening devices; all things are filled with nets—the devil has filled everything with his snares ... Jesus, seeing a great crowd of men trammelled by nets not to be cut by anything except himself, subjected himself to the nets of the world [*retibus mundi*]'. (This passage is from a translation by Jerome of Origen's commentary on The Song of Songs, ii, 9, which in the version Origen knew had the Greek equivalent not of Vulgate *prospiciens per cancellos* 'looking through the lattices' but of *prospiciens per retia*. Professor Roy Porter informs me that the Septuagint error arose through confusion of the similar Hebrew words for lattices and nets.) The idea that these nets may be easily broken is implicit in the Origen (*PG*, XIII, 183-4): Jesus breaks the nets, giving 'confidence to his Church, that it may venture to break through the nets'.

6325–34 **Bithinke ... it** the story, derived from *Vitae Patrum* (*PL*, LXXIII, 1022) is in the 13th-century Jacques de Vitry, *Exempla* (Crane, p. 34, no. 76), e.g. in London, British Library, MS. Harley 463 (described in Herbert [1910] p. 5), f. 1; it is also found in medieval Spanish (Keller, K943).

6327–8 **þe ... þus** has no precedent in F11,754, as Dr Walls noted.

6336 **Peeter** I Pet. v 8.

seecheth F11,770 *circuie* 'circles'. The reading could be [*sercleth*], if τ was misread by χ.

6336–7 **what ... deuowre** JMO's *wham he may deuoure* may be influenced by the ME Bible: according to Forshall and Madden, the 'Wycliffe' Bible has *sechinge whom he schal deuoure*; the earlier version differs only in spelling.

6343–4 **a ... bal** F11,783–4 *Une damoiselle sote, / Ce sembloit qui' une pelote / Portoit* 'a foolish girl, it seemed, who carried a ball'.

6344 **rouh** τ read F11,78 *duvee* 'downy' as *drue(e)*: (see 6361)?

6347 **If** in view of F11,791 *Se* 'If', I assume that τ's *Yif* was misread by χ as CGJMOS's *Yis*. The spelling is C's.

6349–50 **Who ... I** F11,795 *Si estes (vous), dis je, si gento* ' "You are", I said, "so gentle" '. τ misread *Si* as *Qi*?

6353 **of ... doinge:** F11,802 *de put afaire* may imply prostitution.

6354 **Jeonenesse** in view of F11,803 *jeunece*, and JMO's ambiguous *Iuuenesse* (? *Iunenesse*) it is just possible that the form should be *Jeouenesse*, for *Joifnes*—see *MED junesse, joifnes*; *MED jolines(se)* (d) cites only C's substitution at this point. It is hard accurately to record G^3's glosses to the word: they occur here (f. 88^r/33) and on ff. 89^v/11, 91^v/26, 92^r/9 but are never quite legible, the difficulty being the letter before *-the* in ? in *ȝougthe*. Following G, the spelling here and at 7106 is replaced by *Joenenesse* at 6439, 6594, 6614, 6616.

fonne F11,805 *saillant* 'jumping one' var. *faillant* (lit. 'lacking') MS. *y*.

6356 **trippe** om. F11,809 *et queur* 'and run'.

6357 **trice** F11,809 *bale* 'dance' suggests that this is a form of *trace* 'to pace or step in dancing; to tread a measure'. *OED trace* v.^{1}2 records no form in *tri-*, but since there is *trais(e)*, and the ME MSS are unanimous, I do not emend.

6358 **joynpee** *MED* records this only here and in Lydgate's *Pilgrimage*.

with þe ferþeste F11,812 *au plus loins* 'furthest'.

6359 **dych** F11,814 *mur(et) ou haie* 'wall or hedge' is a legal phrase denoting boundary.

EXPLANATORY NOTES 495

6359-61 **and ... anoon** F11,815-18 *Se des pommes a mes voisins | Veul avoir, tost en leurs gardins | Sui saillie et sur .i. pommier | Sui tost rampee et de legier* 'if I wanted some of my neighbours' apples, I quickly jumped into their gardens, and rapidly and lightly climbed into an appletree'.

6361 **rouh** see 6344.

6362 **feþered** om. F11,820 *Es pies* 'on the feet': τ avoids repetition.

6363 **Azael** II Kings ii 17-23: Azael, famous for his speed, was killed by the retreating Abner, whom he pursued to despoil.

6368-9 **þerof ... priued** the minimum age for ordination to the priesthood, and so to the episcopacy, was thirty (Gratian, *PL*, CLXXXVII, 377-8).

6370 **A ... with** F11,835-6 *Vne croce me faut a souler*. τ's *crooked staf* destroys the word-play on 6371 *croce*: to the responsibilities associated with the bishop's crosier Youth prefers a toy for playing a game in which some form of 'cross' was used (Tobler *coler*: '*coler de la crosse*'). *OED Chulle* mentions only a kind of football; *MED chollen* gives no certain meaning).

6374 **to gadere floures** F11,843 *D'aler quillier* 'of skittling'.
to bigile F11,843 *d'aler billier* 'of playing ball'.

6376 **ioye** om. F11,848 *et plus deduit* 'and more delight': τ avoids repetition.

6380 **quod ... more** in view of F11,856 *dis je, [plus] de rien*, MO's word-order, supported by J's variation, is accepted.

6382-4 **Shal ... þee** in view of F11,859-63 '*Vous me porterez, qu'avez dit, | Dit je, damoiselle? Petit | Fais porter mie ne voulez, | Quant de porter moi vous parlez*', JMO's reading is accepted, α having omitted the passage by eyeskip from 6382 *þee* to *þee* in 6384.

6386 **Mors**[1] is in large lower-case letters in C.

6388 **in** F11,870 *a* 'to' var. *en* MS. *o*.

6397-8 **nice, foolisshe** F11,888 *nice* offers no precedent for *foolisshe*: JMO's omission of it could be accepted, assuming it to be a gloss in α.

6398 **Cyrtim** (*Cyrtes* at 6403) Syrtes, sandbanks or quicksands (*OED syrtis*, which does not record this example) on the north coast of Africa (*Muir's Historical Atlas*, 'Medieval and Modern', Map 2 Gg).
Caribdim and Cillam (*Caribdis* and *Cilla* at 6411, 6423 etc.) Scylla and Charibdis of the idiom; in Greek legend, dangerous rocks on the Italian side of the Straits of Messina, and a whirlpool on the Sicilian side, both personified as female monsters. Scylla was composed below the waist of barking dogs (the sea on rocks—6430).
Bitalasson (*Bitalasso* at 6423, *Bitalassus* at 6424). F11,890 *Bitalassum* var. *Bitalasom* MS. *o*, *Bitalasson* MS. B. *Thesaurus*

Lingua Latinae s.v. *bithalassus* 'between two seas' (i.e. where two currents meet, or an isthmus is submerged). The derivation may be Acts xxvii 41 which in at least one Vulgate manuscript refers to Paul's ship running aground (the prow 'sticking fast') *in locum bithalassum*.

6399 **Sirenam** (*Sirena* at 6437) Sirens of Greek legend were sea-nymphs bird-bodied below the waist, whose sweet singing so charmed hearers that they died of starvation. See Rowland, pp. 139-41 for the medieval confusion of Sirens and Mermaids, apparent for example in the Pseudo St Victor's account of three kinds of Siren (two half-fish, one half-bird); both kinds often appear in The Bestiary (e.g. *A Thirteenth-century Bestiary in the Library of Alnwick Castle*, f. 14) which lists pleasure and music among their lures for travellers.

6403 **as sand** in view of F11,898 *comme sablon*, G's reading is accepted against C's *as a sand* ('like a sandbank' though *OED sand* does not record this sense in sg. until 1555?). The ME variants are ambiguous: JMO's *a sande* appears to support C, but only M's *þat a sond* echoes the original construction, and I assume it to be a corruption of *þat as sond*: cf. 6407 *It is sond* (F11,907 *Ce est sablon*).

6404 **a wawe cometh** F11,900 *on cuide passer* 'one thinks to pass': τ read *cuide* as *unde*.

6408 **binemeth** F11,910 *tot* 'all' var. *toult* 'takes away' MSS *AMG*: this is another example of the *o*-type MS *not* being τ's sole source: *o* has *tant*.

6414 **idem** F11,925 *idem* MSS *oTLGH* (Lat. 'the same', used to avoid repetition of names, words, etc.). *MED* renders *in here idem* by '? in their own way'; it seems to mean 'in their aforementioned movements'. The world's affairs endlessly alter as a result of the movements just described, also this flux produces repetition of similar events: essentially unproductive activity.

6417 **Salomon** Eccl. i 2-11.

6418 **souhte aboute** F11,927 *circuia* 'went round', referring to Eccl. i 6.

6421 **wrong** F11,936 *entorteillant* 'entangling'.

6427 **peynted on walles** e.g. four years after the *Pèlerinage* was written, Laurent de Boulogne painted a Wheel of Fortune in the castle of Hesdin (Evans, 1948, p. 181). Published examples in French wall paintings are elusive, but 13th-century relief wheels can be seen round rose windows at Amiens (a half-wheel over the south porch window) and at Beauvais and Basle (Mâle, *xiii*^{e} *siècle*, pp. 93-7). Rochester Cathedral contains one of the best-known (12th-century) painted examples in England.

6430 **possed** F11,950 *expose* 'exposed [to the waves]'. The reading could just possibly be *exposed*, if χ read *se exposed* as *see pposed*.

EXPLANATORY NOTES

6434 **cleyey** C offers no precedent for the spelling; there is no other example in C of an adjective formed from a noun ending in -y. The reading could be *cleyy* (cf G's *clayy*).

6438 **hire** om. F11,966 *Et bon chemin laissier leur fait* 'and makes them leave their safe route'.

6456 **corowne** Is. xxii 18 'he will crown thee with a crown of Tribulation'.

6460 **set** F12,003-4 *mise ... et assise*: τ avoids repetition.

6465 **goldsmithesse** the image of Tribulation embodying the functions of God as goldsmith is developed until 6549. Perhaps originating in Ezek. xxii 19-22, Is. i 25, Jer. vi 29-30, it appears in Alanus de Insulis (*PL*, CCX, 453; Moffat p. 43): *Deus ... tanquam mundi elegans architectus, tanquam aureae fabricae faber aurarius, velut stupendi artificii artifex artificiosus, velut admirandi operis opifex ....*

6473 **Persecucioun** the pilgrim has progressed spiritually (II Tim. iii 12).

6476 **Job** Job i-xlii.

6477 **þilke ... kalender** saints with feasts during the liturgical year.

6483 **defouled** F12,046 *qui est foule* 'which are pressed [in a wine-press]'.

6484-5 **þat ... messangere** F12,048-50 *Que par le conduit en descent / De lermes (un) grant pressourage / Qui de (la) douleur est message* 'by the conduit descends a great [wine-]pressing of tears which declares sorrow'. τ read *ou descent* 'where [the tears] descend' for *en descent*. His awkward literal rendering is reflected in GJMO, accepted against G³'s correction (also in CS).

6486 **Hountee and Confusioun** may be two names, or one.

6487-8 **so ... hamered** in view of F12,054 *tant forgie et martele* I accept MO, assuming that α rationalised to *beten him and hamered him*.

6489-90 **put ... bodi** F12,056-7 *mis a mort / Ou civile ou corporelle* 'put to either civil or bodily death' var. *mis a mort / cheuille ou corps corporelle* 'put to death or racked in the physical body'.

6490 **it** om. F12,059 *A sa pel acheter le fais* 'I make him pay for it on the skin': τ avoids repetition.

6491 **þe ...** F12,061 *la couenne* 'thick hide [of which a smith's apron is made]'. G left the space he found in α. I assume that τ left a space which he doubtless intended to fill later—but perhaps α could not read what τ had written. G³ wrote *vacat* 'there is a space' over the gap; CS wrote *vacat* in the text; β omitted the whole phrase.

al oon F12,062 *.i. forain devantel* 'one external apron'. Man's skin as Tribulation's working apron recalls Christ as anvil (see n. 2125).

6492 **þilke ... am** F12,063 *Connoist on cil que je parsui* 'one can tell whom I pursue': τ read *Connoist cil qui je sui?*

6502 **Þe lawe** F12,082 *l'essai* 'the trying [of the metal]' var. *la loi* MS. *o*.

6503 **Adonay** the divine name, often used in the Hebrew Bible, and instead of 'Jehovah'; Christian liturgy applies it to the Son.

6506 **today** F12,087 *Mes hui* 'henceforth'.

6511 **Þilke ... also** *quod I* has no precedent in F12,095 *Celle voul je savoir aussi*: τ misread *savoir* as *l'avoir*, and turned preterite narrative into direct speech.

6512 **I ... boþe** F12,096-8 *je la vi; | Toutes .ii. (les) lu* 'I saw it; I read them both'.

6514 **hath ... eclips** F12,100 *De qui le pouoir point n'eclipse* 'whose power is not at all eclipsed' var. *Qui a le pouvoir en l'esclipse* MS. *o*. The light of truth is unaffected by suffering, though apparently obscured, as Christ/the sun is unaffected by eclipse.

6517-18 **stepdame ... Virtu** this title links Prosperity with Idleness (3724).

6521 **hange** F12,114 *pendre* a pun in F and ME on 'hanged/hung about with' (see 6544-5)?

6522 **garnisonis** (F12,116 *garnisons*) the minims after *o* are undifferentiated. The reading could be *garnisoins* (G has *garnysouns*).

6522-6 **þat² ... Paradys** F12,116-22 *que de piec'a | Nous et nostre Grace avions | Mis en diverses regions. Pou avion de bons chastiaus | Que n'eussion mis aucuns vaissiaus | Es quiex emplage avion mis | Des grans tresors de paradis* 'that we and our Grace established once in various regions. We had very few good castles in which we had not placed some vessels in which we put the fulness of the treasures of Paradise'. τ's *where* in 6524 is explained by F12,120 *Pou* var. *Ou* MSS *ABM¹LM*, and *goode* in 6525 by F12,120 *aucuns* var. *de boins* MS. *M*. τ's reading (confused by F corruption) appears in JMO, G's rare omission being due to eyeskip from 6524 *we* to *we* in 6525. G³ (followed by CS) made five substitutions in a long correction no doubt from F² (note the 'correct' use of the royal *we* and *oure* in 6523), still without reaching overall sense.

6528 **macier** F12,127 *machiere* lit. 'crusher', as if Tribulation were God's hit-woman; MO's reading (supported by J) is accepted, assuming that τ saw var. *macier* 'mace-bearer [who keeps order in a law-court]' MSS *BL*, and used the F form instead of ME *macere*. But G's *matiere* (? 'concern' *OED Matter* 19b) could be accepted on the assumption that it derives from F var. *matiere* MS. *G*.

stoones F12,126 *pierre* var. *pierres* MSS *TM¹GH*.

EXPLANATORY NOTES 499

6529 **sergeauntesse** F12,128 *machecriere* 'female butcher' var. *chambelliere* MS. *A*.

6538–9 **here² ... tobroken** F12,145 *despecies | (Sont) leur armes ou desmaillies* 'their armour is broken up and taken apart [lit. unlinked]'. τ read *desmaillies* as a sb.

6561 **eche ... hauen** the lack of concord derives from F12,185 *ont chascun*.

6562 **þei wolen do ... þider** F12,188 *(Il) feront*: var. *Y feront* MS. *o* may explain þider.

6573–4 **I ... herd** F12,208 *veues | Diligaument o et leues* 'I had seen [them] and read [them] diligently' var. *leues | Diligaument oy et veues* MS. *o*.

6574 **took hem ayen** conceals acceptance of an alternative reading: although CS's *took hem ayen to hire* accurately renders F12,209 *li rendi*, I accept GMO, assuming that τ saw var. *les rendi* MS. *o*, CJ(S) adding *hem* to clarify.

6574–5 **and² ... hire** has no precedent in F12,209.

6570 **Judas** Acts i 16–18.

6577 **triacle and venym** Adonay's commission to Tribulation, written at the Fall, is for a treatment only. In contrast, Satan's commission is for destruction of those aspiring to heaven, so it was written only at the Redemption. Their means are similar, their effects different.

6582 **þou wolt haue** F12,224 *(tu) mues* 'you change' var. *tu weus* (for *veus*) MS. *o*.

6585 **Theophile** Theophilus, legendary bishop of Adana in Cilicia, sold himself to the devil, and despaired even as he gained his desires: on repenting, he was assisted by the Virgin, who returned Theophilus's bond. His story was common in literature and art: see Fryer (p. 290, n. 1) for a summary of its literary history from the 10th century, which includes Rutebuef's *Miracle de Thèophile*, and for a broad account of its visual history from the 12th century (see also Mâle, *The Gothic Image*, p. 261). It occurs twice at Notre Dame, Paris (Fryer, Pls III, IV).

6590 **sergeaunte** OED cites only this example of the v. (from, *pace* OED, F12,241 *sergenterai*); see 6581 (F12,222 *sergante*).

6593 **couenaunt** om. F12,246 *me* 'to me', absent in MS. *o*.

6600 **handes** om. F12,259 *En donnant du leur volentiers* 'giving of theirs gladly'.

6602 **grete²** F12,264 *lointains* 'far off'.

6617 **ledde ... me²** F12,292 *me conduisoit*. A rare creation of repetition: was *ledde* was once a gloss, so that and *ledde me* should be rejected?

6618 **suffred ... forge** F12,293–4 *me fist porter | A la sote parmi la mer* 'allowed myself to be carried over the sea by the foolish one' var. for *sote: force* MS. *o.* τ misread *force* as a reference to the anvil which the pilgrim had become for Tribulation's blows, so he began a new sentence at *To*, substituting *she hath brouht me* for the then puzzling *parmi la mer*. Alternatively, his source had, instead of *parmi la mer*, an accidental repeat of the last three words of F12,293.

6621 **Noe ... Diluvie** refers not only to the protection of Noe's family from the Flood, but also to its signification, the Church's protection of mankind against sin (see *MED ark(e)* 3b).

6623 **shadwe ... restinge** F12,301–2 *esconsal, | Un abri et un repostal* 'a resting-place, a shelter and a refuge': τ reduced repetition.

6624 **if ... it** F12,305 *se de toi ne le veus faire* 'you do not wish to make [a shelter for me] of yourself'. τ misconstrued *veus*.

6631 **any** F12,317 *aucun* is masc., *feulles (leves)* fem., so *any* refers not to a leaf but to a person (desiring heaven).

6632 **falle** om. F12,320 *Comment que soit* 'whatever the reason' (lit. 'however it may be').

6634 **to keepe him** has no precedent in F12,323.

6640 **I drawe** τ read F12,333 *je chace* 'I chase' as *je trais*?

6641 **to²** F12,336 *(a)* 'by'.

6641–2 **Sterre Tresmountayne** Pole Star (? Mary, *stella maris*): 'Over-the-Mountain', North being over the Alps in Italy, the name's origin.

6642 **holding ... handes** F12,337 *jointes mains* 'hand in hand'. τ thought the hands of those being led were joined in prayer.

6668 **man ... michel** F12,384–5 *ausi mal gist | Hons com chievre par trop grater* Hassell, C140.

6670–1 **þe ... flowinge** F12,389 *le temps de (ton) deluge* 'the time of your disaster [lit. flood]' referring to 6621. Reading *temps* as *camps* (for *champs*), τ was baffled by *deluge*.

6675 **soo** has no precedent in F12,396.

6685 **wey** τ read F12,416 *haie* 'hedge' as *voie*.

6697 **I pray yow** has no precedent in F12,439.

6701 **arryuaile** F12,445 *rivage* 'shore'. *OED arrival* 2 gives only one example: 'landing place'. If *a* in G's *aRyuaile* is otiose, the reading should be the commoner *ryuaile* (*OED rival* sb. 1).

6703 **freted** F12,448 *fretee* 'showing metal fittings'.

6704 **to¹,²** F12,451–2 *trop ... touz* 'too ... all' var. *trop ... trop* MS. *A*.

6709 **arches** F12,462 *archieres* 'arrow-slits'; see n. 6904.

6711 **veyle** puns on a nun's veil (see 6724–5, 6734 and notes)?

6714 **am** om. F12,470 *mout* (Stürzinger *mont*) 'greatly'.

6719 **þe ... name** F12481 *La nef, dist elle, par son non*: as Dr Walls noted, τ was misled by the masc. pron., though correctly making

EXPLANATORY NOTES

the ship fem. in 6720.

6722 **To ... cleped** F12,487 *De relier (elle) est nommee* 'it takes its name from *relier*', referring to the etymology of *religion* (*religare*).

6723 **soule** F12,489 *La vie* 'life' MSS to*AMB¹GLH* var. *L'ame* MSS *TL*.

6724-5 **þe olde** τ read F12,491 *les veus* 'the sails' as *les vieus*.

6725 **religiows** F12,492 *relieurs* 'binders' var. *religioux* MS. *L*.

6733 **hem¹** om. F12,507 *Ou les despiece* 'or breaks them up', reducing repetition.

6734 **olde** F12,509 (see n. 6724-5).

6738 **almost noone** F12,517 *mes nus* 'none any more'.

6743 **religious** F12,526 *relieures* 'binders' var. *religieurs* MS. *A*.

6749 **Gildenemouth** St John Chrysostom ('Goldenmouth' from his powers of oratory), *PG*, LI, 78, gives an extended metaphor in which Christ guides the ship/church through tempest. The reference is however probably to his sermon on the Spirit: commenting on II Cor. iv 13 (*habentes autem eumdem Spiritum fidei*), he speaks of a ship battered by storm, attacked by pirates and torn with internal conflicts, led back to tranquillity by the 'right hand of heaven' (*PG*, LI, 292).

6751 **Cluigni ... Cistiaus** Cluny, the great Benedictine early 10th-century foundation; Citeaux, the Cistercian Abbey in central France founded in about 1097 by St Robert of Molesme. As Locock noted, the idea of a monastery as *l'antichambre du Paradis* may derive from the 13th-century Huon de Mery's 'Tournement of Antichrist' (Huon de Mery, p. 104), a Psychomachia drawing on Raoul de Houdenc's allegories, in which this title is given to the Abbey of St Germaine des Prés when the protagonist finally enters it.

6765 **maace** F12,564 *plommee* 'cosh' [lit. 'lump of lead'].

6775 **goodshipe** F12,582 *sapience* 'wisdom': τ tried to avoid repetition?

I haue out in view of F12,583 *Je boute et chace* 'I drive out and chase away', G's reading is accepted (*OED haven* 8b), rather than substitutions.

6778 **maace** om. F12,589 *et (ma) plommee* 'and my cosh'.

6779 **Þe² ... Helle** F12,591 *des paines d'enfer l'Orreur* 'Horror of the Pains of Hell'.

6807 **to** om. F12,642 *pauser et* 'rest and'.

6810 **scripture** see 1341.

6813 The 8 monastic virtues (9, with Charity) somewhat resemble the Pseudo St Bernard's 'Eight Points of Perfection' (*PL*, CLXXXIV, 1181-6).

ÞE LYFE OF ÞE MANHODE

6818-19 **Þilke ... bare** F12,663-4 *Celle au gambeson estoit nue* 'She in the gambeson was naked'. Only MS. *A*⁷ (not MS. *o*) explains τ, inserting two lines: *Celle au gambeson estoit | Aus degrez et la matendoit | Dautres dras estoit toute nue* — but see n. 6819-20.

6819-20 **saue ... inne** F12,664 *Fors tant qu'elle en estoit vestue* 'except insofar as she was clothed in it [the gambeson]' var. *Force du pourpoint dont estoit vestue* MS. *A*⁷. τ's reading here is not explained by MS. *A*⁷ but by the main text (e.g. MS. *o*). τ's source must have been close to MSS *oMA*⁷, but not among Stürzinger's MSS. Perhaps *inne* should read *[in it]*, on the assumption that χ misread τ.

6824 **steled** in view of F12,673 *aceree* 'sharpened on a steel', GJMO's reading is accepted. C misread, and so took *stiked* as part of the following adverbial clause; S 'improved' to *stiking*.

6826 **mete croumed** τ read F12,677 *viande enmiellee* 'honeyed meat (or food)' as *viande enmiette* (see n. 56, to which this image relates).

6833 **serued** an error for *seruede*, C's normal pa. t. sg.?

6835 **disporteresse** *MED* records only this example.

6865 **wel** has precedent only in F12,750 var. *bien* MSS *TAM*¹*GL*.

6868-9 **ordre ... hardy** F12,754-5 *l'ordre | Que ... on ne s'amorde* 'order, so that one is not anxious ...' or 'the Order, so that there is no desire ...'.

6874 **name** Prudence (see 2432).

6884 **she wolde** F12,780 *veus* 'you want' var. *veult* MS. *A*.

6904 **archere** τ read F12,814 *Archiere* 'arrow-slit' as *Archier*. See n. 6709.

6906-8 **whoso ... cast** τ translates as if F ran 12,822, -21, -19, -20 instead of F12,819-22 *Plus hardie ell' en est assez | Contre les dars qui sont getez. | A main armee bien convient | Que soit a l'huis dont l'assaut vient* 'In them she is much stronger against thrown darts. It is very fitting that with armed hands she should be at the door from which the attack comes'. The var. *souuent* 'often' for F12,821 *convient* robbed τ of a main v. in F12,821-2, and made him misconstrue *est* in F12,819 as main v. in a sentence beginning at F12,817. τ also read F12,822 *Que* as *Qui*, so had to write *he* in 6907 (F12,819 *ell'*).

6908 **name** Continence (see 2295).

6914 **suthselerere** *OED* records only this example.

6918 **þat ... parchemyn** F12,838-9 *qui mise est | En vaissel fait de parchemin* 'which is placed in a vessel made of parchment': the image perhaps combines the picture of food held in a twist of 'paper', and of Scripture written on a scroll. τ read *qui mise est* as *qui i mise est* and so compounded his error, reading *En* as *Et*.

6923 **whyt culuer** the Spirit inspired the writing of Scripture (hence

EXPLANATORY NOTES

the common image of dove at the ear of an Evangelist scribe), he assists in its interpretation, and his gifts are the result of its study.

6939 **thanke** F12,877-8 *mercier* / . . . *et regracier*: τ avoids repetition.

6941 **with . . . handes** F12,882 *A tout le mains* 'at the very least': the living should pray for the souls of those who when alive earned them material benefits. Taking *mains* for 'hands' τ totally misconstrued.

6942 **quod she** F12,883 *te di* 'I say to you' (still in direct speech).

doon; heerinne in view of F12,883-4 *fait,* / *Ceens* I accept MS's *heerinne* modifying *hast seen*, against CG's *doon heerinne;*.

6950 **perce** is G's reading (supported by MO) accepted against CJS's 'improvements'.

sweeteliche F12,898 *doublement* 'doubly' var. *doulcement* MS. *A*.

6952 **þei haue** F12,901 *il en ont* 'from this they have'.

6961-2 **and . . . she is** F12,919-20 *De li voir messagiere elle est* / *Et procurresse, quant temps est* 'truly she is his messenger and advocate when the time comes': τ misconstrued *De li voir . . . quant temps est* as 'when it is time to see him'.

6963 **him** τ read F12,922 *Se* as *Le*, compounding the error which made him think Prayer is obtaining audience for the supplicant.

6963-4 **sheweth . . . him** F12,923 *Nunce ce qui li est commis* 'she announces that [message] which is committed to her'. τ saw not *commis* but var. *promis* MS. *o*, and misconstrued *Li* as 'to him'.

6971 **theef** Luke xxiii 42-3.

6976-8 **þat²... rise** F12,945-8 *qui esveille* / *Le roy toute(s) fois quil sou(b)melle;* / *Par son juper et son corner,* / *Se trop se gist, le fait lever* 'who wakes the king whenever he oversleeps; by her blowing and trumpeting she makes him get up if he lies [in bed] too long'. Var. *Par son juper et par son corner* made τ construe the first three words as modifying *esveille*, last four as modifying *fait?*

6980 **In adiutorioun** F12,952 *in adjutorium* var. *in adiutorion* MS. *A*¹. Ps. lxix 1: *Deus in adiutorium meum intende* 'Oh Lord, come to my aid'.

at euery hour this psalm begins each of the Canonical Hours (which are based on the Psalms, hence punning references in 6981, 6983, 6984 to *þe begynnynge, sawtrye* and *psalmodye*).

6982 **deliteth . . . melodye** F12,956 *(la) melodie en desclique* 'the melody issues from it [the *organes*]' var. *(la) melodie en deslice* MSS *A*¹*L*.

6987 **organe** F12,965 *orguenerie* MSS *toBA*¹*dM*¹*G*, *organeriee* MSS *LM*. Tobler '*organe*-playing' (see n. 4137), but the mingling of instruments in 6983 suggests the *organum* (strictly part-singing)

ÞE LYFE OF ÞE MANHODE

of polyphonic instrumental music.

6988-90 **he ... jogeloresses** F12,968-70 *De celle qui en joue a fait | (Sa) principal esbateresse, | (Et s')especial jouglerresse* uses singulars: τ (unable to visualise a one-woman band?) made them pl.

6991 **þei blowen** τ read F12,972 *il convient* 'it is fitting' as *il cornent*.

6996-7 **espye ... nouht** F12,982 *pas espier | Ne vous vieng* 'I do not come to spy on you' var. *pas espier | Ne vous veulz* MS. A^1.

7005 **quod she** has no precedent in F12,998.

7019 **strof I nothing:** F13,026 *n'escrirai je rien* puns on *escrier* 'cry out', 'protest', and *escrire* 'write': the poet does not protest or write about what will happen.

7026 **Benedicite** a blessing which must precede any valid suspension of the rule of silence. 'De Taciturnitate Discipulorum' in the 6th-century *Rule of the Master* (known to St Benedict) describes how brothers wishing to address their superior stand before him silently until *os clave benedictionis aperiant* (Vogüé, I, pp. 407-9). *Decreta pro Ordine Benedicti* mentions how *Post sextam nullus in claustro loquatur donec ... minimus alta voce Benedicite dicat* (Lanfranc, *PL*, CL, 446).

7027 **hem** F13,039 *des dames* 'the women'.

7031 **leced** *MED* cites only this example.

a ... afterward this phrase implies the pilgrim's entire life as a religious. The Cistercian silence just embraced by him finds its parallel in his poem, for we go from his vows straight to his death.

7038 **to tourneye** F13,057 *nuncier* 'to make an announcement' var. *tournoier* MS. *o*.

7040 **haue** om. F13,061-2 *batu | Et* 'beaten and'.

7060-1 **him**[1,2,3]: F13,099-100 *li ... | ... li ... li* may be masc. or fem., but are fem. here, referring to *Sante (Hele)*.

7061-2 **Oon ... him** F13,101-2 *Une heure jus elle m'abat | Et une heure je la rabat* 'Sometimes she strikes me down, and sometimes I strike her down' (sometimes the speaker, Infirmity, and sometimes her adversary Health, wins—both are female). CGJOS show that τ correctly wrote *she*, but having made the error described in n. 7060-1, thought *elle* referred not to Health (in the wrong gender, as in 7068) but to the third woman present, Infirmity's companion Old Age: 'sometimes she (Old Age) overcame him (Health), and at other times I beat him (Health)'. G^3 unfortunately altered *sche* in 7061 back to *he*.

7062 **fewe** τ took F13,103 *pou* 'little' as pl. sb. (in spite of sg. v.).

7063 **Medicine** om. F13,105 *enhuvetee* 'hooded'.

7063-4 **coumfort, whiche** F13,104 *aucun confort ... li* 'some comfort to her [Health] who': τ's ignoring *li* results in *whiche* relating to *Medicine*, not *Hele*.

EXPLANATORY NOTES

7067 **þe** τ read F13,113 *ses* 'her' as *les*.

7068 **empassionementes** F13,115 *empocionnemens* 'potions' var. *enpacionnemens* MS. *o*. β sensibly corrected to *pocions*, but GC, and S's omission of the phrase, confirm τ's echo of the meaningless F var. *MED* cites only this: '? medicinal potions'.

7071-2 **His ... ete** may be a parody of the eucharist as foretold in John vi 54-7; Infirmity's consumption of the body is a kind of inversion of the spiritual growth resulting from consumption of the Body and Blood in the Host (cf. 7088-90 where, surprisingly, we do not actually see the pilgrim receive the Viaticum before his death).

7078-9 **bringeth ... þerof** loses the word-play of F13,133 *les (gens) desvoies ravoie* 'brings back to the path those who have lost the path'.

7082 **þilke** F13,140 *mon* 'my'.

7091 **hire** I accept JM's reading, because at 7103 τ has apparently realised that Death is female, and because *him/hire* confusion is easy; perhaps *him* (supported by O) should be retained.

7094 **bodi** F13,161 *terriere* 'earthly appearance'.

7103 **to hire** without precedent in F13,175 could be omitted, as in JMO(S).

7106-7 **of ... me** has no precedent in F13,182.

7117 **Vilesse** in view of F13,201 *Vieillece* G's reading is accepted: C(S) misunderstood it as 'Vileness', and β substituted *Elde*.

dotede τ read F13,201 *redoutee* 'feared' as *rado(u)tee*.

7121 **Þis ... glose** F13,209 *Ce sont ... les gloses* is pl.

7128 **Ysaie cursed me** Is. lxv 20 (see n. 1246-9).

7140 **temporal** F13,242 *corporel* 'corporal'. τ's error is retained, as if he misread F; the reading could be *[corporal]*, as if χ misread τ.

7143-5 **þat¹ ... nouht** F13,249-51 starts a new sentence: *Qui d'une part est soustenu, | Se d'autre part il est feru, | Pas si legierement ne chiet* 'He who is supported on the one side does not fall so easily if he is hit on the other'. τ read *Qui* as *Que*, so (as GC³ show) added *ne* to complete his sense '[I do not thrown them down so quickly] that they are not supported on one side [even] if they are struck on the other, so they do not fall so easily ...'.

7149 **him³** om. F13,259 *jus trebuchier | ... et* 'fall down and'.

7153 **to pinche)** F13,266 *pousser* 'to push' var. *penser* (for *pincer*) MS. *B*.

7173 **for ... bileevinge** F13,304 *Pour avoir en aucun remain* 'in order to have some people left' (lit. 'in order to have a remainder in some') referring to the survival of Noe and his family, and to the rainbow which was God's sign of a new covenant (Gen. ix 8-17).

7174 **corde ... accord** retains the word-play of F13,305-6 (cf. *A.B.C.* 5858-65). The bow is unstrung as a sign of peace. After *accord* τ om. F13,307-10 *La corde en tieng, l'arc devers li. | Est onques archier je ne vi | Qui en tel guise peust traire, | Se (de) vers li ne vouloit traire* (my punctuation): 'I hold the cord of it with the bow on his side [in heaven]; I have never seen an archer who could draw it in such a way—without drawing it towards him'. One cannot draw a bow while holding the wood, rather than the string, near the body. There may be a glance at the Judgement image of God seated on a rainbow, the 'wood' of the bow rather than the 'string' thus being towards him. τ eyeskipped from *concorde* at the end of F13,306 to the end of F13,311 *De la corde dont encorde*, and was doubtless confused also by F13,307, beginning similarly with *La corde*.

Hitherto F couplets or lines were it usually syntactical units: henceforth F is more ambiguous, often using enjambement.

7174-6 **With ... þerinne** the bow-string becomes the means by which Mercy raises sinners to heaven. In the *Soul*, a rope made from Faith, Hope and Charity draws souls from Purgatory to Heaven (*Guillaume de Deguileville*, f. xxxviii^(r,v))—cf. George Herbert's reference in *The Pearl* to 'thy silk twist let down from heaven to me'.)

7179 **foul wrecchednesse** F13,318 *sent(in)e orde* 'foul lowest deck': sinners are drawn up from the bilges, as it were, of the Church (the ark—see 7173).

7182 **þere** should perhaps be emended to *[þer]*, the unstressed form: but possibly C felt that in the interrogative construction it carried more stress than usual.

7188 **Aristotle seith** *De Generatione Animalium* (trans. A. Platt, Vol V of Ross), 777A.

7198 **al ... shewe it** I assum that τ followed the syntax of F13,353-4 *n'estoit pas mestier: | Pour monstrer la, il fist*, but it is possible that, expecting the now more frequent enjambement, he wrote what appears in all the MSS: *al were it nouht neede to shewe it. He maade ....*

7201 **eche** om. F13,360 *cretien* 'Christian'.

7201-2 **Come ... come forth** F12,360-1 *Tieng! | Qui veut alaitier viengne avant!* 'Come! Come forward, anyone wishing to suck'. Perhaps τ thought *alaitier* inf. after imperative *Tieng*, and wrote *Haue, whoso wole, souke—come forth*, but I have assumed that he knew that *alaitier* is governed by *veut*. In this case his first *Come forth!* is otiose.

7204 **profite** the speech of the breast may continue until *brest* in 7205.

7204-5 **ne ... brest** F13,366 *Ne tel mammelle n'aleta* 'nor did such a breast ever give milk'.

7208-15 **hunger ... syknese** the 7 Corporal Works of Mercy (*ODCC*,

EXPLANATORY NOTES

p. 394).

7225 **I trowe wel** is misplaced by τ, according to F13,408-10 *et point ne te lairont. / Je pense bien qu'avant la mort / Venra qu'aies d'elles deport* 'and they will [not] leave you at all. I really think they will not give you respite until Death comes'. Either τ's source had the neg. that sense requires (age and infirmity will persist until death), or τ corrected intelligently.

7238-9 **quod ... anoon** om. C by eyeskip from *anoon* in 7238 to *anoon* in 7239.

7239 **taryinge** F13,434 *vielle (veille)* 'watching' ('staying awake', 'waiting', 'watching by the dead'). τ unnecessarily loses the word-play.

7243 **eerþeliche** F13,442 *terribles* 'terrible' var. *terrestres* MS. *M*.

7246 **stinkinge to wormes** F13,448 *Aus vers puans* 'to stinking worms'.

7247 **ordeyned** F13,451 *expose*.

7251-2 **þat¹ ... togideres** F13,459-60 *L'uis est estroit, (le) cors et (l')ame / Ne pourroient passer ensemble* 'the door is narrow: the body and the soul could not pass in together'. Perhaps the first clause was illegible to τ: he read *L'uis* as *L'un(e)*, and then guessed *est le cors et l'autre ame*?

7258 **sumtime** see 84.

7260 **wel** has no precedent in F3,475 *tu eus chier*. Grace refers to 95-103.

7263 **hire** in view of F13,480 *li* 'to her', the reading of GJM (supported by O) is accepted in place of C's *heer* over erasure.

7264 **purgatorie**, the place or state where those who have died in a state of grace expiate temporal punishment still due to them for venial sin before receiving the Beatific Vision, is presented in Book 2 of the *Soul*. See *NCE*, XI, 1034-9.

7267 **he** in spite of F13,489 *La mort, elle*, τ has apparently forgotten that Death is female.

7268 **Wel ... supprysed** F13,490 *Je le seu bien, je fu suppris* reveals *þat* as demonstrative pron., not conj.

7269 **þe soule** F13,492 *m'ame* 'my soul'.

7272 **orlage** clearly refers to a bell-sounding mechanism (either one employing an escapement, or a water-controlled klepsydra) which may have sounded only the canonical hours. In the late 12th-century *Chronicle of Jocelin of Brakelond* a clock, having woken the sacristan at the time for Mass, is used as a source of water to put out a fire, so is undoubtedly a klepsydra (Jocelin, pp. 107-8). For terminology and an analysis of early references to horology see Howgrove-Graham; for illustration of a klepsydra from the *Bible Moralisée* of c. 1285 see Drover.

7273 **Matyns** the 1st Canonical Hour, at midnight (in Benedict's

ÞE LYFE OF ÞE MANHODE

    Rule, 2 a.m.).

7289-90 **Faire ... chastysed** F13,531-2 *Biau, se dit on (il) se chastie / Qui par autri (si) se chastie* 'He who has himself by someone else chastises himself well'. G's awkward *Faire chastiseth ...* may reflect τ, other scribes having normalised.

7295-300 **Heere ... Amen** a F equivalent is found only in three Stürzinger manuscripts, and the exact equivalent only in MS. A^7.

7299 **wherinne ... enclosed** is a quotation from *Le Roman de la Rose*, line 2.

GLOSSARY

The glossary explains only the more unfamiliar words and senses (so that Middle English pronouns, for example, are normally excluded). Some unusual spellings of commonplace words are, however, included. When a word occurs with both familiar and unfamiliar meaning, only the latter is recorded, so that it should never be assumed that the meaning given is the only one which a word has in the text. Orthographical variants are included, being relatively few: common ones immediately follow the headword, rarer ones are at the end of each entry. No attempt has been made to give complete inflexions: additional parts are included only if change of meaning, or significant change of form, makes it necessary. Thus, instead of:

bete *v*. beat 3165. *pr. l sg*. 4278. **beten** *pl*. 6303. **beet** *pa. t. l sg*. 1123. **beete 2 sg**. 391. **bete** *pl*. 4921. *pp*. 1446. **beten** embroidered 120.

the entry is simply:

beten *pp*. embroidered.

Line references are usually to the first occurrence of the form, inflexion or meaning cited, but sometimes a later occurrence is cited instead, if it is part of a phrase. Sometimes 'etc.' is used to indicate that though an example ends an entry there are many examples of it. The sign ~ stands for the headword or phrase in any of its forms. In the arrangement, consonantal *i* is treated as *j*; þ follows *t*; *u* and *v* are separated according to function; vocalic *y* is treated as *i*, vocalic *w* as *u*; consonantal *y* and *w* have their usual places. Abbreviations used are conventional, and will be found in the List of Abbreviations: important is the distinction here between 'n.' meaning 'noun', and 'n' after a line reference, meaning 'see note at or near this line number'. Proper nouns are listed at the end of the glossary.

a poynt *adv. phr*. properly 2134–5; *wel* ~ right 1374n.
a soursaut *adv. phr*. without warning 7231.
aas *n*. ace 2013.
abaaten see **abate**.
abashe *v. refl*. feel ashamed 774; feel afraid 5686. **aba(s)she** *intr*. 3978. **abasheth** *tr. pr. 3. sg*. alarms 6050. **abashed** *intr. pa. t. sg*. was amazed 213. *refl*. in *of nothing she* ~ *hire* she was not a bit discouraged 1556. **abashed** *pp*. dismayed 51; **abasht** surprised 3589; **abaasht** 2101.
abate *v*. put an end to 3165. **abaaten** *pr. pl*. defeat 7048. **abated** *pp*. diminished 958.

abayeth *pr. 3 sg.* bays 5028. **abayinge** *pr. p.* barking 6430.
abeescede *pa. t. sg.* lowered 6081.
abeye *v.* obey 2852.
abetter *v.* improve 987.
abide(n), abyde *v.* remain 1149; *in her I wole* ∼ I will abide by her teaching 2621. **abitte** *pr. 3 sg.* waits 7267. **abo(o)d** *pa. t. sg.* remained waiting 2604. **abidinge** *vbl. n.* delay 541; dwelling 1240.
abiggeth *pr. 3. sg.* pays for 6490. **abouhte** *pa. t. sg.* paid for 6364. **abouht** *pp.* 6657.
abitte see **abide**.
able *adj.* in *to merci* ∼ fit for mercy 6017.
abo(o)d see **abide**.
abouht(e) see **abiggeth**.
aboute, abowte *adv.* around the outside 24; all round 26; round 837. *prep.* around 1996.
abstracto Lat. *n.* in *in* ∼ in theory 5694-5.
accident *n.* in *bi* ∼ by virtue of a non-essential relation 3315n.
ac(c)ord *n.* agreement 7174; *of* ∼ in agreement 5358.
accroche *v.* haul in 5105.
accrocheres *n. pl.* those who acquire property illegally 5094.
acloyed *pp.* harassed (lit. shod) 6487.
acounte *n.* statement of accounts 928.
acustomed *pp.* customary 5209; *nouht* ∼ strange 2655.
ad aliquid Lat. (∼ *esse*) *adv. phr.* to be relative 715n
adaunted *pp.* subdued 3444.
adiutorioun (for Lat. *adiutorium*) *n.* help 6980n.
affeccioun *n.* emotions (the faculty of the soul concerned with emotion and volition) 2334.
aferre *adv.* distantly 4083.
affiched *pp.* in ∼ *to* braced against 2036.
afforce *v. refl.* do (one's) best 2181.
af(f)ray *n.* fear 4394.
affraye *v.* in *made me* ∼ attacked me 5489. **afrayed** *pp.* disturbed 6153.
aferd *pp. adj.* afraid 6698.
afrighte *intr. pa. t. sg.* became frightened 2453. *tr.* **afryght** frightened 7232.
after *adv.* later 8; then 57. *prep.* in imitation of 371; according to 646; for 808; by 4005; ∼*þat* as 607; in a manner proportionate to 2218; ∼ *his riht* to fit it 2138-9.
afterward *adv.* secondly 1385; thirdly 2479; ∼ *yit* thirdly 1393.
ageynseyn see **ayensey**.
agilt *pp.* sinned against 5955.
ago(on) *pp.* in *be* ∼ have gone 2731; *ben* . . . ∼ have passed away 1979.
aiourne *imp. sg.* order me to appear (in court) 5991.
al *conj.* although 979; ∼ *were* (*it*) 537; ∼ *be* (*it*) in spite of its being 2263; ∼ *be it þat* however 2240-1.
al *n., adj., adv.* see **al(le)**.
alder *adj. gen. pl.* in *oure* ∼ of all of us 5917.

GLOSSARY 511

aleyes *n. pl.* narrow streets 23.
algates *adv.* all the while 47; nevertheless 356; yet 1472; all the same 1587; anyhow 1960; at all events 1991.
alight *pp.* descended 215.
aliquid see **ad.**
al(le) (It is often impossible to distinguish *n.* from *adv.*, as at 659, 1078, or *adj.* from *adv.*, as at 1130). *n.* everything 145; totality 1622; ~ *togidere* the world as a whole 861; *of* ~ everything 1054; *in* ~ in every way 2043; ~ *togideres* everything at once 2587; (*from*) ~ *to* ~ totally 3938, 4018. *adj.* every 28; ~ *nihtes* every night 6890; ~ *poyntes* 4523 see **poynte.** *adv.* in ~ *ooþerwise,* ~ *ooþerweys* in quite a different way 777n, 1728; intensive in ~ *only* 2514-15 etc.
allegeaunce *n.* relief 1120.
allegge *v.* in *herd* ~ heard given in evidence 607n.
alleggeth *pr. 3 sg.* alleviates 6957.
alleweys see **alweys.**
alliaunce *n.* bond of friendship 5891.
almesse *n.* charity 1084.
almused *pp. adj.* (invented, as if from hypothetical ME *almessan*) distributed as alms 1479.
aloyngne *v. refl.* go far away 3662; **alonygne** 2710n, 2976. **aloyned** *pp.* 5740.
alosed *pp.* esteemed 3991.
alowe *v.* be valued 4076. **alowed** *pp.* recognised 2198.
alowh *adv.* below 1377; low 5507.
alphabeti Lat. *n. gen.* of the alphabet 5833.
als see **as.**
also *adv.* ? in the same way 424.
alþerfirst *adv.* first of all 2470.
alweys *adv.* nevertheless 1812; in every way 3572; **alleweys** 1361.
amase *v.* confuse 3005.
amelle *n.* enamel 123.
amende *v. intr.* reform 627; improve 5184. *tr.* correct 5221. **amended** *pp.* atoned for, forgiven 1385. **amendinge** *vbl. n.* correction 1255.
amyrall *n.* admiral 6555.
ammenuse *v.* decrease 5134.
ammynistrede *pa. t. sg.* dispensed 1451, **aministreden** *pl.* cared for 2957.
amoneste *v.* warn 2850. **amonesteth** *pr. 3 sg.* exhorts 2248. **amonested** *pa. t. pl.* in ~ *me of hem* advised me (to wear) them 2516. **amonestinge** *vbl. n.* counsel 628.
amonges *prep.* in ~ *alle* of all 2324.
ancille *n.* handmaid 5942.
and *conj.* if 78; *and . . . and* both . . . and 7045.
anevelte *n.* anvil 2093.
ang(e)les *n. pl.* fish-hooks 6679.
anglet *n.* small corner 1197.
anything *n.* any 1086.

anything *adv.* at all 324; in any way 2478.
annoy(e) *n.* suffering 1325; harm 6493; **anoye** disturbance 229; irritation 3861; **annoy** 6041.
anoynede *pa. t. sg.* anointed 544.
anoon *adv.* at once 131; suddenly 147; as soon 411; straight 438; now 2074; ~ *after* immediately 110; **anon** 2738.
answere *pr. 1 sg.* explain 1026. **answeringe** *vbl. n.* in *as* ~ in correspondence as it were 618-19.
apayed *pp. adj.* pleased 1781; satisfied 2266; *euel* ~ displeased 2643.
aperceyue(de), aperseyued see **ap(p)erceyue**.
apert *adj.* obvious; *in* ~ plainly 2986.
apertliche *adv.* clearly 923; **apertlyche** 276.
apese *pr. subj. sg.* settle 1391. **apeseth** *imp. pl.* reassure 1950. **appesed** *pa. t. sg.* 1885.
apeshipe *n.* an apelike act 4325.
apparamens *n.* apparel 849.
appare *v.* disguise 2913. **appareth** *pr. 3 sg.* 2883.
apparence *n.* show 1692.
appel *n.* pupil of the eye 1740.
ap(p)erceyue *v.* see 1378; perceive 1750; understand 2442.
apperede *pa. t. sg.* became evident 1964.
appesed see **apese**.
appreeued *pp.* sanctioned 2198; **ap(p)r(o)ved** confirmed (as if a document?) 1962n; witnessed to 6473.
appropred *pa. t. sg.* arrogated 5161.
aqueyntee *n.* friend 76.
aray(e) see **ar(r)ay(e)**.
arayour *n.* craftsman 3525.
araseth *pr. 3 sg.* tears away 5070. **arased** *pp.* obliterated 1389; torn 5077.
arauhte see **areechin**.
arblast *n.* crow-bow, catapult 4611.
areechin *pr. pl.* hold out 5781. **arauhte** *pa. t. sg.* 5776.
areynest *pr. 2 sg.* reproach 3732. **are(y)ned(e)** *pa. t. sg.* interrogated 2593.
aresone *v.* question 1663. **aresoned** *pa. t. sg.* called to account 1628.
argue *v.* accuse 964; prove wrong 1591; **arguen** blame 911. **arguest** *pr. 2 sg.* reproach 1700. **arguinge** *pr. p.* finding fault with 967.
aryed *pp.* brought to shore 6676.
armure *n.* weaponry 5726.
ar(r)ay *n.* magnificence; decoration 216; equipment 1105; clothing 4042.
ar(r)aye *v.* arrange 3527; clothe 3105. *refl.* present myself 4172. **arayeth** *tr. pr. pl.* order 2335. **arraye** *refl. imp. sg.* prepare 7155. **arayed** *pa. t. sg.* decorated 122; well arranged 1478; equipped 2610.
arretten *pr. pl.* attribute 5341.
arryuaile *n.* landing place 6701.
as *rel. pron.* that 2703, 4135n. *adv.* as if 273; ~ *answeringe* corresponding 618-19; *is* ~ *michel to say* ~ means 1275; ~ *for himself* about what is his responsibility 1296; ~ *to regard of* in comparison with 1464; ~ *to*

GLOSSARY

þe body in body 3289-90; ~ who seith so to speak 3729; ~ ayens as is appropriate to 4849; ~ bi myn avys to my mind 5182; ~ of with regard to 5260; ~ bi riht legally 5855; pleonastic in ~ at this time 1940 etc; **als** as 64. **as** *conj.* that 2656.
askepe *v.* escape 222.
asketh *pr. 3 sg.* in þe cas ~ circumstances demand 652-3; ~ *him* questions about 964. **askinge** *pr. p.* asking for 141.
aslewthed *pp.* neglected 6598.
aspye(d) see **espye**.
asquynt *adv.* sidelong 4087; **asqwynt** 6190.
assaye *n.* in to ~ (F *a essai*) for the attempt (on the walls) 196.
assaye *v.* find out 378; try 4338; test 4792; assess 5587. **assayede** *pa. t. sg.* made an effort 2457.
assyse *n.* in þe grete ~ the Last Judgement 5869.
assoile *v.* refute 1744. **assoileth** *pr. 3 sg.* clarifies 4215.
assured *pp.* in ~ *of* recovered from 5502.
astone *v.* stun 1177. **astoned** *pp.* bewildered 2471.
at *prep.* in ~ *his wille* as he pleased 31; as pleased him 778-9; at his disposal 1712; ~ *eye* with (*poss. pron.*) own eyes 195; *preyse* ~ *a bodde* 255-6 see **preyse**; ~ *hir lust* what she likes 1362; ~ *þe fulle* absolutely 1519; ~ *his devys* according to his inclination 1912; ~ (*poss. pron.*) *rihtes* properly 1942; ~ *þe shortest* as briefly 2001; ~ *short wordes* briefly 2485; ~ *alle poyntes* completely 2762; ~ *þe laste* eventually 2805-6; *holde*... ~ *fable* regard as fiction 2992; ~ *þe eerþe* on the ground 3361; ~ *þe e(e)nde* in the end 4073; *at* (*poss.*) *time* when necessary 5702; *at* (*poss.*) *cours* in turn 5725; ~ (*þe, þis*) *neede* in emergency 5877; *sette* ~ 6224, *sette*... ~ *a glooue* 6355 see **sette**; *sitten*... ~ *herte* 6814 see **sitte**.
atamed *pp.* pierced 2431.
ateynt *pp.* in ~ *to þe herte* speechless with rage 2926.
attemprede *pa. t. sg.* restrained 2275. **atempree** *pp.* controlled 2275.
awmenere, awmeneer *n.* almoner 1420.
availe *v.* help; *pr. subj. sg.* in ~ *what* ~ *may* come what may 5191-2.
auale *v.* swallow 2477; **avale** descend 3270. **aualeth** *pr. 3 sg.* sinks 5592.
avaunt *v. refl.* boast 467. **avauntinge** *pr. p. adj.* boastful 4078.
avauntour *n.* boaster 4211.
Aue Marie (for Lat. *ave maria*) Hail Mary (a prayer to the Virgin) 5937.
auenaunt *adj.* well designed 1883; suitable 2811.
avented *pp.* vented 4177.
aventour *n.* vent 4178.
avys *n.* reaction 257; thinking 904; judgement 3238; mind 5182; advice 6160; **avyis** 6159.
avise *v. refl.* consider 1631. *tr.* tell 327; caution 349. **avised** *intr. pp.* explained (to) 579; warned 636. *as adj.* wary 3726.
avisement *n.* counsel 638; *for* ~ in explanation 1761; *bi* ~ 678 see **bi**.
avisiliche *adv.* sensibly 2685; watchfully 4859.
auoir, auoyr, avoir *n.* possessions 1067.
avowe *v.* acknowledge 3923.

awaite *n.* ambush; *ley me in* ~ lie in wait 1249.
awurþe *v.* become; *euele* ~ 1672-3 see **euele**.
ayemaunt *n.* adamant 3065.
ayen *adv.* again 193; (often modifying *v.* as in *counforted* ~ 578, *tolde* ~ 1796, *turne* ~ 2195: see the verbs).
ayenputtinge *vbl. n.* pushing (*sb.*) back 1451.
ayens *prep.* in time for 849; towards 850; against 2789; *mistake* ~ 835-6 see **mistake**; *as* ~ 4849 see **as**.
ayensey *v.* refute 2690; *to yow* . . . ~ argue with you 2689. **ayensseith** *pr. 3 sg.* objects 5152. **ageynseyn** *pl.* attack the validity of 1080. **ayenseyinge** *vbl. n.* complaining, opposition 1276, 6551; **ayenseynge** 1441.
ayenward *adv.* conversely 3406; back again 6899.
axe *v.* ask for 5953.

bachelere *n.* young gentleman 2830.
baconresse *n.* one who flays or smokes (victims) 5074n.
baishtnesse *n.* perplexity 3264.
baleys *n. pl.* switches 3758.
banere *n.* banner; inner sign 136n.
baret *n.* deception 2334; disturbance 2354.
barm *n.* chest, lap; ~ *fell* leather apron 6486.
baselique *n.* basilisk 4459n.
basonettes *n. pl.* bascinets 4029.
baudryk(e) *n.* baldric, sword-belt 2403; **baudrike** 4716.
baundoun *n.* control, power 3349.
beausire fair sire (with irony) 2858; **beawsire** 2824.
bebled *pp.* bloodied 3673.
beede *v.* offer 5943.
beesme *n.* besom, broom 1098; **beseme** 3753.
belygh, beligh *n.* bellows 3956. **belyes** *pl.* 3998; **belies** 4166; **belwes** 4152.
bended *pp. adj.* blindfolded 6150.
Benedicite Lat. bless you! 7026n.
benefet *n.* kindness 582.
benigne, benyngne *adj.* gentle 136; gracious 284.
beringe *vbl. n.* behaviour 3433. **beringes** *pl.* in ~ *up* flatteries 4078.
berne *v.* store in a barn; *made it* ~ 1539 see **make**.
beseme see **beesme**.
betake(n) see **bitake**.
beten *pp. adj.* embroidered 120.
bi *prep.* in 56; according to 375; from 819; with 891; on account of 1143; into 1158; as a result of 1388; ~ *as miche as* because 139; ~ *order* one by one 224; ~ *especial* particularly 522-3; ~ *avisement* with due consideration 678; ~ *riht* rightly 683; ~ *ouht þat I haue herd speke* as far as I know 790-1; ~ *leysere* with deliberation 853-4; ~ *long time* long 1128; ~ *hire rihtes* as is her due 1362-3; ~ *likenesse* as follows 1594; ~ *sum wey* somehow 1673-4; ~ *defaute of* without 1675; ~ *þin*

GLOSSARY

oth honestly 1705; ~ *resoun* logically 1725-6; ~ *couenaunt* on (such) terms 1990; ~ *swich condicioun* in that case 2076; ~ *no wey* at all 2620; ~ *semblaunt* in appearance 2815; ~ *existence* in reality 2920; ~ *felonye* wrongly 2922; *sette þe lasse* ~ 3018 see **sette**; ~ *certeyn avys* with sure judgement 3238; ~ *accident* 3315n; ~ *þere* where 3459; ~ *yowre wille* with your permission 3484-5; ~ *so michel* to that extent 3749; ~ *þe morwe* in the morning 3851; ~ *þe eerþe* along the ground 3940; ~ *no wey* under no circumstances 4205; ~ *no wise* in no way 4242; ~ *my folage* 4390n; ~ *me* with my help 4441; *as* ~ *myn avys* in my opinion 5182; *as* ~ *riht* 5885; ~ *gesse* without due consideration 6129; ~ *þat oone side* on one side 6806; **by** in ~ *especial* particularly 4369-70. **bi** *conj.* ~ *þat þat* since 5209.
bicchede *pp. adj.* cursed 4557.
bidropped *pp.* sprinkled 1962.
bigge *v.* buy 5326. **bouhte** *pa. t. sg.* bought 5950.
biggere *n.* buyer 5324.
bigile *v.* wile away time 6374.
bigilouresse *n.* female deceiver 3010n.
bihated *pp.* detested 167.
biheetinge, beheighten, bihight see **bihoote.**
biholdinge *vbl. n.* gaze 65; attention 1748; perception 2738; mind 6199; appearance 7160.
biho(o)te *pr. 1 sg.* promise 1258. **biheetinge** *pr. p.* 7262. **bihyghte** *pa. t. sg.* 3943. **biheighten** *pl.* 445. **bihight, bihyght** *pp.* 1888. **bihotinge** *vbl. n.* 5289.
biknowe *pr. 1 sg.* acknowledge 6658. **bikneewe** *pa. t. sg.* 2388.
bilefte *pa. t. sg.* remained behind 3078. **bileevinge** *vbl. n.* remainder 7173n.
bilymed *pp.* caught with bird-lime 3785.
bille *n.* judgement (in court) 5892n; petition 5943.
bimeene *v. intr.* feel regret 3393. **bimenynge** *pr. p.* lamenting 116.
bineme *v.* take away 337. **binemen** *pl.* deprive 1018. **binome** *pp.* 5463.
bipleyne *v.* mourn 3706.
biscorn *n.* two-horned beast 4107n.
bisiliche *adv.* fervently 1071; minutely 1834; carefully 2264; eagerly 2487; **bisyliche** solicitously 297.
bisorwede *pa. t. sg.* regretted 2455.
bitake *pp.* given 3114; **bitake(n), betaken** in *yuele* ~, *euele* ~ wretchedly placed 2191, 2652, 5631.
bithinke *v. refl.* bear in mind 331; reflect 633. *pr. 1 sg.* remember 876. **bithouht(e)** *pa. t. sg.* remembered 110; thought 707; **bithowhte** 4999. **bithouht** *pp.* in *was* ~ *of hire* called her to mind 1565.
bitimes, bitymes *adv.* early 3194; *al* ~ all in good time 757; in plenty of time 2500.
biyo(u)nde *n.* in *þe wey of* ~ the wrong path 3728. *adj.* in *þe wey* ~ 3756; *þe londe of* ~ the other world 6924. *prep.* in ~ (*þe*) *see* on the other side of the sea (of the world) 3539, 3601.
blak *adj.* in ~ *abbeye* Benedictine abbey 5267.

blame *v.* find fault with 964; reprove 1591; censure 1694. **blamed** *pp.* reproached 1589.
blecched *pp. adj.* blackened 4002.
bleederes *n. pl.* those who bleed, martyrs 1979.
bleynte *pa. t. sg.* ducked, foiled attack 6226.
blynde *n.* blind thing 3330; purblind 4040; *pl.* blind people 6277.
blisse *v.* bless; *made* ∼ *me* (see **make**). **blisseth** *imp. pl.* in ∼ *yow* cross yourselves 6168. **blissedest** *pa. t. 2 sg.* blessed 395. **blissede** *3 sg.* made the sign of the cross on 283.
blow *interj.* pshaw! 4302n.
bobaunce *n.* boast 5917.
bocherye *n.* slaughter-house 4569.
bodde see **preyse**.
bodiliche *adv.* physically 1768.
boistous *n.* one who limps 3855. *boistouse pl.* those who limp 4039. *adj.* coarse (F *drus*) 2140; violent 6219; stubborn 7083; **boystows** 4862.
bokeler(e) *n.* shield 36, 2446n. **bokeleres** *pl.* 6520.
bole *n.* bull 5607.
bolt *n.* arrow from a cross-bow 3785.
book *pa. t. sg.* baked 1574.
boongree mawgree *adv. phr.* whether (you) like it or not 5448.
boord *n.* table 305.
bordoun see **burdoun**.
bot *pa. t. sg.* bit 4697.
boþes *n*, in *youre boþes* both your 5916.
bouche *n.* hump 5424; a back-pack (hump) 5426; **bowche** 5415, 5418.
bouched *pp.* humped 5592, 6408; in ∼ *biside here rule* perverted from their Rule (lit. crooked along their ruler) 5441; **bowched** spiritually deformed 5419; **bowchede** perverted (lit. lumpy) 5421. **bouched** *pp. adj.* hump-backed (owing to a back-pack) 5456; **bouchinge** *vbl. n.* opening, mouthing, bulging 5560n.
bouchede *n. pl.* hump-backed people 5439, 5443n.
bowke *v.* soak 1134. **bowkinge** *vbl. n.* solution 1133n; **bowkynge** 6066.
bounde *n.* boundary 835.
bounde *v.* make a boundary round 932. **boundeth** *pr. 3 sg.* restricts 931.
bountee *n.* good breeding 133; virtue 2327; grace 5940; kindness 7222; **bowntee** 5899.
bowe *n.* rain-bow 7173.
bras *n.* brass 1201n; copper (or brass) coins 4866.
bred(de) see **brode**.
brede *n.* breadth 4313.
bredinge see **brode**.
breketh *pr. 3 sg.* destroys 5070.
brenne *v.* burn 5202; burn at the stake 6210.
brybes *n. pl.* bribes/pieces of bread 5215.
bridel *n.* bit; *shake his* ∼ be impatient 3068. **brydel** in *rounginge on my* ∼ chafing at my bit 4836n.
broche *n.* prick 4732; prickle, spear 4742. **broches** *pl.* spines 4730.

GLOSSARY

brode *v.* breed (interest) 5133n. **bredde** *pa. t. sg.* incubated 3995. **bred** *pp.* 3994. **bredinge** *vbl. n.* incubation 3996.
bronnched *pp. adj.* crouched 5637.
brose *v.* smash 1158. *pr. 1 sg.* crush 1113. **brusede** *pp. adj.* as *n.* afflicted people 294. **brosed** *pp.* broken 1155; **brused** 1546.
bulte *v.* sift 1553.
bultel *n.* garment of loosely-woven cloth (of the kind used for sifting) 4863.
burdoun *n.* pilgrim's staff 111; **bordoun** 114.
burgh *n.* country place 1558; *in* ~ *or in toun* anywhere 1558-9.
buryelles *n.* tomb 4293. **buryell** 3146n.
but *conj.* and indeed 1n; except 176; only 409; unless 442; indeed 574; rather 1520; on the contrary 1682; *non* ~ *passe* no one who did not go in 47; ~ *only* except 88; ~ *if* unless 93; ~ *þat* unless 1077; as long as 2098; ~ *of so michel* except to say 2179; but that 2385; intensive in ~ ... *oonliche* 1503-4; *nis* ~ is only; pleonastic in ~ *of as michel* except insofar 3030; ~ *algates* yet 5373.
butour *n.* pelican/bittern 5608n.

caliouns, caliown(e)s *n. pl.* flints 4758.
camen see **come**.
can see **kunne**.
canoun *n.* Canon Law 1643n.
canst see **kunne**.
care *n.* in *of gret* ~ burdened by work 3522.
careful *adj.* fearful 4818.
careynes see **karayne**.
carmen Lat. *n.* song 4741n; poem 5833.
carolle *pr. 1 sg.* dance (and/or sing) in a circle 6356.
cas *n.* situation 652. *pl.* (F *les cas, divers cas*) matters 616; circumstances 626.
caste(n) *v.* shoot 2242; put forth 3231; spit 4457; emit 4758; ~ *hire chere* look 131; ~ *out* rescue 1334; release 1853. **caste** *pr. 1 sg.* in ~ *out* emit 4179. **kaste** *pa. t. sg.* pulled 3521; **kast** in ~ *out* released 5809. **cast** *pp.* in ~ *out* cleansed 1269; ~ *on* turned towards 4537.
cause *n.* adequate reason 414; reason 443; a court case 594; the originator 1535; *suich* ~ something having such an effect 1778; *for* ~ *of* by 1870; *for* ~ *of necessite* of necessity 6268-9; *for* ~ for the sake of 7174.
caused *pp.* given cause; *þou were þanne* ~ you would then have been justified 2571-2.
ceened *pa. t. sg.* dined 1290.
cene *n.* (Last) Supper 1290.
certeyn *adj.* particular 443; reliable 1242; *for* ~ assuredly 1621; *in* ~ confidently 3683; surely 5627-8. *adv.* indeed 58; certainly 180; in fact 1041.
certes *adv.* indeed 5861; certainly 5888.
cesse *v.* stop 956; *maden* ~ interrupted 449. *subj. sg.* in ~ *of* abandon 2851.

ÞE LYFE OF ÞE MANHODE

chayere *n.* the front of the raised chancel 579n; throne 1572.
chambere(re) see **chaumberere**.
chamberleynes *n. pl.* chamberlains 512n.
chambre see **chaumbre**.
chambrere see **chaumberere**.
champyoun, cha(u)mpioun(s) see **chaumpioun**.
chanownes *n. pl.* Canons Regular of St Augustine 59.
charbuncle *n.* ruby 1879; **charboncle** 6025; **charbouncle** 6123.
charge *v.* load 3375; ~ *it with* impose on it 625. *pr. 1 sg.* direct 1497. **charged** *pp.* imposed 685; weighed down 6250.
chasteleyne *n.* castellan 6903.
chaufest *pr. 2 sg.* warm 3121.
chaumberere *n.* handmaid 923; **chamb(e)rere** 928, 1138.
chaumbre *n.* residence 1239; **chambere** room 1439; **chambre** 1089.
chaumpe *n.* background 1964.
chaumpioun *n.* athlete (representing his lord?) 255n; warrior 2525; **champion** combatant 396; **champyoun** champion (representing a nobleman in single combat) 1658. **cha(u)mpiouns** *pl.* 41, 293.
chaunge *n.* in *make ~ of* exchange 5316.
chaunge *v.* ? transform (by art or alchemy), ? exchange 3547.
cheer(e) *n.* expression 817; *she made me ~ þat* she looked as if 5502; *to which men ouhten make good ~* who should be welcomed 7075-6; **chere** in *caste hire ~* 131 see **caste**.
cheere *adj.* cherished 1336; *þe more ~ I haue hem* the more I love them 4574; **chier** in *þou haddest wel ~* you admired 7260.
cheerliche *adv.* carefully 1293.
cheertee *n.* charity; *holt in ~* 1316 see **holde**.
cheese(n) *v.* distinguish 599; **chees** *pa. t. sg.* chose 6763; **ches** 5941. **chose(n)** *pp. adj.* in *most ~* choicest 2324. **cheesinge** *vbl. n.* choice 3604.
cheke(e)r *n.* chess 3438; Exchequer/game of chess 4916n.
chere see **cheer(e)**.
cherl *n.* peasant 2772.
cherliche *adj.* stubborn, ignorant 4278.
chevachyes *n. pl.* cavalry raids 4028.
cheuentayn, cheuenteyn *n.* commander 4027; leading letter 5264.
cheuesaunce *n.* sustenance 5375; **cheuishaunce** means of control 3847.
chevice *v. refl.* provide for (oneself) 3550.
chide *v.* give vent to anger 821; quarrel 891; complain 980; *to yow . . . to ~* to rebuke you 823; *~ to* rebuke 961. **chideth** *imp. pl.* 989. **chidde** *pa. t. sg.* in *~ to me* rebuked me 1496; *~ with me* complained loudly against me 1585.
chidere *n.* scold 920.
chylde *v.* bear a child 885. **chyldinge** *vbl. n.* bearing of a child 883.
chyldhode *n.* extreme youth 2560; childish occupation 4908; youth 6126. **chyldhodes** *pl.* childish exploits 4021n.
cite *v.* summon (to appear in court) 3050.
cleer *adj.:* bright; **cleere** 5921.

GLOSSARY 519

cleyme *pr. 1 sg.* call 5214.
clepe summon 179; call 683; call on 1014; describe 1523; **clepen** calle 620. **clepinge** *pr. p.* calling 885. *vbl. n.* summons 2952.
clerk *n.* scholar 1590. **clerkes** *pl.* scholars 60; clerics 2668.
cleue *v.* split 5435; **clyve** 4045.
clogge *n.* block of wood (tied to an animal to restrain it) 5046.
clogged *pp. adj.* restrained by a block of wood 5045.
cloystreres *n. pl.* monastics 6860.
clomben see **cloumben**.
cloos *n.* city wall 98; **clos** 4636.
close *v.* enclose 3621. **closeth** *pr. 3 sg.* encloses 500.
closure *n.* enclosure 489; *vnder litel* ~ within small confines 1580.
cloþes *n. pl.* table-cloths, altar-cloths 528.
cloumben *pa. t. pl.* climbed 70. **clomben** *pp.* 4322; **clumben** 7231.
clout *n.* piece of fabric, rag 4216n. **cloutes** *pl.* rags 4863; patches 5224.
clouted *pp.* mended 4863.
clumben see **cloumben**.
coadiutowres *n. pl.* assistants 524.
coife *v.* put a covering over, hood 4357.
cokard *n.* simpleton 3020.
cokardy *n.* stupidity 3566.
colee *n.* stroke made with the flat of a sword (as in the dubbing of a knight) 6792.
coleyinge see **koleye**.
colys *n.* clear meat broth 4603.
collacioun *n.* edifying lecture 5417.
coltes *n. pl.* young animals 468.
coluber Lat. *n.* a snake 4675.
coluer *n.* pigeon (dove) 3146; **culuer** dove 6827.
comaundinge *vbl. n.* in *in* ~ as an order ?2849.
come(n) *v.* come; *fulliche* ~ get all the way 109; *do* ~ 246 see **do**; ~ þere as þow art approach you 401; ~ *neer (nyh)* approach 453; ~ *to* end in 472; *to what end I shulde* ~ what I should achieve 694; ~ *þer ny(g)h* approach it 1283; ~ ... *þerto(o)* reach 2029-30; overtake it 6727. **cometh** *pr. 3 sg.* in ~ *to my lust* takes my fancy 1047; ~ *not so to knowleche* is not for this reason apparent 5092-3; *it* ~ *hire of kynde* it is her nature 5353; *w(h)ennes* ~ *it yow* 824, 869, 2784-5, *whens* ~ *it þat* 2768, *whens þis* ~ *yow* 5786-7 see **w(h)ennes**. **come** *subj. sg.* in ~ *fulliche* to reach 180; ~ *to my lust* takes my fancy 960; *þat euele passioun* ~ *to hire* a plague on her 4412. *pl.* in ~ *þei raþe*, ~ *þei late* sooner or later 4969; **comen** should come 5601. **come** *pa. t. 2 sg.* came 1646; *euele* ~ *þou here* it was a bad day for you when you came here 4546-7; **com** *3 sg.* in ~ *upon* attacked 4394; ~ *me* entered me 5496. **kamen** *pl.* came 1457. **comynge** *vbl. n.* in ~ *out* origin 733; ~ foorth 3234.
commissarye *n.* representative (of Grace) 2854.
committe *pr. 1 sg.* entrust 2621. *pl.* commission 6533; **comitte** 6529. **committede** *pa. t. sg.* gave the authority 3237.
commune *adj.* shared 564; public 565; general 987; generally accepted 1714; generally available 5158; *al* ~ universal 7246.

communion *n.* spiritual fellowship 1858.
competent *adj.* suitable 2852.
compleyne *v.* lament 1115.
comprehendeth *pr. 3 sg.* includes (both) 5287.
conclude *v.* convince 1738.
concreto Lat. *n.* in *in* ~ in reality 5695.
condicioun *n.* nature 3153; quality 3227; status 3678; state 4666; *bi swich* ~ 2076 see **bi. condiciouns** *pl.* attributes (tools of the trade) 4268.
condyt *n.* duct (for blood or air) 3365.
conduye *v.* guide 6629.
conduyeresse *n.* ruler 6745; **condyeresse** 4027.
conferme *v.* prove 1007. **confermed** *pp.* ratified (it) 1409.
confused *pp. adj.* frustrated 2314.
confusioun *n.* error 472; humiliation 2684; pudenda/mock embarrassment 4173n; disgrace 5851; *put to* ~ destroyed 3037.
congruitee *n.* correctness 288n.
conquere *v.* gain 251; obtain 5301. **conqueredest** *pa. t. 2 sg.* won 393.
conscience *n.* remorse 1174n; heart 1238.
consideratioun *n.* attention 1166.
constablesse *n.* controller 4028.
constreyneth *pr. 3 sg.* impels 2332. **constreyned** *pa. t. sg.* urged 5472.
continue *imp. sg.* in ~ *on us þi* . . . *eyen* go on looking after us 5921.
contract *pp. adj.* paralysed 3148.
contracte *n.* burden (helpless body) 3350n, 3383
contrarie, contrarye *n.* opposite 659; difficulty 3405; opponent 3406; *remeved to þe* ~ rescinded 2941.
contrarie, contrarye *adj.* harmful 238; in opposition 7115; *al* ~ completely backwards 6205.
contrarye *v.* resist 3409.
contrarious *adj.* damaging 810.
contricioun *n.* (with both literal 'battering' and metaphorical 'remorse' connotations) contrition 1113n; ~ . . . *make of* 1152, *make of* . . . ~ 1165-6 crush (it).
contrite *pr. 1 sg.* crush (it) 1146n. *pp.* crushed (contrite) 1132; **contrit** in *make* ~ crush 1168; **contryte** 1184.
conuersioun *n.* transformation (Transubstantiation) 787.
conuerte *v.* turn away 2333; turn 5137; change (his) attitude 6057. *refl.* in ~ *hem* be converted 3036; ~ *þee* change your mind 5773. **conuerted** *tr. pp.* turned my attention 1224.
conuoye *v.* convey 5392.
corage *n.* mind 713; heart 5753; *meeved al mi* ~ 1946 see **meeved.**
corn *n.* grain 804.
corownement *n.* crowning 2162.
correcte *v.* punish 615; overrule, eradicate 5872n.
corteynes *n. pl.* bed-curtains; *leyn in* ~ slept in the curtained beds 3821.
coste *v.* skirt 6167. **costinge** *pr. p.* following 3717; **costynge** skirting 6244. **costed** *pa. t. sg.* ran alongside 3515.
costlewe *adj.* costly 3113.

GLOSSARY

cowchen v. in ~ *him* lay him to rest 5451.
cowde(st), cowþe see **kunne**.
cowuele see **kowuele**.
coude, coudest see **kunne**.
counfort n. help 2536; **coumfort** 7063.
counforte(n) v. assist 4506; **comforte** 6886; ~ *ayen* ease 2639, **coumforteth** pr. 2 sg. rests 1898. **coumforte** imp. sg. in ~ þee relax 1952. **counforted** pp. in ~ *ayen* reassured 578.
countenaunce n. behaviour 3522, 3574; expression 4089; bearing 4723; **cuntenaunce** composure 2190.
counterfete v. assume 4564; dissemble 5231. **counterfetinge** pr. p. pretending 4327. **counterfeted** pp. adj. defective 3148.
counterpeis n. the equivalent 7013.
courbe adj. crippled 7135.
courreyinge pr. p. adj. good for improving things by beating 1097n.
cours n. course 6089; *at here* ~ 5725 see **at**.
courseth pr. *3 sg.* condemns 1248.
couenable adj. appropriate 2302; good 2943; suitable 6968.
couent n. monastery 7272.
couertour n. covering 5697; **couerture** 2876.
crabbe n. in ~ *tree* crab apple tree 2773n.
craft n. job 2658; skill 3549; function 4393. **craftes** pl. 1279.
criaunce n. in *in ful* ~ fully believing 5894.
crye v. complain 981; cry out 1119; squeak 4358. pr. *1 sg.* in *I* ~ (*yow*) *mercy* I beg (your) pardon 200. **cryede** pa. t. sg. in *I* ~ *to God mercy* begged God for mercy 6629. **icryed** pp. lamented 2539. **cryinge** vbl. n. lamentation 3920; outcry 4224.
Cristene adj. Christian 1856.
croce n. cross 6371; **croos** crosier 4923; **crois** Cross 5893; *make a* ~ *to cross* (myself) 3657.
crochet n. hook 4875.
cro(o)ked(e) see **crooke**.
crook n. hook 4616.
crooke pr. *1 sg.* distort 4620. **cro(o)ked(e)** pp. adj. hook-shaped 279; rude 2804; misshapen 3004; crooked (like a shepherd's crook) 4561; bent 5232; wrong 5903; sinuous 4676; **krookede** 4925.
crosse v. make the sign of the Cross on 250. **crossed** pp. adj. in *seyl* ~ set sail (making a Cross-shape) 6746.
croume n. the soft part of a loaf 865.
croumed(e) pp. adj. crumbled 56n, 6826n.
cumpany n. in *into* ~ as a companion 555.
cumpasede pa. t. sg. fashioned 1880.
cuntenaunce see **countenaunce**.
cuntre n. territory 3428; *bi* ~ overland 4803; *þe* ~ *aboue* heaven 6262.
cuppe n. chalice 518.
curat n. an ecclesiastic responsible for the spiritual welfare of another ecclesiastic 771.

cure *n.* authority 1655; *of swiche I have no* ~ I have no liking for those 177; ~ *of* desire for 490, liking for 1238; *take him in* ~ look after him 5437; *of no wiht hath* ~ has no liking for anyone 6901.
curen *v.* remove 1205. **cureth** *pr. 3 sg.* treats 1219.
currowres *n. pl.* couriers 7056.
cursede *n.* cursed woman 6200. *pl.* wicked people 1448.
cursinge *vbl. n.* excommunication 630n.
curteys *adj.* refined 4169; considerate 7142. **curteis** as *n.* courteous man 785.
curteysye, curteisye *n.* kindness 1653; *doon* ~ show consideration 5203.
curteisliche *adv.* in *wel* ~ with great dignity 1099-1100.
customableche *adv.* habitually 2433.
custome *n.* in *leese hire* ~ deviate from her usual practice 811. **customes** *pl.* usual habits 873.
customed *pp.* in *hadde not* ~ was not used 2454; *I haue* ~ *to sakke* I have been used to putting in my sack 5553.
customere *n.* frequenter 401.

day *n.* daylight 3268; *no* ~ 334 see **no**; *þis* ~ today 583. **dayes** *pl.* in ~ *of youre lyue* all your lives 441.
dart *n.* point 2240; thrust 2749; spear 5494.
daunger *n.* hesitation 789; arrogance 1400; ~ ... *make* object 2676-7; *in any ooþeres* ~ under obligation to anyone else 2955; **daungere** difficulty 96; **dawngere** power 64.
daungerous *adj.* particular 2265; difficult 2841. as *n. pl.* the sick difficult to treat 1287.
debonaire, debonayre *adj.* gentle 332; friendly 920. as *n.* kindly one 1108, gracious lady 5839.
debonairliche *adv.* meekly 1319.
debonayrtee *n.* graciousness 5787.
declyn *n.* in *putte it al in* ~ overthrow it completely 7244-5.
decoccioun *n.* in ~ *of heete* changing (its) nature by boiling 7189.
decoloured *pp. adj.* in *wel* ~ cut very low at the neck 4035.
dede *n.* death; attributive in ~ *beddes* deathbeds 295.
dediedest *pa. t. sg.* dedicated 395.
dedlich *adj.* mortal 1397; ~ *skyn* perishable leather 2383.
dedliche *adv.* mortally 629; *al* ~ (F *tout mortement*) very sadly 1792; **dedly** mortally 176.
dee *n.* die (*sg.* of dice) 2013.
def *adj.* empty; *a* ~ *note* an empty nut 5505n.
deface *v.* do away with 780. **defaced** *pp.* obliterated 1389; sullied 2999.
defamowse *adj.* dreadful 1135.
defaute *n.* lack 1051; error 1073; fault 4097; *bi* ~ *of* 1675 see **bi**; *put in* ~ 6964 see **putte**; **defawte** 5808. **defautes** *pl.* sins 4097; needs 6855.
defence *n.* prohibition 2938; *made* ~ *þat non took* forbade anyone to carry 2952.
defended *pa. t. sg.* forbade 413.

GLOSSARY 523

defensable *adj.* fortified 6753.
deffye *subj. sg.* may treat with contempt 4026.
defouled *pp.* disfigured 1914; tormented 2590; defiled 5493; trodden in a wine-press 6483; trampled on 6635.
degree *n.* level 1395; *gret* ~ exalted position 4322. **degrees** *pl.* rungs 70; steps 6816; *in alle* ~ in every respect 3217.
deingne, deygne, deyn(gn)e *v.* think (it) proper 3145. **deyned** *pp.* thought it proper 4250.
deyntees *n. pl.* delights; *his* ~ *he maketh* he takes delight in 2106.
del *n.* part; *leueth not* ~ do not leave anything out 998.
delitable *adj.* delightful 569.
delitous *adj.* delightful 3113.
deliuere *v.* give 2954, 5569. *refl.* in ~ *him of* discharge his duty towards 531-2; *shortliche to* ~ *me* the long and the short of it is 2484; *I would* ~ *me* I should like to leave 7239. **deliuerede** *tr. pa. t. sg.* provided 866. **deliuered** *pp.* satisfied 532; ~ *to* in the power of 4815.
delt *pp.* in ~ *about* distributed 6029.
demaundes *n. pl.* questions 7265.
dene see **eerþe.**
departe *v.* open up 606; distribute 5026; *from him ye must* ~ you must leave it 490; ~ *of* distribute 1084; ~ ... *out of* emerge from 4447. **departeth** *pr. 3 sg.* marks out 502; separates 837. *refl.* in ~ *hire from* leaves 5764. *tr.* **departede** *pa. t. sg.* distributed 3510. **departed** *pp.* taken 6339; ~ *yow* distributed among you 584-5. **departinge** *vbl. n.* divorce 442; opening up 604; **departynge** separation 2408.
departere *n.* distributor 1434.
deposed *pp.* put down, demoted 4318.
depriued *pp.* excluded 5979.
desceyte *n.* deception 1695; *withoute* ~ exactly 1618; **desceite** in *withoute* ~ free of any mistake 1916; **disceyte** concealment 1303.
deserue *v.* perform 526. **deserueth** *pr. 3 sg.* executes 590. **deseruede** *pa. t. sg.* in *neuere* ~ *I to yow* I have never deserved from you 5778.
despyt(e), despite *n.* contempt 962; insult 2494; resentment 4451; *do* ~ *to* defy 4446; *dooth to God* ~ disobeys God 5318; *in* ~ *of* despite 5699.
despoile see **dispoile.**
despreise *v.* disparage 6742.
destroyinge *vbl. n.* in *bi* ~ as a result of the suppression 1388.
deveer, deueir see **deuoir.**
deuynale *n.* something to be divined, a riddle 1697.
deuocioun *n.* desire 3377.
deuoir, devoir, devoyr, deveer, deueir *n.* duty 1021; best 3743.
dide(n), didest see **do.**
diffamacioun *n.* dishonour 5705.
diffame *v.* slander 4599.
difference *n.* distinction 2874.
dight *pp.* adorned 159.
digneliche *adv.* in the proper manner 1288.
dimes, dymes *n. pl.* tithes 405.

dine v. eat 527. **dyned** pp. eaten 1083.
diner, dyner(e) n. the meal 531n.
disalowe v. denigrate 6742.
disceyte see **desceyte.**
discerne v. distinguish 600; judge 606; perceive 908. **discerned** pp. distinguished 465.
disceuered pp. separated 1542.
discharge v. unburden 680.
disclosed pp. hatched 3997n; exposed 4296.
discomfyt see **discoumfyte.**
discomfort n. discouragement; haue ~ of feel discouraged by 2016.
disconfort see **discoumforte.**
discordinge pr. p. adj. incompatible 2510.
discoumfyte v. defeat 2074. **discomfyt** pp. 6318; **discounfited** discouraged 2636.
discoumforte, disconfort v. refl. be uneasy 1951; be dismayed 3968. **discounforted** pa. t. sg. disturbed 30; alarmed 217. **discounforted** tr. pp. 561; **discomforted** 6234; in pain 7210.
discrecioun n. discernment 593; sound judgement 61.
discreteliche adv. with discernment 682; **discretliche** 921.
disdeynowes adj. contemptuous 4056.
disencresen v. deprive 5276.
disese n. discomfort 2468; dide ~ harmed 3029; men don it any ~ he is harmed at all 3033.
disgise(e), disgysee adj. new-fangled 1606; extraordinary 1609; strange 4842; elaborately prepared 5522; **disgisy** obscure 2655; misleading 3009; **disguysee** monstrous 4715.
disgisyliche adv. horribly 1544n.
disguised pp. malformed 4858, 6171.
dishoneste adj. unreasonable 1807.
disioynct pp. adj. in ~ ... is sawen (F est desjointe et sciee) cut apart 4780.
diskeuere v. display 2392.
disordeynee adj. wrong 2356.
disparpoylinge vbl. n. dispersion 4156.
dispende v. pay out 4989. **dispendeth** pr. 3 sg. consumes 5218.
dispendere n. treasurer 5103.
dispense n. sustenance 5079.
dispense(e)r(e) n. distributor 1420; almoner 6020; treasurer 6028.
dispitous adj. haughty 1399.
displeasaunce n. in hath ~ is offended 3033-4.
displese v. refl. be offended; of nothing ye ~ yow you are not offended at all 2467. tr. offend 977. **displeseth** pr. 3 sg. offends 1596. **displesed** pa. t. sg. in ~ to angered 386; **displesede** upset 1946.
dispoile v. refl. strip 1329; **despoile** 97. tr. 404; make ~ 849. **dispoylinge** vbl. n. taking (it) off 2151.
disporteresse n. entertainer 6838.
disseyuable adj. misleading 2499.

GLOSSARY

disseueringe *pr. p.* isolating 501.
dissolute *adj.* weakened 6723.
dist see **do**.
distracte *adj.* confused 2023.
disturbaunce *n.* hindrance 2784.
diuerse *adj.* various 626; differing 646; different 1199; several 1748; vicious 3149; **diuers** unusual (F3838 *desguisee*) 2091; disagreeable 2809.
diuers(e)liche *adv.* differently 2386.
divinynge *vbl. n.* consultation of augury; *goinge* ~ having resort to guesswork 1619.
diuise, divise *v.* suggest 1790; explain 4728; ~ *to* (F *diviser . . . du*) ? contemplate, describe 2663; **diuisen** in ~ *of* consider 314. **diuisede** *pa. t. sg.* in ~ *of* described 1943; ~ . . . *myself* talked to myself 2626. *pp.* **diuised, divised** explained 1304.
do(n), doo(ne) *v.* administer 341; cause 5529; behave 4683n; ~ *come bring* 246; *I should* ~ *riht gret wysdom* it would be as well 267; ~ *his jugement* give sentence 607-8; *to* ~ to be done 660; *maketh* ~ 810 see **make**; ~ *to me homage* be grateful to me 924; ~ . . . *awey* remove 956; *leue to* ~ neglect 990; ~ *almesse* give alms 1263; ~ *sum abstinence* abstain a while 1265; ~ . . . *peyne* do penance 1276; *maad* ~ 1322 see **make**; ~ *so miche* make sure 1402; *in* . . . ~ put in 1562-3; ~ *awey* put an end to 1914; *with which I shulde* ~ *me profyte best* which would be most use to me 2086; ~ . . . *þi pleyn wille* do what you think best 2176; ~ *it upon* put it on over 2213-14; ~ *on* put on 2217; ~ *so* behave like that 2396; ~ *þi wurshipe* gain honour 2420; *her plesaunce* ~ please her 2456; ~ *hem of* take them off 2470; *of* . . . ~ take off 2588; ~ *þe to wite* prove to you 2819-20; ~ *peyne* try hard 2939; *litel* ~ *with* have small use for 2948; ~ *yow good* help you 2982; ~ *him his ese* soothe him 3120; ~ *him disese* hurt him 3140-1; ~ *þee riht* give you justice 3442; *counfort you shulden* ~ *me* you would give me peace of mind 3483-4; *hath to* ~ *with* has use for 3760; *it wolde nothing* ~ it would not move 4164-5; ~ *his miht* pit his strength 4254; ~ *at my wille* do what I like 4339; ~ *him lettinge* hinder him 4681; ~ *so michel toward* so succeed in (petitioning) 5797; ~ *from þee* remove from you 5801; ~ . . . *from* separate 6385; ~ *my message* perform my errand 7066. *pr. 1 sg.* in ~ *him (un)wurshipe* (dis)honour him 5010-11. **doost** *2 sg.* in ~ *þe vicarishipe* are the representative 362; ~ *as þe wise* are a wise man 2716; ~ *me lettinge* hinder me 3902. **dooth** *3 sg.* ~ *þee nothing* is no use to you 2054-5; ~ *his profyt with* takes advantage of 2102. ~ *businesse* devotes herself to 5133; ~ *al his entente* tries hard 6290; **do(o)n** *pl.* find 2102; ~ *me despyt* show me contempt 966; ~ *to wite* mean 1379-80; ~ . . . *encumbraunce* hinder, restrict 2506; ~ *me counfort of* ease 5781. **do** *subj. sg.* should do 6872. **do(o)** *pl.* ~ *no foly* do not do anything stupid 163; ~ *we* let's work 4649; ~ . . . *shame* humiliate 5476; ~ *we peyne* let's be careful 5479. **dooth** *imp. pl.* in ~ *me to haue* give me 1824; ~ . . . *execucioun* carry out 2839. **doynge, doinge** *pr. p.* in ~ *away* getting rid of 2144. **dide** *pa. t. 1, 3 sg.* gave 118, put 1994; *fulliche* ~ completed 543; *so michel I* ~ I had such an

ÞE LYFE OF ÞE MANHODE

effect 1124; ~ *so michel* was so successful 1571; *so miche we* ~ we achieved the result 3349-50: ~ *þerwith* used it 5491; ~ *not my iorney* did not make my journey 6131; ~ *hire couenaunt* kept her promise 6593. **didest** *2 sg. so michel þow* ~ you were so successful 1647; **dist** 1162. **dide(n)** *pl.* put 530; caused 1957; behaved 2997; ~ *miche ayens* greatly offended 884; *so michel* ~ succeeded 1966-7; *so miche we* ~ we achieved the result 3349-50. **dide** *subj. sg.* in ~ *me of of* took me away from 3329. **do(one)** *pp.* committed 1222; put to death 1851; caused 2609; left 2615; taken 5031; acted 5411; performed 6603; *had* ~ *it awey* removed it 953; *maad* ~ 1322 see **make**; ~ *of* stripped from 1542-3; *so michel* ~ managed to arrange 1613; ~ *it* ensured 1614; ~ *out* removed 4775; **idoo** 706; **ydoon** 4199. **do(o)inge** *vbl. n.* behaviour 968; function 1299; ~ *of þe execucioun* imposing the penalty 593-4; *of yuel* ~ malicious 1045; *wel* ~ generosity 4093; **doinges** *pl.* actions 1700; activities 4393; *of* ~ in behaviour 2998.

doble *adj.* in *in* ~ *partye* in two 617.

doctours *n. pl.* learned churchmen 54.

doinge(s), doyinge, do(one), doost, dooth see **do.**

doluen *pa. t. pl.* dug 4957.

dore *v.* dare 1689. **durst** *pr. 2 sg.* 3824. **durre** *3 sg.* 6531. **dorre** *subj. sg.* 6716. **durste** *pa. t. sg.* dared 1477; (as *subj. sg.*) 2599; **durste, dorste** 995, 4961.

dortour *n.* dormitory (of a convent or monastery) 6805.

dortowrere, dortorere *n.* chambermaid 5664, 6893.

dote *v.* lose (one's) reason 7127. **doted** *pp.* out of (your) mind 902; stupid 1502; ~ *hire* made her senile 1587; **dotede** (as *n.*) senile old woman 7117.

doubled *pp.* given two parts 2297. *pp. adj.* consisting of two parts 2303.

doubleliche *adv.* in two different ways 5312.

doun *adv.* at the bottom 1373.

dounward *prep.* down the side of 75; down in 6609.

doute *pr. 1 sg.* in *I* ~ *not . . . ne* I am quite sure 499; **dowte** *imp. sg.* in ~ *not þat þat ne* you can be certain that 373-4.

doutows *adj.* vague 153.

drauht *n.* move (in a board-game) 4540; hooking movement 5092.

drawe *v.* pull 3874; approach 3932; draw in 4166; extend 5385; take 7074; ~ *doun bi* trail along 3940. *refl.* approach 1424. *intr. pr. 1 sg.* in ~ *for oon* put my opponent at a disadvantage 4150n. *tr. out . . .* ~, ~ *. . . out* extend 5381, 5388. **draweth** *3 sg.* ropes in 3890; ~ *of* draws nourishment from 5351. **drawe** *subj. sg.* in ~ *bakward* be shy 10. **dro(o)uh** *pa. t. sg.* led 5004; drew out 7205; **drowh** pulled 3349. *refl.* **droowh** went 456; **drouh** 6664. **drowe** *subj. sg.* went 3940. *tr.* **drawe(n)** *pp.* brought 1886; derived 3588; drawn out 4867; pulled apart 5077; hanged 5123; **ydrawe** drawn 4470. **drawinge** *vbl. n.* in ~ *out* having (eyes) put out 2337.

drawestere *n.* in ~ *and hangestere* (female) executioner 3922n.

drede *n.* doubt 4204; *made I . . . drede* was I afraid 5738.

drede *v.* respect 589; *to* ~ to be feared 6433. *pr. 1 sg.* in ~ *of* doubt 3333; *whi made I . . .* ~ why did I fear 5738. *refl.* feared 4316. *tr. imp.*

sg. in ~ *nouht* you may be sure 1213. **ydred** *pp. adj.* feared 1108.
dredinge *pr. p. adj.* amazing 1845n. *vbl. n.* doubt 198.
drenche *v.* drown 4363; swallow 5534. **dreynt** *pp.* drowned 6158.
dresse *v. refl.* in ~ *him ayens* oppose 963. **dressede** *pa. t. sg.* prepared for action 3927. **dressed** *tr. pp.* set 69, 6746.
drestes *n. pl.* refuse of pressed grapes 6483.
dropped *pp. adj.* spotted 1982.
dubble *n.* in *selleth to þe* ~ at double the price 5142.
dueliche *adv.* in the proper way 508; fairly 634; quite rightly 759.
dulle *adj.* lethargic 6637.
dulle *v.* make numb 3871. **dulleth** *3 sg.* stupefies 3864.
dure *v.* last 5929.
durre, durst(e) see **dore**.
dwellere *n.* inhabitant; *vntrewe* ~ squatter 389.
dwellinge *n.* container 1614. **dwellinges** *pl.* accommodation 27.
dwellinge *vbl. n.* waiting 1829.

eche *adj.* every 31; ~ *oon* all of you 1207; **iche** in ~ *wight* everyone 14. **eche** as *n.* every one 47. as *pron.* 440.
edifyinge *vbl. n.* structure; *her maketh his* ~ it is built 716.
eek *conj.* also 5967, 5974, 5996, 5999 only.
eelde *n.* old age 1586.
eelded *pp.* aged 5698; **elded** 1456.
eende see **ende**.
eendinge *n.* death 302.
eerþe *n.* in ~ *dene* earthquake 4218; **erþe** 3224; **eerthe** 4309.
ees *n.* bait 6297.
ey *n.* egg 803.
eye *n.* in *at* ~ 195 see **at**; *to þe* ~ in appearance 1696; *haue to me his* ~ should give me attention 4041; *after þat I see with* ~ as I see it 6203. **eyen** *pl.* sight 2730; *upon yowre* ~ on (pain of losing) your eyes 1080n; *to þine* ~ from your point of view 2684; **yen** 2627.
elded see **eelded**.
elleswhere *adv.* anywhere else 105; ~ *þan to himself* outside himself 715-16.
embosed *pp.* hunch-backed 4974; **enbosed** 4862. **embosede** as *n.* 4040; **enbosede** 5439.
empassionementes *n. pl.* ? medicinal potions 7068n.
empeche *v.* prevent 7117; **enpeche** in ~ ... *of* hinder 2781; **empecheth, enpecheth** *pr. 3 sg.* hinders 3373. **empeched** *pp.* impeded 2060.
empechement *n.* obstacle 488; obstruction 3357.
empeyringe *vbl. n.* damage 2430.
emplastres *n. pl.* poultices, plasters 7068.
empressed *pp.* crowded 4084.
enamelure *n.* piece of enamelling 1839; enamel work 1865.
enchaunte *v.* bind in a spell 3005.
enchesoun *n.* reason 7139; *for noon* ~ on any pretext 2412-13; *with a litel* ~ on a slight pretext 4742.

encline *v.* in ~ *to* show inclination for 2356. **enclineth** *pr. 3 sg.* leans 5390.
encline, enclyn *adj.* submissive 3042; *were* ~ showed a desire 1441.
enclosed *pp.* contained 7299. *pp. adj.* shut off 572.
enclowed *pp.* fastened with nails 2207.
encombraunce, encumbraunce *n.* hindrance 2063; difficulty 2506. **encombraunces, encumbraunces** *pl.* obstacles 182.
e(e)nde *n.* consequences 696; goal 2949; conclusion 5295; *to þat* ~ so that 399; *to what* ~ *I shulde come þerof* 694 see **come**; *drawe to* ~ come to an end 845; *þe laste* ~ finally 3151; *without* ~ endlessly 5616; *put to þe* ~ finished 5619; *make* ~ finish 6140; *þei strecchen nouht to oon* ~ they do not serve the same purpose 6577.
endente *v.* in *I made . . . endente it* I had it serrated 4769.
enduringe *vbl. n.* in *þe long* ~ *of hem* their durability 5139.
enfamined *pp. adj.* hungry 1706.
enfermerere *n.* infirmarian 7216.
enforce *v. refl.* try 2531.
engendre *v.* breed 5134. **engendred** *pa. t. sg.* sired 5016. *pp.* conceived 1172; *was . . .* ~ had (its) origin in 730; *pp. adj.* developed 4974.
engyn *n.* skill 1753.
enhabite *v.* take up residence 3241; ~ *in* inhabit 5639. **enhabiteth** *pr. 3 sg.* is contained 1742. **enhabiten** *pl.* live 4460.
enioyned *pp.* imposed 686; charged 7039.
enlargise *v.* in ~ *it* give it away 1085.
enlumineth *pr. 3 sg.* lights up 2022. **enlumined** *pp.* in *beth* ~ have light shed on them 2024. **enlumyned** *pp. adj.* illuminated 5906n.
ennoye, ennuye *n.* harm (F *envier*) 2300n; *do* ~ create trouble 4238.
en(n)oye, ennuye *v.* harrass 2781; *lasse* ~ (F *mains ennuier*) weary you as little as possible 1941; ~ *to* harm 4636. **enoyeth** *pr. 3 sg.* grow boring 2754. **enoye** *subj. sg.* in ~ *yow nouht* may not bore you 4844.
enoyinge *vbl. n.* (F *ennuier*) boredom 3597.
enoorned *pp.* equipped 5744.
ennuye see **e(n)oye**.
enoyntinge *adj.* (F *moles*) soothinge 4513.
enpeche(th) see **empeche**.
enquerouresse *n.* (female) investigator 2814,
enrichesse *v.* enrich the spiritual life of (someone) 1688.
enseled *pa. t. sg.* sealed up 701.
entame *v.* cut into 5912.
entencioun *n.* in *I haue myn* ~ I have made my point 1011; *of þis . . . was litel myn* ~ this . . . was not at all what I had had in mind 2422.
entendaunt *adj.* subordinate 3316n.
entende *v.* pay attention to 2391; ~ *þerto* see to that 3335. **entenden** *pr. pl.* try 7090. **entende** *imp. sg.* attempt 3387; listen 5771; ~ *nouht* pay no attention 3347. **entendeth** *pl.* in ~ *hider* listen to me 457.
endended *pa. t. sg.* paid attention to 3983.
entente *n.* mind 2335; *hath set hire* ~ is careful 1309; *to þat* ~ in the hope 2727, in order to 4192; *in gret* ~ seriously meaning 4873; *with so gret* ~ so seriously 5154; *doth al his* ~ does his best 6291.

ententyf *adj.* attentive 2369.
entermedlinge *pr. p.* blending sounds 6983. **entermedled** *pp.* mingled 3515.
entermete *v. refl.* in ~ *me of* busy myself with 4524. **entermeteth** *pr. 3 sg.* interposes 5360. **entermeted** *pa. t. sg.* interfered 864. *subj. sg.* 831.
entre *n.* entrance 32; *make me* ~ gain entrance for me 6763.
entringe *vbl. n.* entrance 92.
envenyme *v.* poison 4458. **envenymed** *pp.* poison-bearing 4753.
envye *n.* malice 1547; *whoso euere hath þerto* ~ whatever anyone says 461; *haue noon* ~ do not be annoyed 576-7.
envyous *adj.* irritable 2149.
envirowned *pp.* haloed 125; surrounded 4083.
equipolle *adj.* equivalent 2296.
equipollence *n.* the equivalent 6686.
equitee *n.* righteousness 6556; *in* ~ fairly 85; *bi* ~ according to the proper interpretation of the law 375.
er *adv.* before 1949, *conj.* 180. *prep.* in ~ *þis* before now 170; in times past 872; long since 2667.
erbes *n. pl.* weeds 6149.
ere *v.* plough 3697.
eren, eres *n. pl.* ears 3262, 4406.
erliche *adv.* early 846.
erraunt *adj.* wandering 1085.
erre *v.* wander 2354.
erst *adv.* until now 887; *while* ~ a while ago 3169.
eschawfed *pp.* excited, inflamed 6111.
ese *n.* comfort 4434; *do him his* ~ 3120 see **do**; *holde him in* ~ stay resting 3570.
ese *v.* comfort 1803. **esed** *pp.* relieved, made comfortable 5025.
esement *n.* refreshment 567.
especial *adj.* in *bi* ~ 522-3 see **bi**.
espye *v.* to detect 3464; spy on 6996². **aspye** catch sight of, ambush 2171.
espyour *n.* waylayer 2810; a person who lies in ambush 2843.
espyowresses *n. pl.* women who lie in wait 4843.
esta(a)t(e) *n.* position 2415; prosperity 4317; retinue 4918.
euel(e) *n.* disease 5341; **yuele** evil 2725; **evell** vice 4665.
euel(e), yuel(e) *adj.* bad 337; miserable 3894; *þat* ~ *passion smyte it* see **passioun**; ~ *wil* resentment 3463; *of* ~ *feith* deceitful 3489-9.
euel(e), yuel(e) *adv.* terribly 1496; badly 1948; regrettably 2791; disastrously 3816; unpleasantly 3825; wickedly 4047; wretchedly 5769; uncomfortably 6668; ~ *iled* brought to harm 301; ~ *sittinge* most unsuitable 597; *me thinketh* ~ it is intolerable 861; *I shulde be* ~ *serued* it would be hard luck on me 1060-1; *it is* ~ *bifalle þee* it is unfortunate for you 1669; ~ *þow woldest awurþe with me* you would turn nasty 1672-3; ~ *bitaken* 2190-1 see **bitake**; ~ *apayed* 2643 see **apayed**; **evele** 4729.
euene *adj.* balanced 1774; straight 3537; equal 6220; *in þe* ~ *lyne* level 1373-4.

euene *adv.* straight 58; steadily 2007; right 2237; directly 2807; pleonastic in *riht* ~ *bihynde* 2093; **evene** 1442.
euenenesse *n.* equity 653.
euident *adj.* unmistakable 6087.
excepted *pp.* with the exception of 615. **exceptinge** *vbl. n.* excluding 1451.
excited see **exiteth.**
excusacioun *n.* excuse 5252.
excuse *v. refl.* make excuses 3487; ~ *yow of dispenseer . . . mown ye not* you cannot cry off (just) because you have no distributor 6028.
execucioun *n.* application 307; penalty 594; *dooth pleyn* ~ publicly carry out 2839-40.
exersise *v.* apply 1635.
exile *n.* ruin 404.
existence *n.* in *bi* ~ 2920 see **bi.**
exiteth *pr. 3 sg.* awakens 1929. **exite** *pl.* drive 891. **exited** *pa. t. sg.* roused 2311. **ex(c)ited** *pp.* prompted 138; anxious 1827.
explicit Lat. *pr. 3 sg.* in ~ *carmen* the poem is ended 6018.
expose imp. explain 5210.

fable *n.* falsehood 2992; *withoute* ~ accurately 649, to tell the truth 2423. **fables** *pl.* nonsense 2498; stories 3691.
facioun *n.* shape 1370; appearance 1868; design 2091; making 3238; *his* ~ the way it was made 1877.
faile(n) *v. intr.* lack; ~ *of* miss 5897; *litel or nothing I shulde* ~ I should lose little 6130. **faileth** *pr. 3 sg.* is lacking 734; *nothing* ~ *him* he lacks nothing 171; *me* ~ I lack 6454. **failede** *pa. t. sg.* was lacking 379; *me* ~ I lacked 111. *subj. sg.* in *I* ~ *. . . but litel* I should not be far out 3128. **fayled** *pp.* in *nothing is* ~ *us* we lack nothing 2965. **failinge** *pr. p. adj.* in *be not* ~ *to me* do not fail me 6613.
fayn *adj.* glad 1876.
fain, fayn *adv.* gladly 150, 2653.
fair(e) *adj.* beautiful 6; attractive 57; splendid 216; good 264; dear 344; fine 392; elegant 1087; pleasant 1088; skilled 1656; pleasing 2841; ~ *to yow* suitable 500; **fayr** in ~ *semblaunt* favour 264-5. as *n.* lovely one 1107; **faire** 3628. **fairere** *adj. comp.* more gracious 265. **faireste** *superl.* in *þe* ~ *of þe pley* an advantage 3776.
faire *adv.* gently 2551; richly 5492; carefully 6919; properly 7289; *wel and* ~ 1936 see **wel.**
fair(e)ye *n.* magic 3183; witchcraft 4926.
fairnesse *n.* beauty 118; clear statement 3007; brilliance 3577; **fayrnesse** brightness 6588.
faitourye *n.* (F. *fetardie*) ? idleness 3436n.
fallas *n.* pretence 369. **fallaces** *pl.* logical quibbles 2896.
falle *pr. subj. sg.* in *it* ~ *þee not in foryetinge* it may not fall into oblivion 399. **fel** *pa. t. sg.* declined 2438; ~ *him* came to him 4993. **falle(n)** *pp.* fallen 174; lapsed 2668; *is* ~ has happened 2877.

GLOSSARY

fals(e) *adj.* counterfeit 749; wrong 1621; deceitful 3936; artificial 4537²; dishonest 5100; unfaithful 5999; ~ *feste* 5342-3 see **feste**; **fauce** only in ~ *visage* 4401 etc.
falsed *pp.* proved wrong 1714.
falsnesse *n.* error 3006.
fame *n.* reputation 4665.
familier *n.* household servant, associate 5352.
fanned *pa. t. sg.* winnowed 1540.
fantome *n.* delusion 4927.
fardell(e) *n.* pack, burden 679.
fardelled *pp. adj.* in a pack 3882.
faste *adv.* firmly 78; loudly 561; hard 707; securely 2414; ~ *bi* (*by*) nearby 277. **fastere** *comp.* more safely 2401.
fastned *pp.* placed 1375.
faucoun *n.* falcon 3812.
faucowners *n. gen.* falconer's 3813.
feebelnesse, feebilnesse *n.* softness 2509.
feeblesse *n.* infirmity 2526.
feeblished *pp.* enfeebled 2544.
feedere *n.* in ~ *of briddes* gamewarden 53.
feedinge *vbl. n.* food 55; nourishment 1619. **feedinges** *pl.* 4132.
feelinge *vbl. n.* touch 1212.
feers see **fers**.
feerste(e) *n.* arrogance 1042.
feyne *v.* simulate 459. *refl. pr. 2 sg.* shirk 6035.
feith *n.* in *in good* ~ in all honesty 2168; *in* ~ truly 3106.
fel see **falle**.
felawe *n.* companion 4044; friend 5474.
fell *n.* hide; see **barm**.
felle *adj.* fierce 323.
felnesse *n.* ferocity 328; harshness 334.
felonye *n.* rage 476; *bi* ~ committing a crime against me (your feudal superior) 2922.
felthe(s) see **filthe**.
fen *n.* mire 2059. **fennes** *pl.* 5639.
fenestralle *n.* window (of the body), sight 3287.
fer(re) *adj.* far away 538; distant 1826.
fer(re) *adv.* a long way away 22; a long way 2080.
fered *pa. t. sg.* terrified 3945.
ferforth *adv.* in *so* ~ to such an extent 6003.
fermerye, fermorye *n.* infirmary 6806.
ferred *pp.* a long way away 3624.
fers *adj.* arrogant 898; violent 2352; **feers** 1052.
fersliche *adv.* aggressively 899; arrogantly 1074.
feste *n.* in *maken a fals* ~ give (it) pointless respect 5342-3. **festes** *pl.* holidays (saints' days) 3688.
feture *n.* shape 5700.
feþere *v.* provide with wing-feathers; *make* ~ cause to be winged 193.

fiat Lat. *pr. subj. sg.* let (him) be 4675.
ficched *pp.* fixed 4395; **fichched** in ~ *to* concentrated on 7277.
figure *n.* form 1406; likeness 3218; example 4781; shape 4856; letter 5264; foreshadowing 6002; *in* ~ prefiguration 5927.
figured *pp.* shown 1377; represented in a diagram 1405; given the form of 1493; indicated 1507; formed 6172; represented 6174; *well propirliche* ~ of exactly the same appearance 549-50. **ifigured** *pp. adj.* in *wel* ~ ? well made 5490.
fylleth *pr. pl.* fill 2104.
fillinge *vbl. n.* fill; ~ *sufficiaunt* its fill 1469; ~ *to sufficance* something large enough to fill (it) 1713.
filthe *n.* disgusting thing 1059; lasciviousness 1088; corruption 1147; wickedness 5990; stain 6902; *make* ~ void excrement 5702.
fyn *adj.* pure 4598.
firmament *n.* sphere of the fixed stars 955.
firste *adj.* in~ *bigynnynge* very beginning 2095; *at þe* ~ at first 6415.
fix *pp.* established 5842.
flatere *v.* beguile 3251. **flateringe** *vbl. n.* beguiling speech 3245; flattery 4077; *withoute* ~ bluntly 313.
flee(n) *v.* flee 4280, ?5874n, 5981, 7009. **fleeth** *pr. 3 sg.* flees 5835. **fleeinge** *pr. p. adj.* avoiding 1449, ? fleeing 5874n. **flowen** *pp.* fled 3411n. At 5874 and at 4225, 4490, 5719 it is impossible to distinguish between this verb and the one in next entry.
flee *v.* fly (with wings) 62; **fleen** *pr. pl.* 189. **fleih** *pa. t. sg.* flew 3352; **flygh** 6595. **flyen** *pl.* 57. **fleeinge** *pr. p. adj.* at a run 1458, flying 3221; **fleinge** 5582.
fleen *n. pl.* fleas 3262n.
flees *n.* fleece 504.
fleschliche *adj.* carnal 477.
flewmatyk *adj.* phlegmatic (affected by the predominance of phlegm, one of the four physical 'humours') 4748.
floyte *n.* flute, shepherd's pipe 4362n. **floytes** *pl.* 4157.
foisoun, foysoun *n.* a wealth 126; crowd 4536; ~ *of good* supplies 7209-10.
folage *n.* folly (+pun on *foliage*) 4390n.
folye *n.* idiocy 459; stupidity 3546; *no* ~ nothing silly 163; **foly** (an) absurd thing 1068; **folie** fool's style 460.
foliliche *adv.* stupidity 1074.
fonne(d) *adj.* imbecile 1503; as *n.* fool 6354.
fool *adj.* silly 2239.
foolhardiment *n.* rashness; *of* ~ foolhardy 595.
foorbishour *n.* burnisher (person or object?) 3585.
foorbushed see **forbisheth**.
fo(o)rth *adv.* on 2469; *putten hem* ~ 10-11 see **putte**; *passe* ~ 184, *passe heer* ~ 242-3 see **passe**; *putte hire* ~ 1552 see **putte**; *bere it* ~ 1678-9 see **bere**; *bring* ~ produce 2900; *comynge* ~ 3234 see **come(n)**; *euene* ~ straight 6828.
for *conj.* because 11; so that 254; ~ *þat* because 156; ~ *as miche* 1141-2. *prep.* because of 31; what with 55[2]; by 227; as a result of 627; as 922[2,3];

GLOSSARY

against ? 4946, 6624, 6661; pleonastic in ~ *to* 62; *as* ~ *himself* 1296 see as; ~ *which* why 1297; *nouht* ~ *þanne* 1321-22 see **nouht**; ~ *yow* on your account 1599; ~ *cause of* by 1870; ~ *nothing* not for anything 1958; ~ *whi* which is why 2111; *ordeyned* ~ *wele* 2502 see **ordeyne**; ~ *Seint Germeyn* by Saint Germain! 2861; ~ *my loue* to please me, now 3268; *oo* ~ *to seye* 3390 see **oo**; ~ *til* until 3883; ~ *no peny* (not) for any money 4100; *drawe* ~ *oon* 4150 see **drawe**; ~ *þus michel* for this reason 4491; ~ *to haue* having taken 4880; ~ *to speke (of)* to be mentioned 5679; *pas* ~ *pas* 6076 see **pas**; *I sey* ~ *me* speaking for myself 6170; ~ *cause* because 6268; ~ *cause of* for the sake of 7174. **fore** 1626, 3546.

forbere *v.* spare 1179; tolerate 1309; bear with 1657; *ben to* ~ are to be treated tolerantly 908. **forbar** *pa. t. sg.* spared 3939. **forbore, forborn** *pp.* put up with 871; tolerated 2724; **forboren** 4388. **forberinge** *vbl. n.* concession 3345.

forbeten *pp.* well worn 3676.

forbisheth *pr. 3 sg.* burnishes 6871. **furbished, foorbushed** *pp. adj.* burnished 33, 546.

fordoon *pp.* destroyed 4950.

fore see **for.**

forfeted *pp.* sinned 1119; ~ *nothing* not sinned at all 3223.

forfeture *n.* offence 910.

forge *v.* make, design 1053; create 4593, **forgede** *pa. t. sg.* created 2196. **forged** *pp.* beaten into shape 2124.

fors *n.* in *of . . . I made no* ~ 3793, *gret* ~ *made I nouht* 5761 see **make.**

forsake *v.* give up 2333. *pr. 1 sg.* deny 3993. *subj. sg.* refuse 2584.

forseide, forseyde *adj.* afore-mentioned 290, 699.

forshetteth *pr. 3 sg.* prohibits 931.

forsooth *adv.* indeed 5174.

forsters *n. pl.* foresters 5106.

forsworn *pp.* committed perjury 5407.

forth see **fo(o)rth.**

fortheringe *vbl. n.* aid 5201.

forthinketh *impers. pr. 3 sg.* in *me* ~ I regret 888. **forthouhte** *pa. t. sg.* in ~ *me* regretted 83; *to þe . . . olde it forthouhte* it displeased the . . . old woman 6039. **forthouht** *pp.* regretted 4054; (? by Nature) 4974.

forthward *adv.* on my way 1826.

forto *prep.* until 704.

foruey(n)e *v. intr.* go astray 2353; *kepten hem to* ~ should avoid straying 7289. *refl.* 3663. **forveyed, forueyed** *intr. pa. t. sg.* strayed 3624, 5756. **forveied** 175. **forueyinge** *vbl. n.* straying 7290.

forwh *n.* rut 2063.

foryete *v.* forget 362. **foryat** *pa. t. sg.* forgot 3792. **foryetinge** *vbl. n.* in *it falle þee not in* ~ it is not forgotten 399; *sette . . . into* ~ forgot 3711; *put in* ~ forgotten 7077-8.

foryive, foryiue *v.* forgive 334.

foryifte *n.* forgiveness 4626.

foul(e) *adj.* stained by sin 245; wretched 3542; dirty 3576; shameful 3801.

foule *adv.* rudely 906; horribly 4868.
founded *pp.* as *n.* (F. *enfondu*) in þe ∼ the one affected by swollen throat-glands 3856.
foundement *n.* foundations 24; basis 6775; *make þi* ∼ 2559 see **make**.
fourchede *pa. t. sg.* forked 3510.
fourmede *pa. t. sg.* planned 1397. **fourmed** *pp.* 1366.
fraud *n.* dishonesty 1232; deception 1675; insincerity 2333.
fre *adj.* great 425; easy 2243; honourable 4902; **free** generous 5845.
fredom *n.* generosity 1683.
freytour *n.* refectory 6805.
fretoreere, freytoureere *n.* manager of the refectory 6854, 6929.
fretted *pp.* secured 6703.
fro(m) *prep.* against 2430; *michel* . . . ∼ far away from 1730n; ∼ *al to al* utterly 4018; ∼ *hand to hand* ? by the personal approach 5247n.
froren *pp.* as *n.* in þe ∼ those who are frozen (paralyzed) 3856.
frosshes *n. pl.* frogs (or toads) 5639.
frote *v.* caress 4526. **froted** *pp.* massaged 5565.
frounced(e) *pp. adj.* knit (brows) 2773; scowling 2848; wrinkled 5699.
ful *adj.* in ∼ *maad* (F *parfais*) completed 1404; ∼ *of* filled by 1474; *make* . . . ∼ 1719 see **make**; ∼ *of* loaded with 4406; covered with 5697. *adv.* very 1102; fully 1569; ∼ *wel* really 710; clearly 2005; ∼ *seid* finished 1440.
fulfille *v.* completely fill 1467; carry out 1570; *hire pleasaunce* . . . ∼ do what she wanted 2456. **fulfilled** *pp.* full up 1114; completely filled 1462. **fulfillinge** *vbl. n.* satisfaction 5039; filling 6525.
fulle *n.* fill 6373; *at þe* ∼ 1519 see **at**.
fulliche *adv.* completely 1472n; ∼ *come, come* ∼ reach 109, 180; ∼ *dide þat* successfully performed (the ceremony) 543.
furbished see **forbisheth**.

gabbe *v.* deceive 277.
gaynpayn *n.* gauntlet 2303.
gambesoun, gambisoun *n.* gambeson (quilted jacket worn under armour) 6459, 6817.
game *n.* amusement 998; *halt no* ∼ takes very sriously 408; *is þe* ∼ *so turned ayenward* the course of events is reversed 3405.
garnement *n.* garment 2101.
garnisonis *n. pl.* fortresses (occupied by armed defenders) 6522n.
gastlich *adj.* devilish 4400.
genderes *n. pl.* in. ∼ *of Dame Venus* members of Venus' race 5610.
generacioun *n.* propagation 952n.
generalliche *adv.* collectively 2291; *eche wight* . . . ∼ each and every one 28-09.
genievre *n.* juniper 3866.
gentel *adj.* noble 1464; well-bred 4000; kind 5060. as *n.* gracious one 6349.
gerdel see **girdel**.
gerner *n.* barn 4997. **gerne(e)res** *pl.* 2104.

GLOSSARY 535

gesse *n*. in *bi* ~ (F *par assente*) by instinct 6129.
gesse *n. pl.* jesses (fastened to a hawk's legs) 7007; **gessis** 3814.
gile, gyle *n*. trickery 1675.
girdel *n*. sword-belt 2399; **gerdel** 2366.
glade *v. intr.* (F *esjouir*) rejoice 7159. *refl.* 984. **gladed** *pp*. pleased 3355.
gladshipe *n*. gladness 28.
glasses *n. pl.* windows 3284.
glee *n*. music, delight 5933.
gleedes *n. pl.* embers 819.
glene *v*. gather 5035.
glist(e)ringe *pr. p. adj.* sparkling 1880, 2022.
glose *n*. commentary 5211; interpretation 7121; *without* ~ clearly 479.
glose *v*. deceive 3607.
go see **go(on)**.
gobet *n*. fragment 1156; lump 3864.
god see **good**.
goinge, gon(e) see **go(on)**.
good(e) *adj*. excellent 431; genuine 1407; reliable 2002; right 2301; proper 2342^{1,2}; *with* ~ *wille* eagerly 212; patiently 2118; ~ *leue* full permission 350; ~ *passage* safe crossing 366; *in* ~ *pees* quiet 804; ~ *pees* serenity 1388; *in* ~ *feith* 1433 see **in**; *bi* ~ *riht* with good cause 4378; *þow were* ~ it would be best for you 4582; ~ *wille* right intention 7004. as *n*. good thing 144; good fortune 1631; goodness 1896; reward 3385n; *þi* ~ the benefit to you 574; *souereyn* ~, ~ *souereyn* absolute good 1765, 1772; *so miche* ~ *þow coudest* 2681 see **can**; **god** 1719, 1721. **goodes** *pl*. acts of goodness 3478n; advantages 4149; benefits 6956.
goodliche *adv*. kindly 129; graciously 204; properly 2263.
goodshipe *n*. kindness 582; good thing 4130; goodness 4436. **goodshipes** *pl*. blessings 29.
goomes *n. pl.* (F *taillans*) jaws 2258.
go(on) *v*. walk 859; travel 1874; ~ *out of* leave 2355; ~ *for nouht* be useless 2547; *to* ~ ... *leue* give up the idea of going 2741; ~ *to nouht* fail 3848; ~ *to waste* (F *a gast*) go to ruin 5799. *pr. 1 sg.* in ~ *softe* move slowly 7110. **go(o)th** *3 sg*. in oo*þerweys it* ~ it is not a bit like that 2940; ~ *to flihte* takes flight 4227. **gon(e)** *pp*. ago 1978; **go** 3839.
goinge *vbl. n*. path 4096; ~ *divinynge* having to resort to guesswork 1619.
goot, got *n*. goat 3024, 6668.
gorge(e)r(e), gorgier(e) *n*. gorget (throat armour) 2219.
gorgered *refl. pa. t. sg.* in ~ *him* put on his gorget 2081.
goth see **go(on)**.
gostlich(e) *adj*. spiritual 3288.
goutous *adj*. gouty 3855.
gouernayle *n*. controller 3318.
gouernaunce *n*. control 942; behaviour 5597.
gouernement *n*. control 5596.
gouernour, gouernowr *n*. controller 3321, steersman 3844.
gouernouresse, gouernowresse *n*. she who controls 172.

graces *n. pl.* prayers (of thanksgiving) 5782.
graciows, gracious(e) *adj.* attractive 1346. as *n.* friendly one; *þe* ~ *litel plesaunt* the gentlewoman who hurts 1109.
graffed *pp.* grafted 2026.
graunt *n.* permission 1993.
graunt(e), grawnte *v.* agree with 4389.
graueresse *n.* female engraver 5099.
grees *n. pl.* steps 6818.
greet see **gret(e)**.
gre(e)vaunce, greuaunce *n.* pain 2142; injury 3033; displeasure 5896.
greeve, greeue, greven *v.* harm 2232; hurt 2468. **greevinge** *pr. p. adj.* painful 2422.
greevous *adj.* painful 2155; serious 5853.
greisiler *n.* gooseberry bush 4738.
gret(e) *adj.* grown 233; serious 601; much 1157; fat 2141; mature 2582[2]; ~ *wunder* amazement 124; ~ *wysdom* a very wise thing 267; *to* ~ excessive 319; *in* ~ as a whole 1154[1,2]; *þe* ~ *cene* The Last Supper 1290; *þe* ~ *Thursday* Maundy Thursday 1291; *riht* ~ *wunder* very surprising 1612; ~ *riht* good reason 2566; ~ *neede* necessary 2694; *I hadde* ~ *wrong* 2889 see **haue**; *of* ~ *care* 3522 see **of**; ~ *wille* determination 4279; ~ *estate* important position 4321; ~ *degree* high rank 4322; ~ *foysoun* large numbers 4536; *in* ~ *entente* 4872 see **entente**; ~ *weyes* main roads 5225; *haue* ~ *wrong* 5358 see **haue**; ~ *bred* coarse bread 5551; ~ *metes* coarse food 5554; ~ *fors made I nouht* 5761 see **make**; *þe* ~ *assyse* The Last Judgement 5869; *I made nouht riht* ~ *viage* 6167 see **make**.
gretliche *adv.* very much 203; hard 1475; most 1844; severely 2485; profoundly 2510; **gretli** 3589.
gretnesses *n. pl.* enormous things 1735.
gretteste *adj.* strongest built 2563; most important 6138.
grevaunce see **gre(e)vaunce**.
greven see **greeve**.
gryndinge *vbl. n.* (F *emolument*) making 2161n.
grinnes *n. pl.* snares 7016.
grynte *v.* gnash 2835. **grinte** *pa. t. sg.* in ~ *with þe teeth* ground his teeth 2927.
gronded *pp.* felled 6799.
ground *n.* foundation, source 5920.
grucche *v.* complain 961. *pr. subj. sg.* may protest 5062. **grucchinge** *pr. p.* in ~ *of* complaining about 1059; ~ *to* being angry with 4586. **grucched** *pp.* in ~ *me* opposed me 2805. **grucchinge** *vbl. n.* complaining against 6583.
grummynge *pr. p.* grumbling 3078. **grummede** *pa. t. sg.* grumbled 2833. **guerdoun** *n.* reward 1862.
guerdoned *pp.* repayed 6952.
guste *n.* appetite, organ or sense of taste 5556n.
gusten *v.* have an appetite for, taste 5568.
habite *n.* attire (? habit) 3310.

GLOSSARY 537

habite *pr. 1 sg.* live 4309.
haboundinge *pr. p. adj.* intense 5968.
hachees *n. pl.* anguish 1159.
hadde, hadden, haddest see **haue**.
haf see **heue**.
haleth *pr. 3 sg.* in ~ *him* lifts him up 5901.
half *n.* side 1855; *by þe* ~ by half 3085.
halp see **helpe**.
halt see **holde**.
halte *adj.* as *n.* in *þe* ~ the lame 4039.
halte *v.* be lame, limp 4662. **haltinge** *pr. p. adj.* lame 5371. *vbl. n.* crippling 5372.
haluelinge *adv.* half 3792.
halwedest *pa. t. 2 sg.* consecrated 395.
halwen *n. pl.* saints 4734.
han see **haue**.
hand(e) *n.* in *sette* ~ 5082 see **sette**; *from* ~ *to* ~ 5247 see **from**; *into þin* ~ to you 5913; *set* ~ 6518 see **sette**; *leue of his* ~ 7172 see **leue**.
handlinges *n. pl.* caresses 2286.
hange(n) *v.* in *of þei* ~ they relate to 1914; ~ *hem with* hang themselves about with 6521n. **heeng** *pa. t. sg.* hung 213. **hongen** *pl.* 2374; **heengen** hanged 5122. **hanged** *pp.* hung 2120; hanged 5112; ~ *with* hanged by (? hung about with) 6545 see 6521n. **hanginge** *vbl. n.* in *hath his* ~ 733 see **haue**.
hangestere *n.* (female) executioner 3922n.
hanselled *pp.* in *of him I was* ~ I was endowed with it 4232.
hap *n.* favour, good opinion 4319n.
hard *adj.* in *I make me* ~? I become energetic 5042.
harde *v.* harden 4279.
hardement *n.* courage 6653.
hardi, hardy *adj.* bold 1259; *þei be not* ~ they should not have the temerity 6869.
hardied *refl. pa. t. sg.* plucked up courage 1479.
hardiliche *adv.* freely 996; bravely 3054; **hardily** 4517.
hardliche *adv.* vigorously 6499.
hardnesse *n.* inflexibility 1143; rigidity 2509.
hardshipe *n.* hardness 6058.
harm *n.* suffering 1322; infirmity 5233; injury 5343. **harmes** *pl.* ills 173; troubles 1910.
harrow *interj.* Help! 3910; Allas! 4881; Halloo! (hunting cry) 5474.
hassok *n.* mound 4914.
hast(e) see **haue**.
hasted *pp.* speeded up 5197.
hastelet *n.* piece of meat (on a spit) 5522.
hastyf *adj.* impetuous 854. **hastyfe** 4551.
hastliche *adv.* soon 2170.
hateful *adj.* malevolent 4737.
haterel *n.* nape of the neck; *hire* ~ *bihynde* the back of her head 2630.

hath see **haue.**
hatte *pr. 1, 3 sg.* am (is) called 3855, 5711. **hatteth** *3 sg.* 2002 (see note 2661). **highte, hyghte** *pa. t. sg.* 1954, 4990.
haubergeoun *n.* habergeon, coat-of-mail 2184. **hawbergeoun** 3904.
hau(n)teyn *adj.* loud 537; arrogant 3160.
haunteth *pr. 3 sg.* in ~ *me* comes to me 5458. **haunted** *pp.* travelled 4244.
haue(n), have(n) obtain 408; reach 472; find 1120; experience 1325; meet with 2158; ~ *pitee of* feel pity for 357; ~ *wurshipe* be respected 469; ~ . . . *esement* refresh 567; ~ *it in havinge* possess it 1359; ~ *in mynde of* remember 1657; ~ *his mesure* be contained 1580; ~ *of* receive 1801; ~ *in þi memorie* remember 1922; ~ *discomfort* be troubled 2016; ~ *thirst* be thirsty 2273; *I wende wel* ~ *ben* I really thought I was 3403; *of me þou shalt* ~ *it* I am going to attack you 3816; ~ . . . *out of* release 4548; ~ *of* feel 4732; ~ *shame* be shamed 4812; *for to* ~ 4880 see **for**; ~ *þin herte to* turn your thoughts to 5805; ~ *affray* be afraid 6173; *to* ~ *in sum bileevinge* to have some left 7173n. **haue** *pr. 1 sg.* in ~ *no cure* 177 see **cure**; ~ *wrethe to myn herte* am mortally enraged 867-8; ~ *myn entencioun* haue made my point 1011; ~ *gret lust* am most anxious 1824-5; ~ *leeuere* would rather 2491; ~ *ioye* am pleased 2589; ~ . . . *in despyte* despise 4060; *þe style I* ~ I use the correct methods 5386; ~ *wil þerto* desire it 5807; ~ *out* drive away 6775n. **hast(e)** *2 sg.* in *bataile þou* ~ *to* you are at war with 3244. **hath** *3 sg.* receives 1524; ~ *þerto envye* 461 see **envye**; ~ *(no) reward* 715 see **reward**; ~ . . . *his hunginge of* depends on on 732-3. **haue(n), have(n), han** *pl.* know 654; possess 1752; keep 1928; *men* ~ *not taken him* 507 see **men**; ~ *knowing of* know 4068; ~ *here issue* emerge 4456-7; ~ *here thouht* intend 5520; ~ *here hoodes wrong turned* are blind 6534. **haue** *subj. sg.* has 634; may feel 2063; *þat God* ~ *part* God help us! 2887; *I* ~ *wrong* it would be useless 3578; ~ *to me his eye* should pay me attention 4041; *faile me nouht þat I ne* ~ make sure I have 5243; *whosoeuere* ~ *be here fader* whoever their father was 5517-18; *I* ~ *leeuere* I should rather 5658; ~ *defaut of* lack 6029-30. *imp.* keep 370; hold 2678; ~ *noone envye* 576 see **envye**; ~ *youre herte neuere þe more feers* you can stop being angry 1051-2. **hauynge, havinge** *pr. p.* in ~ *part* sharing 828. **had(de)** *pa. t. 1, 3 sg.* in ~ *in metinge* saw in my dream 74; ~ *gret wunder* was amazed 124; ~ *not customed* 2454 see **customed**; ~ *gret wrong* should be much at fault 2889; ~ *doon* did 3734; ~ *it to his mete* eaten it 4021; *I wende nouht . . . to haue* ~ I did not think I had 4656; ~ *needed* needed 5498. **hadden** *pl.* in ~ *gret stryf* fought fiercely 1661-2; *so michel diden þat þei* ~ succeeded in obtaining 1966-7. **hadde** *subj. sg.* would have 169; *ne* ~ *I* had I not 170; ~ *levere* would rather 415-16; *al at his wille he* ~ *it* he did have it completely at his disposal 1712; *ne* ~ *be* had it not been for 3866. **hadde(n)** *pl.* in *ye* ~ *do* you might just as well have done 6090; ~ *ben* were 3451. **havinge** *vbl. n.* receiving 295; experience 2668.
he *interj.* alas! 5742.
heef see **heue.**

GLOSSARY 539

heelde(n) see **holden**.
heeng(en) see **hange(n)**.
heerafter *adv.* after this 1990; later 2752.
heerafterward *adv.* later 1093.
heerayens *adv.* in comparison 1505.
heerbi *adv.* this way 243.
heerbifore *adv.* in time past 2305.
heerde *n.* shepherd 504. **heerdes** *pl.* sheep 503.
heerfore *adv.* for this reason 1272.
heerinne *adv.* in this matter 370; in this place 6857.
heerne *n.* cranny 1997.
heerof *adv.* about this 2633.
heeron *adv.* about this 799.
heff see **heue**.
heggeward *n.* in *to þe* ∼ towards the hedge 3941.
hele *n.* healing 5913.
hele *v.* heal 6047. *imp. sg.* 5337. **heled** *pp.* healed 6070.
hele *v.* conceal 2761, 2872. **heled** *pp.* concealed 1198. **helinge** *vbl. n.* concealment 2905.
helpe *intr. pr. 1 sg.* in *to whom I* ∼ whom I assist 1495. *refl.* in *wel he coude* ∼ *him þerwith* he could make good use of it 35; *to* ∼ *me* for my use 970; ∼ *me with* make use of 1039-40; ∼ *þiself* defend yourself 2446. **halp** *pa. t. sg.* helped 553. **helpe** ? *subj.* 4111n. **holpen** *pp.* 5123.
hep *n.* circumference (F *masure*) 1610n.
her *n.* hair 3252.
herberwh *n.* accommodation 264. **herberwes** *pl.* resting-places 1810.
herberwe *v.* conceal 2380; live 3356. *refl.* 6807. **herberwede** *tr. pa. t. sg.* housed 6808.
herd *pp.* in ∼ *seyd* heard tell 2935; ∼ *speke it* heard it said 4377; ∼ *speke* 5176.
hering(e) *n.* herring 6777; *a red* ∼ a brass farthing (F *un harenc sor* a smoked herring) 2439.
herinne *adv.* into this place 6777.
heritage *n.* portion 454.
herte *n.* mind 999; attitude 1399; courage 2983; *haue wrethe to myn* ∼ 867-8 see **haue**; *haue youre* ∼ 1051-2 see **haue**; *with* ∼ earnestly 1802; *in þin* ∼ inwardly 2157; *myn* ∼ *al afrighte* my heart failed me 2453; *to þe* ∼ absolutely 2926; *with good* ∼ willingly 2982-3; *to myn* ∼ extremely 3791; *lyth me on* ∼ preoccupies me 5191; *hadden me neuere sithe in* ∼ never liked me since 5644; *haue þin* ∼ 5805 see **haue**; *with good* ∼ confidently 5816; *with verrey* ∼ sincerely 5824-5; *sitten me . . . at* ∼ were most important to me 6814.
heu Lat. *interj.* alas! 4927.
heue *v.* lift 4182. **heve, heue** *pr. 1 sg.* 4088. **haf, heef** *pa. t. sg.* lifted 4877, 6020. **hoven** *pa. t. pl.* 2692. **houen** *pp.* 2691.
heuene *n.* in ∼ *queen* queen of heaven 5982.
heuenlich *adj.* unworldly 4308.
hevy *adj.* distressing 1989.

hevy v. distress 1062. **hevyede, heviede** pa. t. sg. angered 1585, 1798.
hid, hyd pp. hidden 199; obscure 595. 1110n.
hideles, hydeles n. secrecy 4471. pl. hiding places 5452.
hidouschipe n. horror 4417n.
hy(e) adj. loud 3983; lofty 4390; top 6121; *þe ~ cuntre* heaven 2196.
 hy(gh) as n. *in an ~* high up 25. **hye** as adv. *in þe ~ honged* the one hanging high in the air 3866n; *~ raueshed* spiritually transported 4308.
hyed pp. extolled 2388.
highte, hyghte see **hatte(th)**.
hynesse n. high-handedness 811; authority 833.
hippe pr. *1 sg.* hop along 5386n. **hippinge** pr. p. limping 5371.
hol see **ho(o)l**.
holde(n) v. think 962; keep 1227; *~ parlement* speak 882; *~ at (in) regard* as 1245. refl. remain 3570; *~ me* restrain myself 147; *~ me stille* remain silent 269; *in my purpose I wole ~ me* I will maintain my purpose 3011-12; *~ ... to* stay on 3774; *~ me seised of* keep a grip on 5634. pr. *1 sg. in to þee I ~ me* I hold on to you 6126. tr. *in ~ ... speche* speak 6688. **holt** *3 sg.* pinches 2138; *~ in cheertee* loves 1316; **halt** *in ~ no game* takes very seriously 408; *it ~ not of hire* it is not due to her 6031; *on þee it ~* it depends on you 6586. refl. *in ~ him* pays attention 918. **holden** tr. pl. *in ~ in viletee* despise 1316-17. **heelde** refl. pa. t. sg. *in ~ hire stille* had stayed still 6649. tr. subj. pl. *in ye ~* if you would stay on 3480. **holden** refl. pp. *wolde haue ~ me in good pees ynowh* would not have said a word 804. **holdinge** vbl. n. *in þe manere of þe ~* the way it is held 1193.
holi adj. *in ~ fame* a reputation for virtue 4665.
holliche adv. completely 488.
holt see **holde(n)**.
homage in *do to me ~* 924 see **do**.
honeste adj. genuine 2945.
hongen see **hange(n)**.
ho(o)l adj. complete 137; healed 5338; *keep ... ~* 2226 see **keepe**; *~ of* free from 2766; *~ lookinge* good sight 6202.
hoot adj. hot 5382.
hoper n. machinery 1545n; flour hopper 1551.
horned(e) adj. as n. horned one (the bishop/Moses) 558; *þe grete ~* the bishop (? pope) 616; *þe ~ of helle* the Devil 384-5.
hose v. put leggings (or stockings) on 3116.
how adv. in which 1338; no matter how 1578[1,2]; *~ iit was bifalle* what had happened 138; *~ he dide* what he did 536; *~ þat* however 1127; *~ ye understonden* what you mean 2146; *~ miche þat euer* however much 3114; *~ it euere be* whatever happens 3276, interj. what! 4559.
houpe v. give hunting calls 6181.
hour(e) n. *in þilke same ~* that very moment 206-7; *oon ~* one moment 1255; *in þis ~* right now 6232; *at euery ~* at the start of every canonical hour 6980n.
hous, hows n. home 1; container 1616; *hem of þe ~* þe members of the religious community 5253. **houses** pl. monasteries (or convents) 6530.

howse *v.* build 1041.
howwe *n.* mattock 4923.
howweden *pa. t. pl.* dug with mattocks 4957.
hoven, houen see **heue**.
hucche *n.* cupboard 1830.
humblesse *n.* humility 133. **humblisse** 70.
humour *n.* sap 878.
hunte *n.* hunter 4222, 6304. **huntes** *gen.* 5546.
hurt(e)le *v.* thrust down, butt 342. *pr. subj. sg.* cast 6533.

ybounden *pp.* bound 709.
ybroken *pp.* broken 2205.
iche see **eche**.
icryed see **crye**.
idel, ydel *adj. absol.* in *holde it in* ~ treat it lightly 1245; *in* ~ in jest 6458.
idem Lat. *adj.* the same; *in here* ~ ? in their own way (? in their aforementioned movements) 6414n.
idoo, ydoon see **do**.
ydrawe see **drawe**.
ydred see **drede**.
yen see **eye**.
if *prep.* in *but* ~ 93 see **but**; ~ *it ne were* but for it 3039.
ifigured see **figured**.
yherd *pp.* heard 898.
yhurt *pp. adj.* hurt 5501.
yknowe see **know(n)**.
yle *n.* place (F *ille*) 1110n.
iled see **lede**.
ylost see **leese**.
imaad see **make**.
ymaginatyfliche *adv.* in the mind (F *imaginauement*) 1758n.
ymet see **mete**.
ymped *pp.* set 4409.
implicacioun *n.* complexity 6412.
impotent *adj.* helpless 7135.
in *prep.* on 16[1]; at 396; into 529; to 917; by 1158; with 1223[1,2]; for 1411; about 1884; as 1983; ~ *good pees* 804 see **holde**; ~ *al times* always 1014; ~ *no wise* at all 1022; ~ *þat winne ye nothing* that does not do you any good 1030; ~ *swich wise* like this 1297-8; ~ *þe euene lyne* level with it 1373-4; ~ *swich manere þat* so that as a result 1383-4; ~ *oo degree* at the same level 1396; ~ *good feith* honestly 1433; *I haue* ~ *myn* vsage I am used 1524; ~ *litel quantitee* small 1529; *haue* ~ *mynde* 1657 see **haue**; ~ *no time* never 1869; ~ *what manere* how 1918; *haue* ~ ... *memorie* 1922 see **haue**; ~ *alle places* everywhere 1955; ~ *eche (ne) sesoun* all the time 2003, never 2413; ~ *al* 2043 see **al** *n.*; ~ *oo tyme* some day 2169; ~ *hire* ... *abide* 2621 see **abide**; ~ *comaundinge* 2849 see **comaundinge**, ~ ... *daunger* 2955 see **daungere**; ~ *apert* clearly

2985-6; obviously 4682; ~ *vsage* familiar 3100; common 5148; ~ *alle degrees* completely 3217; ~ *sum poynt* sometime 3630; ~ *certeyn* 3683 see **certeyn**; ~ *negligence* 3710 see **sette**; ~ *litel time* soon 3723; *neuere* ... ~ *no time* never ever 3823; ~ *sesoun* useful 3905; *haue* ... ~ *despyte* 4060 see **haue**; ~ *sori time* it was unlucky that 4247; ~ *wise of* like 4606; ~ *gret entente* 4872-3 see **entente**; ~ *hande* in cash 5190; ~ *no place* never 5217; ~ *þee it is* it is up to you 5632-3; *hadden* ... ~ *herte* 5644 see **haue(n)**; ~ *point is* ... *to* is about to 5881; ~ *figure* 5927 see **figure**; ~ *þis hour* 6232 see **hour**; ~ *defaute* 6964 see **putte**; ~ *foryetinge* 7085 see **putte**; ~ *sum bileevinge* some people left 7173n. pleonastic in ~ *seyinge* 290, *entre* ~ 672, ~ *techinge* 786, *studie* ~ 2308; *adv.* pleonastic in *entre* ~ 687; **inne** inside 1702; ~ *and out* inside out 3521.
incestus Lat. *n.* incest 5712.
incipit Lat. *pr. 3 sg.* (it) begins 5833.
indignacioun *n.* in *hauen* ... ~ grow angry 5253.
indulgence *n.* forgiveness 1859.
inobedient *adj.* disobedient 2345.
inouh, ynouh, ynow(e), inow(e), inowh, ynow(h) *adj.* plenty of 272; enough 804; *by* ~ a good deal 5679. as *n.* 1155. *adv.* fully 825; very 2660; *maad* ~ well enough built 2767.
instrument *n.* implement 4127.
interiectioun *n.* outcry 4930.
intermete *refl. pr. 1 sg.* take it upon myself 4330.
interpretation *n.* meaning 682.
into *prep.* to 1849; ~ *cumpany* 555 see **cumpanye**; ~ *þe time þat* until 2989; ~ *þi viage (pilgrimage)* on your journey (pilgrimage) 3376-7; ~ *foryetinge* out of mind 3711; *may* ~ can get into 5570; ~ *wey* on the right path 6638.
ypreised see **preyse**.
yrayne *n.* spider 5072.
irchoun *n.* hedgehog 4716.
yrened *pp.* tipped with iron 1884n.
irows(e) *adj.* angry 661.
ysee *v.* look at 5886. **iseyn** *pp.* seen 684; **yseye** 3293.
ysen *v.* leave 1214; ~ *out of* 392n; come out 1129. **ysede** *refl. pa. t. sg.* in ~ *me out* came out of 113. **ysed** *pp.* issued 1131. **ysinge** *vbl. n.* in *withouten any* ~ without going out at all 114.
ysheþed *pp. adj.* sheathed 708.
yspoke(n) *pp.* spoken 897, 1070.
issue *n.* exit 5299; *haue here* ~ 4457 see **haue**.
ystreight see **strecche**.
ythouht see **thinke**.
yuel(e) see **euel(e)**.
ywriten *pp. adj.* written 4986.

jakkes *b. pl.* gambesons (F *gambesons*) 2082 (note 2091).
jangeleresse *n.* talkative woman 3721.

GLOSSARY

iangle *v.* chatter 4210: **jangelinge** *pr. p.* contradicting 2992.
jape *n.* joke 400.
japere *n.* trickster 4099.
jogelorye *n.* music 6988.
jogelour *n.* entertainer 4360. **iogelours** *pl.* 3642.
jogelo(u)resse *n.* female entertainer, musician 4360; **jowgleresse** 6838.
ioyngtliche *adv.* in *oon* ~ united in one 2916n; **ioyntliche** together 4929.
joynpee *adj.* with feet together 6358n.
iuste *adj.* as *n.* good man 1895.
justice, iustice, iustyse *n.* in *do* ~ *of* administer justice to 351; **Hy Justice** Chief Justice 623.
iustifye *v.* execute justice upon 624.

kaccheres *n. pl.* grabbers 5094.
kamen see **come**.
kan see **kunne**.
karayne *n.* corpse 5646. **careynes** *pl.* 4573.
kast(e) see **caste(n)**.
keembe *v.* comb. **kembest** *pr. 2 sg.* in ~ *him* make him elegant 3122. **kembed** *pp.* in *euele* ~ unkempt 4728; **kempt** in *wel* ~ elegant 5669.
keep *n.* notice 64; *taketh* ~ pay attention 4849.
keepe *v.* guard 1293; protect 2234; maintain 2939; wish for 4582; *made* ~ 85 see **make**; ~ ... *hool* protect 2226. **keepe** *pr. 1 sg.* in *of* ... *I* ~ *noon* I do not care at all for 4044. **keepeth** *3 sg.* secures 2415; wishes 5437; **keepith** in ~ *not* does not care 1320. **keepe** *subj. sg.* in (*so*) *God* ~ *yow* for heaven's sake 943; God help you 2808. *refl.* in ~ *him wel* pay careful attention 1296; *pl.* in ~ *yow fro* avoid 480. **keep(e)** *imp. sg.* in ~ *þi* be careful 308; *tr.* in ~ *þi mouth* watch your tongue 2267. **kept(e)** *pa. t. sg.* in *ne* ~ *hem* ? did not remain 2669n; ~ *not* did not care 6406. **kepten** *pl.* in ~ *hem to forueye* prevented themselves from straying 7289. **keeping** *vbl. n.* protection 2715.
kernelles *n. pl.* battlements 43.
herue *v.* cut 745; divide up 755; cut out 850. **kervinge** *pr. p. adj.* cutting 610; *wel* ~ sharp 546. as *n.* cutting edge (F *taillant*) 628.
keuereth *pr. 3 sg.* covers 2233.
kynde *n.* nature 3229.
kindelinge *vbl. n.* ? encitement 4734n; **kyndlinge** kindling brand 4756.
kyte *m.* red kite (F *escouffle*) 1706n.
kitte *v.* in *make* ~ *hem* have them cut up 5200.
knet *pp.* knotted 75.
knyt *pp.* tied; ~ *in* associated with 730.
knokke(n) *v.* beat 2174; *to* ~ beating 2166.
knorred *pp. adj.* gnarled 4276n.
know(en) *v.* understand 5704. **knew(e)** *pa. t. subj. sg.* in ~ *hem not wel* did not examine them thoroughly 1148n; *if I* ~ *not a flye in mylk* if I did not see the obvious 2888. **knowe(n)** *pp.* experienced 2288. *pp. adj.* **yknowe** in *nouht* ~ unknown 594. **knowinge** *vbl. n.* in *ye haue* ~ *of youreself* you know yourself 4068.

koleye v. look round from side to side 3778. **coleyinge** pr. p. 3782.
kouerynge, koueringe vbl. n. disguise 2880; pretext 5208.
kowele n. vat, tub; **cowuele** 6088.
kunne v. be able 3464; know 4068; þer shulde noon ~ no one could 791; shal nothing ~ diuise will not be able to ask (of me) 1790. **can, kan** pr. 1, 3 sg. is fully aware of 1586; ~ ... on has skill in 36. **canst** 2 sg. understand 3438. **kunne** pl. in ~ nothing cannot do anything 1502. subj. sg. in ~ a smith neuere so wel forge however well a smith can forge 4594; ~ he neuere so michel caste however well he can throw 6755. **cowþe** pa. t. 1 sg. had been able 5026. **cowde** could 1555. **cowde, kowde, kowþe** subj. 1, 3 sg. in whoso ~ wel biholde it if it is rightly regarded 6433. **cowdest, coudest, kowdest** 2 sg. in if so miche good þow ~ if you have any sense 2681. **cowde** pp. understood 7125.
kunnynge n. skill 655; intelligence 966; knowledge 2669.

la(a)ces n. pl. cords 4284, 6866.
labelles n. pl. strips 392n.
laboure v. carry out, work at 3523. **labowred** pp. tilled 1538.
lace v. part with (F laissier) 5658n.
lache adj. negligent 7003.
lachesse n. laziness 6881.
lakketh impers. pr. 3 sg. in ~ me fails 800; litel ~ þat I ne were I am not far off 863; þer ~ þe you want 1482; me ~ I need 1483. intr. in litel ~ it ne it almost 4037.
langage n. words 2801.
langour n. sickness 5840; in ~ distressed 1287.
languetted pp. chattered 5408. **langwetynge** vbl. n. glib talking 5401.
languishe v. grow weaker 4615.
lappes n. pl. loose sleeves 3700.
largeliche adv. extensively 5111.
largesse n. abundance 5846.
lasse adj. minor 602; smaller 1601. as n. in sette þe ~ þi have a lower opinion of 3018. adv. in þe ~ less 252; neuere þe ~ no less 1980; neyþer more ne ~ not at all 3260; of neiþer more ne ~ nothing at all 4185. **lase** in was neuere þe ~ nevere decreased 4995.
laste adj. in ~ ende far end 1393-4; at þe ~ eventually 2805-6; in þe ~ ende finally 3151; at þe ~ at the end of life 3385-6.
lattere adv. later; neuer þe ~ (F non pour quant) nevertheless 1018.
law(g)he v. laugh 4524. **lo(o)wh** pa. t. sg. laughed 3079; ~ of 561; ~ not did not rejoice 2739. **lawghinge** vbl. n. smile 4537.
lauendere n. laundress 1138.
lawe n. civil law 1643. **lawes** pl. monastic Rules 2341n.
leced pp. adj. leashed 7031n.
leche n. healer 173; **leeche** 297.
lede v.[1] take 1014; bring 2601. **led** pp. brought 2644; **iled** 301.
lede v.[2] dull 3868. **leded** pp. adj. 3869.
leef adj. dear 3023; it were riht ~ to him it would give him great joy 157; be ~ wish 3699. **le(e)uere** comp. in I hadde ~ I would rather 423;

GLOSSARY

levere 416. **leeuest** *superl.* in *it was me not* ~ it was not my preference 3531.

leese *v.* lose 573; ~ *þe lyfe* die 423; ~ *hire custome* 811 see **custome**; ~ *my peyne* waste my efforts 1215. **leeseth** *pr. 3 sg.* in ~ *purpose* quails 2189. **lese** *subj. sg.* in ~ *not* should not waste 6061. **leese** *imp. sg.* ~ *it for nothing* do not on any account lose it 2378. **ylost** *pp.* lost 958.

leeue see **leue**.

leeue, leeve *v.*[1] believe 1517. *subj. sg.* 2214; **leue** 5125n. **leeue** *imp. sg.* (F *crois*) 3673.

leeue *v.*[2] allow; *pr. subj. sg.* in *God* ~ God grant 3667.

leeuere, leeuest see **leef**.

lefte see **leue**.

legittime *adj.* legitimate 4667.

ley *v.* in ~ *doun* take off 2490; *make* ~ *doun* cause to be laid down 1110-11. *refl.* in ~ *þee* lay yourself down 2638. *pr. 1. sg.* in ~ *me in awaite* 1249 see **awaite**. **leith** *3 sg.* 5689. *tr.* 4129. **leyde** *pa. t. sg.* in ~ ... *doun* removed 2488. **leyden** *pl.* laid out 528. **leyd** *pp.* laid on 318; pawned 5281.

leiser(e), leysere *n.* time 271; *bi* ~ 853-4 see **bi**; *at* ~ at your leisure 957.

lemman *n.* concubine 4987.

lene *v.*[1] lend; *subj. sg.* in *ne* ~ does not lend 1901. *imp. pl.* 5244.

lene *v.*[2] *refl.* (+ to) lean on 2006; rely on 2726. **lened** *pp.* in *was* ~ *hire* was leaning 1478n. *tr.* in ~ *to* supported by 2036; ~ *on* rested on 5359. *pp. adj.* ~ *at* leaning at 7065.

lerne *v.* show 1762; get used to 2508; teach 3102. **lerned** *pp.* been led to expect 130; understood 2656; ~ *of* accustomed to 2507. **lernynge** *vbl. n.* instruction 688.

les see **la(a)ces**.

lese *n.* in *in* ~ on a leash 6860.

lesinge *vbl. n.* falsehood 2992; *withoute* ~ in fact 670; without deceit 1303; *al withoute* ~ with complete honesty 2751. **lesinges** *pl.* fictions 3689.

lete *v.* allow 844; *he þe lyf shal* ~ he dies 5905. *imp. sg.* in ~ *hem go ligge* ignore them 1503. *pp.* in ~ ... *go dounward* dropped 6609.

lette *v.* delay ? 2777n, hinder 3763; ~ *him to clymbe* prevent his climbing 4013. **letted** *pa. t. sg.* in ~ *hire nothing* did not get in her way at all 1102. **lettede** *subj. sg.* in ~ *hem not* must not obstruct them 429. **letted** *pp.* in ~ *to go* prevented from going 2493. **lettinge** *vbl. n.* delay 1993; hindrance 3446; *þou doost me* ~ you hinder me 3902.

lettere *n.* writing 1092; Epistle 1248n, 2010.

leþie *adj.* pliant 3878.

leue *v.* give up 15; hesitate 990; remain 1149; leave 2976; *to go ... I wolde not* ~ I did not want to abandon the idea of going 2741; ~ *of his hand* relent 7172; **leeue** 1344n; **leve** put down 2939. **leueth** *pr. 3 sg.* gives up 497. **levinge** *pr. p.* omitting 324. **leue** *subj. sg.* 5125n. **leueth** *imp. pl.* omit 998. **lefte** *pa. t. sg.* remained 1289; stopped 3792. **leftest** *2 sg.* neglected 1924.

leuere, levere see **leef.**
lewed(e) *adj.* unlearned 60. as *n.* ordinary people 13; laymen 1465.
lich *adj.* equal 783; like 914; **liche** 751; **lych** 6097. **lich** *adv.* similarly 2317.
licour see **likour.**
lye *n.* lye (alkaline solutions made by leaching ashes, used in washing) 6066.
lyflode *n.* victuals 5068; livelihood 5220.
lift(e) *adj.* left 521.
lyfte *pa. t. sg.* lifted 50.
ligge *v.* lie 295; *let hem go* ~ 1503 see **lete. lyth** *pr. 3 sg.* is to be found 641; *youre profyite* ~ *þerinne* you will benefit from it 581; ~ *þerinne* is inherent in it 611-12; ~ *me on herte* is on my mind 5191; ~ *euele* has no rest 6668; **lith** 6892.
light *n.* vision 2630.
light *adj.* active 2657. as *n.* in *þe lyghte* the active one 6354.
lighted *pp.* ? illuminated 5907.
lightliche *adv.* easily 750.
lightnesse *n.* brightness 3270.
like *v. impers.* (+ dat.) please 99. **liketh** *pr. 3 sg.* in *it* ~ *me nouht* I do not like it 870; *me* ~ I like 972; I am glad 2369; ~ *me* I want to 2472. **like** *subj. sg.* in ~ *or not* ~ whether you like it or not 7132. **likinge** *vbl. n.* pleasure 3129.
liknesse *n.* in *took þerof* ~ took it as an example 1042; **likenesse** in *bi* ~ 1594 see **bi.**
lilour *n.* liquid 1141; **licour** 5333.
limited *pp.* assigned 4933.
lynage *n.* descent 4903.
lyne *n.* in *þe euene* ~ 1373-4 see **in.**
lysted *pp.* edged 1836.
lystes *n. pl.* battleground 5918n.
litel *adj.* poor 1401; *in* ~ *quantitee* looking small 1529; ~ *(a) closure* small form 1580, 1609. as *n.* ~ *lakketh þat I ne were* 863 see **lakketh;** ~ *or nouht it is to me* I could not care less 988; *for* ~ at the least excuse 6609; **litele** 1773[1,2]. **litel** *adv.* slightly 1163; ~ *is woorth* is futile 1057; useless 2409; *þe graciowse* ~ *pleasaunt* 1109 see **graciowse**; *of . . . was* ~ *myn entencioun* this . . . was hardly what I had had in mind 2421-2; **litele** 316, 1903.
litel-beloued *adj.* little-loved 1108.
lyth, lith see **ligge.**
litterarum Lat. *n. pl. gen.* in ~ *alphabeti* letters of the alphabet 5833.
live *pr. 1 sg.* in ~ *with* use as sustenance 4427. **lyvinge** *vbl. n.* life 4133.
liueliche *adj.* vigorous 638.
localliche *adv.* in respect of place 1753n, 1757.
logge *v.* live 6751. **logged** *pp.* established 6776.
loyne *n.* leash 5240.
loke(de), lokest, lookinge see **looke.**
lokyere *n.* locksmith 5100.

GLOSSARY

londe of biyonde see **biyonde.**
long(e) *adj.*[1] tedious 881; *riht long* ~ for far too long 1825; (*bi*) ~ *time* long 385; ~ *time gon* a long time since 1977-8.
long *adj.*[2] in ~ *on* owing to 463; *on me . . . it is not long* it is not my fault 3771; *if it ne be* ~ *on my self* unless I prevented it 5786.
longe *adv.* a long while 886; *as* ~ *as* provided that 466; while 177; *as* ~ *as . . . so* ~ as long as 2431; ~ *lerned* quite accustomed 2507; ~ *þat* long since 6678.
longe *v.* belong (to); ~ *to þee* be your responsibility 380. *pr. 1 sg.* in *I* ~ *nothing to* I have nothing to do with 5412-13. **longeth** *3 sg.* in ~ *wel to þin office* is certainly your responsibility 351; *to whom þe ded* (*office*) ~ whose responsibility it is 768[1,2]; *it* ~ *not to me* it is not my job to do so 937; ~ *freeliche to me* is wholly my responsibility 942; *þis* ~ this function is proper (to) 3346.
looke *v.* read 1924. *pr. 1. sg.* make sure 1068. *subj. sg.* in *God* ~ God keep you 3632. *imp. sg.* mind 354; consider 2182; ~ *wel on* fix your eyes on 2007; **lok** 3645. **looketh** *pl.* consider 2182; ~ *wel* make quite sure 677. **lookede** *pa. subj. sg.* in *I* ~ *wel* I must be very careful 703. **lookinge** *vbl. n.* to look 1154; seeing 1212; glance 4087; *only my* ~ *was* I could only see 81; *hool* ~ accurate sight 6202; **lokinge** eyes 1530.
loos *n.* honour 2194.
looseth *pr. 3 sg.* loosens 4127.
loowh see **lawgh.**
lopen *pp.* in *I am* ~ I spring up 6360.
lopyns *n. pl.* morsels 5533.
lordinges *n. pl.* sirs 313; gentlemen 457.
lordship(e) *n.* authority 729[1,2]; control 827; power 959. **lordshipes** *pl.* positions of authority 731.
lordshipinge *pr. p. adj.* (F *seignourissant*) in authority 725.
los *n.* destruction 5529.
loth *adj.* angry 831. *quasi-adv.* reluctantly (F *envis*) 830, 5764.
lowe *n.* in *oþer hye or* ~ rich or poor 5234.
lowe *adj.* low down 5473.
lust *n.* longing 692; pleasure 977; wish 4267; desire 5685; *at hire* ~ 1362 see **at**; *haue gret* ~ am very anxious 1824-5; *þer took me no* ~ *to* I had no desire to 4896.
luste *impers. pr. 3 sg.* in *me* ~ *not to foryete* I will not forget 882; **lusteth** is pleasing 4930. **lust** *pers. pa. t. sg.* wished 6005.
lusty *adj.* attractive 4980.

maad(e) see **make.**
maat *adj.* overcome 2805; powerless 7041; *check and* ~ checkmate 3439; **mate** 3437.
macier *n.* ? mace-bearer 6528n.
mad(en), madest see **make.**
magnifye *v.* praise 4219.
mai, may see **mown.**
maide *n.* virgin 3536.

mayl *n.* link 2205.
mailet *n.* mallet 1096.
mailure *n.* chain-mail 2254.
mayme *n.* injury 2766; spiritual disfigurement 4329.
mayresse *n.* a high (female) official 2813.
maister *n.* person of authority 277; craftsman 1049; teacher 2447; **mayster** 4793. **maistres** *pl.* learned men 54.
maisterman *n.* clever operator 2261n.
maistrye *n.* control 827.
maistrieth, maistryeth *pr. 3 sg.* overpowers 2475.
make *v.* in ~ ... *deye* kill 636; *contribucioun* ... ~ *of*, ~ *of* ... *contricioun* crush (it) 1152, 1165-6; ~ *anything þerof* do anything with it 1652-3; ~ ... *ful* fill 1719; ~ *yive me* have me given 1803; ~ ... *answer* answer 2070; *how þou shalt* ~ *þi foundement* what you must base your argument on 2558-9; ~ ... *mugoe* build up (their) fund 2666n; *daunger* ... ~ 2676-7 see **daunger;** ~ *gret wundringe* be amazed 3311; ~ *him chek and maat* checkmate him 3438-9; ~ *a cross* cross (myself) 3657; ~ *him shadwe* protect him 4639; ~ *flight* to fly 4865; ~ *kitte hem and araye hem* have them sawn and stacked 5200; ~ *chaunge of hem* change them round 5316; ~ *filthe* defecate 5702; ~ *restinge* pause 6133; ~ *a restinge* pause 6133; ~ *passage* set sail 6701-2; ~ *me entre* let me in 6763; ~ *habitacioun* live 6968; ~ *good cheer* welcome 7075; *maad* ~ *it* had it composed 7300. *pr. 1 sg.* in ~ *semblaunt* pretend 4062; ~ *it queynt* swagger 4091; ~ *þe wey to prepare the way for* 4111-12; ~ *it place* make room for it 4170; ~ *drenche and perisshe* drown and destroy 4363; ~ *drive hem out* have them driven out 5604; ~ *þe queyntrelle* 5677 see **litel;** ~ *remember on* call to mind 7077. **makest** *2 sg.* ~ *it ayen* repair it 3543. **maketh** *3 sg.* in ~ *his edifyinge* 716 see **edifyinge;** ~ *do* is the cause 810; ~ *his norture* find his food 1172; *deyntees he* ~ *of* 2106 see **deyntees;** ~ *clepe him* is called 2842; ~ *weene* seems 3278; ~ *do and counterfete* causes to be imitated and performed 4324; ~ *him gentel* assumes gentleness 5056; ~ *no ioye of* does not like 5436. **maken** *pl.* in ~ *þe touchinges* ... *and þe tastinges* touch and feel 2289-90; ~ *synge masses* have masses sung 5288. **make** *subj. sg.* in ~ *him queynte* behaves elegantly 2878; ~ *him simple* behaves as if honest 2879; ~ *he neuere so michel debaat* however much he may protest 3439. *pl.* ~ *him* ... *ouerthrowe* unseat him 4653. *imp. sg.* ~ *þat* ... *be tobroken* have ... broken 1747-8; ~ *gret sorwe* lament 4962. *pl.* in ~ *yive* have me given 5242. **ma(a)de** *pa. t. 1, 3 sg.* enabled 365; was giving 447; ~ *keepe* saw was kept 85; ~ *me fayr semblaunt* was most gracious to me 264-5; ~ *blisse me* ... *and marke me* had me marked with the sign of the cross 286; ~ *arme þee* had you armed 387-8; ~ *take þee* had you given 388; ~ *him bounde* had him bound 1327; ~ *tacche* cause to be nailed down 1330; ~ *my solace* enjoyed 1349; ~ *berne it* had it brought into the barn 1539; ~ *me sermoun* explained 1999; ~ *defence þat non took* forbade anyone to carry 2787; *of* ... *I* ~ *no fors* I paid no attention to 3793; ~ *hire* became 4411; ~ ... *endente it* had it serrated 4769; ~ *roste* had roasted 5462; ~ *me cheere þat* behaved as if 5502; ~ *me*

GLOSSARY

fisshinge fished 5556; ~ *I euere drede* did I ever fear 5738; ~ *not riht gret viage* did not get very far 6167-8; *men* ~ *of you saale* you were for sale 6350; **maade** 1397. **madest** *2 sg.* in ~ *him ysen* drove him out 392; ~ *brenne* caused to burn 6210. **ma(a)den** *pl.* helped 80; was due to 2315; ~ *ceese* brought to an end 449; ~ ... *requeste* asked 450. **ma(a)d** *pp.* complete 674; ~ *do* caused 1322; ~ *to* turned by 1547; ~ *semblaunt* showed signs 2623; ~ *me a shewinge of* displayed to me 2653; ~ *ynowh* 2767 see **ynowh**; *so* ~ of such a shape 4860; ~ *ayens Nature* unnatural 5132; ~ *it be so miche in her bowkinge* so soaked it 7095; **imaad** 803; **maked** 5973. **makinge** *pr. p. adj.* in ~ *noise* a sound of their being made 1368. *vbl. n.* in *in* ~ in the making 674; **makynge** 3750.
makere ayen *n.* repairer 3524.
manasest *pr. 2 sg.* threaten 3830. **manaseth** *3 sg.* stands as a warning 2331. **manas(s)inge** *vbl. n.* threats 3924; *without* ~ without warning 6564.
mane(e)re *n.* behaviour 1088; kind 3046; circumstances 3804; state of affairs 5257; nature 5284; *haue* ~ know how to go about it 347; *þe* ~ *of* about 1038; *þe* ~ *of þe holdinge* the way it is held 1193; *in swich* ~ *þat* in that 1918; *shoop her* ~ prepared 5486; *þe* ~ *how* the way in which 5818; *haue þi* ~ react 6582.
manhode, manhede *n.* human nature 38; human form 3236; ? human body 7199; *bodi of þe* ~ human body 620; *lyfe of þe* ~ human life 7296.
manward *adv.* in *to* ~ towards man 6219.
marchaleth *pr. 3 sg.* fakes up for sale 5325.
margery *n.* pearl 1975.
marigh, mary *n.* marrow 5072, 7071
market *n.* in *nygh a shrewed* ~ about to come off badly 3781n.
marmoset *n.* idol 4901.
masowned *pp.* built 210.
mast *n.* mast (the fruit of any forest tree, as eaten by pigs) 915.
matere *n.* ingredients 866; materials 4592; ~ *whereupon þou mihte werche* responsibility / material to work on 762-3; *not a* ~ *of wratthe* nothing to be angry about 1062. **mateere** 4592.
mattere *n.* mat maker 3605.
maugracious *adj.* ugly 3796.
maugre, mawgre *prep.* in spite of 7067; ~ *nature* unnaturally 4974; ~ *hem* against their will 6221; *adv.* in **boongree mawgree** whether you like it or not 5448.
mawmet(e) *n.* idol 4875; *ydole* ~ image 5445.
maundement *n.* a commission 2849.
me *pers. pron. acc.* and *dat.* (see relevant verb for use in various reflexive and impersonal constructions such as *passe me* and *me thowht*); for me 1995; to me 5739; *bettere* ~ *is* I had better 994; ~ *were bettere haue been* I would have been better off 3965; **mee** 5848.
medle *v.* be concerned 935. *refl.* interfere 2987; busy yourself 6669. **medled** *pp. adj.* mingled 3118.

mees see **mes**.
meete *adj.* the right size 2214.
me(e)te *v.* dream 7, 7283. **mete** *pr. pl.* in ~ *ye* are you dreaming 3179. **mette** *pa. t. sg.* 108. **met, ymet** *pp.* 3179, 7282. **me(e)tinge** *vbl. n.* 74, 277.
meeue, meeve *v.* worry 1193; *to haue aught to* ~ *him* he ought to want 1395; ~ *þee* put you off 1499. **meeued** *pa. t. sg.* removed 944; ~ *me* I wanted 105; ~ *al my corage* made me angry 1946. **meevinge** *vbl. n.* movement 6415.
meyne *n.* household 248; faculties 2335.
men *pron. indef.* people 14; they 92; in passive constructions such as ~ *han not taken him* he has not been given 507; *þe* ~ mankind 1324.
mendivauns *n. pl.* beggars 1263.
mene *n.* intercessor 5958.
mene *adj.* intervening 488; moderately serious 602.
menest *pr. 2 sg.* in *þer þou* ~ to which you are going 6682. **ment** *pp.* ? gone (F *tendu*) 7257.
mercy, merci *n.* compassion 1691; good gracious 2501; *crye yow* ~ ask your pardon 200; *miche(l) grant* ~ thank you very much 1823, 2720; ~ *I pray yow* have pity 2467; *to* ~ *able* 6017 see **able**.
merciable *adj.* compassionate 329.
mere mayden *n.* mermaid 4362n.
merelle *n.* counter (in the game of merels) 4150. **merelles** *pl.* merels 3643.
merlyoun *n.* merlin (F *esmerillon*) 3813.
merthes see **mirthe**.
merveile *refl. pr. 3 sg.* in ~ *hire* is astonished 1613.
mes *n.* a serving of food 778; a household (F *mes*) 431n; *grete* ~ a great quantity of food 2273; **mees** food 789. **mes** *pl.* 2272.
mesel *adj.* diseased 4867.
meselrie *n.* disease 601.
message *n.* in *do hire* ~ fulfil her mission 6961.
mesure *n.* limit; *withoute* ~ immeasurably 21; *haue his* ~ be contained 1580; *out of* ~ incredibly 2482; *passede* ~ was immeasurable 3952.
met(e) see **me(e)te**.
mete *n.* meal 777; food 798.
metinge see **me(e)te**.
metyerde *n.* measuring rod 5312.
meward *adv.* in *to* ~ see **to**.
miche *n.* in *kan he neure so* ~ *on* 36 see **kunne**; *bi as* ~ *as* 139 see **bi**; in pleonastic phrase *so* ~ 728; *so* ~ *þer is þat* 1192-3 see **so**; *do so* ~ 1402 see **do**. *adj.* great 241; a great deal of 1092; *so* ~ *good þow coudest* 2681 see **kunne**. *adv.* greatly 94; ~ *nedeth* is most essential to 15-16; ~ *graunt mercy* 1823 see **mercy**; *so* ~ *we dide . . . þat* 3349-50 see **do**; *so* ~ for such a long time 7095.
michel *n.* in *so* ~ *I* (*þow*) *dide*(*st*) 1124, 1647 see **do**; *so* ~ *til* 1177-8 see **so**; *as* ~ *as to sey* 1275 see **as**; *dide so* ~ 1571 see **do**; *so* ~ *diden* 1966-7 see **do**; *but of so* ~ 2179, *but of as* ~ *as* 3030 see **but**; *so* ~ such 3091;

make he neuere so michel 3439 see **make**; *ne litel ne* ~ not in any way 3493; *bi so* ~ 3749 see **bi**; *for þus* ~ in order to imply 4491; *do so* ~ *toward* 5797 see **do**; *so* ~ *I sey you* I can tell you 6176; *as* ~ *of heres as* as much of their property (? as many of their people) as 6565; *kunne he neuere so* ~ 6755 see **kunne**; *as* ~ *as she was cloþed in* what she was wearing 6819. **mychel** 5376. *adj.* great 595; many 1484; large 2144; ~ ... *from* large in comparison with 1730. as *n.* the grand 1401. *adv.* a great deal 31; much 217; very 597; greatly 631; ~ *out of þe wey* far strayed 5708.

midday *n.* the highest point of the sun's course (? south) 5760.

middes *n.* centre 123.

might, myght see **mown.**

miht *n.* power 739; *in* ~ strong 2410.

millewardes *n. pl.* millers 5108.

mynde *n.* in *haue in* ~ remember 1657; *þer be alwey* ~ of constant attention should be given 2395.

mynde *refl. pr. 1 sg.* remember 1732.

mynede *pa. t. sg.* undermined 4922.

mynged *pp.* reminded 2284. **mynginge** *refl. pr. p.* remembering 2383.

ministre *n.* administrator 248. **ministres** *pl.* assistants 523.

ministres *pr. 2 sg.* in ~ *him* provide him with 3469.

mir(r)e *v. refl.* look in a mirror; ~ *him* look at himself 2012; ~ *þee* see yourself reflected 2014.

mirthe *n.* amusement 5524. **mirthes, merthes** *pl.* 3122, 6380.

mis *adv.* in *go* ~ go astray 6158.

mysbifalleth *pr. 3 sg.* turns out badly 320. **misbifallen** *pl.* come to grief 7145. **bisbifel** *pa. t. sg.* in *how it* ~ *hem* what disaster overtook them 1453.

misbileeued *pp.* as *n. pl.* unbelievers 5979.

mischaunce *n.* misery 5093; evil 5918.

mische(e)f *n.* a dangerous thing 2534; harm 3032; affliction 4850.

miscleped *pp.* misnamed 3817.

misdo(on) *v.* do wrong 1422; do farm 2240; mysdo 1284. **misdoinge** *vbl. n.* in *withoute* ~ when no harm has been done (by them) 1322.

misericorde *n.* mercy 5858.

misese *n.* trouble 1811.

misfel *pa. t. sg.* in ~ *me* misfortune befell me 3788.

mishapneth *pr. 3 sg.* in ~ *(him)* has the misfortune 6633.

misliketh *imper. pr. 3 sg.* displeases; *me* ~ I am annoyed 1620; *nothing* ~ *me þerinne* I have nothing against it 1991-2; *it* ~ *me* I am upset 2047.

misseith *pr. 3 sg.* slanders 5585. **missey** *imp. sg.* in ~ *of* 2267.

missittynge pr. p. adj. inappropriate 1780.

mistake *v.* in ~ *ayens* offend 835-6. **mistakest** *refl. pr. 2 sg.* in *of nothing* ~ *þee* you are quite right 1720. **mistake** *pr. subj. sg.* in ~ *þee* not make no mistake 308. **mistooke** *pa. t. sg.* in ~ *þee* did wrong 1163. **mistake(n)** *pp.* trespassed 912; ~ *me to* offended 3101. **mistakinge, mystakinge** *vbl. n.* offence 1625; doing wrong 1699; *withoute* ~

faultless 1088; correctly 2330; legitimately 5205; *no* ~ nothing wrong 1778. **mistakinges** *pl.* errors 1596.
misterman *n.* kind of man 2774n.
mo(o) *n.* more 3001; *withoute* ~ 1049-50 see **withoute**.
moldewerp *n.* mole.
moneyden *pa. t. pl.* minted 2126. **moneyed** *pp.* 2124.
more *n.* in *today* ~ henceforth 998n; *withoute* ~ 1049 see **withoute**; *þe* ~ greater 4952; *not . . . ~ ne lasse* not at all 6348.
mort *n.* in *A la* ~ (a battlecry) 4546.
moste in *shalt* ~ see **shal.**
mouht *n.* mouth 1189.
mown *v.* be able 954; *ye shul wel* ~ it is all very well for you 467. **may** *pr. 3 sg.* in *it* ~ *not be þat þou (þei) ne be be(eth)* you (they) will inevitably 167, 300; ~ *not be* is impossible 185; ~ *not be þat he ne haue* he cannot fail to have 1288-9n. **miht** *2 sg.* in ~ *not* will not be able 183; ~ *nothing do* cannot do anything 2713. **miht(e)** *pa. t. 1. 3 sg.* in ~ *no more* could do no more 1798; ~ *I haue* if I had 1120.
mugoe *n.* fund 2666n.
murmur(e) *n.* complaint 1058.
murmuringe *pr. p.* in ~ *with here teth* snarling through their teeth 6431.
musard *n.* dolt 2850.
muse *v.* ponder 3766; believe 4325; to idle away time 5650.
museryes *n. pl.* amusements 3644n.
muste *pr. 1, 3 sg.* in *I ne* ~ *caste* I cannot but emit 4758; *it ne* ~ *go* it has to go 5146. **moste** 2587.
mutacioun *n.* transformation 792; change 854.
nailes *n. pl.* hooves 4678.
nakenen *v.* rob 869. **naked** *refl. pa. t. sg.* stripped 91. *tr. pp. adj.* open 368; loose 747; uncovered 770.
named *pp.* in ~ *to do miracles* given the reputation of performing miracles 5334.
nameliche *adv.* particularly 986.
nart *adv.* + *pr. 2 sg. (ne art)* are not 5859. **nis** + *3 sg.* is not 1975n, 3193. **nere** + *subj. sg.* were it not for 6013.
nature *n.* 807n; His physical nature 1851n.
ne *adv.* not 37n; ~ *were* if it were not for 906; ~ *seechen but* seek nothing but 2394; pleonastic in double negs., e.g. ~ ~ *misdede nouht* neither did he sin 245.
neede *n.* in *at þe* ~ 2408 see **at**; *when it shal be* ~ when necessary 2550; *is most* ~ *of* is most essential 3551. **needes** *pl.* business 1017.
neede *v. intr.* be necessary 935.
needes *adv.* necessarily 5535; *I muste* ~, ~ *I muste* I would be (was) obliged 46, 218.
neewe *n.* in *of* ~ recently 2840.
neewe *adv.* recently; ~ *wexe a fool* just gone silly 902; **newe** again 1948.
neewed *pp.* renewed 4031.
neighe, neyghe *v.* go near 568. **neihede, neighede** *pa. t. sg.* 816, 4701.

GLOSSARY 553

neiþer, neyþer *conj.* in ~ *inne ne oute* the inside or outside of 1702; ~ *more ne lasse* not at all 3492. **noþer** 6904.
nempne *v.* name 684.
nere see **nart**.
nestle *v.* nest 4225.
neuere *adv.* not at all 726; no 1065; ~ *so (adj.)* however *(adj.)* 36; ~ *oon* no-one at all 568; ~ *þe more* 1052 see **haue**; *ye witen* ~ 1105 see **wite**; *it was* ~ *þat I ne was* I was always 5655-6; **neuer** 1018n.
newe see **neewe**.
next *prep.* in ~ *me* immediately below me in rank 6859.
nice, nyce *adj.* stupid 3589; frivolous 6344; ignorant 6936.
niceliche *adv.* foolishly 905; ? indolently 5636; wickedly 5637.
nygh, nigh, nyh, nih *adv.* at hand 402; near 542, 1343n; nearly 2344; close 2350; firmly 3974; *of so* ~ so closely 1845.
nis see **nart**.
no *adv.* not at all 324; ~ *more* any more 89. *adj.* in ~ *day* (not) at any time 334; ~ *game* 408 see **holde**; ~ *wise* any way 1022; *in* ~ *time* 1869 see **in**; ~ *wiht* anyone 1978; *for* ~ not by any 2204; *by* ~ *wey* 2620 see **bi**; *for* ~ *peny* (not) for any money 4100; **noo** 7287.
nobleche *adv.* splendidly 2611.
noblesse *n.* nobleness 3223; the nobleman 5257.
noces *n.* wedding (F *noches*) 880n.
nolde *adv.* + *pa. t. sg.* (*ne wolde*) would not 5864.
no(o)n(e) *pron.* no-one 35; not one 2323; not any 2588; *neuere* ~ never anyone 99; ~ *lich* no parallel 783; ~ *of us* neither of us 835; ~ *swich* (in multiple neg.) its equal 1066; one like it 2092[1,2]. *adj.* no 1; any (in multiple neg.) 2412; *ne* ~ *ooþer* nor anyone else 183:, ~ *ooþer* no one else 767; ~ *ooþer thing* nothing else 1024; ~ *ooþerweys* not for any other reason 2069; ~ *so litel* the slightest 4757. *adv.* in *shal þee* ~ *neede* will not be necessary for your 2448; *wule he oþer* ~ whether he likes it or not 3443-4.
norice, norish *n.* nurse 1312.
norishe *v.* take care of 2676. *pr. 1 sg.* feed 4533.
norture *n.* food 4580; *maketh his* ~ 1172 see **make**.
note *n.* nut 5505. **notes** *pl.* 3637.
nothing *n.* in *gabbed me of* ~ did not lie to me about anything 262; *of* ~ in nothing 1720; by nothing 3062; *haue* ~ have no business 422; *for* ~ not for anything 1958; *dooth þee* ~ 2058-5 see **do**; *leese it for* ~ 2378 see **leese**; *ne* ... ~ nor ... anything 2477; *in* ~ not in the least 2717-18; ~ *of tomorwe in me* no future for me 3913; **nothinge** 755. **nothing** *adv.* not at all 1102; ~ *woorth* useless 1399.
noþer see **neiþer**.
nouht *n.* nothing 205; *ne* ~ *is woorth* ... nor is ... any use 1400; *for* ~ *be they not* not for nothing are they 1923; *setten* ... *at nouht* 2202-3 see **sette**; ~ *it is worth* it is no good 2619-20n; *serueth me of* ~ is no use to me 5027. *pron.* no one 2982. *adv.* not 156; not at all 870; ~ *þan* nevertheless 37n; ~ *for þanne* (F *non pour quant*) nevertheless 1321-2; ~ *for þat* not that 2504; ~ *acustomed* 2655 see **acustomed**; **nowht** 695.

nouelries *n. pl.* innovations 839.

o see **oo**.
obeisaunt *adj.* obedient 6551.
obley-makere *n.* wafer-maker 1459n.
of *adv.* in *doon* ∼, *did(e)* ∼, ∼ ... *do* see **do**.
of *prep*, from 42; about 66[1]; by 118; in 145; out of 288[2]; on 357; as regards 410[1,2]; at 561; with 666; as one of 762; for 924; some of 1821; by means of 2737; proper to 3206[1,2]; on account of 3263; *cure* ∼ 176 see **cure**; ∼ *sooth* indeed 281; *hath his hanginge* ∼ 732-3 see **haue**; ∼ *yuel doinge* 1045 see **do**; ∼ *all* everything 1054; ∼ *nothing* 262 see **nothing**; ∼ *so nyh* 1845 see **nyh**; ∼ *þat* because 1946; *but* ∼ *so michel* 2179 see **but**; *out* ∼ *mesure* 2482 see **mesure**; ∼ *newe* 2840 see **newe**; ∼ *what* in what way 3015; *but* ∼ *as michel as* 3030 see **but**; *drede* ∼ 3333 see **drede**; ∼ *euele feith* dishonest 3498-9; ∼ *gret care* very responsible 3522; *neede* ∼ necessary 3551; ∼ ... *I made no fors* 3793 see **make**; ∼ *me* ∼ *þou shalt haue it* 3816 see **haue**; ∼ *alle thinge* particularly 3933-4 *of* ... *feele* experience 4727; *wolt not* ∼ 4809 see **will**; *serueth me* ∼ *riht litel* is of little use to me 4828; ∼ *kynde* naturally 5353; ∼ *acord* 5358 see **ac(c)ord**; *art* ... ∼ belong to 5443; *assured* ∼ safe from 5502; ∼ *verrey riht* according to strict justice 5873; *assaiyede* ∼ *alle* tried everything 6418; *vse* ∼ *boþe* use both 6576; ∼ *wheþer þou wolt vse* which you will use 6576; pleonastic in *many* ... ∼ 26-7, *hadd(e)* ... 28-9.
offence *n.* wrong-doing 2720; *withoute* ∼ legitimately (? without violence) 2073.
ofte-times *adv.* often 2552.
oynement *n.* healing agent (? the eucharist) 3907n. **oynementes** *pl.* oils 289.
oynture *n.* ointment 4357n.
olde *n.* old woman 3807; ? **oolde** 4342n.
on *prep.* about 36; into 632; at 2007; in 3318; *long* ∼ 463 see **long**; *witnesse* ∼ 856 see **witnesse**; ∼ *oo side* one way 1063-4; *bithouhte* ... *on* see **bithinke**; ∼ *þat ooþer side* (F *d'autre part(ie)*) moreover, in addition 1601n; *take* ∼ 5853 see **take**; *an* only in ∼ *hy* high up 50; at the top 1870.
oncloþed *refl. pa. t. sg.* undressed 91.
ones see **oones**.
onhede see **oonhede**.
onlyue *adj.* alive 2576.
oo *adj.* one 3360, 3390n; ∼ *time* sometimes 647-8; **o** 5325; (perhaps on occasions = article).
oon *adj.* one 440; the same 1031; in unity 2410; ∼ *hour* sometimes 5277; *hire* ∼ *brest* one of her breasts 7161. *pron.* one 496; person 816; a person 2390; someone 2595; *neuere* ∼ 568 see **neuere**; *eche* ∼ 1207 see **eche**; **on** 2119n, 2601n.
oones *adv.* once 2960; **ones** 7213.
oonhede *n.* unity 1858; **onhede** 4780.

GLOSSARY

ooþer *adj.* different 4856; another 6959; *noon* ~ *thing* nothing else 1024; *on þat* ~ *side* 1601 see **on**; **ooþer** *pl.* other 54. **ooþer** as *pron.* the other 441; *ne noon* ~ nor anyone else 183; *þat oon and þat* ~ 702 see **þat**; *þat* ~ *the next* 1200. **ooþere** *pl.* others 78. **ooþeres** *gen.* other people's 716. **ooþer** ? as *adv.* otherwise 4512.
ooþerweys *adv.* as *adj.* not the case 2518. *adv.* in terms of quite different circumstances 1695; differently 1698; in different ways 1757; for any other reason 2069; the opposite way 4071; in another way 6711; *al* ~ 1728 see **al**; ~ *þan dueliche* off the proper path 2733. ~ *it goth* it is quite the opposite 2940; *al* ~ *turned* reversed 2941. **ooþerweyse** 6175.
ooþerwise *adv.* in any other way 608; *al* ~ see **al**; **ooþerwyse** 178.
openliche *adv.* publicly 1408; clearly 1964.
opned *pp.* explained 1818.
ordeyne(e) *adj.* controlled 2245n; correct 2355.
ordeyne *v.* order 1036; to be ordained 2786n; *to* ~ *of yow* to have control over you 5802n. **ordeyned** *pa. t. sg.* arranged 784; instructed 1447. *refl.* decreed 3229. *tr. pl.* made arrangements about 310. *pp.* arranged 525n; appointed 1634; established 1644; ~ *for wele* carefully planned 2502; ~ *to* destined for 7247. *refl.* prepared 2762.
ordeynowr *n.* controller 5803.
ordinem Lat. *n.* order 5833.
organe *n.* instrument (especially the portative organ) combining sounds 4138; ? polyphonic music 6987n. **organes** *pl.* (? *sg.* sense) pipes 6981.
orlage *n.* clock 7272n.
orphanitee *n.* orphanhood 5771.
oseres *n. pl.* osiers, willow twigs 6704.
oþer *conj. 3;* **oþere** 471. *adv.* pleonastic in ~ . . . *or* 352.
oþerwhile *adv.* sometimes 4236.
ouht *pron.* anything 4162; *bi* ~ *þat I haue herd speke* 790-1 see **bi**. *adv.* at all 1323; *þat* ~ *shal availe* that shall be worthwhile 1891.
ouhte see **oweth**.
out *adv.* in *comyng* ~ 733 see **come(n)**; *cast* . . . ~ 1269 see **caste(n)**; *gon* ~ 2355 see **go**; ~ *of mesure* 2482 see **mesure**; ~ *shet* excluded 3217; ~ *of þi wey* off your path 3470-1; ~ *of myself* confused 3729; *don* ~ removed 4775; (with ellipsis of *intr. v.*) come out 5298; ~ *of witte* insane 5577; ~ *of* escape from 6186; *was* ~ went 6552.
outerliche see **vtterliche**.
outrage *n.* intemperance 5164. **outrages** *pl.* extravagances 5529.
outrageous *adj.* undisciplined 2257.
outtaketh *pr. 3 sg.* makes an exception 764. **outtakinge** *pr. p.* 1232.
owttaken *pp. adj.* in *any* ~ exception 12.
ouer *adv.* moreover 2100.
ouer *prep.* in ~ see abroad 2251; ~ *alle* in everything 1075; above all 6196. **over** in *more* . . . ~ *more* . . . *than* 2060-1.
oueral *adv.* completely, as is required 297n; everywhere 1559.
ouerbigge *v.* pay too much for 6351.
ouerflowe *v.* overrun 1723.
ouertrede *v.* subdue 7061.

ouertrowinge *vbl. n.* over-confidence 2784.
owen *adj.* in *here* ~ their rights 1661.
oweth *pr. 3 sg.* in ~ *wel to* really should 6792. **ouhrte** *pa. t. sg.* owed 40, 5488. *impers.* in *us* ~ we should have 5952.
owher *adv.* anywhere 223.

paas *n.* way in 244; paragraph, chapter 610; way out 1206; path 2006; **pas** 672, 5688. **pases** *pl.* 1809.
palet *n.* shovel 1228.
parcenere *n.* sharer 3386.
parde *interj.* (reduced form of *par dieu*) indeed 6713.
paresis *n.* the Parisian denier 5137n.
paringall *adj.* equal 4043.
parlement *n.* discussion 315; speech 1414.
part *n.* portion 454; *havinge* ~ being concerned 828; *þat God haue* ~ God help us 2887.
parte *v.* set out 491n; divide (something) 495; share 3385n. *pr. 1. sg.* in ~ *fro* leave 2738.
partere *n.* distributor 1282n.
partye *n.* portion 494; *double* ~ two parts 617; *in* ~ partly 1770.
pas *n.* in ~ *for* ~ step by step 6076. (See also **paas**).
passage *n.* entrance 39; crossing 366; *make* ~ set sail 6702; *hard* ~ a hard time 7001.
passe *v.* cross; go through 1401; ignore 2786; ~ ... *foorth* get through 184; cross 242. *refl.* in *shortliche to* ~ *me* in short 29; *I* ~ *me* I deal with it briefly 2358-9. **passinge** *tr. pr. p.* in ~ *my wille* ignoring my wishes 875. **passede** *pa. t. sg.* in ~ *mesure* was immeasurable 3952. **passe** *intr. subj. pl.* in ~ *we ouer* let us not pursue the matter 5196.
passioun *n.* painful disease; *þat euele* ~ *smyte it* a plague on it 2474-5.
Pater Noster Lat. *phr.* Our Father (the Lord's prayer) 4785.
patroun *n.*[1] design (F *patron*) 1371.
patroun *n.*[2] patron, superior in the monastery (F *parrain*) 2270.
pauteneers *n. pl.* purses 5224n.
payage *n.* payment 40n.
paye *v.* in ~ *ayen to* repay 5095-6. **payed** *pp.* in *as wel he hadde be* ~ he was as satisfied 2271.
peyne *n.* in *leese my* ~ 1215 see **leese**; *do* ~ try hard 2939. **peynes** *pl.* punishments 685; anguish 2187.
peyne *v. refl.* take pains 3325. **pewyneden** *pa. t. pl.* went to great efforts 1956.
peynture *n.* painting (of the surfaces) 4293.
peys *n.* weight 3870.
peise *v.* weigh down 5036. *refl. pr. 1 sg.* 5043. *tr.* **peiseth** *3 sg.* weighs 5043. **peise** *pl.* sell by weight 5207. **peysede** *pa. t. sg.* was heavy 5124.
penauntes *n. pl.* penitents 687.
peny *n.* coin 4427; (*noon*) ... *for no* ~ (not) for any money 4100.
penselles *n. pl.* pennons 44n.
peramowres *adv.* with a great love (perhaps with echo of original meaning 'by the love of God') (F *par amours*) 573.

perauenture *adv.* perhaps 657.
perche *n.* rack 2079.
perished *pp.* destroyed 4502; **peresshed** 6622.
pestilencial *adj.* dangerous, disease-producing 5574.
pye *n.* magpie 4224.
pyer *n.* (Gallicism) stone 2737n.
pighte *pa. t. sg.* struck 5996.
pike *n.* pickaxe 4952.
pikois(e), pykois(e) *n.* pickaxe 4924.
pile *n.* (F *pel*) stake 2098n.
pipe *n.* musical pipe 804n.
pistel *n.* Epistle (read at Mass) 6282n.
pitaunceere *n.* distributor of rations 6913.
pitous(e), pitowse *adj.* compassionate 329.
place *n.* in *put . . . into swich* ~ bring to the point 3828; *make . . .* ~ *more* give more room 4081; *in no* ~ never 5217. **places** *pl.* squares 27.
placebo Lat. *fut. 1 sg.* as *n.* ('I will please') flattering behaviour 4352n.
platte *n.* flat 637.
platte *pr. 1 sg.* flatten out 6470.
ple *n.* in *holt* ~ is arguing 5475. **ples** *pl.* suit or actions at law 5384.
pley *n.* amusement 943; game 4287; *þe faireste of þe* ~ the best bet 3776.
pleydeden *pa. t. pl.* went to law 5399.
pleye *v.* make play 2444; handle (it) 2447; ~ *at* handle 2446.
pleyn *adj.* honest 2839; direct 2853; *do þi wille* 2176 see **do**.
pleine *refl. pr. 1 sg.* complain 1022.
plente *n.* abundance 92.
plesaunce *n.* in *do her* ~ 2456 see **do**.
plyt *n.* in *out of* ~ from (their) scroll (or folds) 2829.
plounginge *vbl. n.* immersing 5532.
poynynges *n. pl.* piercings 2111.
poynt *n.* in *a* ~ see **a**; *in sum* ~ to some extent 3630; *in* ~ *is* is about 5881; *in þis* ~ at this moment 6188. **poyntes** *pl.* topmost part 2015n; *of alle* ~ completely 2605; *at alle* ~ completely 2762; *in alle* ~ all the time 4523.
polishest *pr. 2 sg.* make refined 3122.
pomel(le) *n.* knob 1878.
pondre ? *n.* 5134n.
poopet *n.* lad 2562n. **popettes** *pl.* lasses 3684.
poorge *v.* clear out 1225. **purgeth** *pr. 3 sg.* cleanses 1219. **poorginge** *vbl. n.* purification 394; **purginge** 6071.
popettes see **poopet**.
porter *n.*[1] door-porter 33.
porter *n.*[2] bearer 1282.
portreyed *pp.* carved 1046.
posse *v.* pat 6378. **possed** *pp.* battered 6430.
potage *n.* soup 4604.
potentes *n. pl.* crutches 7032.
pouce *n.* pulse 3364.

poudre *n.* flour 3859.
pound *n.* ? pound's-worth of time 5167n.
powere *n.* in *to my* ~ as far as I can 3743.
preche *v.* in ~ *me* explain to me 794; *to* ~ preaching 1103.
precious *adj.* too proud 857.
predicacioun *n.* assertion (in logic) of something about a subject 5294.
predicament *n.* Predicament (of Aristotle) 714 (see note 715).
preeue, preeve *v.* approve 1612; test 4163; **prooue** prove 940; ? **preue** 3379. **preeue** *refl.* try 2583. **preeued** *pp. adj.* confirmed 1983; **proued** 2839.
preyse, preise *v.* respect 2618; *litel to* ~ of little value 1693; *michel to* ~ of great value 1974; ~ *at a bodde* give a fig (lit. bud) for 255-6; *litel þei wolde* ~ they would not think much of 1603-4. *pr. 1 sg.* in ~ *not* . . . *at thre verres* do not give a fig for 3010-11n. **preysede** *pa. t. sg.* admired 1877. **preysed** *pp.* honoured 2388. *pp. adj.* **ypreised** 1109. **preysinge** *vbl. n.* public adulation 4073.
presentliche *adv.* actually 1768.
presse *n.* in *in* ~ gripped 6607.
pressinge *pr. p.* constricting 2466. **pressed** *pp.* pinched 2590. **pressinge** *vbl. n.* pressing (of wine) 6485n.
pressour *n.* wine-press 6483.
pryded *pp.* filled with pride 6559.
prik(k)inge *pr. p.* spurring 3984. **prikked** *pp.* sewn 2120. **prik(k)inge** *pr. p. adj.* sharp, prickly 352.
prime *n.* spring; ~ *temps* (Gall.) Springtime 848n.
prys, pris *n.* renown 2194; reward 3067; honour, respect 4043; price 5179.
prise *pp. adj.* (Gall. taken); *blowe* ~ sound the hunting call signifying that the prey is taken 4183.
priued *pp.* excluded 6369.
priue(e) *adj.* secluded 1430; private 2348; **pryue** in ~ *chambre* room containing a close-stool 5700n.
priuees *n. pl.* intimate friends 2350.
priueliche *adv.* furtively 1448; **priuely** secretly 1687; **priuiliche** 6778.
priuytees *n. pl.* secrets 3253.
procuracioun *n.* document giving (her) legal authority to act on (his) behalf 6965.
procuresse *n.* agent 6961.
profyt(e), profite *n.* benefit 158; **profyite** in *youre* ~ *lyth þerinne* it is to your advantage 581; **profyt** in *do me* ~ 2086 see **do**.
profitable *adj.* beneficial 569.
profite *v. intr.* be of benefit 572; **profiteth** *tr. pr. 3 sg.* in ~ *me anything is any good to me* 2478.
prooue see **preeve**.
propeliche, properliche see **propirliche**.
propir, propre *adj.* appropriate 1917; ~ *wil(le)* individual will 6403.
propirliche, properliche *adv.* appropriately 549; accurately 1371; **propeliche** 3865.

GLOSSARY

prouidence *n.* store 2667.
psalmodye *n.* the singing of psalms 6984.
publican *n.* tax collector 4329.
pulle *v.* strip 5079. **pulleth** *pr. 3 sg.* pulls up 6295.
purblynd(e) *adj.* one-eyed 6190n.
purchace *v.* bring about 4024. **purchaceth** *pr. 3 sg.* obtains 5220. **purchasedest** *pa. t. 2 sg.* deliberately procured 1164.
purgeth, purginge see **poorge**.
purpoynt *n.* pourpoint 2111n.
purposed *pp.* intended 2741.
purueye *v.* (+of) provide 1815.
puruiaunces *n. pl.* stocks, provisions 5065.
putte *v.* prod 342; ~ . . . *into swich place* bring to the point 3827-8; ~ *al in* rely entirely on 3847. *refl.* set out 2043. **puttest** *pr. 2 sg.* go 2733. **putteth** *tr. 3 sg.* pushes 1219; thrusts 1221; ~ *me to vnwurshipe* disgraces me 5590. **putte** *subj. sg.* in ~ *me to serue* make myself servant 4900-1. *refl. pa. t. sg.* in ~ *hire forth* came forward 1552. **put** *pp.* in ~ *him vnder* submitted to 1251; ~ *to þe ende* brought to an end 5619; ~ *in defaute* left unrepresented in court 6964; ~ *in foryetinge* neglected 7077-8; **putt** 6918.
puttok *n.* kite 5064n.

quantite(e) *n.* size 1693; *litel* ~ small form 1529.
quassen *pr. pl.* override 1597.
queynteliche *adv.* exquisitely 159; cleverly 1837; splendidly 2611.
queintise *v.* beautify 2884; adorn 3117. **queyntisinges** *vbl. n. pl.* finery 4031.
queyntrelle *n.* in *a litel make þe* ~ behave a bit like a fine lady 5676-7.
quik *adj.* living 783; **quik** 4763. **quike** as *n. pl.* the living 1855.
quykene *v.* liven up 4121. **quikned** *pp.* kept alive 1292.
quinzimes *n. pl.* periods of fifteen days 5166.
quod *pa. t. sg.* said 142.

ra(a)ge *n.* insanity 4668; violent desire, mania 5543.
rad see **rede** *v.*[1]
raptus Lat. *n.* rape 5711.
rathe, raþe *adv.* swiftly 830; early 4969.
rau(g)ht(e), rawhte see **reeche**.
raunpen *v.* crawl 860.
raunsome *n.* debt, toll 40; **raunsoum** ransom 2125.
rauished, raueshed *pp.* transported 3351.
recche *v. intr.* in *it thurt not* ~ there is no need to trouble 1760; it does not matter 3554; ~ *of* think much of 3613; worry about 6315. *tr. pr. 1 sg.* care 3599. *impers.* in *it shulde nothing* ~ *þee* you should not mind 2157-8. *refl. imp. sg.* in ~ *þee neuere* 1981. **roughte** *pa. t. sg.* in *þerof* ~ *me nothing* 3079. **rouht** *impers.* in ~ *hire of* she cared for 3523.
recomaunded *pp.* commanded again 2943.
recoupeth *pr. 3 sg.* interrupts 4212n.

recouere v. restore 1914; **rekeuer** return to 3944.
recreaunt adj. defeated 6696.
rede v.¹ read 1093. **rad, red** pp. 5, 1199.
rede v.² advise; pr. 1 sg. 242.
rederes n. pl. lectors 515n.
redye v. prepare 1902. **redynge** vbl. n. preparation 3924.
redresse v. bring back to the right course 175. refl. return to the right path 3670.
redressere n. guide 5442n.
reeche pr. 1 sg. give 5771. **raught, rauhte** pa. t. sg. gave 6021; stretched out 6033.
refreyneth pr. 3 sg. restrains 2233.
refuit see **refute**.
refuse v. be refused 2128. **refused** pp. rejected 5447.
refute n. refuge 5847. **refuit** 5866.
regent n. ruler 2329.
reioyse v. take pleasure in 495; cheer 5934. **reioysede** refl. pa. t. sg. in ~ me of was delighted by 2085; **rejoycede** 3390.
rekenynge n. account (of one's conduct, given to God at the Last Judgement) 5965.
rekeuer see **recouere**.
releef n. sustenance (distributed to the poor) 1084n; remainder of the food 1289.
releeue v. rescue 5770.
religioun n. the state of life bound by religious vows; an Order 17.
religious n. pl. members of religious Orders 60; **religiows** 6725.
reme(e)ve v. violate 824; transform 974; move 3147. **remeved** pp. altered 2941. **remeevinges** vbl. n. pl. transformations 881.
remembre v. refl. recollect yourself 1926; make ~ on 7077 see **make**.
remenaunt n. rest 499.
remordinge pr. p. adj. gnawing (with remorse) 1175.
rennere n. one who runs about 6354.
renomed pp. in of ... ~ renowned for 4660.
repele v. take back 4047; to ~ it for it to be recalled 1359n.
repreeved, reprooved pp. invalidated 1621.
representatyfliche adv. in a representative way 1759.
reprouable adj. disgraceful 4942.
residue n. remainder of an estate when all charges, debts and bequests are paid 5104.
resyne pr. 1 sg. give 5913.
resortinge refl. pr. p. in ~ him to taking his power from 3316n.
resoun n. the measure by which a miller makes his toll 2872; no(t) ~ illogical 1600; bi ~ 1725-6 see **bi**.
respyt n. reprieve 641; **respite** 4545.
respiten v. in ~ me of reprieve me from 5782.
restinge vbl. n. perch 3146n; resting-place 6623; make a~ 4846 see **make**.
reuthe n. pity 5960.

GLOSSARY

rewm *n.* kingdom 6515.
reuelle *n.* delight 5576; merry-making 6357.
reuye *pr. 1 sg.* place a higher stake (in a game of dice) 5615n.
reward *n.* regard; *hath* ~ *elleswhere þan to himself* is concerned with matters relating to others 715-16; *hath no* ~ pays no attention 915.
rewe *n.* row 7127.
rewelles *n. pl.* rowels (on a wheel-spur) 3958.
rial *adj.* royal 5977; **ryal** 3556.
rialliche *adv.* in reality 1768.
rialtee *n.* royalty 5277.
ri(g)ht *n.* justice 2433; reason 2566; truth, accuracy 7282; *bi* ~ 683 see **bi**; *after his* ~ 2138-9 see **after**; *to his* ~ 2148 see **to**. **rihtes** *pl.* in *bi hire* ~ 1362-3 see **bi**; *at here* ~ 1942 see **at**.
ri(g)ht *adv.* very 22; just 50; as soon 267[2]; absolutely 954; exactly 1574; ~ *so* so in exactly the same way 1013; so absolutely 1575; accordingly 1775; ~ *went* behaved virtuously 5375; **ry(g)ht** 1882, 1883, 1943, 3983, 4737.
rihte *v.* correct 2150; ~ *þee* improve the fit of 2160. **rihted** *pp.* fitted 2120.
rihtful *adj.* just 5864.
ringeres *n. pl.* small bells (F *sonets*) 1908.
riot *n.* lack of control 1586.
ryot(t)ous *adj.* uncontrolled 2140; undisciplined 2149.
ryuaile *n.* shore, landing-place 6648.
riueled *pp.* shrivelled 5698. **rivelede** as *n.* shrivelled one 4753.
rochet *n.* long dress 120n.
roile *v.* roll 5606.
romaunce *n.* story (in the vernacular) 6n.
rouht(e) see **recche**.
rouken *v.* crouch 5521.
roundeth *refl. pr. 3 sg.* curls into a ball 4730. **rownded** *intr. pp.* hunched 4729.
roundliche *adv.* steadily 2553.
rounge *v.* gnaw 4481; *stint to* ~ stop gnawing 1177n. **rounginge** *pr. p.* in ~ *on my brydel* chafing at the bit 4836n. **rounged** *pp.* 4572n.
roungere *n.* filer 5098.
rownynge *vbl. n.* whispering 1549.
rude *adj.* rough 322; crude 1043; untutored 2924.
rudeliche *adv.* roughly 321; aggressively 822; in simple terms 3027.
rudeshipe *n.* roughness 320.
rudesse *n.* uncouthness 5554n.
russet *n.* cloth 5243n.

sa(a)f *adj.* as *n.* place of safety 436. *adj.* in *vouched* ~ 5860 ~ see **vouched**.
sa(a)ftee *n.* in ~ where it can do no harm 49n.
say(e) see **sey**.
salue *v.* greet 4350.

salwh *adj.* dirty (F *salis*) 1456.
same *adj.* in *in þilke* ~ *houre* then and there 206-7; *þe* ~ that very 260.
sanctificatur Lat. *pass. pr. 3 sg.* it is sanctified 4319n.
saule *v.* satisfy 1711.
saulee *n.* satisfaction of appetite 102.
sautree, sawtree, sawtrye *n.* psaltery 4138n.
saue, save *v.* help 913; *pr. subj. sg.* in *so God* ~ *þee* for heaven's sake 2785; ~ *youre grace* (formal greeting) 4074.
savouringe, *vbl. n.* taste 1500; **savowringe** 1212.
scaffold *n.* platform 4093; *in* ~ as if on a platform 1382.
scarmushe *v.* skirmish 2445.
scauberk *n.* scabbard 2370.
science *n.* knowledge 7122.
scoole *n.* University Faculty 1640; **scole** 713n.
scotte *n.* a contribution (of money) 5217.
scrippe *n.* pilgrim's satchel 111; **scryppe** 1890; **skrippe** 270.
scripture *n.* document 1091; Scripture 1198; writing 1839.
sechim see **sethim.**
secrees *n. pl.* secrets 1650.
secundum Lat. *prep.* following 5833.
seeche *v.* search 680; seek out 1231. *intr.* in *to whom I* ~ to whom I have recourse 5911.
seeinge *pr. p.* in *cleer-*~ clear-sighted 3220; *nouht* ~ blind 4744.
seelde(n) *adv.* seldom 3502.
seemynge *pr. p.* looking 851.
seemynge *vbl. n.* appearance; *bi* ~ to all appearances 1567; *to my* ~ it seemed to me 1471; *it is to þi* ~ does it seem to you 1705.
se(e)rcle *n.* circle 485.
seeste *pr. 2 sg.* (+ enclitic pron.) do you see 158. **se(e)** *imp. sg.* in ~ *here this is* 1785. **seigh, sey(g)h, s(e)ih, sigh, sy(g)h** *pa. t. sg.* saw. **seyen** *subj. pl.* 751. **seyn, seen** *pp.* seen 6.
seeten *pa. t. pl.* sat 4399.
seew *pa. t. sg.* sowed 1537.
sey(e), seyn *v.* say 269; tell 382; **sei** 5191; **seyne** 7178. **sey** *pr. 1 sg.* in *specialliche þis I* ~ notice particularly 1846; *I* ~ *þee wel* I assure you 1976. **seiste** *3 sg.* (+enclitic pron.) do you say 226. **seyn** *pl.* 606. **saye** *subj. sg.* may say 458. **seyinge, seyinge** *vbl. n.* statement 494.
seye, seyen, seigh, sey(g)h, s(e)ih see **seeste.**
seyn see **seeste, sey.**
seyntes *n. pl.* Christians 1858.
seised *pp. adj.* in *holde me* ~ *of þee* keep hold of you 5634.
seiste see **sey.**
selde *pa. t. subj. sg.* sold 5181.
seleeres *n. pl.* stores 2105.
selfe *pron.* itself 5111.
semblable *adj.* similar 5822.
semblaunt *n.* appearance 3961; *made . . .* ~ 264-5 see **make**; *bi* ~ in appearance 2815.

sentences *n. pl.* opinions 4214.
sequestre *v.* separate 3344.
sercelich *adv.* in a circle 6415.
sergeaunt *n.* servant 247.
sergeaunte *v.* perform (my) duty 6590n.
sermonynge *n.* the giving of a sermon 643.
sermoun *n.* talk 367; explanation 1278.
serteyn *adv.* certainly 1731; (and in various intensive senses): clearly 752; indeed 798; really 1095; exactly 1685; to tell the truth 1705; etc.
sertes *adv.* well now 2368; plainly 2495; indeed 3142.
serue *pr. 1 sg.* in *wherof I* ~ what my function is 1305; ~ *of* serve up 4746. **seruen** *pl.* in ~ *of nouht* are no use 6730. **serued** *pp.* in *euele* ~ 1060-1 see **euele**.
sesoun *n.* year 114; opportunity 3172; *in eche* ~ for all occasions 2003; *ne in no* ~ nor for any reason 2413; *in* ~ timely 3905.
sethim *n.* in *tre of* ~ shittim (acacia wood, the wood of the shittah-tree) 1869n; **sechim** 2004.
sette *v.* in *at yow . . .* ~ attack you 894. *pr. 1 sg.* in ~ *þe lasse bi* think less of 3018; ~ *þee* present 3314; ~ *. . .* at a glooue disregard 6355; ~ *litel acounte bi* take no notice of 6494-5. *pa. t. sg.* put into the oven, baked 865; put 1396; ~ *hond to* took hold of 3348; ~ *al in negligence* completely forgot 3710; ~ *so gret busynesse* was so active 6309; **setten** *pl.* in ~ *. . . at nouht* held in contempt 2203. **set(te)** *pp.* placed 25; was seated 1855; assigned 2925; set down 7281; ~ *hand in* invaded 6518. **settinges** *vbl. n. pl.* traps 6335.
sewe *v.* follow 2692. **suinge** *pr. p.* (writing) later on 3057; **seuynge** behind 3797.
shadden see **shede**.
shadewe *v.* hide 5675. **shadewed** *pp.* obscured 3266.
shadwe *n.* in *make him* ~ protect him 4639; **shadewe** 6673.
shake *pp.* brandished 2357.
shal *pr. 1, 3 sg.* will 180; can 2075; ~ *nothing kunne* 1790 see **kunne**; ~ *wel kunne espye* will cleverly detect 3464; *it* ~ *like him wel* he will be very pleased 3923; ~ *wel kunne redye* will efficiently prepare 6967; ~ *neuere noon mowe* no one at all will be able 7180-1. **shalt** *2 sg.* in *þou* ~ *moste* you will have to 3343; *þou* ~ *wel mown* you will easily be able 3445; *þou* ~ *haue þe hegge thikkere* the thicker the hedge will be 3748. **shul** *subj. pl.* in *ye* ~ *wel mown* you may well 467. **shulde** *pa. t. 1, 3 sg.* in ~ *ete* was going to eat 517; ~ *go* am to go 6997. **shuldest** *2 sg.* in ~ *wel thinke* may well imagine 2563. **shulde** ? *subj. sg.* in *þat . . . he ne* ~ *be* without his being 37.
shalmuses *n. pl.* shawms 4157n.
shape *v.* make 1053. **shape(n)** *pp.* formed 1046; fitted 2148. **shoop** *pa. t. sg.* in ~ *hire manere* prepared 5486.
sharp *adj.* keen 1899.
sharpliche *adv.* smartly 2554.
shede *v. intr.* let something fall 6919. **shode** *refl.* in ~ *me* part my hair 3687. **shadden** *tr. pa. t. pl.* let fall 56. **shed** *pp.* scattered 4174.

she(e)nde v. spoil 4599; destroy 5435. **sheendinge** pr. p. injuring 2483. **shente** pp. adj. rotten 4584.
sheete v. shoot.
shet see **shitte**.
shewe v. describe; explain 266; point out 1595; display 5339. subj. sg. in ~ it make it look 1695. **shewinge** vbl. n. explanation 688; verrey ~ the full admission 677.
shitte v. close 3843. **shet** pp. adj. in ~ withoute excluded 3216; out ~ 3217.
shode see **shede**.
shof see **showve**.
sholdred pp. adj. shouldered; ~ ynowh strong enough in the shoulder 2521.
shoop see **shape**.
shorene pp. adj. as n. tonsured men 509.
shorte adj. brief; at ~ wordes 2485 see **at**. **shorteste** superl. in at þe ~ 2001 see **at**.
shortliche, shortlych(e) adv. briefly 83; ~ to passe me 29, passe me ~ 2359 see **passe**.
showve v. thrust 5549. refl. cast 6623. **shof** pa. t. sg. 2460. **shoven, shouen** pp. 3259, 5602.
shrewe n. evil woman 4411.
shrewed(e) adj. wretched 2474; evil 2647; **shrewed** harmful 2349; a ~ market 3781 see **market**.
shrifte n. confession 677.
shrive pp. adj. absolved 1253.
shul(dest) see **shal**.
shuldren n. pl. shoulders 4089.
side n. in on þat ooþer ~ 1601n see **on**. **sides** pl. edges 650.
si(g)h, sy(g)h see **seeste**.
syhinges n. pl. sighs 1159.
syke adj. as n. the sick 1287.
siker adj. sure 191; reliable 4736.
sikerliche adv. firmly 2003; certainly 5663.
similacioun n. illusion 1769.
simphanye n. hurdy-gurdy (or similar instrument) 4137n. **simphaunes** pl. 3640.
simple adj. honest 2879.
singuler(e) adj. unique, individual 1056, 4042.
sithe adv. afterwards 263; then 269; later 849; **sithen** 62, 5950; **sitthe** 4231. conj. since 754.
sittinge pr. p. adj. appropriate 112; proper 288n; yuel ~ 597 see **euele** adv.; ~ to right for 1882.
skant adj. niggardly 6008.
skirme pr. 1 sg. in ~ þerwith brandish it 4266. **skirmynge** pr. p. adj. darting about 34.
skorche v. flay 506.
skorcheresse n. (female) skinner 5074.

GLOSSARY 565

skrippe see **scrippe**.
sle v. kill 747; beat 1176. **slo(o)w(h)** pa. t. sg. 2579, 4424, 4503.
  slo(o)wen pl. beat 1960²n.
sley(g)htes n. pl. special methods 68.
slewthede pa. t. sg. neglected 3852.
slo(o)wen, slo(o)wh see **sle**.
slugged adj. sluggish 3447.
smellinge vbl. n. sense of smell 1210.
smerte pr. 3 sg. hurts 5985.
smyþthiere, smithiere n. smith 4771.
so see **soo**.
sobirliche adv. moderately 474.
soden pp. boiled 7194.
softe adj. soothing 317; gentle 319.
softe adv. gently 318; slowly (F *belement*) 2551; luxuriously 3507.
soiourne v. dwell 5993.
solempnysed pp. performed 1857.
sonere compar. adj. in þe ~ quickly 3913.
so(o) adv. this 83; like that 127; such 130; then 179; in such a way 1162; neuere ~ miche however much 36; ri(g)ht ~ 955 see **ri(g)ht**; ~ michel I (þow) dide(st) . . . þat 1124, 1647 see **do**; ~ michel tel (þat) until 1177-8, 1572-3; ~ miche þer is þat probably 1192-3; if it were ~ þat if 1374; ~ it is in fact 1554; but of ~ michel 2179 see **but**; if ~ miche good þow coudest 2681 see **kunne**; til ~ miche þat until 4552; if ~ be if it happens 4903; pleonastic in ~ miche 728; ~ God saue (keepe) you (þee) 913. conj. as long as 97.
sook see **souke**.
sool adj. alone 3205.
soomer n. beast of burden 2697; **soomeer** 5244.
sooth n. truth 909; in ~ really 150; indeed 1703-4; indeed 1703-4; I can tell you 1877; of ~ in fact 281; sey me ~ tell me honestly 1729; wite ~ truly now 3188; **sooþe** 1250; **soth** 3469, 5970; **soothe** 5540.
sooth adj. true (F *bien voirs*) 865; **soothe** 3690.
sooth adv. yes indeed 5665.
soothliche adv. in fact 820; to tell the truth 1483; really 1603; yes indeed 1719; exactly 2744; **soothli** 4905.
soothness n. the truth 950; in ~ in actual fact 1937.
sophistre n. pseudo-philosopher 1605.
sore adj. painful 2153; **sor** 4049. **sorere** comp. more painful 4608.
sore adv. intensely 83; severely 4692; heavily 6364.
sorweful adj. poor 3646.
soth see **sooth** n.
soudyours n. pl. soldiers 6519.
souke v. suck 5079; yiveth ~ suckles 3125; **sowke** 7186. **sook** pa. t. sg. 7204.
sounde v. heal 2638.
sowne v. make a sound 6500.
sownere n. person in a faint 3878.

soupe *v.* sip 4603.
souprised *pp.* overcome 2486.
sourdeden *pa. t. pl.* arose 1910.
soursaut see **a soursault**.
souereyn *adj.* supreme; royal 4736; ~ *good, good* ~ Supreme Good, *summum bonum* 1765, 1772; **sovereyn** 1719. as *n.* **souereyn** Superior 738.
spayere *n.* opening in a garment; ?armhole 3519n.
sparinge *vbl. n.* forgiving 324; mercy 629; *in* ~ mercifully 592.
spaulinge *pr. p.* moving up and down 4089n.
spaueyne, spaveyne *n.* spavin (bony tumour on the legs of horses) 5351.
spaveyned *pa. t. sg.* in ~ *me* gave myself a spavin 5369. **spaueynede** *pp.* as *n.* those afflicted with a spavin 4039.
speeres *n. pl.* spheres 829.
speke *v.* discuss 3049; argue 3067; *herd(e)* . . . ~ heard tell 791; heard it 5176; *to* ~ speaking 1103; *nouht for to* ~ *(of)* unmentionable 5679, 5713. *pr. 1 sg.* say 2069. **speketh** *3 sg.* in ~ *to perce* talks of piercing 3669. **speke** *pa. t. sg.* spoke 3090. **speken** *pl.* 310. **yspoke** *pp.* 897. **spekinge** *vbl. n.* talk 2257; **spekynge** 2259.
sperhauk *n.* sparrowhawk 3813.
spilt *pp.* lost, destroyed 6013.
spore *n.* spur 4243.
sporeth *pr. 3 sg.* spurs 2553.
spreynt *pp.* sprinkled 1533.
springaldes *n. pl.* missiles 2242.
sqwire, squyre *n.* square, right-angled tool 1372, 1404.
stable *adj.* reliable 2201.
stablisshe *pr. 1 sg.* strengthen 5772.
stal *pa. t. sg.* stole 5003.
staunch *v.* quench 1711.
stede *n.* in *in* ~ 331 see **stonde**.
steere *n.* rudder 3845.
steyn see **stye**.
steled *pp. adj.* steel-toothed 6824.
stelen *v.* creep about 5106.
stended *pp.* stretch 6241n.
stenderesse *n.* stretcher out (to lengths not originally woven) 5319n.
stepdame *n.* stepmother 3724.
stercheth *pr. 3 sg.* strengthens 6312.
stye *v.* climb 3412; rise up 6572. **steyn** *pp.* ascended 1854.
stiked *pp.* set 70; ~ *in* attached to (by the piercing of the satchel's fabric) 1904.
style *n.* necessary legalistic tone 5386n.
stille *adj.* inactive 889; *holde me* ~ 269 see **holde**.
stilleliche *adv.* secretly 3838.
stinte *v. intr.* stop 1177. *tr.* bring to an end 5896.
stire *v. refl.* get moving 1825; move 3303. *tr. pr. 1 sg.* encourage 7211. **stirest** *2 sg.* twist 3006. **stiren** *intr. pl.* become excited 2257. *stiryinge*

GLOSSARY

pr. p. 4090. **stired** *refl. pp.* grown angry 1074. **stirringe** *vbl. n.* excitement 1164.
stiwest *pr. 2 sg.* soak 3121.
stok *n.* in *upon þe* ~ growing 5177. **stokkes** *pl.* fetters 7015.
stonde *v.* in ~ *in stede* be of use 331; ~ *to God* rely on God's judgement 335; ~ *stille in estaat* remain in an unchanged condition 845; *let me* ~ leave me alone 3010. **stont** *pr. 3 sg.* in *it* ~ ... *in no stede* it is no use 3932.
stour *n.* field of battle, battle 6110. **stoures** *pl.* ? 4028n.
stowpe *v.* lower 5455. **stowpeth** *pr. 3. sg.* curves down 373.
strang(e)led *pp.* devoured 4571, 6339.
strauhte see **strecche**.
straunged *pp.* ? banished 4019n; removed 5740.
straungeres *n. pl. gen.* in *þe* ~ those of just anybody 753n.
straw *n.* in *for a* ~ at the touch of a mere twig 411; *dredden a* ~ care a fig for 2213.
strecche *v.* hang out 6679. **streccheth** *pr. 3 sg.* in ~ *nouht to þat* is not sufficient 2503. **strecchen** *pl.* reach out 5238; ~ *nouht to oon ende* do not have the same purpose (or effect) 6577. **strauhte** *pa. t. sg.* stretched out 5487. **streighte** *pp.* extended 3513; **streiht** 6831; *at þe eerþe* ~ flat on the ground 3361; **ystreight** 6710.
streyne *v.* hold firm 2377n.
streyt(e) *adj.* narrow 84; constricting 2133; tight-fitting 4033.
streitliche *adv.* carefully 1293.
strike *v.* stroke (in putting on) 3686.
strof *pa. t. sg.* in *of þat* ~ *I nothing* I did not cavil at all at that 7019.
strogle *pr. 1 sg.* make violent attempts to escape from restraint 6357.
stronde *n.* shore 6164.
studie, studye *v.* study (spiritual material) 6925. **studyede** *pa. t. sg.* thought hard 2798.
stumblinge *n.* obstacle 4281.
stuprum Lat. *n.* violation 5711.
subject *n.* subordinate 738. **subgis** *pl.* 730.
subiectioun *n.* obedience *in* ~ subordinate 736.
subsidies *n. pl.* taxes due to the sovereign 4958.
substaunce *n.* property 5143; essential being 5920n.
subtile *adj.* narrow 91; fine 1636; skilful 1638; clever 1645; ingenious 1686.
subtilitee *n.* skill 1564.
subtil(l)iche, subtylliche *adv.* discerningly 1506; skilfully 1567.
suer see **sure**.
suerliche see **sureliche**.
suette *n.* tallow 6589.
suffice *v.* satisfy 421; cope with 2180. **sufficeth** *intr. pr. 3 sg.* in ~ *nouht* will not be enough 611.
sufficience *n.* enough 4936.
sufficient *adj.* able 2953; competent 4064.
suffisance *n.* sufficient quantity; *to* ~ completely 1713-14n.

suffre v. allow 416; tolerate 888; endure 2616; *wolde wel* ~ *þat* would be quite happy if 2581. **suffreden** *pa. t. pl.* in ~ *to dismembre hem* allowed themselves to be torn apart 1968.
suich(e) see **swich**.
suinge see **seuyinge**.
sum *adj.* in ~ *ooþer thing* otherwise 4471. *pron.* in *in* ~ *bileevinge* some people left 7173n.
sumtime *adv.* once 244; sometimes 321; **sumtyme** 504.
sumwhat n. something 269.
superflue *adj.* superfluous 5420.
supplaunte v. in ~ *him* bring him down 3437.
sup(p)rysed, suppprised *pp.* overcome 4018; tricked 6329.
surcotes n. *pl.* outer garments (often of rich material) 4034.
sure *adj.* reliable 2210; secure 3326; *I am not* ~ *to telle* I cannot rightly say 79; **suer** certain 2816- **surer** *compar.* safer 243.
sureliche *adv.* confidently 2037; safely 2401; **suerliche** 2193.
surenesse n. catch (F *serreure*) 2416.
surer see **sure**.
suretee n. confidence 6125.
surmownted *pp.* overcome 4816.
surplu(i)s n. in *þe* ~ the rest of his activities (associated with his staff) 2851; remainder 6464.
surquideoures *adj.* presumptuous 596.
surquidrye n. presumption 3789.
suscited see **sussited**.
suspeccionous *adj.* misleading 154n.
suspecioun n. doubt 2916; **suspessioun** uncertainty 2828.
sussited *intr. pa. t. sg.* rose from the dead 1854 (see note 1849); **suscited** *tr.* brought back to life 4547.
susteyne v. support 2039; endure 2116; **susteen** maintain 5855. **sustene** *refl. pr. 1 sg.* 4264. **susteyneth** *3 sg.* holds 2411.
susteynour n. supporter 2727.
suthselerere n. subcellarer 6914.
swelwe *pr. 1 sg.* swallow 5542, 5559.
sweringes n. *pl.* oaths 5407.
swevene n. dream 7; **sweuene** 4.
swich(e) *adj.* such 101; like that 727; such and such 1159; like it 1486; as follows 6897; *noon* ~ 1066 see **noon**; *in* ~ *wise* 1297-8, *in* ~ *manere* 1383-4 see **in**; *bi* ~ 2076 see **bi**; ~ *and* ~ (F *et tex et quiex*) a person of such a nature 2785; ~ *time þer was þat* for a moment 6224; **suich(e)** like this (F *tel*). **swiche** as *pron.* people like that 176. **suich** *adj.* the same 6415.

taarges see **targe**.
taast(e) see **taste**.
tables n. *pl.* backgammon 3643.
tablettes n. *pl.* flat pieces of jewellery 3117.
tacche v. be fastened down 1330. **tac(c)ed** *pp.* tied.

GLOSSARY

T(h)au, Tahu *n.* Tau 274n, 283.
take *v.* apply 325; give 719; take hold (of) 3942; ~ *þe weye* travel 161; ~ *þi wey* go (on) 238; *made* ~ *þee* 388 see **make**; *of him . . .* ~ *ensaumple* follow his example 2557; ~ *no gret keep* pay very little attention 3465; **taken** 15. **take** *imp. sg.* in ~ *him* put it on 3387. **took** *refl. pa. t. sg.* in ~ *him up* began 4142; ~ *hire to flee* flew 6394. *tr.* in ~ *ayen hire woordes* went on 4587. **take** *pp.* in ~ *on me* brought against me 5853; ~ *it* got it from 6082; ~ *hardiment* found courage 6653; **taken** in ~ *upon* (this was) based on 7298.
takere *n.* successful hunter 3805.
tale *n.* account 1800; *telle hire* ~ have her say 1301.
tale *n.* ? handle 4071n.
talinge *vbl. n.* chattering 4392.
targe *n.* light shield, buckler 2220. **taarges** *pl.* 2082.
targede *pa. t. sg.* shielded 2440.
tarye, tarie *v. tr.* and *intr.* delay 3497, 4265.
taste *n.* touch 2312; **taaste** 1499.
taste *v.* touch 5360. **tastede** *pa. t. sg.* felt 3364. **tastinge** *vbl. n.* touch 599; touching 2288; sense of touch 2293. **tastinges** *pl.* caresses 2287; physical sensations 2291.
tecche *n.* blemish (F *tache*) 4668.
teche *v.* guide 349. **techinge** *vbl. n.* meaning 611; instructions 2612; wisdom 5596; *yiueth* ~ shows us 592.
teene *n.* irritation, anger 5474; injury 5836.
teeneth *pr. 3 sg.* angers 4430.
telle *v.* say to 483; describe 611; *I am not sure to* ~ see **sure**; *þer shulde noon kunne* ~ *of* no-one has ever heard of 791; ~ *hire tale* 1301 see **tale**. *pr. 1 sg.* in *wel (I)* ~ *yow (þee), I* ~ *yow wel* I tell you straight 634; I assure you 2036. **tolde** *pa. t. sg.* in ~ *ayen* repeated 1796.
temporalitee *n.* material possessions (of the clergy) 5277.
temps see **prime**.
tenure *n.* content, meaning 2835.
tere *v.* cry 3396.
terme *n.* goal 2951.
termininge *vbl. n.* termination 7244.
testat *n.* person who has left a will 5104n.
tete *n.* teat 4431.
thanne see **þanne**.
thar *impers. pr. 3 sg.* in *him* ~ *not* there is no need for him 5909. **thurt** *pa. t. sg.* in *it* ~ *not* it is not necessary 1760.
that see **þat**.
thau see **tahu**.
therof see **þerof**.
thikke *adj.* fat 3096. as *n.* thicket 4489; *þe leste* ~ *of* the thinnest part of 3779.
thikke *adv.* thickly 3514.
thikkeliche *adv.* indistinctly 3491.
thilke see **þilke**.

ÞE LYFE OF ÞE MANHODE

thinke v.[1] *impers.* in *me shulde* ~ *suich a yifte* such a gift seems 1682.
thinketh *pr. 3 sg.* in *me* ~ it seems to me 576. **thinke** *subj. sg.* in *þee* ~ it may seem 2153. **thouhte** *pa. t. sg.* in *me* ~ it seemed to me 21; **thowhte** 19.
thinke v.[2] imagine 30; consider 1153; ~ *to* mean 2354; *shuldest wel* ~ may well imagine 2563-4; ~ *on* consider 3107; remember 5779. **thinken** 751. **thinke** *pr. 1 sg.* intend 1077; ~ *to* intend to go to 3505; **think** in ~ *more to ooþer eende* have another purpose in mind 6402. **thinkest** *3 sg.* in *what* ~ *in þi corage* what are you thinking of 712-13. **thouhte** *pa. t. sg.* in ~ *wel* was certain 819. **thouhten** *pl.* in ~ *wel* fully expected 5727. **ythouht** *pp.* 697.
this see **þis**.
thong *n.* sword-belt 2376n.
thoruh *adv.* absolutely (F *de tout*) 323.
thoruhout *adv.* totally 1502.
thouhte see **thinke**[1,2].
thouhti *adj.* thoughtful 2421; **thouhty** 4655.
thowte see **thinke**[1].
thral *adj.* controlled 415.
thraldom *n.* restriction 428; **thraldom** 1033.
thrist *n.* thirst 6086.
throsshen *pa. t. sg.* threshed 1540.
thuartinge see **thwartinge**.
thurt see **thar**.
thus see **þus**.
thwart *adj.* ? haughty (sliding across its object) (F *de travers*) 4086.
thwartinge *pr. p. adj.* crossed 6202. **thuartinge** *vbl. n.* opposition 7047.
thwartouer *adv.* crookedly 6189nn.
til *prep.* to 5733.
tile *v.* till 3697.
time *n.* in *whan my* ~ *cometh* at the right time 270; *long* ~ for ages 385; *seeth* ~ sees the time is right 760; *bi long* ~ 1128 see **bi**; ~ *was* it was time 1352; (*in*) *no time* never 1869, 6245; *þe* ~ *bifore* time gone by 1906; *long* ~ *gone* a long time ago 1978; *þat* ~ in those days 2210-11; *it were wel* ~ it is more than time 2449; ~ *comynge* future 2662; *olde* ~ past 2663; *a* ~ once 3289; *in þat* ~ then 3606-7; *in litel* ~ soon 3723; *as at þis* ~ for the moment 3883; *of euel* ~ in an evil hour 4246; *in sori* ~ *he hadde* it was a pity he had 4247-8; *of bifore þis* ~ for some time 4967; *into þe* ~ *þat* until 5102; *for long* ~ (at a price increased only) by the passage of time 5184; *o* ~ sometimes 5325; *at his* ~ when he feels the need 5702; *at þe firste* ~ first 5777; *swich* ~ *þer was* 6224 see **swich(e)**; *forto þe* ~ until 6254; **tyme** in *in my* ~ while I am alive 422; *in oo* ~ on one occasion 2169. **times** *pl.* in (*in*) *alle* ~ always 403; whenever 972; *many* ~ often 643; *ofte* ~ often 2879; **tymes**.
tissue *n.* rich band 121.
to *prep.* (often to be found under the verb it precedes or follows); for 115; of 119; in 203[2]; as 493[1,2]; at 517; on 1823; into 2668; against 3244; ~ *meward* on my side 82; in my direction 131; appropriate to me 304;

GLOSSARY

where I am concerned 308; ~ *assaye* 196 see **assaye**; *to þat ende* (. . .) *þat* so that 399; *fair* ~ *yow* 500 see **fair**; ~ *what ende I shulde come* 694 see **come**; ~ *thre thinges* in three ways 1380; ~ *haue ouhte* ~ *meeve him* he ought to long for 1395; *as* ~ *regard of* 1464 see **as**; ~ *þi seemynge* 1705 see **seemynge**; ~ *sufficaunce* 1713-14 see **sufficaunce**; ~ *his riht* completely 2148; ~ *þine eyen* 2684 see **eye**; *as* ~ *þe body* physically 3289-90; *as* ~ *þe soule* spiritually 3290; ~ *þi rihtes* as you should 3562; ~ *here powere* as far as they can 4116-17; often pleonastic as in ~ *þilke* 1; *vnderstonde* ~ 382; *displesede* ~ 386 etc. *adv.* too 319.
tobreke *v.* destroy 3527. **tobroke(n)** *pp.* broken up 1748.
tobreste *v.* break up 5434. *pr. subj.* 5849.
toclouted, toclowted *pp.* completely patched, tattered 5022.
todrawe *pr. 1 sg.* tear apart 4602.
tofore *adv.* earlier 1771.
tokeneth *pr. 3 sg.* signifies 374.
tokne *n.* sign 284; *in* ~ as a sign 398. **tokenes** *pl.* meanings 1243.
tolde see **telle**.
tonell *n.* cask 5486n.
toode *n.* toad 4753.
took see **take**.
tooþer see **þat** *adj.*
topulle *pr. 1 sg.* pull apart 4602.
toragged *pp.* completely ragged 5021.
torell *n.* turret 1603.
torent *pp.* torn to pieces 6204.
touche *n.* capacity for sensation 5575.
toucheth, towcheth *pr. 3 sg.* is relevant to 11. **touchinges** *vbl. n. pl.* caresses 2286; physical contacts 2289; **towchinges** 5561.
tournements *n. pl.* ? displays of power 4190n.
tourneye *v. intr.* take part in a tournament 7038.
tprw *interj.* (the cry of a hen) 4196.
trauaile *n.* pain 624; trouble (F *paine*) 2511; labour 3062.
trauaile *v. refl.* labour 2547. *intr.* 1264. **trauailed** *pp.* in ~ *of* tired by 6263. *pp. adj.* tired by labour 6696.
trauailour *n.* task-master 3610.
tre(e) *n.* wood 1869.
trespas *n.* offence 1271.
tretable *adj.* affable 371.
trewa(u)nde *v.* beg idly 5235.
trewaundes *n. pl.* idle beggars 5255, 5335. **truwauntes** 1285.
trewe *adj.* honest 3555.
treweliche *adv.* honestly 3554.
trewes *n.* truce 5469.
triacle *n.* salve, antidote 4598.
tributarie *n.* one who gives tribute 4960.
trice *intr. pr. 1 sg.* tread a measure 6357n.
trist(e) *n.* trust 1531; *in* ~ *of* by relying on 2727.
triste *pr. 1 sg.* trust 4827.

troubel *adj.* troubled 6482.
trouble *v.* disturb 4745; ∼ *myn vnderstondinge* rack my brains 1475.
trouthe, trowthe *n.* loyalty 3254; truth 5552; *bere* ∼ *to* be faithful to 441.
trowe *pr. 1 sg.* believe 6; expect 151; think 342; am sure 581; assure you 2601.
trusse *v.* make into a bundle 3342. *refl.* load myself up 5042.
trusses *n. pl.* ropes 3806.
truwauntes see **trewaundes**.
tumbistere *n.* female tumbler or dancer 6354.
tunder *n.* tinder 4759.
tunneth *pr. 3 sg.* puts into a cask 5592.
turne *v.* bring 1032; change 1142; knead 1555. *intr.* change 845; ∼ *to flight* retreat 2195. **turneth** *2 sg.* in ∼ *to wundringe* becomes the object of amazement 788. **turne** *intr. subj. sg.* in ∼ *ayen* return 1268n.
turned(e) *tr. pa. t. sg.* made 1576. *refl.* in ∼ *me ayen* turned round 795. **turnyng(e)** *vbl. n.* in *þe* ∼ *ayen* the reversal 2959.
twey(e) *num.* two 2036.
tweyes *adv.* twice 4328.
tweyne *num.* two 292; both 310; *boþe* ∼ both 7044.

þanne *pron. dem.* in *nouht* (*not*) *for* ∼ 1322-3 see **nouht**.
þanne *adv.* then 113; **thanne** 206.
þat *pron. rel.* what 607[1,2]; who 10; since 3126n.
þat *pron. dem.* the one 2799; *to* ∼ *ende* so 399; ∼ ∼ (*dem.* + *rel.*) what 1789; (*rel.* + *dem.*) that which 3306. *adj. dem.* in ∼ *oon* the 260; one 496; ∼ *ooþer* (*þe tooþer*) the other 5, 373; *That ooþer* 1217n; ∼ *oon and* ∼ *ooþer* the first and the second 702; ∼ *time* in those days 1962; at that moment 3606-7; ∼ *ben þilke* those are they 6250.
þat *conj.* so that 327; since 3412[2]; ∼ . . . *I ne wolde wite* (*sey*) (after neg.) without knowing (saying) 147, 269; *as* ∼ as the fact that 144; *for* ∼ because 156; ∼ *I ne were* 863 see **lakketh**; *but* ∼ unless 1077; as long as 3223; *without* ∼ *it greeuede* without its hurting 2362-3; ∼ *euele passioun smyte it* a plague on it 2474-5; ∼ *God haue part* God help us 2887; *of* ∼ for the fact that 3070; from the fact that 3447; *who* ∼ he who 4208; *so* ∼ as long as (F *puis qu'*) 4536; pleonastic in *who* ∼ 1880; *before* ∼ 722; *oþer* ∼ 635; *when* ∼ 972; *what* ∼ 1036; *and* ∼ *which* ∼ 4307; *er* ∼ 5849; *albeit* ∼ 7125.
þer (unstressed), **þere** (stressed) *adv. dem.* there 27n; **ther** 4789; **þeere** 6052. **þer(e)** *rel.* or *conj.* whereas 415; where 517, 3186.
þeraboute *adv.* about it 4495; ∼ *as* in a place where 4679-80.
þerafter *adv.* accordingly 1411.
þerbi *adv.* that way 87; by it 503; as a result of this 740; by means of it 1511; from this 2441; **þerby** 2885.
þereas *conj.* where 401; whereas 3247; **þeras** 5993.
þerfore *adv.* for that purpose 303; as a result 1979; for this reason 2061; for it 3557; **þerfor 2718**.
þerforth *adv.* by that place 236.

GLOSSARY 573

þerinne *adv.* in it 14; there 422; by it 573; inside 1086; in that 1691; about it 1992; inside it 2471; on it 4410; *youre profyite lyth* ~ 581 see **profyt(e)**; **þerin** 5298.
þernyh *adv.* near 1283.
þerof *adv.* of it 86; in this 117; about that 287; as a result 694; about it 798; in it 828; for that 980; from it 1042; by it 1578; in that 1720; free of it 2895; *daunger* . . . *make* ~ object to it 2677; *I wole not* ~ I will not have anything to do with that 3616; *speken no* ~ did not mention it 3682; **Thereof** 2659.
þeron *adv.* on it 980: about it 2497; with it 3559.
þerto *adv.* to it 461; about it 974; to the point 1363; to that 2069; on it 3017; at it 3341; *go* ~ approach it 1422; *come* . . . ~ 2029-30, 2030-1 see **come**; **þertoo** 1634 etc.
þervnder *adv.* under it 6088.
þerwhiles *adv.* meanwhile 2756.
þerwith *adv.* with it 35; in addition 3143; with them 3758.
þider *adv.* to that place 81; **þidir** 6752.
þiderward *adv.* in that direction 1216.
þilke *pron. dem.* he 88; the one 548; that one 549; that 1290; one 2056; anyone 2061; ~ *of reyn* the rainy sort 2755; **thilke** 2187. *adj. dem.* (+*pl. n.* or *v.*) those 678, 6250; **thilke** 47 etc.
þis *pron. dem.* this reason 1041; ~ *is þat* this is the reason why 1625; This 1475. **þis** *adj. dem.* in ~ *day* today 583; ~ *hundreth winter* the next hundred years 948-9; *at* ~ *time* here and now 1077; **This** 2119 etc.
þiself *pron.* you yourself 407; *of* ~ by your own power 2384.
þouh *adv. (conj.)* although 184; even if 577; if 3419; *not gret wunder* ~ not surprising that 1612; **þowh** 2467.
þus *adv.* like this 268; in this way 1961; ~ *doon* done all this 455; **Thus** 1796; ~ *miche* this much 4288; ~ *michel* this reason 4491; this 7284.
vnbynt *pr. 3 sg.* loosens 7026.
vncharged *pp.* unburdened 3351.
vnclosed *pp.* made known 316; revealed 676.
vncorded *pp.* unstrung 7175.
vncowche *v.* in ~ *him* take him out (of his container, or storage) 5452.
vnder, under *prep.* within 1609; ~ *hir sides* on her hips 818; *put him* ~ 1251 see **putte**; ~ *litel closure* 1580 see **closure**; ~ . . . *holt* overcomes 3247; ~ *hire spayere*? tucked into her armhole 3519; ~ *hire side* at her side 3802; ~ *keye* locked up 5005.
vnder *adv.* underneath 6062.
vnderputte *v.* submit 3167.
vndersettere *n.* supporter, upholder 4369.
vnderstonde *v.* pay attention to 267; mean 1009; **vnderstande** 13; **vndirstande** 720. **vnderstant** *pr. 3 sg.* understands 4212. **vnderstonde** *pp.* listened to 992. **vnderstondinge** *vbl. n.* comprehension 800; mind 909.
undertake *v.* quarrel with 2558. **vndertaken** *pr. pl.* rebuke 911. **vndertake** *pp.* taken upon yourself 2789. **vndertakinge** *vbl. n.* objection 72.

vndertakere *n.* reprover 4048n.
vndo *pr. subj. pl.* in ~ *wel þe liddes* open your eyes wide 922.
vnenpeched *pp.* unhindered 3930n.
vnfold *pp.* revealed 675; ~ *it* spread it out 1092; **vnfolden** brought out 2451.
vnfounde *v.* dissolve, undermine 4943.
vnheled *pp. adj.* exposed 487; uncovered 743.
vnhelere *n.* one who guts a house (to the point where it is roofless) 5098n.
vnioyned *pa. t. sg.* divided 4782.
vnyrened *pp.* without an iron tip 2056.
vnkeuere *v.* uncover; *may men come to* ~ may be uncovered 758.
vnkynde *adj.* unnatural in behaviour, ungrateful 5999.
vnknytte *v.* untangle 3794.
vnknowe *pp. adj.* unknown 595.
vnkunnynge *pr. p. adj.* unskilled 660.
vnlikynge *adj.* dissimilar 2510n.
vnmaken *pr. pl.* destroy 1369.
vnnestleth *pr. 3 sg.* dislodges 4131.
vnneþes *adv.* with difficulty 6758.
vnplytede *pa. t. sg.* unfolded, opened 5827.
vnresoun *n.* injustice 2873.
vnscrippe *v.* in ~ *here scrippes* take their satchels away from them 2844n.
vnshette *pa. t. sg.* opened 4485.
vnstaunchable *adj.* insatiable 5038.
vnthrift *n.* shiftless one 3330; fault, evil (F *laidure*) 2498. **vnthriftes** *pl.* inadequacies 4292.
vnthryfti, vnthrifty *adj.* deformed (F *contrefaite*) 5458.
vntrewe *adj.* false; ~ *dwellere* squatter 389. as *n.* false one 400.
vntreweliche *adv.* dishonestly 5108.
vntrussed *pp.* untied 675; unburdened 3351.
vnwarnished *pp.* unprovided 4504.
vnwemmed *pp. adj.* immaculate 5924.
vnwounden *pp. adj.* undone 742.
vnwurship(e) *n.* indignity 1033; disgrace 2907; *putteth me to* ~ 5590 see **putte.**
upon *prep.* on 81; over 2130; at 2779; ~ *yowre eyen* on your honour, cross your heart; **vpon** 2120.
upriht *adv.* the right way up (and uprightly) 6146; *euene* ~ straight up 58.
vsage *n.* use 699; the usual practice 807; practice 812; *haue in myn* ~ am used to 1524; *in* ~ customary 3100. **vsages** *pl.* traditions 425.
vse *n.* in *in* ~ common 5149.
vsede *pa. t. sg.* in ~ *in pleyinge* toyed with 3520. **vsed** *pp.* in *hath* ~ *to hide hem* has customarily taken refuge 6643.
vsereres *n. pl.* usurers 5017.
vsshere *n.* porter 693; **vussher** keeper 3636.
vtaues *n. pl.* periods of eight days 5166n.

vtterliche *adv.* straight out 3301; **outerliche** in *al* ~ totally 800.
vussher see **vsshere.**

vanitee *n.* that which is worthless 6284.
variable *adj.* flashing as it moved 547n.
varie(n), varye(n) *v.* wander 829; change 846; change position 6413; uarie 941n.
vauntynge *pr. p. adj.* boastful 2394.
ve (for Lat. *vae*) *n.* woe 4741n.
veyle *n.* sail 6711n.
veyn(e) *adj.* useless 3232; worthless 6282.
vele(y)nye see **vileynye.**
venge(n) *v. refl.* in ~ *him* get his own back 596. *tr.* avenge 1184.
vergeous *n.* the juice of unripe fruit 4746.
verres *n. pl.* glasses 3011n.
verrey *adj.* true 666; correct 682; proper 5701; **verry** 6421. **verrey** *adv.* truly 96.
verreyliche, verriliche, verryliche *adv.* in truth 1768; really 3158.
vertu *n.* moral strength 2614; power 3316; power to act 3362; *for* ~ to make itself strong 4730.
vertualliche *adv.* in essence 1758; **virtualliche** 1754n.
vertuous, vertuows(e) *adj.* strong 2411; powerful 2326; morally powerful 2616.
via Lat. *n.* path 4675.
viage *n.* journey 1807.
vicair, vicarie, vicary *n.* representative 278; God's representative 5973.
vicarishipe *n.* position as representative; *of whom þow doost þe* ~ whose position you hold 362.
vileynye, vileynee, vele(y)nye, vyleynye *n.* ill 2156; injustice 1674; *seith* ~ uses wicked (or obscene) language 5585.
vileynesliche *adv.* without dignity 4895.
viletee, vilitee *n.* disgusting appearance 4336; *holden in* ~ 1316-17 see **holde.**
vintere *n.* vintner 5587.
virly *n.* a light dance (or sport accompanied by dancing) 5371n.
vitaile *n.* food 1892.
void, voyd *adj.* empty 518; **voide** 4158.
voide *v.* abandon 477; get rid of 1141; empty 5520; leave 6227.
vouched *pa. t. sg.* in ~ *sa(a)f* condescended 5860.

wacche *n.* bird scare 4490 (see note 4489).
wafrere *n.* seller of thin cakes 5466.
wagen *pr. pl.* pledge 5278.
waymentinge *pr. p.* lamenting 4836. *vbl. n.* lamentation 1223.
waite *n.* watchman 6976.
waite *v.* watch for (F *gaitier*) 5455.
waytere *n.* ambusher 2843.
wakinge *vbl. n.* waking period; *in* ~ while awake 5.

wales *n. pl.* scabs 3693.
war *adj.* careful 6328.
warde *n.* guard 3467. **wardes** *pl.* teeth (on a key) 753.
warne *v.* refuse 5844. **werne** *pr. 1 sg.* 7187.
warnished *pp.* equipped 2747.
wasshene *pp. adj.* as *n.* the one who is pure 6900.
waste *v.* wear away 5144.
wastel *n.* cake or loaf of the finest flour 4160.
wawe *n.* wave 6404.
waxe, waxinge see **wexe**.
weel see **wel**.
weene *v.* think; imagine 1514; *maketh* ∼ makes it seem 3278. **weenest** *pr. 2 sg.* expect 5826; **wenest** 2499. **wende** *pa. t. 1 sg.* 710. **wendest** *2 sg.* 2923. **weenynge** *vbl. n.* in *to my* ∼ in my opinion 2057.
wey *n.* path 14; journey 2947; *take þi* ∼ go 238; *bi sum* ∼ 1673-4 see **bi**; *brouht ayen to* ∼ redirected 2023; *bi no* ∼ 2620 see **bi**; **weye** 161.
weylate *n*, crossroads 5702.
wel *adj.* satisfactory 2458.
wel *adv.* used as an intensitive to strengthen the action of the verb, e.g.: thoroughly 5; really 6; carefully 9; ∼ *poynt* 1374 see **a**; ∼ *and faire* perfectly well 1936; **wol** very 717; **weel** 2902.
wele *n.* the general good 2502; profit 3384; reward 3385.
welle *n.* well 565; source 571; fountain 5959.
welþe *n.* well-being 3389.
wenche *n.* serving-girl 861.
wende, wendest see **weene**.
wennes see **whennes**.
wente *pa. t. sg.* went along 116; was going 140; ∼ *out of* left 2314; **went** 1480. **wente** *refl.* 541.
werche *v.* work 763. **werching** *vbl. n.* work 855; making 5414.
were *n.* fish trap 5299.
were *pa. subj. sg.* in *al* ∼ *(it)* 537 see **al**; *ne* ∼ *(it)* if it were not for 906; ∼ *it neuere so strong* however hard it was 2212; *I ne* ∼ I have not been 1825-6. *pl.* in ∼ *his handes neuere so enoynted* however slippery his hands were 77; *ne* ∼ did not exist 718; *þow* ∼ *good* 4582 see **good**.
wered *pa. t. sg.* wore 2119n. *pp.* worn away 4337.
weri, wery *adj.* upset (F *lasse*) 832; *not* ∼ pleased 4505.
werinne see **wherinne**.
werkes *pl.* creations 1081.
werne see **warne**.
werpeth *pr. 3 sg.* twists into rope 6311. **worpen** *pp.* made up of 4313.
werre *n.* conflict 300, battle 2201; *ye shulde right soone haue þe* ∼ I would make something of it (F *tost eussiez la guerre*) 893-4; *to* ∼ by way of attack 5949n.
werrye *v.* fight against 3648. *pr. 1 sg.* make war on 4446. **werred** *pp.* ravaged (F *guerroie*) 1390.
wex *n.* wax 6588.
wexe *v.* grow 543. **waxe** *pr. 1 sg.* become 5464. **wex** *pa. t. sg.* grew 1538. **woxe** *pp.* enlarged 5427. **waxinge** *vbl. n.* growth 5186.

GLOSSARY

what *pron.* whatever 458; **whatt** 1805. *adv.* how 1119; why 2991 (sometimes perhaps merely emphatic introduction to question). *conj.* in ~ *up* ~ *doun* the long and the short of it was 1647.
whatsoeuere *pron.* whatever 1622.
wheel *n.* circular path 836.
when(ne)s *adv.* where from 914; ~ *cometh it yow* what business is it of yours 859; ~ *cometh it* why is it 2768; **wennes** 824; **whenes** 240.
wherfore *adv. rel.* and so 63; on which account 1626; so that 2623. *adv.* why 4616.
wherinne *adv. rel.* in which 69; **werinne** 4930.
wherof *adv. rel.* as a result of which 51; in which 884; in what connection 1305; about which 1639; of which 1934; in what capacity 2808.
wheron *adv. rel.* on which 6460.
wherto *adv. interrog.* where 562; for what reason 2511. *rel.* in which connection 610.
wherupon *adv. rel.* on which 763.
wherwith *adv. rel.* with which 2042.
wheþer *pron.* which (of the two) 3599. *conj.* whether or not 198; if 2147; ~ *euere I shal* shall I ever 2537.
which(e) *pron.* who 33; whom 281; those 1921; of whom 4424; with which 7175; *þe* ~ 1446-7; ~ *þat* whatever 4541; **wiche** 3872; **wich** 6445, **which(e)** *adj.* what 4912.
while *n.* in *allas þer* ~ (expression of grief) 5887. **whiles** *pl.* in *The* ~ *while* 4580.
who *pron. rel.* whoever 132; someone 1176; ~ *þat euer,* ~ *þat* whoever 1880, 2192; *as* ~ *seith* 3729 see **as. whom** *acc.* in *of* ~ by whose authority 362.
whoso *pron.* anyone who 170; if anyone 1969; if one 1372; ~ *wel seeth* it is obvious to anyone 1035; ~ *it euere were* never mind who 2595.
whosoeuere *pron.* whoever 461.
wich(e) see **which(e)**.
whichche *n.* witch 5582.
wi(g)ht, wy(g)ht *n.* person; *eche (iche)* ~ everyone 14; *no* ~ no one 168; *any* ~ anyone 354; *sum* ~ someone 747.
wiket *n.* gate 6850.
wylde *adj.* fierce 2189; **wyilde** waste, desolate 16.
wil(le) *n.* intention 973; desire 1801; *with good* ~ gladly 212; *at his* ~ 31 see **at**; *passinge my* ~ 875-6 see **passe;** *haue* ~ *þerto* wish it 5807; will 2334.
wilne *v.* desire 3175.
winne *v.* gain 1030; earn 2479; profit 5331; *nothing* ~ gain no advantage 1794.
winter *n. pl.* in *hundredth* ~ hundred years 945.
wise *n.* manner 1609; *þe beste* ~ as well as possible 196; *in no* ~ not at all 1022; *in swich* ~ like this 1298. **wises** *pl.* ways 1764.
wisse *pr. subj. sg.* show 5988.
wist(en) see **wite**.
wit see **wit(te)**.

wite *v.* know 148; realise 348; understand 1378; *þou miht* ~ you should be able to tell 197; *þat mown ye wel* ~ you can be sure 492; *don to* ~ 1378 see **do**. **wot** *pr. 1, 3 sg.* in *I* ~ *neuere* I do not in the least know 901; *I* ~ *wel* I am sure 1023; **woot** 132. **wost** *2 sg.* 1952. **wiste** *pa. t. sg.* knew 211. **wist** *pp.* experienced 2288.

with *prep.* by 1955; by means of 3292; ~ *herte* 1802, ~ *good herte* 2982 see **herte**; ~ *þe bettere wille* more willingly 5228-9; *see* ~ *eye* see for myself 6203; ~ *þis* in this matter 6428; ~ *owres* by virtue of our hands (lifted in prayer) 6941.

withdraw *v. refl.* in ~ *him* detach himself 1265. *tr.* draw out 3760; remove 5000. *intr.* in ~ *with* contract 5231. **withdrough** *pa. t. sg.* removed 5003.

withholde *v.* remember 721; hold back 4284; prevent 6883. *refl.* in ~ *him* restrain himself 4261. *tr. pr. 1 sg.* reserve 307. **withholt** *3. sg.* 3415. **withheeld** *pa. t. sg.* retained 2606; restrained 3930. **withholde(n)** *pp.* reserved 336; reserved (for himself) 616². *pp. adj.* special 616¹.

withholdinge *vbl. n.* leaving 1227; hindrance 3414.

withinne *prep.* inside 98; in 3790. *adv.* inwardly 368; in (it) 1776; *man* ~ the inner (spiritual) man 621.

withoute *prep.* in ~ *mesure* immeasurably 21; ~ *fable* accurately 649; to tell you the truth 2423; ~ *lesinge* in fact 670; honestly 1466; ~ *daunger* unstintingly 789; ~ *more*, ~ *mo(o)* only 1049-50, merely 1767; at once (? in particular) 3885; at once 4144; at once (? alone) 4244; alone 5560, 6586, 6814; ~ *misdoinge* although no offence had been committed 1322; ~ *spot* flawless 2010; ~ *annuye* fully protected 2300; ~ *drede* certainly 4204; ~ *woodshipe* sane 4719; ~ *mistakinge* 5205 see **mistake**; ~ *stintinge* ~ *ende* continuously 5578-9, 5616; ~ *any forberinge* mercilessly 5747; **withouten** 12; **without** 185. **withoute** *adv.* outside 97; outwardly 368; *man* ~ outer (physical) man 620; **without** out 626.

withseye *v.* contradict 1724.
withsitte *v.* resist 3435.
withstond *pr. subj. sg.* resists 2852.
witing(e)liche *adv.* deliberately 2685.
witnesse *n.* evidence; ~ *on Resoun þe wise* Reason, who is clever, will give proof of this 856; *in* ~ in acknowledgement 5976.
witnesse *pr. subj. sg.* in ~ *hem* furnish them with proof of 5395.
wit(te) *n.* intelligence 800; mental capacity 1561; mental skill 1671; ability 2486; understanding 2667; *out of* ~ mad 1101; **witt** faculty 1503; **wyt** cleverness 1668. **wittes** *pl.* faculties 1501; minds 3041.
woke *n.* week 4328. **wookes** *pl.* 5166.
wol see **wel**.
wole *v. pr. 1, 3 sg.* will 4; wishes 100; wants 495; *whoso* ~ *bineme it* anyone taking it 337; *I* ~ *wel* I am very willing 2819; *I* ~ *not þerof* 3616 see **þerof**; **wol** 145; **wule** 382; **wil** 934n. **wolt** *2 sg.* in ~ *þou oþer ne* ~ *þou* whether you like it or not 3047-8; *þou* ~ *not of* you refuse 4809; *if þou* ~ if you please 5240; **wult** 2308. **wolde** *pa. t. 1, 3 sg.* would 148; should like 2367; *he* ~ *for nothing* he would not under any circumstances 1958; **wold** 2219; **wode** 6164. **wolde(n)** *pl.* in ~ *sey*

meant to say 1008. **wolde** *subj. sg.* in *if* . . . *I* ~ *do al awey* if . . . I were to remove everything 956; ~ *God* would to God 6737. **wold** *pp.* 2786n.
wombe *n.* bowels 3158; belly 4015. **wombes** *pl.* stomachs 5607n.
wombed *adj.* bloated 4080.
woninge *vbl. n.* in *hath his* ~ dwells 5978.
wont *pp.* in *was* ~ used 5730; *I hadde not be* ~ *to be* I was not used to being 7008; *as it was* ~ as usual 7273.
wood *adj.* insane 863; **woode** 476.
woodeth *pr. 3 sg.* goes mad with fright 2189.
woodshipe *n.* madness 2256.
wookes see **woke**.
woord *n.* statement 556; command 640; information 1170, *of* ~ in what was said 706. **woordes** *pl.* in *took ayen hire* ~ 4587 see **take**; *wordes* in *at shorte* ~ briefly 2485.
woorth *n.* value 2442.
woorth *adj.* valuable 856; *(riht) litel is* ~ is (absolutely) useless 1057; *it is nothing* ~, *nouht is* ~ it is no use having 1399, 1400; *nothing* ~, *litel* ~ useless 2114, 6875. **worth** 499.
woot see **wite**.
wordes see **woord**.
wordliche *adj.* worldly 6273; earthly 6518; ? secular 6543; **worldliche** 6412; **wordlich** 6435.
wormes *n. pl.* mites (of scabies) 3696.
worpen see **werpeth**.
worth see **woorth**.
worthi see **wurþi**.
wost, wot see **wite**.
woxe see **wexe**.
wrat(t)h(e) *v.* anger 984. **wrathþe** *refl.* grow angry 774; **wretthe** 5410.
wrechche *adj.* wretched 5767.
wretthe see **wrat(t)h(e)**.
wryinge *pr. p.* twisting.
writhen *pp.* twisted 4276. **wriþen** *pp. adj.* 75.
wrong *n.* in *hadde* . . . ~ should be at fault 2889.
wronge *adj.* bent 5370. **wrong** *adv.* in ~ *shapen* deformed 4862; *hauen here hoodes* ~ *turned* are blind 6534.
wroth *adj.* very angry 556.
wule, wult see **wole**.
wunder *n.* in *it is not riht gret* ~ it is not very surprising 1612.
wunder *adv.* extremely 91.
wunder, wundre *v.* blunder about 4379; ~ *upon* be astonished about 1973. **wundrede** *pa. t. sg.* was amazed 1095. *refl.* was puzzled 65. **wundringe** *vbl. n.* in *turneth to* ~ 788 see **turne**; *make gret* ~ be much amazed 3311.
wurche *pr. 1 sg.* function 2737.
wurmode *n.* wormwood (*artemisia absinthium*) 4755.
wurshipe *n.* reputation 433; respect 469; honour 514; *your* ~ to your credit 1618; *do þi* ~ gain respect for yourself 2420; **wurship** 1034.

wurshipe *v.* do honour to 1047; **wurshipen** 5472. **wurshiped** *pp.* graced 519.
wurþen *pp.* in ~ *up* mounted 4660.
wurþi *adj.* important 126; high 1665; excellent 2635; notable 4193; deserving of 5856; ~ *to haue* worthy of 2958; ~ ... *to* equal to 6109; **wurthi** good 415; proper 686; **worthi** 4631.
wurþilyche *adv.* correctly 1523.
wurþinesse *n.* virtue 2870; *neuere of gret* ~ not very honourable 1665.

yaf see **yive**.
yate *n.* gate 43.
yelde, yilde *v. intr.* leave (the body) 1332. *refl.* surrender 3244; admit yourself 3246. *tr.* return 5295. *pr. 1 sg.* make 1124; give 5771. **yelt** *3 sg.* in ~ *invisible* makes (me) invisible 2729. **yelde, yilde** *pr. subj. sg.* in *God* ~ *hire* may God reward her 2694-5. **yelte** *pa. t. sg.* 5293. **yolde** *refl. subj. sg.* were to surrender 6756. **yolden** *tr. subj. pl.* might give 927.
yerde *n.* rod 279; (? Birch)-cane 1096; **yerd** 383.
yeue see **yiue**.
yilde see **yelde**.
yit *adv.* still 65, yet 346; moreover 353; in addition 382; further 995; more 1000; ~ *a litel* a little longer 345; ~ *more* another thing 934; on top of that 1457; ~ *in helpinge* besides helping 977-8; *afterward* ~ thirdly 1393; *neuere* ~ not until now 1805; *ne* ~ nor indeed 2198; ~ *also* and another thing 2529. *conj.* nevertheless 185; pleonastic in *neuerþeless þouh* ... ~, *þouh* ... ~ 238, 1657-8.
yiue, yive *v.* give 161; kick 4683; *make* ~ *me* have me given 1803; **yiven** in *to* ~ to be given 2166-7. **yiueth** *pr. 3 sg.* in ~ *techynge* makes it clear 592. **yif** *imp. sg.* 5240. **yaf** *pa. t. sg.* in ~ *to ete to alle* fed everyone 788. **yeuen** *pl.* 6852. **yaf** *subj. sg.* were to give 1366; **yeue** might give 6159.
yivere *n.* giver 1434.
yolde(n) see **yelde**.
yore *adv.* in *ful* ~ very long ago 5983.

INDEX OF NAMES

Aaron 278n, 876n.
Abner 4503n.
Abstinence 6929.
Achimelech 2306n.
Acordaunce to þat þat Men Seyn 4383 see **Resonance**.
Adam 3594, 4241, 6015, 6552, 6556.
Adonay 6503n, 6514, 6559.
Amalech 4274 (see note 4273).
Amason Amasa 4503n.
Ambrose 416n.
Annoye of Lyf 3863n.
Apemendeles 4983n.
Appocalipsis 4861n.
Architriclyn 880n.
Argus 4174n.
Aristotle 949n, 1590n, 1593, 1628, 1682, 1792, 2569, 7188.
Athenes 1728.
Attemperaunce Temperance 2231, 2234n, 2251, 2295, 5603.
Austyn Augustine 52.
Auarice 5019, 5020, 5472, 5475, 5477, 5724, 6251.
Azael 6363n.

Babiloyne 4125.
Barabas 4796n.
Baret Conflict 5307, 5357.
Beel 5544n.
Beneyt, Beneit Benedict 68, 2339, 2363, 2375; **Seint ~** 2866.
Bernard 2309n, 3724.
Besachis 4983n.
Bitalasso(n), Bitalassum 6398n, 6423, 6424.
Blaunche 6901.
Boloyne þe Grace 4075n.

Caribdim, Carybdis 6398n, 6400, 6411, 6421.
Castel Landoun 4100n.
Castrimargye 5530n, 5531.
Cerastes 4676n.
Chaalit, Chalyt 18n, 2269.
Charite(e) 666, 1315, 1361, 1413, 1440, 1442, 1447, 1449, 1534, 1539, 1552, 1564, 1569, 1572, 1574, 1689, 1788, 4446, 6808, 7179, 7192, 7203, 7207.
Chastite(e) 5647, 5652, 5657, 5662, 6903.

Cherubyn 32n, 48, 63, 190, 236, 548, 654, 656, 684.
Chidinge 4761, 4765.
Cilla 6423n, 6424, 6426, 6428; **Cillam** 6398.
Cirtes 6400 (see note 6398), 6403, 6409; **Cyrtim** 6398n.
Cistiaus Citeaux.
Cleeruaus Clairvaux 3875n.
Cluigni Cluny 6751n.
Confusioun 6487.
Constaunce Faithfulness 2407.
Continence 2295n.
Continuacioun see **Feruent**.
Contricioun 1186.
Coquinerie 5213n.
Corde of Wrecches Cord for Those in Need 7178n.
Correccioun 4772.
Coupe Bourse Theft 5086-7n.
Coueytise, Couetise Covetousness 5018, 5019.
Cristes gen. 5932; **Crystes** 5861; see **Ihesu**.
Crueltee 4106.

Daan Dan 4675n, 4676.
Dalida Delila 3250n.
Dame Blaunch 6900; see **Blaunch**.
Dame Glotonye 5641; see **Glotonye**.
Dame Justice 4771; see **Justice**.
Dame Peresce 3684; see **Peresce**.
Dame Resoun 2800; see **Resoun**.
Dame Venus 5610, 5619-20; see **Venus**.
Daniel 4860n.
Dauid 2305, 2486, 2556, 2566, 2567, 2570, 4451, 6097.
Desperacioun 3887.
Despyte Resentment 4760, 4766.
Deth 4420, 4438, 4440, 7037, 7043[1,2], 7047, 7049, 7069, 7073, 7090, 7092, 7113, 7133, 7156, 7226, 7242, 7247, 7267, 7268.
Detraccioun 4601, 4657, 4689.
Diluvie Flood 6621.
Disceyuaunce Deception 5308.
Discipline 6868.

Eeue see **Eue**.
Egipcian Marie 6068n.

582   ÞE LYFE OF ÞE MANHODE

Egipte 4276.
Envye 4420, 4468, 4475, 4543, 4566, 4580, 4695.
Epicurie 5516n, 5518.
Equite 5364, 5601.
Esau 1508n, 4781.
Esdras 4987.
Esperaunce Hope 2002, 2190.
Etiques *Ethics* 2569n.
Eue 4244; **Eeue** 4241.
Euele Wil Unnatural Desire 5690.
Ezechiel 281n, 4860n.

Falsetee 4365.
Fardrye Make-up 5698.
Femyne Land of Women (of the Amazons) 3964.
Feruaunt Continuacioun Sincere Perseverance 6948-9.
Flaterye 4364, 4392.
Foy Faith 1890.
Force 2200.
Fortune 6425.
Fraunceys St Francis 73.

Gabrielles *gen.* Gabriel's 5948n.
George see **Seynt George**.
Germeyne see **Seint Germeyn**.
Giesy 5262n.
Giezetrye 5286.
Gildenemouth St John Chrysostom 6749n.
Glotonye 2256, 5525, 5541, 5641, 5719, 5723. **Glotoun** 5590.
God 201, 247, 335, 428, 454, 488, 491, 493, 585, 721, 722, 723, 913, 943, 1137, 1190, 1258, 1286, 1290, 1670, 1841, 1843, 1903, 1908, 1910, 1919, 1933, 1938, 2046, 2333, 2499, 2501, 2540, 2542, 2608, 2614, 2694, 2785, 2808, 2831, 2887, 2963, 2993, 3045, 3185, 3217, 3225, 3235, 3425, 3475, 3504, 3632, 3667, 3713, 3780, 3911, 3962, 4017, 4135, 4315, 4329, 4734, 4785, 4825, 4881, 5118, 5120, 5217, 5304, 5318, 5337, 5599, 5763, 5778, 5860, 5864, 5941, 5970, 5971, 5978, 6120, 6153, 6160, 6184, 6257, 6575, 6580, 6583, 6611, 6622, 6625, 6629, 6641, 6653, 6736, 6779, 6961, 7293.
Goddes *gen.* 275, 516, 1848.
Golias Goliath 2579n.
Grace (Dieu) 178, 222, 262, 264, 286, 312, 386, 397, 404, 408, 430, 537, 551, 552, 554, 558, 560, 578, 582, 663, 711, 781, 783, 809, 822, 897, 991, 996, 1022, 1026, 1070, 1079, 1208, 1226, 1235, 1476, 1633, 1787, 1800, 1887, 1943, 1994, 1999, 2045, 2078, 2466, 2533, 2538, 2603, 2609, 2617, 2620, 2627, 2634, 2694, 2708, 2837, 3014, 3015, 3022, 3031, 3089, 3100, 3448, 3485, 3590, 3737, 3751, 3775, 3792, 3908, 3968, 4281, 4811, 4830, 4835, 5156, 5276, 5279, 5509, 5737, 5764, 5783, 5796, 5830, 6020, 6021, 6022, 6033, 6043, 6081, 6099, 6161, 6187, 6227, 6243, 6244, 6343, 6459, 6523, 6617, 6621, 6625, 6630, 6641, 6644, 6648, 6667, 6713, 6760, 6766, 6785, 6815, 6840, 6856, 6992, 6998, 7009, 7012, 7026, 7216, 7236, 7240.

Grece Greece 1728.
Þe Gryselichhede of Helle The Horror of Hell 6779.
Guileuile see **Thomas of Guileuile**.
Þe Gulf 5611.

Helye Elias 3865n.
Heresye 6194.
Hye Iustyse The Judge at the Last Judgement 5870.
Holicherche 6366.
Holi Gost 5926, 5947, 6748, 6923; **Holy Gost** 4446.
Holi Writ 6917.
Homicidye 4797.
Hountee Shame 6486n.
Humilitee 2379.

Impatience 4766.
Infirmitee 7059.
Iniquitee 4365, 6556.
Inobedience Disobedience 4240.
Þe Inuocacioun of Dieu Calling upon God 6979.
Ypocrysie 4311.
Ire 4753, 5863.
Ysaak Isaac 1507n, 6002n.
Isaye Isaias 962; **Ysaie** 4101n, 7128n.
Israel the Israelites 365; Israel 4252, 6086.
Israel Jacob 4675n.
Yueresce Drunkenness 5611n.

Jacob 1511 (see note 1508), 4424n, 4688; **Iacob** 4781n.
Jacobines 58n.

INDEX OF NAMES

James, Seynt St James of Compostella 2552n.
Jeonenesse Youth 6354n, 7106; **Joenenesse** 6439, 6594, 6614, 6616.
Jeremie, Jeremye, Jerome St Jerome 4956n, 4969, 6317n.
Jerusalem 20, 139, 186, 227, 3535, 5751, 6750, 6997.
Ihesu, Jhesu, Ihesus 1323, 1416, 1426, 2119, 2948, 6971; ~ **Crist (Cryst)** 520, 640-1, 1848, 2009, 5269, 5783, 6748. ~ **Cristes** *gen.* 2200; see **Cristes**.
Joab 4503n.
Job 6476n, 6566.
Joenenesse see **Jeonenesse**.
Johan, Seint 4637, 4643.
Ioye of Ooperes Aduersitee 4450.
Joseph 5525n.
Judas 3888n, 3937, 4504, 5048, 5119, 5291, 5292, 6570.
Justice 2323, 4771, 5600, 5863.

Labour 3598.
Landoun see **Castell**.
Larescyne Larceny 5087n.
Latria Lat. Worship 6978.
Laurence 5462n.
Lessoun 6916, 6926.
Letargie Lethargy 3877n.
Liberalitee 4990.
Longis, Longius Longinus 4455n, 5996.
Lucifer 3995.

Magdaleyne Mary Magdalene 1126, 6067, 6282.
Magus see **Simon**.
Mahoun Mahomet/Idol 4886, 4889.
Malischique ? Blabber-mouth 5583n.
Malevoysigne ? Old Malmsey, ? Bad Neighbour 5583n.
Marie see **Egipcian** for Mary of Egypt.
Marie 1342; **Virgine** ~ 2020; **Seinte Marye** 5599.
Martyn, Seint 1311.
Maungepayn Breadeater 5214n.
Medicine 7063.
Memorie 2661, 2697, 2742, 4808, 6475, 6874, 6881.
Mensonge Falsehood 5350, 6356[1,2].
Menterye Lying 5354n, 5363; **Mentirye** 5372.
Mercury 840.
Misericorde (Corde of Wrecches) Mercy 7178.

Moyses, Moises Moses 278, 305, 365, 430, 434, 443, 447, 449, 455, 510, 531, 541, 542, 584, 697, 699, 758, 776, 803, 877, 1083, 1090, 1280, 1419, 1447, 1450, 1495, 1803, 2701, 2705, 5922, 5926, 6811; **Moiseses** *gen.* 6084.
Mors Lat. Death 6386.

Nabal 3037n.
Nabugodonosor 4124n.
Nature 808, 819, 897, 898, 910, 991, 999, 1070, 1496, 1595, 1613, 1617, 1620, 1625, 1633, 1636, 1650, 1654, 1786, 1796, 1798, 5132, 5135, 5410[1,2], 5413, 7080.
Neemye The Book of Nehemias (II Esdras) 1204n.
Negligence 3877.
Nicolas, Seint 4547n.
Noe 3596, 6621.
Noli Me Tangere Lat. Touch Me Not 4741n.

Obedience 3093, 6862.
Obstinacioun Obstinacy 2847, 4272.
Occisioun Slaughter 4798.
Ocupacioun 3599.
Ogiers *gen.* 2325n.
Oiseuce Idleness 3573, 3686, 3709, 3720, 3895. **Oyseuce** 4831.
Olyueeres *gen.* Oliver's 2326n.
Orgoill, Orguill Pride 2846, 4104, 4340, 4343, 4369, 4378, 4420, 4628, 6247.
Orisoun Prayer 6958, 6972.
Ortigometra "Mother of Quails" 6262n.
Oure Lady 5599.

Paour de Dieu Fear of God 6773.
Paradys, Paradise 1853, 4019, 4436, 5431, 5988, 6467, 6526, 6540, 6773.
Patience 2114.
Peeter 1121; **Saint** ~ 86; **Seint** ~ 6067, 6336.
Penitence 1109, 1303, 1421, 1443, 1449, 3167, 3170, 3754, 4282, 5737, 5738, 5800, 6065, 6069, 6602, 6686, 6699, 6789, 7014, 7077, 7094, 7262.
Peresce Sloth 3684, 3855, 4284, 4334, 4706, 4822, 5116, 5123.
Periurement Perjury 5350, 5355, 5357, 5362, 5404.
Persecucioun 6473.

Perseueraunce 2406n.
Pharao(n) Pharaoh 427, 3038, 4251.
Þe Pilgrimage of þe Lyfe of þe Manhode The Pilgrimage of Man's Life 7295-6.
Pite 7185.
Pontifex Bridge-maker 381n.
Poul(e), Seynt St Paul 2, 1894, 1926, 2248.
Pouerte 5437, 6877.
Preyere 6959.
Propertee 5437.
Prosperitee 6517, 6530, 6535.
Prouerbe The Book of Proverbs 5319n.
Prudence 2432.

Rapyne Robbery 5056.
Rebellioun 4240.
Religioun The Religious Life 6720.
Renard Reynard the Fox 4319n.
Resonance and Acordance to Þat Þat Men Seyn Echoing and Agreeing with What Is Said 4383n.
Resoun Reason 312, 338, 345, 434, 447, 456, 465, 509, 579, 691, 711, 712, 776, 794, 819, 856, 2800, 2807, 2817, 2838, 2856, 2861, 2864, 2866, 2873, 2875, 2893, 2898, 2903, 2910, 2928, 2940, 2996, 3013, 3020, 3027, 3048, 3053, 3079, 3081, 3088, 3163, 3183, 3265, 3272, 3336, 3348, 3358, 3368, 3398, 3422, 3767, 3792, 4271, 4658, 5109, 5509, 5599, 7177.
Rolandes gen. Roland's 4229n; **Rowlandes** 2326n.
Romayns Romans 1927.
Þe Romaunce of the Rose 7298.
Rude Entendement Untutored Understanding 2842, 2915, 2919, 3042, 3054, 4270.
Rudeness Ignorance 2923.

Salomon Solomon 852, 2433, 4623, 4763, 6281, 6417; **Salomon** 3056.
Sampson 3249 (see note 3250).
Samuel 4237n.
Sapience Wisdom 1559, 1570, 1574.
Sathan Satan 6290, 6333. **Sathanas** 4421, 4792, 5016.
Saul 2563n, 2567, 2578, 4273n, 4450n.
Science Knowledge 1644.
Silence 7025.
Symeon, Seint 2864n.

Simon (Magus) 5262n, 5264, 5268.
Symonye Simony 5268, 5286n, 5287.
Sirena(m) Siren 6399, 6437.
Sobernesse 5602.
Sobirtee, Sobrietee Sobriety 2250, 6930.
Soothnesse Truth 5601.
Sterre Tresmountayne Pole Star (? Virgin) 6641-2n.

Theophile Theophilus 6585n.
Thomas of Guileuile 3226.
Thomas, Seynt Saint Thomas of Canterbury 412.
Tobye Tobias 3289n.
Treccherie Treachery 5307, 5352.
Tresoun Treachery, Betrayal 4539n, 4648, 4657, 4686, 4697; **Tresouns** gen. 4364.
Trewaundrie Begging 5213.
Tribulacioun 6472, 6516, 6557, 6647, 6675.
Tricot Trickery 5307n.
Triphon 4505n.
Tristesse Melancholy 3857.

Vndernemynge of Euele Reproof of Wickedness 6870.

Vantaunce oþer Void Paunche Boasting or Empty Belly 4181.
Veynglorie 4121, 6246.
Þe Vengeaunge of God and Þe Gryselichhede of Helle The Vengeance of God and The Horror of Hell 6779n.
Venus 840, 5610, 5620, 5641, 6894.
Verite Truth 5363.
Vertu 6518.
Vilesse Old Age 6387, 6388, 7117.
Virginitee 5643, 5654.
Void Paunch see **Vantaunce**.

Werynesse and Letargie 3877n.
Wilful Pouerte Voluntary Poverty 6876-7.
William, Seint 2270n.
Wrathe of Ooþeres Ioye Anger at Others' Happiness 4449.

Xpc Christ (from the Greek letters representing CHRistoS) 5994n.

Zacharie Zacharias 6010n.

APPENDIX

The Melbourne Manuscript's additions and variants from 7264.

After *too* in line 7264, M adds on f. 93ᵛ a prose passage of fourteen and a half manuscript lines, and on ff. 94ʳ-95ʳ a poem forming a prayer to Christ at the moment of the pilgrim dreamer's death. The poem, which is 2271.4 in Robbins and Cutler, is published in Roberts, pp. 106-8, but in the interests of completeness, and since I do not agree with Roberts in some details, it too is included here. The rest of the text, which takes us to the end of *Þe Pilgrimage of Þe Lyfe of Þe Manhode*, also shows major variants, described below. Capitalisation and punctuation, which is often doubtful, are mine. Transcription follows the practice adopted for MS. M in the critical apparatus, except that the *þ/y* confusion is corrected here, and in the absence of parallel forms in O as a guide I expand all, not only some, of the flourishes after final *-m, -n, -r*.

'A, dere Aungel,' quod I, 'where ert þou now, þat I haue no com-/fort of þe? For now I see wele, me must be mawene with þe syth of dede / whilk is here present and abydes oonly for me.' Neuerlesse I spake vnto Grace / Dieu and saide vnto hire in þis wyse: 'Swete lady, with all myne hert I / biseke yow to graunt me space, of your gentresse, for to make a supplicacione / vnto God and to his modire (whilk er euer mercifull) þat þei wold vouchsafe / to be my socoure, what tyme þat I shall passe fro hence; for trewly I am / right aferde of þat dredefull houre when my body and my soule shall / departe.' 'Now,' quod Grace Dieu, 'sithene I see þat þou art sore repentynge, / I graunt þe space to say fully þine entent—and I shall enforme þe here / of a shorte prayere whilk is gude to ilk creature forto say, what tyme / þei fele þeme vnbelappyd with cordeȝ of deth as þou art at þis tyme.' / And þen Grace Dieu tuke to me a litill roule writyne on þis manere / with golde letters, and I bigan to rede and say on þis wyse knelynge / deuoutely opone both my knese.

Here is þe prayere of þe pilgryme / þat he sayes afore his deth.[71]
[f.94ʳ]

       My souerayne saueoure to þe I call,
       My refute and my proteccione:
       Eternall kynge and immortall,
       In þe is myne affeccione;
5   Ihesu, for þat dileccione
       Bitweyne þe and þi modere dere,
       Þi mercy now lat on me apere.

       Thi mercy I aske for myne offence,
       For deth now shewed has his duresse.
10   Shew on me þi beniuolence:

Lat never þe fende my soule oppresse.
He besy is to haue me in destresse;
His malice fro me lorde now distreyne
Þat for me soffrid moste greuouse peyne.

15 To þe I crye with all instaunce
And tremell spirite of humblenesse
As þou for me soffrid grete noysaunce
And drank drynk of grete bittirnesse,
And as scripture beris witnesse
20 Vnto þi fadire þi spirite gan ȝelde:
Be now my socoure and my belde —

Of þi precious bloede effusion
Some drope at þis necessite
To extingue þat by collusion
25 Þe fals fende has infectid me.
Þis worldis mutabilite
Me has dissayued, bot, lorde, þi grace
May quench al malice and manace.

Moste mercifull lorde called in scripture
30 Is þou full of benignyte;
Þi myght and mercy shall euer endure
Moste hyeot ert þou of dignyte.
Now, lorde, represse malignyte
Of all þat is to me noysaunce: [f. 94v]
35 My prayere be nowe to þi plesaunce.

I haue offendid þe greuously
And made noon satisfaccione;
Þe tyme is comene þat me must dy,
Þere is now no retraccione.
40 Deth hastes hym with coacion
My spirite fro me now for to pryve:
Help now lorde for þi woundeȝ fyve.

For synners, þou incarnacioun
Assumyd of flessh virginall,
45 And also suffrid þi passione
To fredome þem þat for synne were thrall;
No tonge þe gudnesse may tell all
Of þi debonaire humblenesse:
Now helpe me lorde in þis distresse.

50 Here now my deprecacione,
Þou immolate lambe immaculate,
To be now of saluacione
Þin owne dere child predestinate;
And if I be contaminate,

GLOSSARY 587

 55 Receife lorde my contricion
  By merite of þi dere passion;

  And for þat wounde of þi right syde
  Fro whilk þer rane both watere and blode,
  Be my socoure now at þis tyde,
 60 My ioy, my hope, my faith, my fode.
  Ihesu, þat for me died on rode
  And was with blode made roseate,
  Help me now þus angustiate.

  Graunt now fro my cors corruptible
 65 In faith my spirite forto procede
  Vnto þi blisse þat is infallible
  Where þou rewardis for all gude dede.
  In þi grace fully I putt my mede: [f.95r]
  Þi dome on me þou mollify
 70 On crosse for me lorde þat gan dy.

  Now Mary, qwene of virginite,
  Þat bare both verrey god and man
  And conceyued thurgh humilite,
  Be my help as þou may and kan.
 75 Socoure and safe me fro wikkid Sathan,
  Restreyne his horribilite:
  My socoure now lady þou be.

  Lorde Ihesu graunt me þat grace,
  For þi dere passione þou soffrid for me,
 80 No wikkid powere my spirite enbrace
  Fro þi presence forbarred to be.
  Graunt me þi blissed face to see,
  And to þe, lorde, now at myne ende
  My spirite holy I commende. Amen.

Here þe pilgryme endes his dremynge on þis wyse.[72]

The disagreements with Roberts are as follows, my own reading being represented by the lemma: 8 Thi] This (clearly so: the scribe's characteristic dotting of *i*, easily mistaken for an abbreviation mark, is apparent in line 20). 14 moste] most. 29 Moste] Most; mercifull] masterfull. 32 Moste] most. 35 prayere] prayers.

The relationship between M and the main text from line 7264 to the end is not adequately represented by formal Variants: M cuts some sentences, transposes others, and inserts one from an earlier place. The variations are as follows. Omitted from M are lines 7264-6:
 Now I telle yow, if I mihte haue spoke I hadde maade hire
 many demaundes of whiche I hadde doute and kneewe nouht.

The next sentence, in 7266-7,

> It is folye for to abide to þe neede. Whan men weenen þat
> Deth be riht fer, he abitte at the posterne; wel I wiste þat: I
> was supprysed.

is omitted at this point, but is inserted (all but he last two clauses) later in M: after 7289 *chastysed*. Instead of the portion omitted in 7264-7, M has:

> And onoon as I hadde endyde þis shorte prayere,

going straight on to

> Deth lete þe syth rynne, and made þe soule departe fro / þe
> body as me thoght.

in which the last three words are the equivalent of the beginning of the next sentence in the main text's 7271:

> Þus me thouhte as I mette, but as I was in swich plyte . . .

which then becomes in M:

> Þen I was in swylk plyte . . .

at which point a normal relationship to the main text is re-established.

BIBLIOGRAPHY

The Bibliography lists all works cited, and a few others. Three dots at the end of a title indicate that it has been curtailed.

Manuscripts

Cambridge: Fitzwilliam Museum, MS. 62; Hours (with scenes from Deguileville).

Magdalene College, MS. Pepys 2258; 17th-century abridgement of the ME prose Pilgrimage.

St John's College, MS. 189 (G.21); Þe Pilgrimage of þe Lyfe of þe Manhode (J in the stemma).

Trinity College, MS. R.3.20 (once part of London: Sion College MS. Arc.L40.2.E.44)

University Library, MS. Add.6681; ME Bible.

University Library, MS. Add.6684; ME Bible.

University Library, MS. Ff.5.30; Þe Pilgrimage of þe Lyfe of þe Manhode (C in the stemma).

University Library, MS. Ff.6.30; 17th-century abridgement of Þe Pilgrimage of þe Lyfe of þe Manhode.

University Library, MS. Mm.2.15; ME Bible.

Glasgow: University Library, MS Hunter 239; Þe Pilgrimage of þe Lyfe of þe Manhode (G in the stemma).

London: British Library, MS. Add. 31,840; Le Roman de la Rose.

British Library, MS. Add. 39,677; Durandus, Pontificale of Mende.

Sion College Library, MS. Arc. L24.1/SI.7M; Catalogus Librorum Omnium M.M.S.S. in Bibliotheca Hac de Sione apud Londinenses. / Per I.S. Bibliothecarium Collectus 1650.

Sion College Library, MS. Arc. L40.2.E.4; Catalogus Librorum Omnium Quotquot in Hac Bibliotheca

Collegij Sionensis in Studiosorum vsum extant. S.S.S. Per Ioh: Spencerum Bibliotheca (Quanta Potuit Diligentia) Ordine Alphabetico Collectus (1632).

Sion College Library, MS. Arc. L40.2.E.5(2); Catalogus Librorum Omnium Qvotqvot in Biblio-theca Collegij Sionensis sub Arctiores Custodelâ in Archivis Asservantur MDCLVII. Sed Anno MDCLVI [Eodem Qvo Maxima Pars Londinij] Perierunt Incendio.

Sion College Library, MS. Arc. L40.2.E.44; Þe Pilgrimage of þe Lyfe of þe Manhode (S in the stemma).

Sion College Library, MS. Arc. L40.2.E.58(1,2); Catalogus Librorum a Bibliothecâ Collegij de Sione ad Hospitium Suttonianum [Vulgò Charterhouse] Londino Conflagrante Calendis Septembris Anno MDCLXVI, Transmissorum.

Sion College Library, MS. Arc. L40.2.E.62(1,2,3); J. du Moulin, The Catalogue of the Books in Durdens Librarie. Made by Iames dv Movlin Dr of Physick: Begvn Septembre 27 and Compleated the 3rd Octobre 1667.

Sion College Library, MS. Arc. L40.2.E.64; Book of Benefactors; no title page.

Sion College Library, MS. Arc. L40.2.E.62.1,2,3; Catalogve of the Books in Dvrdens Librarie, made by Iames dv Movlin Dr off Physick begvn Septembre 27 Compleated the 3rd Octobre 1667.

Melbourne: State Library of Victoria, MS. *096 G94; Þe Pilgrimage of þe Lyfe of þe Manhode (M in the stemma).

Oxford: Bodleian Library, MS. Add.C.29; Le Pèlerinage de la vie humaine (Vie^2).

Bodleian Library, MS. Auct.D.3.8; Vulgate + Interpretationes nominum Hebraicorum.

Bodleian Library, MS. Auct.D.4.9; Vulgate + Interpretationes nominum Hebraicorum.

Bodleian Library, MS. Auct.D.5.14; Vulgate + Interpretationes nominum Hebraicorum.

Bodleian Library, MS. Bodley 270ᵇ; La Bible Moralisée.

Bodleian Library, MS. Douce 300; Le Pèlerinage de la vie humainne en francois (*Vie*¹).

Bodleian Library, MS. Laud Misc.556; Catalogue of Laud Donations.

Bodleian Library, MS. Laud Misc.691; Catalogue of Laud MSS.

Bodleian Library, MS. Laud Misc.705; Catalogue of Laud's First and Second Donations.

Bodleian Library, MS. Laud Misc.740; Þe Pilgrimage of þe Lyfe of þe Manhode (O in the stemma).

St John's College, MS. Registrum Benefactorum Bibliothecae Coll: D. Iohannis Oxon. [No shelfmark].

St John's College, MS. Wood donat.5; Catalogue.

Secondary Material

Alanus de Insulis. See Cornog, and Moffat.

Albertus Magnus. 'Liber de Sacrificio Missae.' In *B. Alberti Magni, Ratisbonensis Episcopi, Ordinis Praedicatorum, Opera Omnia* .... Vol. XXXVIII. Paris, 1899, pp. 1–189. See also Best.

Allen, H. E. *Writings Ascribed to Richard Rolle Hermit of Hampole, and Materials for His Biography*. MLA Monographs, 3. London, 1927.

The Alnwick Bestiary. See Millar.

Amos, F. R. 'The Medieval Period.' In her *Early Theories of Translation*. New York, 1920, pp. 3–46.

Analecta Bollandiana. See Hooff.

Andrieu, M. *Le Pontifical romain au moyen-âge*. 4 vols. Vatican, 1938–1941.

——. 'Les Ordres Mineurs dans l'ancien rit romain.' *Revue des sciences religieuses*, 5 (1925), 232.

Aquinas, Thomas. *The 'Summa Theologica' of St. Thomas Aquinas Literally Translated by the Fathers of the English Dominican Province*. 2nd edn. 22 vols. London, 1921–1932.

——. See Gilby [for a parallel text in progress].

―――. *Liber de Veritate Catholicae Fidei Contra Errores Infidelium seu 'Summa Contra Gentiles'.* Ed. P. Marc and P. Carmello. 3 vols. Turin, 1961.

Aristotle. See Cooke, and W. D. Ross.

Attwater, D. *A Dictionary of Saints.* 2nd edn. London, 1958.

Aubert, M. *Stained Glass of the XIIth and XIIIth Centuries from French Cathedrals,* Art and Nature in Colour. London, n.d. [*c.* 1937].

Augsburger, D. A. 'Rutebeuf et la 'Voie de paradis' dans la litterature française du moyen âge.' Diss. Michigan 1950.

Avino, V. d', ed. *Rationale Divinorum Officiorum . . . Accedit aliud Divinorum Officiorum Rationale a Joanne Beletho . . . .* Naples, 1859.

Baisier, L. *The Lapidaire Chrétien, Its Composition, Its Influence, Its Sources,* Catholic University of America Studies in Romance Languages and Literature, 14. 1936; rpt. New York, 1969.

Barber, Malcolm. *The Trial of the Templars.* Cambridge, 1978.

Baring-Gould, S. *The Lives of the Saints.* Rev. edn. Edinburgh, 1914.

Barrois, J., ed. *La Chevalerie Ogier de Danemarche.* Romans des Douze Pairs de France, 8,9. 2 vols. Paris, 1842.

Bartholomaeus Anglicus. See Trevisa.

Battaglio, S. *Grande Dizionario della Lingua Italiana.* Vol. VI. Turin, 1970.

Baudouin de Condé. 'La Voie de Paradis.' In *Baudouin de Condé.* Vol. I of *Dits et contes de Baudouin de Condé et son fils Jean de Condé* . . . . Brussels, 1866, pp. 205-31.

Bernard of Clairvaux. See Burch for *The Steps of Humility.*

Berthélemy, C., trans. *Rational ou manuel des divins offices de Guillaume Durand évèque de Mende au treizième siècle, ou raisons mystiques et historiques de la liturgie catholique.* 5 vols. Paris, 1845.

Best, M. R., and F. H. Brightman, eds. *The Book of Secrets of Albertus Magnus: Of the Virtues of Herbs, Stones and Certain Beasts also a Book of the Marvels of the World.* Oxford, 1973.

Bible Moralisée. See Laborde.

Biblia Pauperum. See Avril Henry.

Biblia Sacra Vvlgatae Editionis Sixti V. et Clementis VIII. Pontt. Maxx. Ivssv Recognita atque Edita. Rome, 1861.

Biblia Sacra iuxta Vulgatam Clementinam Nova Editio. 4th edn. Biblioteca de Autores cristianos. Madrid 1965.

Bibliothecae Cleri Londiniensis in Collegio Sionensi Catalogus, Duplici Forma Concinnatus. London, 1724.

Blair, C. *European Armour circa 1066 to circa 1700.* London, 1958.

Bloomfield, M. W. *The Seven Deadly Sins: an Introduction to the History of a Religious Concept, with Special Reference to Medieval English Literature.* East Lansing, 1952.

Blum, A., and P. Laur. *La Miniature française aux xve et xvie siècles.* Paris, 1930.

Blythe, J. H. 'The Influence of Latin Manuals in Medieval Allegory: Deguileville's Presentation of Wrath.' *Romania*, 95 (1974), 256–83.

Bömer. See Deguileville.

Bonaventura, St. 'The Journey of the Mind to God.' In *Mystical Opuscula*. Vol. I of *The Works of Bonaventura Cardinal Seraphic Doctor and Saint, Translated from the Latin by José de Vinck* .... Paterson, 1960, pp. 3–58.

Bond, F. B., and B. Camm. *Roodscreens and Roodlofts.* Vol. I. London, 1909.

Bossuat, R. *Manuel bibliographique de la littérature française du moyen âge.* Melun, 1951.

Boyd, B. *Chaucer and the Liturgy.* Philadelphia, 1967.

Bozon, N. *Les contes moralisés de Nicole Bozon frère mineur: publiés pour la premiere fois d'après les manuscrits de Londres et de Cheltenham* .... Société des anciens textes français. Paris, 1889.

Bradley, Sr R. 'Backgrounds of the Title 'Speculum' in Medieval Literature.' *Speculum*, 29 (1954), 110–15.

Brault, G. J. *Early Blazon: Heraldic Terminology in the Twelfth and Thirteenth Centuries with Special Reference to Arthurian Literature.* Oxford, 1972.

Brockington, L. H. *Ezra, Nehemiah and Esther.* London, 1969.

Brook, S. 'Religious Allegory in Middle English.' Diss. Manchester 1955.

Brown, Carleton. *A Register of Middle English Religious and Didactic Verse.* 2 vols. Oxford, 1916, 1920.

Brown, Carleton, and R. H. Robbins. *The Index of Middle English Verse*. New York, 1943. See Robbins and Cutler for Supplement.

Brusendorff, A. *The Chaucer Tradition*. Copenhagen, 1925.

Burch, G. B., trans. *The Steps of Humility by Bernard, Abbot of Clairvaux*. Cambridge, Mass., 1942.

Cabrol, F. and H. Leclercq, eds. *Dictionnaire d'archéologie chrétienne et de liturgie*. 15 vols. Paris, 1907-1953.

Cahier, C., and A. Martin. *Monographie de la cathédrale de Bourges*. Pt. I. *Vitraux du xiiie siècle*.... Paris, 1841-1844.

Canuteson, J. A. 'The Conflict Between the Body and the Soul as a Metaphor of the Moral Struggle in the Middle Ages.' Diss. Florida, 1975.

Carcopino, J. *Le Mystère d'un symbole chrétien: l'ascia*. Paris, 1955.

A Catalogue of the Manuscripts Preserved in the Library of the University of Cambridge. 5 vols. Cambridge, 1856-1867; rpt. Munich, 1980.

Catalogus Universalis Librorum Omnium in Bibliotheca Collegii Sionii apud Londinenses. London, 1650. [Sion College, Arc.L26.1.SI.7(4) and Arc.L26.1.SI.7 (1,2,3,) all supplemented in manuscript up to A.D. 1666.]

The Catholic Encyclopedia. See Herberman.

Cessolis, Jacobus de. *Libellus de Ludo Scachorum*. Trans. Caxton [from the French]. London, c. 1475.

Chambers, R. W., and M. Daunt. *A Book of London English 1384-1425*. Oxford, 1931.

Chaucer, Geoffrey. See Robinson.

Chesterton, G. K. *Chaucer*. London, 1932.

Chew, S. C. *The Pilgrimage of Life*. New Haven, 1962.

Chrétien de Troyes. *Le Chevalier au lion (Yvain)*. Vol. IV of *Les Romans de Chrétien de Troyes*. Ed. M. Roques. Classiques Français du Moyen Ages, 89. Paris, 1965.

Churchill, W. A. *Watermarks in Paper in Holland, England, France etc., in the XVII and XVIII Centuries and their Interconnection*. Amsterdam, 1935.

Clark, Andrew, ed. *Lincoln Diocese Documents*. EETS, OS 149 (1914).

Clemen, W. *Chaucer's Early Poetry*. Trans. C. A. M. Sym. New York, 1963.

Clubb, M. D., Jnr. *The Middle English Pilgrimage of the Soul*. Diss. Michigan, 1954.

Codex Iuris Canonici Pii X Pontificis Maximi iussi Digestus Benedicti Papae XV Auctoritate Promulgatus, Acta Apostolicae Sedis: Commentorium Officiale, annus IX. Vol. IX, Pt. II. Rome, 1917.

Cohen, G. *Historie de la chevalerie en France du moyen âge*. Paris, 1949.

——. *Mystères et moralités du manuscrit 617 de Chantilly publiés pour la première fois et précédés d'une étude linguistique et littéraire*. Paris, 1920.

——. *Nativités et moralités liégeoises du moyen-âge publiées avec une introduction et des notes d'àpres le manuscrit 617 du Musée Condé à Chantilly (Oise)*. Academie royale de belgique. Classe des lettres. Mémoires, 12. Brussels, 1953.

Colquhoun, K. H. 'A Critical Edition of the Middle English Translation of *Speculum Humanæ Salvationis*.' Diss. London 1964.

Cooke, H. P., ed. and trans. *Aristotle The Organon I: The Categories, On Interpretation*. London, 1949.

Cornog, W. H., trans. 'The *Anticlaudian* of Alain de Lille: a Translation with an Introduction and Notes.' Diss. Philadelphia 1934.

Cottineaux, L. H. *Répertoire topo-bibliographique des abbayes et prieurés*. 3 vols. Mâcon, 1935-1970.

Coxe, H. O. *Catalogi Codicum Manuscriptorum Bibliothecae Bodleianae Pars Secunda Codices Latinos et Miscellaneos Laudianos Complectans*. Vol. II, Pt. 1. Oxford, 1858. [Annotated copy in Bodleian Library at 2590 d.Oxf.1a.15/2].

——. *Laudian Manuscripts*. Vol II of *Bodleian Library Quarto Catalogues*. 1858-1885; corr. rpt. Oxford, 1973. [First printed as *Catalogi Codicum Manscriptorum*].

Crampton, G. R. 'Of Chaucer's A.B.C..' *Chaucer Newsletter*, 1, i (1979), 8-10.

Crane, T. F. *The Exempla or Illustrative Stories from the Sermones Vulgares of Jacques de Vitry*. Publications of the Folklore Society (English), 26. London, 1890.

Crombie, A. C. *Science in the Middle Ages 5th to 13th Centuries.* Vol. I of *Augustine to Galileo.* 2nd ed. 1959; London, 1969.

Cross, F. L., and E. A. Livingstone, eds. *The Oxford Dictionary of the Christian Church.* 2nd edn. London, 1958.

Crum, M. *First-line Index of English Poetry 1500–1800 in Manuscripts of the Bodleian Library.* 2 vols. Oxford, 1969.

Curtius, E. R. *European Literature and the Latin Middle Ages.* Trans. W. R. Trask. London, 1953.

Cust, K. I. *A Modern Prose Translation of the Ancient Poem of Guillaume de Deguileville Entitled The Pylgrymage of Man.* London, 1859.

———. *The Booke of the Pylgremage of the Sowle Translated from the French of Guillaume de Guileville and Printed by William Caxton An. 1483* . . .. London, 1859.

D'Alverny, M.-T. 'Les Peregrinations de l'âme dans l'autre monde d'après un anonyme de la fin du xiie siècle.' *Archives d'histoire doctrinale et littéraire du moyen âge,* 13 (1942), 239–99.

Davis, N. 'Styles in English Prose of the Late Middle and Early Modern Period.' *Langue et littérature.* Les Congrès et colloques de l'université de Liège, 21. Liège, 1961.

Deanesly, M. 'Vernacular Books in England in the Fourteenth and Fifteenth Centuries.' *MLR,* 15 (1920), 349–63.

Dearmer, P. *Fifty Pictures of Gothic Altars.* Alcuin Club Collections, 10. London, 1910.

Deferrari, R. J., trans. *Hugh of Saint Victor on the Sacraments of the Christian Faith (De Sacramentis).* The Mediaeval Academy of America, 58. Cambridge, Mass., 1951.

Deguileville, G. de. See Stürzinger for editions of the *Pèlerinages*; Lydgate for translation of *Vie*^{2}, Guillaume for Caxton's *Pilgrimage of the Soul.*

———. *Dat Boeck vanden Pelgrim* . . .. Delft: Heynrick Eckert van Homberch, 1498.

———. *Le Pèlerinage de l'âme.* Paris: Verard, 1499.

———. *Le Pèlerinage de l'homme.* Paris: Verard. 1511.

———. *Le Pèlerinage die vie humaine.* Lyons: Huss, 1485.

———. *Le Pèlerinaige de Vie Humaine Reproduced in Fascimile from the Printed Book in the Library of the Earl of Ellesmere.* Ed. A. W. Pollard. Roxburghe Club. London, 1912.

———. *Die Pilgerfahrt des träumenden Mönchs aus der Berleburger Handschrift.* Ed. A. Bömer. Deutsche Texte des Mittelalters, 25. Berlin, 1915.

———. *Die Pilgerfahrt des träumenden Mönchs herausgegeben nach der Kölner Handschrift.* Ed. A. Meijboom. Rheinische Beiträge und Hülfsbucher zur germanischen Philologie und Volkskunde, 10. Bonn and Leipzig, 1925.

———. *Romant des trois pelerinaiges.* Paris: Rembolt and Petit, *c.* 1515.

Delacotte, Abbé J. *Guillaume de Digulleville (poète normand) trois romans poèmes du XIVe siècle: Les Pèlerinages et La Divine Comédie.* Paris, 1932.

Delaissé, L. M. J. 'Les Miniatures du Pèlerinage de la vie humaine de Bruxelles et l'archéologie du livre.' *Scriptorium,* 10 (1956), 233-50.

De Ricci, S. *English Collectors of Books and Manuscripts (1530-1930) and their Marks of Ownership.* Cambridge, 1930.

De Ricci, S., and W. J. Wilson. *Census of Medieval and Renaissance Manuscripts in the United States and Canada.* 2 vols. and Indices. New York, 1935-1940.

Des Périers, B. *Nouvelle récréations et joyeux devis I-XC: édition critique avec introduction et notes.* Ed. K. Kasprzyk. Société des textes français modernes. Paris, 1980.

Dictionnaire de Theologie . . . . See Vacant.

Didron, A. 'La Vie Humaine.' *Annales Archéologiques,* 1 (1844), 422-40.

———. 'La Vie Humaine.' *Annales Archéologiques,* 15 (1855), 413-24.

———. *Christian Iconography; or, the History of Christian Art in the Middle Ages.* Trans. E. J. Millington and M. Stokes. 2 vols. London, 1851, 1907.

Dobson, E. J. *Moralities on the Gospels: a Source of Ancrene Wisse.* Oxford, 1975.

Doyle, A. I. 'More light on John Shirley.' *Medium AEvum,* 30 (1961), 93-101.

Doyle, A. I., and G. B. Pace. 'A New Chaucer Manuscript.' *PMLA,* 83 (1968), 22-34.

Drover, C. B. 'A Medieval Monastic Water-Clock.' *Antiquarian Horology,* 1 (1954), 54-7.

Drover, C. B. 'A Medieval Monastic Water-Clock.' *Antiquarian Horology*, 1 (1954), 54-7.

Dudden, F. H. *The Life and Times of St. Ambrose.* London, 1935.

Dulong, M., ed. and trans. *The Trinity College Apocalypse.* 2 vols. London, 1967.

Durandus of Mende. *Prochiron, Vulgo Rationale Divinorum Officiorum, Auctorae Gulielmo Durando, Juris utriusque Doctore Celeberrimo, Mimatensi Episcopo.* Madrid, 1775.

——. See, for Latin, Avino; for French, Berthélemy; for English (Book I) Neale and Webb; (Book III) Passmore.

Durandus of Troarn. See Gallandius.

Eccles, M., ed. *The Macro Plays: The Castle of Perseverance, Wisdom, Mankind.* EETS, OS 262 (1969).

Edghill, E. M., ed. *Categoriae.* Vol I of *The Works of Aristotle. Translated into English under the Editorship of W. D. Ross.* London, 1928.

Einhorn, E. *Old French: a Concise Handbook.* London, 1974.

Einhorn, J. W. *Spiritalis Unicornis: das Einhorn als Bedeutungsträger in Literatur und Kunst des Mittelalters.* Munich, 1976.

An English Miscellany Presented to Dr. Furnivall in Honour of His Seventy-Fifth Birthday. Ed. W. P. Ker, et al. Oxford, 1901.

Evans, Joan. *Art in Mediaeval France 987-1498: a Study in Patronage.* Oxford, 1948.

——. *Dress in Mediaeval France.* Oxford, 1952.

——, ed. *The Flowering of the Middle Ages.* London, 1966.

——. *Life in Mediaeval France.* Rev. edn. London, 1957.

Evans, Joan, and M. S. Serjeantson, eds. *English Mediaeval Lapidaries.* EETS, OS 190 (1933).

Faral, É. 'Guillaume de Digulleville, Jean Gallopes et Pierre Virgin.' In *Études romanes dédiées à Mario Roques par ses amis, collègues et élèves de France*, Société de publications romanes et françaises, 25. Paris, 1946, pp. 89-102.

——. 'Guillaume de Digulleville, Moine de Chaalis.' In *Histoire littéraire de la France* .... Ed. É. Faral. Vol. XXXIX. Paris, 1962, pp. 1-132.

Faral, E., and J. Bastin, eds. *OEuvres complètes de Rutebeuf* (Paris, 1959).

Fleming, J. V. 'The Moral Reputation of the *Roman de la Rose* before 1400.' *Romance Philology*, 18 (1965), 430.

———. *The* Roman de la Rose: *a Study in Allegory and Iconography.* Princeton, 1969.

Flint, M. K., and E. J. Dobson. 'Weak Masters.' *RES*, NS, 10 (1959), 58-60.

Flynn, J. '*Pilgrimage of the Soul*: an Edition of the Caxton Imprint.' Diss. Auburn 1973.

Förster, M. 'Ein mittelenglisches 'Testament Christi'.' In 'Kleinere mittelenglische Texte.' *Anglia*, 42 (1918), 192-7.

Forshall, J., and F. Madden, eds. *The Holy Bible Containing the Old and New Testaments, with the Apocryphal Books, in the Earliest English Versions Made from the Latin Vulgate by John Wycliffe and his Followers.* 4 vols. Oxford, 1850.

Fortescue, A. K. *The Ceremonies of the Roman Rite Described.* 2 vols. 12th edn. London, 1962.

———. *The Mass: a Study of the Roman Liturgy.* 1906; rept. London, 1913.

Fowler, H. N., trans. *Euthyphro, Apology, Crito, Phaedo, Phaedrus.* Vol. I of *Plato with an English Translation.* Loeb Classical Library. London, 1914.

Fox, J. *The Middle Ages, A Literary History of France.* London, 1974.

Francis, W. N., ed. *The Book of the Vices and Virtues: a Fourteenth-century English Translation of the Somme le roi of Lorens d'Orleans.* EETS, OS 217 (1942).

Friedman, L. J. *Text and Iconography for Joinville's Credo.* Mediaeval Academy of America, 68. Cambridge, Mass., 1968.

Fryer, A. C. 'Theophilus, the Penitent, as Represented in Art.' *Archeological Journal*, 92 (1935), 287-333.

Furnivall, F. J. *Autotypes of Chaucer Manuscripts.* London, 1877.

———. ed. 'Proverbs of Good Counsel.' In *A Booke of Precedence etc.* EETS, ES 8 (1869), pp. 68-9.

———. ed. *The Minor Poems of the Vernon Manuscript.* Vol. II. EETS, OS 117 (1902).

Gallandius, A. ed. *Bibliotheca Veterum Patrum Antiquorumque Scriptorum Ecclesiasticorum, Postrema Lugdunensi Multo Loclupletior atque Accuratior.* Venice, CDDCCLXXXI [*sic.*].

Gallandius, A. ed. *Bibliotheca Veterum Patrum Antiquorumque Scriptorum Ecclesiasticorum, Postrema Lugdunensi Multo Loclupletior atque Accuratior.* Venice, CDDCCLXXXI [*sic.*].

Galpin, S. L. 'On the Sources of Guillaume de Deguileville's *Pèlerinage de l'âme.*' *PMLA*, 25 (1910), 275–308.

Gamillscheg, E. *Etymologisches Wörterbuch der franzosischen Sprache.* 2nd edn. Heidelberg, 1969.

Gaston Phoebus. *Le Livre de la chasse de Gaston Phoebus, transcrit en français moderne* . . . . Trans. R. and A. Bossuat. Paris, 1931.

Gayre, R. *Heraldic Cadency: the Development of Differencing of Coats of Arms for Kinsmen and Other Purposes.* London, 1961.

Geissman, E. W. 'The Style and Technique of Chaucer's Translations from the French.' Diss. Yale 1952.

Gewande, H. W. 'Guillaume de Déguilleville, Eine Studies zum *Pèlerinage de la vie humaine.*' Diss. Göttingen 1927.

Gilby, T., gen. ed. *St Thomas Aquinas: Summa Theologicae.* 2nd edn. Vols. I–. New York, 1964–.

Gilles, R. *Le symbolisme dans l'art religieux, architecture, couleurs, costume, peinture, naissance de l'allégorie.* Paris, 1943.

Glorieux, P. *Pour revaloriser Migne.* Mélanges de science religieuse, 9, supp. Lille, 1952.

Godefroy, F. *Dictionnaire de l'ancienne langue française et de tous ses dialectes du ixe au xve siècle* . . . . 10 vols. Paris, 1881–1902.

The Golden Legend. See Voragine.

Goujet, Abbé. 'Guill[aume] de Deguilleville.' In *Bibliothèque françoise, ou histoire de la littérature françoise* . . . . Vol. IX. Paris, 1745, pp. 71–92.

Gower, E. W. 'The Style and Technique of Chaucer's Translations from French.' Diss. Yale 1952.

Grabes, H. *Speculum, Mirror und Looking-Glass: Kontinuät und Originalitët der Spiegelmetapher in den Buchtiteln des Mittelalters und der englischen Literatur des 13. bis 17. Jahrhunderts.* Buchreiche der Anglia, Zeitschrift für englische Philologie, 16. Tübingen, 1973.

Gradon, P. O., ed. *Dan Michel's Ayenbite of Inwyt or Remorse of Conscience: Richard Morris's Transcription Now Newly Collated with the Unique Manuscript British Museum MS. Arundel 57.* Rev. edn. EETS, OS 23 (1965).

Graham, E. A. 'Allegory in Mediaeval French Literature.' Diss. Queen's, Belfast 1955.

Green, R. F. 'Lydgate and Deguileville Once More.' *N & Q*, 25 (1978), 105-6.

Greimas, A. J. *Dictionnaire de l'ancien français jusqu'au milieu du XIVe siècle*. Rev. edn. Paris, 1968.

Gröber, G. 'Histoire de la littérature française.' In *Grundriss der romanischen Philologie*. Vol. II. Strassburg, 1902, pp. 749-54.

Guillaume de Deguileville. The Pylgrymage of the Sowle. Westmestre, William Caxton 1483. Facs. The English Experience, No. 726. Amsterdam, 1975.

Gunn, A. M. F. *The Mirror of Love: a Reinterpretation of* The Romance of the Rose. Lubbock, 1952.

Hagen, S. K. 'The Pilgrimage of the Life of Man: A Medieval Theory of Vision and Remembrance.' Diss. Virginia, 1976.

Halliwell, J. O. *A Dictionary of Archaic and Provincial Words, Obsolete Phrases, Proverbs and Ancient Customs, for the Fourteenth Century*. Vol. I. London, 1847.

Hammond, E. P. *Chaucer: a Bibliographical Manual*. 1908; rpt. New York, 1933.

——. *English Verse Between Chaucer and Surrey*. Cambridge, 1927.

Häring, N. M. 'A Commentary on the Creed of the Mass by Alan of Lille (O. Cist.).' *Analecta Sacri Ordinis Cisterciensis*, 30 (1974), 281-303.

Hassall, W. O., introd. *The Holkham Bible Picture Book*. London, 1954.

Hassell, J. W. *Middle French Proverbs, Sentences and Proverbial Phrases*. Subsidia Mediaevalia 12. Toronto, 1982.

Hastings, J., ed. *Dictionary of the Bible*. 2nd edn. London, 1963.

Heawood, E. *Watermarks Mainly of the 17th and 18th Centuries*. Monumenta Chartae Papyraceae Historiam Illustrantia or Collection of Works and Documents Illustrating the History of Paper, 1. Hilversum, 1950.

Hennecke, E. *New Testament Apocrypha*. Trans. E. Best, et al. Ed. R. McL. Wilson. 2 vols. London, 1963, 1965.

Henry, Albert, ed. *Les Enfances Ogier*. Vol. III of *Les oeuvres d'Adenet Le Roi*. Rijksuniversiteit te Gent Werken uitgegeven door de Faculteit van de Letteren en Wijsbegeerte, 121. Bruges, 1956.

Henry, Avril. 'Chaucer's *A.B.C.*: Line 39 and the Irregular Stanza Again.' *Chaucer Review*, 18, ii (1983), 95-99.

——. 'The Illuminations in the Two Illustrated Middle English Manuscripts of the Prose *Pilgrimage of þe Lyfe of þe Manhode*. *Scriptorium*, 37, ii (1983), 264-73.

——. 'The French Source Manuscript of the Middle English Prose *Pilgrimage of þe Lyfe of þe Manhode*,' *University of Ottawa Quarterly*, 54, iv (1984), 25-33.

——. 'The Structure of Book 1 of *Þe Pilgrimage of þe Lyfe of þe Manhode*.' *Neuphilologische Mitteilungen*, 87, i (1986), 128-41.

——. '*Þe Pilgrimage of þe Lyfe of þe Manhode*: The Large Design, with Special Reference to Books 2-4.' *Neuphilologische Mitteilungen*, 87, ii (1986), 229-36.

——, ed. *The Mirour of Mans Saluacioune* (*Speculum Humanae Salvationis*). London, 1986.

——, ed. *Biblia Pauperum: a Facsimile Edition of the Forty-page Blockbook*. London [Scolar, 1987 forthcoming].

Herberman, et al, eds. *The Catholic Encyclopedia: An International Work of Reference on the Constitution, Doctrine, Discipline and History of the Catholic Church*. 15 vols. New York, 1907-1914.

Herbert, J. A. *Catalogue of Romances in the Department of Manuscripts in the British Museum*. Vol. III. London, 1910.

Hervieux, L., ed. *Phèdre et ses anciens imitateurs directs et indirects*. Vol. II of *Les Fabulistes latins depuis le siècle d'Auguste jusqu'à la fin du moyen âge*. Paris, 1884.

——. ed. *Eudes de Cheriton et ses dérivés*. Vol IV of *Les Fabulistes latins depuis le siècle d'Auguste jusqu'à la fin du moyen âge*. Paris, 1896.

Hill, N., annotator. *The Ancient Poem of Guillaume de Guileville Entitled Le Pèlerinage de l'homme Compared with the Pilgrim's Progress of John Bunyan* . . . . Ed. K. I. Cust. London, 1858.

The Holkham Bible Picture Book. See Hassall.

The Holy Bible Douay Version Translated from the Latin Vulgate (*Douay, A.D. 1609: Rheims, A.D.1582*). London, 1956.

Hooff, G. van, et. al., ed. *Analecta Bollandiana*. I-. Paris, 1882-.

Howgrave-Graham, R. P. 'Some Clocks and Jacks, with Notes on the History of Horology.' *Archeologia*, 77 (1927), 257-312.

Hugh of St Victor. See Deferrari, and Taylor.

Hultman, J. E. *Guillaume de Deguileville en studie i fransk litteraturhistoria*. Uppsala, 1902.

Huon de Méry. *Li Tornoiemenz Antecrit von Huon de Méry, nach den Handschriften zu Paris, London end Oxford*. Ed. G. Wimmer. Marburg, 1888.

Huth, A. H., ed. *The Miroure of Mans Saluacionne: a Translation into English of the* Speculum Humanae Salvationis .... Roxburghe Club. London, 1888.

Illuminated Books of the Middle Ages and Renaissance: An Exhibition Held at the Baltimore Museum of Art, January 27-March 13. Baltimore, 1949.

Incunabula in American Libraries: A Third Census of Fifteenth-Century Books Recorded in North American Collections. Compiled and ed. F. R. Goff. New York Bibliographical Society of America. New York, 1964.

An Inventory of the Ancient Monuments in Caernarvonshire. Vol. I. *East: The Cantref of Arllechwedd and the Commote of Creuddyn*. The Royal Commission on Ancient and Historical Monuments in Wales and Monmouthshire. London, 1956.

Isidore of Seville. *Isidore Hispalensis Episcopi: Etymologiarvm sive Originvm Libri XX*. Ed. W. M. Lindsay. 2 vols. New York, 1911.

James, M. R. *Mediaeval Manuscripts*. Vol. III of *A Descriptive Catalogue of the Library of Samuel Pepys*. London, 1923.

——. *A Descriptive Catalogue of the Manuscripts in the Library of St John's College Cambridge*. Cambridge, 1913.

Jauss, H. R., ed. *La Littérature didactique, allégorique et satirique*. 2 vols. Grundriss der romanischen Literaturen des Mittelalters, 6. Heidelberg, 1968-70.

Jean de Condé. 'Le Dit d'entendement.' In *Jean de Condé*. Vol. III, Pt. II of *Dits et contes de Baudouin de Condé et de son fils Jean de Condé* .... Brussels, 1867, pp. 49-95.

Jespersen, O. *A Modern English Grammar on Historical Principles*. 7 pts. London, 1909-1949.

Jocelin of Brakelond. *The Chronicle of Jocelin of Brakelond Concerning the Acts of Samson, Abbot of the Monastery of St Edmund*. Trans. H. E. Butler. Nelson's Medieval Classics. London, 1949.

Jones, W. R. 'The Heavenly Letter in Medieval England.' In *Medieval Hagiography and Romance*. Medievalia et Humanistica, 6. Cambridge, 1975, pp. 163-78.

Josephus, F. [*Works*]. 9 vols. Trans. H. St. J. Thackeray and R. Marcus. Loeb Classical Library. 1930-1965.

Jung, M. R. *Études sur le poème allégorique en France au moyen âge*. Romanica Helvetica, 82. Bern, 1971.

Jungman, J. A. *The Mass of the Roman Rite: Its Origins and Development* (*Missarum Sollemnia*). Rev. edn. Trans. F. A. Brunner. 2 vols. 1949; rpt. New York, 1951, 1955.

Katzenellenbogen, A. *Allegories of the Virtues and Vices in Mediaeval Art from Early Christian Times to the Thirteenth Century*. London, 1939; rpt. New York, 1964.

Keith, G. H. 'An English Version of a French Moral Treatise (*Voie de Paradis*).' *Romance Philology*, 23 (1969-70), 55-6.

Keller, J. E. *Motif-Index of Mediaeval Spanish Exempla*. Knoxville, Tenn., 1949.

Ker, N. R. *Medieval Manuscripts in British Libraries*. Vol. I. Oxford, 1969.

———. 'Oxford College Libraries in the Sixteenth Century.' *The Bodleian Library Record*, 6 (1959), 459.

Kirschbaum, E., ed. *Lexicon der Christlichen Ikonographie* . . . . 7 vols. Rome, 1968-1974.

Kittel, G. *Theological Dictionary of the New Testament*. Trans. G. W. Bromiley. 1933; Grand Rapids, Mich., 1964-1972.

Kleinefelter, R. A. 'Chaucer's *An A.B.C.*, 25-32.' *Explicator*, 25 (1965), item 5.

Kloss, E., introd. *Speculum Humanae Salvationis: ein Niederländische Blockbuch*. Munich, 1925.

Knox, R., trans. *The Holy Bible: a Translation from the Latin Vulgate in the Light of the Hebrew and Greek Originals, Authorised by the Hierarchy of England and Wales and the Hierarchy of Scotland*. 2nd edn. London, 1956.

Koch, J. *Geoffrey Chaucer's kleinere Dichtungen*. Heidelberg, 1928.

Kolve, V. A. *Chaucer and the Imagery of Narrative: The First Five Canterbury Tales*. London, 1984.

Kundert-Forrer, V. *Raoul de Houdenc, ein französischer Erzähler des XIII. Jahrhunderts*. Studiorum Romanicorum Collectio Turicensis, 12. Bern, 1950.

Kurath, H., et al, ed. *Middle English Dictionary*. [A-O¹]. Ann Arbor, 1952-1980.

Laborde, A. de, ed. *La Bible moralisée conservée à Oxford, Paris et Londres: reproduction intégrale du manuscrit de XIIIᵉ siècle*.... 5 vols. Paris, 1911-1927.

Lafaurie, J. *Les Monnaies des rois de France*. Paris, 1951.

Lamb, W. R. M., trans. *Charmides, Alcibiades, Hipparchus, The Lovers, Theages, Minos, Epinomis*. Vol. VIII of *Plato with an English Translation*. Loeb Classical Library. London, 1927.

Langkammer, H. 'Christ's "Last Will and Testament" in the Interpretation of the Fathers of the Church and the Scholastics.' *Antonianum*, 43 (1968), 99-109.

Langland. See Skeat.

Langlois, Ch.-V. 'Le "Credo" de Joinville.' In *La Vie spirituelle: enseignements méditations et controverses*. Vol. IV of *La Vie en France au moyen âge*.... Paris, 1928; rpt. Geneva, 1970.

———. 'Pèlerinages par Guillaume de Digulleville.' In *La Vie Spirituelle: enseignements méditations et controverses*. Vol. IV of *La Vie en France au moyen âge*.... Paris, 1928; rpt. Geneva, 1970.

Langosch, K., ed. *Die deutsch Literatur des Mittelalters: Verfasserlexicon*. Vol. III. Berlin, 1943.

Lecoy, F., ed. *Guillaume de Lorris et Jean de Meun: Le Roman de la Rose*. Les classiques français du moyen âge. 3 vols. Paris, 1965-1970.

Lefrancois-Pillon, L. *'L'Art du XIVᵉ siècle en France suivi d'un chapitre sur le vitrail par Jean Lafond*. Paris, 1954.

Legge, M. D. *Anglo-Norman in the Cloisters: the Influence of the Orders upon Anglo-Norman Literature*. Edinburgh, 1950.

Leloir, M. *Dictionnaire du costume et de ses accessoires des armes et des étoffes des origines à nos jours*. Paris, 1951.

Lindet, L. 'Les Représentations allégoriques du moulin et du pressoir dans l'art chrétien.' *Revue Archéologique*, 36 (1900), 403-13 and Pls. vi, vii, vii.

Lindsay, D. *The Felton Bequest: an Historical Record 1904-1959*. Oxford, 1963.

Locock, K. B., annotator. *The Pilgrimage of the Life of Man Translated by John Lydgate*. Ed. F. J. Furnivall. 3 vols. EETS,

ES 77, 83 and 92 (1899, 1901, 1904; rpt. as one vol. New York, 1973).

Lofthouse, M. '*Le Pèlerinage de Vie Humaine* by Guillaume de Deguileville with Special Reference to the French MS. 2 of the John Rylands Library.' *Bulletin of the John Rylands Library*, 19 (1935), 170-215.

Lorens d'Orleans. See Francis.

Lorris, G., and J. de Meun. See Lecoy.

Lozinski, G. 'Recherches sur les sources du Credo de Joinville.' *Neuphilologische Mitteilungen*, 31 (1930), 170-231.

Ludolphe le Chartreux. *La Grande Vie de Jésus-Christ*. Trans. M.-P. Augustin. 6 vols. Paris, 1865.

Lutz, J. and P. Perdrizet. *Speculum Humanae Salvationis*. 2 vols. Mulhouse, 1907, 1909.

Lydgate, J. *The Pilgrimage of the Life of Man Englished by John Lydgate, A.D.1426, from the French of Guillaume de Deguileville, A.D.1330, 1355*. Ed. F. J. Furnivall. Roxburghe Club. London, 1905.

———. *The Pilgrimage of the Life of Man Translated by John Lydgate*. Ed. F. J. Furnivall. 3 vols. EETS, ES 77, 83 and 92 (1899, 1901, 1904; rpt. as one vol. New York, 1973).

———. *The Minor Poems of John Lydgate*. Ed. H. N. MacCracken. Vol. I. EETS, OS 192 (1934).

Maas, P. *Textual Criticism*. Trans. B. Flower. Oxford, 1958.

Mackensen, L. *Handwörterbuch des deutschen Märchens herausgegeben unter besonderer Mitwirkung von Johannes Bolte und mitarbiet zahlreicher Fachgenossen von Lutz Mackensen*. 2 vols. Berlin, 1930-1933, 1934-1940.

Maclean, A. J. *The Ancient Christian Orders*. London, 1910.

McCulloch, F. *Medieval Latin and French Bestiaries*. University of North Carolina Studies in the Romance Languages and Literatures, 33. Rev. edn. Chapel Hill, 1962.

Maertens, T. *Histoire et pastorale du rituel du catéchuménat et du baptême*. Bruges, 1962.

Mâle, É. *L'Art religieux du xiie siècle en France: étude sur les origines de l'iconographie du moyen âge*. 3rd edn. Paris, 1928.

———. *L'Art religieux du xiiie siècle en France: étude sur l'iconographie du moyen âge et sur ses sources d'inspiration*. 6th edn. Paris, 1925.

———. *The Gothic Image: Religious Art in France of the Thirteenth Century*. Trans. Dora Nussey from 3rd French edn. 1913; rpt. London, 1961.

Mandeville's Travels. See Seymour.

Marle, R. Van. *Iconographie de l'art profane au moyen age et à la renaissance et la décoration des demeures*. 2 vols. 1931; rept. New York, 1971.

Martial. *Epigrams*. Ed. and trans. W. C. A. Ker. 2 vols. Loeb Library Classics. 1919-1920; rpt. London, 1930, 1927.

Martin, É., ed. *Le Roman de Renart*. Vol. I. 1882; rpt. Berlin and New York, 1973.

Martin, J. R. *The Illustration of the Heavenly Ladder of John Climacus*. Ed. A. M. Friend. Studies in Manuscript Illumination, 5. Princeton, 1954.

Martin P. *Armour and Weapons*. Trans. R. North. London, 1967.

Maskell, W. *Monumenta Ritualia Ecclesiae Anglicanae or Occasional Offices of the Church of England According to the Ancient Use of Salisbury: the Prymer in English and Other Prayers and Forms with Dissertations and Notes*. 3 vols. London, 1846-1847.

Matthews, W. ed. *Later Middle English Prose*. London, 1962.

Meer, F. van der. *Atlas de l'ordre cistercien*. Paris, 1965.

Meijboom. See Deguileville.

Mellinkoff, R. *The Horned Moses in Medieval Art and Thought*. California Studies in the History of Art, 14. Berkeley, Cal., 1970.

Michaud-Quantin, P. 'La classification des puissances de l'âme au xiie siècle.' *Revue du moyen âge latin*, 5 (1949), 15-34.

Middle English Dictionary. See Kurath.

Mielot, J., ed. *Speculum Humanae Salvationis: les sources et l'influence iconographique principalement sur l'art alsacien du XIVe siècle*. 2 vols. Leipzig, 1907.

Migne, J. P., ed. *Patrologiae Cursus Completus ... Series Latina*. 221 vols. Paris, 1844-64.

———. ed. *Patrologiae Cursus Completus ... Series Graeca*. 162 vols. Paris, 1857-1912.

Millar, E. G. *English Illuminated Manuscripts of the XIVth and XVth Centuries*. Paris, 1928.

———., introd. *A Thirteenth-century Bestiary in the Library of Alnwick Castle*. Roxburghe Club. Oxford, 1958.

Moffat, D. M., trans. *Alain de Lille, The Complaint of Nature*. Yale Studies in English, 36. New York, 1908.

Molloy, J. J. *A Theological Interpretation of the Moral Play Wisdom, Who Is Christ*. Washington, D. C., 1952.

Molsdorf, W. *Christliche Symbolik der mittelalterlichen Kunst*. 1926; Graz, 1968.

Mondin, B. *St Thomas Aquinas' Philosophy in the Commentary to the Sentences*. The Hague, 1975.

Le Mont Saint-Michel: poème de Guillaume de Déguileville photographies de Pierre Belzeaux. Les Points Cardinaux, 5. Paris 1962.

Morrill, G. L. ed. *Speculum Gy de Warewyke*. EETS, ES 75 (1898).

Muir's Historical Atlas Ancient, Medieval and Modern Comprising Muir's Atlas of Ancient and Classical History and Muir's Historical Atlas—Medieval and Modern. Ed. R. F. Traherne and H. Fullard. London, 1965.

Munrow, D. *Instruments of the Middle Ages and Renaissance*. London, 1976.

Mustanoja, T. F. *Parts of Speech*. Part I of *A Middle English Syntax*. Mémoires de la Société Néophilologique de Helsinki, 23. Helsinki, 1960.

N. N., trans. *The Rule of the Holy Father Saint Benedict Translated into English*. Douay, 1700.

Neale, J. M. and B. Webb, trans. *The Symbolism of Churches and Church Ornaments: a Translation of the First Book of the Rationale Divinorum Officiorum, written by William Durandus, sometime Bishop of Mende*. Leeds, 1843.

New Catholic Encyclopedia. 15 vols. New York, 1967.

Norton-Smith, J., ed. *James I of Scotland: Kingis Quair*. London, 1971.

Pace, G. B. 'The Adorned Initials of Chaucer's *A.B.C.*.' *Manuscripta*, 23 (1979), 88–98.

Pacht, O., and J. J. Alexander. *Illuminated Manuscripts in the Bodleian Library Oxford*. Vol. III. Oxford, 1973.

Padelford, F. M. 'Spenser and *The Pilgrimage of the Life of Man*.' *Studies in Philology*, 28 (1931), 211–18.

Paris, G. *Esquisse historique de la littérature française au moyen âge (depuis les origines jusqu'a la fin du xve siècle)*. Paris, 1907.

Passmore, T. H. *Sacred Vestments: An English Rendering of the Third Book of the* Rationale Divinorum Officiorum. London, 1899.

Pearce, E. H. *Sion College and Library*. London, 1913.

Pearsall, D. *John Lydgate*. London, 1970.

Perdrizet, P. *Études sur le Speculum Humanae Salvationis*. Paris, 1908.

Perrow, E. C. 'The Last Will and Testament as a Form of Literature.' In *Transactions of the Wisconsin Academy of Sciences, Arts, and Letters*, 17, Pt. I. Madison, 1913, pp. 682-753.

Piaget, A. 'Littérature didactique.' In *Moyen âge (des origines à 1500)*. Vol. II of *Histoire de la langue et de la littérature française des origines à 1900 publiée sous la direction de L. Petit de Julleville* . . . Paris, 1896, pp. 162-216.

——., ed. 'Un poème inédit de Guillaume de Digullville 'Roman de la fleur de lys'.' *Romania*, 63 (1936), 317-58.

Pickering, F. P. *Literature & Art of the Middle Ages*. London, 1970. Trans. from *Literatur und darstellend Kunst in Mittelalter*. Berlin, 1966.

Piehler, P. *The Visionary Landscape: a Study in Medieval Allegory*. London, 1971.

Pilgrymage of Perfeccyon. See Bonde.

Plato. See Fowler, and Lamb.

Plummer, J., ed., *The Hours of Catharine of Cleves*. London, 1966.

Pollard, A. W., ed. *An English Garner: Fifteenth-Century Prose and Verse*. London, 1903.

Porcher, J. *French Miniatures from Illuminated Manuscripts*. Trans. J. Brown. London, 1960.

Pope, J. C., ed. *Homilies of Aelfric: a Supplementary Collection*. EETS, OS 259, 260 (1967, 1968).

Puniet, P. de. *The Roman Pontifical: a History and Commentary*. Trans. M. V. Harcourt. London, 1932.

Purvis, J. S. *Notarial Signs from the York Archiepiscopal Records*. London, 1957.

Quatuor Sermones Reprinted from the First Edition by William Caxton at Westminster. Roxburghe Club. London, 1883.

Quilligan, M. *The Language of Allegory: Defining the Genre.* Ithaca, New York, 1979.

Rahner, Fr. H. 'Das mystiche Tau.' *Zeitschrift für katholische Theologie,* 75 (1953), 386-410.

Randall, L. M. C. *Images in the Margins of Gothic Manuscripts.* California Studies in the History of Art, 4. Berkeley, 1966.

Raoul de Houdenc. See Scheler.

Reading, W. *Bibliothecae Cleri Londinensis in Collegio Sionensi Catalogus . . . .* London, 1724.

Reallexikon zur deutschen Kunst-Geschichte. Ed. O. Schmitt, et al. Vols. I-. Stuttgart, 1937-.

Réau, L., *Iconographie de l'art chrétien.* 6 vols. Paris, 1955-1958.

Regalado, N. F. *Poetic Patterns in Rutebeuf: a Study in Noncourtly Poetic Methods of the Thirteenth Century.* Yale Romantic Studies, 2nd series, 21. New Haven, 1970.

Reiss, E. 'Dusting Off the Cobwebs: a Look at Chaucer's Lyrics.' *Chaucer Review,* 1 (1966), 55-65.

Renclus de Moiliens. 'Roman de Carite.' Ed. A. G. Van Hemel. In *Bibliothèque de l'école des hautes études . . . .* Vol. LXI. Paris, 1885, pp. 1-129.

Renesse, T. de. *Dictionnaire des figures héraldiques.* 7 vols. Brussels, 1892-1903.

Rijk, L. M. de. *The Place of the Categories of Being in Aristotle's Philosophy.* Assen, 1952.

Robbins, R. H., and J. L. Cutler. *Supplement to the Index of Middle English Verse.* Lexington, Kentucky, 1965.

Roberts, P. D. 'Some Unpublished Middle English Lyrics and Stanzas in a Victoria Public Library Manuscript.' *English Studies,* 54 (1973), 105-18.

Robertson, J. C., and J. B. Sheppard. *Materials for the History of Thomas Becket, Archbishop of Canterbury (canonized by Pope Alexander III, A.D.1173).* Rerum Britannicarum Medii Aevi Scriptores (Rolls Series), 67. 7 vols. London, 1875-1885.

Robin, P. A. *Animal Lore in English Literature.* London, 1932.

Robbins, R. H., and J. L. Cutler. *Supplement to the Index of Middle English Verse (Carleton Brown and Rossell Hope Robbins).* Lexington, 1965.

Robinson, F. N., ed. *The Works of Geoffrey Chaucer*. 2nd edn. London, 1957.

Ross, W. D., gen. ed. *The Works of Aristotle Translated into English*. 12 vols. Oxford, 1908-52.

Ross, W. O., ed. *Middle English Sermons*. EETS, OS 209 (1940; rept. 1960).

Rowland, B., ed. *Companion to Chaucer Studies*. London, 1968.

——. *Animals with Human Faces: a Guide to Animal Symbolism*. London, 1973.

Rushforth, G. McN. *Medieval Christian Imagery as Illustrated by the Painted Windows of Great Malvern Priory Church Worcestershire together with a Description of All the Ancient Glass in the Church*. Oxford, 1936.

——. 'Seven Sacraments Compositions in English Medieval Art.' *The Antiquaries Journal*, 9 (1929), 83-100.

Rutebeuf [Rutebuef]. See Faral and Bastin.

Scheler, A., ed. *Dits de Watriquet de Couvin* . . . . Brussels, 1868.

——. *Trouvères belges (nouvelle serie) chansons d'amour, jeux partis, pastourelles, satires, dits et fabliaux par Gonthier de Soignies, Jacques de Cisoing, Carasaus, Jehan Fremaus, Laurent Wagon, Raoul de Houdenc* . . . . Louvain, 1879.

Schell, E. T. 'On the Imitation of Life's Pilgrimage in *The Castle of Perseverance*.' *JEGP*, 67 (1968), 235-48.

Schiller, G. *Ikonographie der christlichen Kunst*. 2nd ed. Vols. I-IV². Gutersloh, 1969-1980. [Vols. I, II are translated by J. Seligman, see next entry. References to these first two volumes are to Seligman]

——. *Iconography of Christian Art*. Trans. from Vols I and II of 2nd German edn. J. Seligman. 2 vols. 1969; London, 1971.

Schneider, A. 'Die Cisterciensische Klosteranlage.' In *Die Cistercienser: Geschichte, Geist, Kunst*. Ed. A. Schneider et al. Cologne, 1974, pp. 68-74.

——. 'Skriptorien und Bibliotheken der Cistercienser.' In *Die Cistercienser, Geschichte, Geist, Kunst*. Ed. A. Schneider et al. Cologne, 1974, pp. 429-46.

Seltzer, L. E., ed. *The Columbia Lippincott Gazetteer of the World . . . with 1961 Supplement*. 1952; New York, 1962.

Severs, J. B. 'Two Irregular Chaucerian Stanzas.' *MLN*, 64 (1949), 306-9.

Seymour, M. C., ed. *Mandeville's Travels*. Oxford, 1967.

Seznec, J. *The Survival of the Pagan Gods. The Mythological Tradition and its Place in Renaissance Humanism and Art*. Trans. B. F. Sessions. New York, 1961.

Shelby, L. R. 'Medieval Masons' Tools: ii. Compass and Square.' *Technology and Culture*, 6 (1965), 236-48.

Shorter, A. H. *Paper Mills and Paper Makers in England 1495-1800. Monumenta Chartae Papyraceae Historiam Illustrantia, or Collection of Works and Documents Illustrating the History of Paper*, 6. Hilversum, 1957.

Simmons, T. F., ed. *The Lay Folks Mass Book*. EETS, OS 71 (1879).

Sinclair, K. V. *Descriptive Catalogue of Medieval and Renaissance Western Manuscripts in Australia*. Sydney, 1969.

Skeat, W. W., ed. *The Complete Works of Geoffrey Chaucer*. 7 vols. 2nd edn. Oxford, 1899.

——., ed. *The Vision of William Concerning Piers the Plowman: in Three Parallel Texts together with Richard the Redeless by William Langland*. 2 vols. 1886; rev. edn. Oxford, 1961.

Smalley, J. 'The Poems of the Middle English *Pilgrimage of the Soul*.' Diss. Liverpool 1954.

Smith, Sr Frances. 'Wisdom and the Personification of Wisdom in Middle English Literature before 1500.' Diss. Catholic University of America, Washington D.C. 1935.

Souvenir of Consecration of Most Rev. Anthony McFreely, D.D., Bishop of Raphoe on 27th June, 1956 at St. Eunan's Cathedral Letterkenny by His Eminence William Cardinal Conway, D.D., Archbishop of Armagh and Primate of All Ireland . . . . Dublin, 1965.

Spalding, M. C. *The Middle English Charters of Christ*. Bryn Mawr College Monographs, 15. Bryn Mawr, 1914.

Speculum Humanae Salvationis. See Kloss, Lutz, and Mielot; for the M. E. version see Avril Henry.

Studer, P., and Joan Evans, eds. *Anglo-Norman Lapidaries*. Paris, 1924.

Stürzinger, J. J., ed. *Le Pèlerinage de vie humaine de Guillaume de Deguileville*. Roxburghe Club. London, 1893.

——., ed. *Le Pèlerinage de l'âme.* Roxburghe Club. London, 1895.

——., ed. *Le Pèlerinage de Jhésucrist.* Roxburghe Club. London, 1897.

A Summary Catalogue of Western Manuscripts in the Bodleian Library at Oxford. Vol. I. Oxford, 1953.

Taylor, J. trans. *The Didascalicon of Hugh of St. Victor: a Medieval Guide to the Arts.* Records of Civilization: Sources and Studies, 64. New York, 1961.

Thesaurus Lingvae Latinae. Vols. I-X. Leipzig, 1900-1980.

Thomas, A. 'Die mystiche Mühle.' *Die christliche Kunst,* 31 (1934-1935), 129-39.

Thompson, Stith. *Motif-Index of Folk-Literature: a Classification of Narrative Elements in Folktales, Ballads, Myths, Fables, Mediaeval Romances, Exempla, Jest-Books and Local Legends.* 6 vols. 1932-1936; rev. edn. Bloomington, 1966.

Tietze, H. 'Die Handschriften der *Concordantia Caritatis* des Abtes Ulrich von Lilienfeld.' *Jahrbuch der k. k. Zentral-Kommission für Erforschung und Erhaltung der Kunst- und Historischen Denkmale.* N.F. 3, ii (1905), 23-63.

Timmers, J. J. M. *Symboliek en Iconographie der christelijke Kunst.* Romen's Compendia. Roermond, 1947.

Tobler, A. *Tobler-Lommatzsch Altfranzösisches Wörterbuch: Adolf Toblers nachgelassene Materialen bearbeitet end mit Unterstützung der Preussischen Akademie der Wissenschaften, herausgegeben von Erhard Lommatzsch.* Berlin, 1925-.

Tolkien, J. R. R., ed. *The English Text of the Ancrene Riwle: Ancrene Wisse, edited from MS.Corpus Christi College Cambridge 402.* EETS, 249. (1962 for 1960).

Traver, H. *The Four Daughters of God: a Study of the Versions of this Allegory, with Special Reference to those in Latin, French and English.* Bryn Mawr College Monographs, 6. Bryn Mawr, 1907.

Trevisa, J., trans. *On the Properties of Things: John Trevisa's Translation of 'Barthomaeus Anglicus De Proprietatibus Rerum'.* Gen. ed. M. C. Seymour. 2 vols. Oxford, 1975.

Trilhe, A., and J.-M. Canivez, eds. *Statuta Capitulorum Generalium Ordinis Cisterciensis ab Anno 1116 ad Annum 1786.* Bibliothèque de la revue d'histoire ecclésiastique, 9-14. Vol. I. Louvain, 1933.

Trojanowska, Z. 'Les Faux Monnayeurs devant La Chambre des Monnaies sous le regne de Louis XI (1461-1483).' In *Proceedings of the International Numismatists' Symposium.* Ed. I. Gedai and K. Biró-sey. Budapest, 1980, pp. 209-15.

Trunzer, F. *Die Syntax des Verbums bei Guillaume de Deguileville. Beitragzur französischen Syntax des XIV. Jahrhunderts.* Coburg, 1913.

Tuve, R. *Allegorical Imagery: Some Mediaeval Books and Their Posterity.* Princeton, N.J., 1966.

Vacant, A., et al. *Dictionnaire de théologie catholique contentant l'exposé des doctrines de la théologie catholique, leurs preuves et leur histoire* . . . . 15 vols. and index. Paris, 1899-1950.

Valois, N. de. 'Jacques de Thérines, cistercien.' In *Histoire littéraire de la France.* Ed. É. Faral. Vol. XXXIV. Paris, 1914, pp. 180-219.

Vincent of Beauvais. *Speculum Naturale.* Venice: Liechtenstein, 1494.

Vloberg, M. *L'Eucharistie dans l'art.* 2 vols. Paris, 1946.

Vogel, C. *Le Pécheur et la pénitence au moyen âge.* Paris, 1969.

Vogüé, A. de., ed. *La Règle du Maître.* 3 vols. Sources chrétiennes No. 105, Serie des textes monastiques d'occident, 14. Paris, 1964-1965.

Voragine, J. de. *The Golden Legend or Lives of the Saints as Englished by William Caxton.* Trans. W. Caxton. Ed. F. Ellis. 7 vols. London, 1900.

Walls, K. M. M. '*The Pilgrimage of the Lyf of the Manhode*: the Prose Translation from Guillaume de Deguileville in its English Context.' Diss. Toronto, 1976.

——. 'Did Lydgate Translate the *Pèlerinage de vie humaine?*' *N & Q*, 24 (1977), 1033-5.

Ward, H. L. D. *Catalogue of Romances in the Department of Manuscripts in the British Museum.* London, 1883-1910.

Watriquet de Couvin. See Scheler.

Watson, A. *The Early Iconography of the Tree of Jesse.* London, 1934.

Wenzel, S. *The Sin of Sloth: Acedia in Medieval Thought and Literature.* Chapel Hill, N. Carol., 1967.

West, M. L. *Textual Criticism and Editorial Technique Applicable to Greek and Latin Texts.* Stuttgart, 1973.

Wharey, J. B. *A Study of the Sources of Bunyan's Allegories with Special Reference to Deguileville's Pilgrimage of Man.* Baltimore, Ma., 1904.

White, T. H. *The Book of Beasts, being a Translation from a Latin Bestiary of the Twelfth Century.* London, 1959.

Whitehead, F., ed. *La Chanson de Roland.* 2nd edn. Oxford, 1946.

Whiting, B. J., and H. W. *Proverbs, Sentences, and Proverbial Phrases from English Writings Mainly Before 1500.* London, 1968.

Wimsatt, J. I. *Allegory and Mirror: Tradition and Structure in Middle English Literature.* New York, 1970.

Woodward, J. *A Treatise on Heraldry British and Foreign with English and French Glossaries.* 2 vols. London, 1896.

Workman, S. K. *Fifteenth Century Translation as an Influence on English Prose.* Princeton Studies in English, 18. Princeton, N.J., 1940.

Wright, C. E. *English Vernacular Hands from the Twelfth to the Fifteenth Centuries.* Oxford, 1960.

Wright, W. A. Three Corrected Proofs of his edition *The Pilgrimage of the Lyf of the Manhode.* [Trinity College Cambridge, Adv.b.18.2].

Wright, W. A. *The Pilgrimage of the Lyf of the Manhode.* Roxburghe Club. London, 1869.

Young, J. and P. H. Aitken. *Catalogue of the Manuscripts in the Library of the Hunterian Museum in the University of Glasgow.* Glasgow, 1908.

Zbozny, F. T. 'The Metrical Structure of Chaucer's *A. B. C.*.' Diss. Pittsburgh, Pa., 1970.

EARLY ENGLISH TEXT SOCIETY

LIST OF PUBLICATIONS
1864–1987

1988

OFFICERS AND COUNCIL

Honorary Director
Professor John Burrow, FBA, Bristol University

Professor J. Bately
Professor L. D. Benson
Professor N. F. Blake
Professor P. A. M. Clemoes
Professor N. Davis, FBA
Dr A. I. Doyle
Dr P. Gradon

Professor D. Gray
Dr A. Hudson
Professor G. Kane, FBA
Professor A. McIntosh
Professor D. Pearsall
Miss C. Sisam
Mr R. A. Waldron

Editorial Secretary
Dr Malcolm Godden, Exeter College, Oxford OX1 3DP

Executive Secretary
Mr T. F. Hoad, St. Peter's College, Oxford OX1 2DL

Assistant Executive Secretary
Mrs Wendy Collier, The Vicarage, Hope, Sheffield S30 2RN

Bankers
The National Westminster Bank PLC, Cornmarket Street, Oxford

Orders from non-members of the Society should be placed with a bookseller. Orders from booksellers for volumes in part 1 of this list should be sent to Oxford University Press, Saxon Way West, Corby, Northants. NN18 9ES. Orders from booksellers for volumes in part 2 of this list should be sent to the following addresses: orders for EETS reprints to Oxford University Press. Saxon Way West, Corby, Northants. NN18 9ES; orders for Kraus reprints to Kraus Reprint & Periodicals, Route 100, Millwood, NY 10546, USA.

EARLY ENGLISH TEXT SOCIETY

The Early English Text Society was founded in 1864 by Frederick James Furnivall, with the help of Richard Morris, Walter Skeat, and others, to bring the mass of unprinted Early English literature within the reach of students and to provide sound texts from which the New English Dictionary could quote. In 1867 an Extra Series was started of texts already printed but not in satisfactory or readily obtainable editions. In 1921 the Extra Series was discontinued and all publications were subsequently listed and numbered as part of the Original Series. In 1970 the first of a new Supplementary Series was published; unlike the Extra Series, volumes in this series will be issued only occasionally, as funds allow and as suitable texts become available.

In the first part of this list are shown the books published by the Society since 1954, Original Series 240 onwards and the Supplementary Series. A large number of the earlier books were reprinted by the Society in the period 1950 to 1970. In order to make the rest available, the Society has come to an agreement with Kraus Reprint & Periodicals, who reprint as necessary the volumes in the Original Series 1–239 and in the Extra Series. Volumes temporarily unavailable are marked in the list with an asterisk.

Membership of the Society is open to libraries and to individuals interested in the study of medieval English literature. The subscription to the Society for 1988 is £15·00 (or for US members $25.00, Canadian members Can. $30.00), due in advance on 1 January, and should be paid by cheque, postal order, or money order made out to 'The Early English Text Society', and sent to Mrs Wendy Collier, Assistant Executive Secretary, Early English Text Society, The Vicarage, Hope, Sheffield S30 2RN. Payment of this subscription entitles the member to receive the new book(s) in the Original Series for the year. The books in the Supplementary Series do not form part of the issue sent to members in return for the payment of their annual subscription, though they are available to members at a reduced price; a notice about each volume is sent to members in advance of publication.

Private members of the Society (but not libraries) may select in place of the annual issue past volumes from the Society's list chosen from the Original Series 240 to date or from the Supplementary Series. The value of such texts allowed against one annual subscription is £22·00, and all these transactions must be made through the Assistant Executive Secretary. Members of the Society may purchase copies of books Original Series 240 to date for their own use at a discount of 25 per cent of the listed prices; private members (but not libraries) may purchase earlier publications at a similar discount. All such orders must be sent to the Assistant Executive Secretary. Orders for Kraus reprints must be for books of a minimum discount price of $15.00.

Details of books, the cost of membership, and its privileges are revised from time to time. The prices of books are subject to alteration without notice. This list is brought up to date annually, and the current edition should be consulted.

LIST 1

ORIGINAL SERIES 1954–1987

OS 240	**The French Text of the Ancrene Riwle,** Trinity College Cambridge MS. R. 14. 7, with variants from Paris Bibliothèque Nationale MS. fonds fr. 6276 and Bodley MS. 90, ed. W. H. Trethewey. 1958 (*for* 1954), *reprinted* 1971.	£8·00
241	**þe Wohunge of Ure Lauerd** and other pieces, ed. W. Meredith Thompson. 1958 (*for* 1955), *reprinted with corrections* 1970.	£6·75
242	**The Salisbury Psalter,** ed. Celia Sisam and Kenneth Sisam. 1959 (*for* 1955–6), *reprinted* 1969.	£13·00
243	**The Life and Death of Cardinal Wolsey by George Cavendish,** ed. R. S. Sylvester. 1959 (*for* 1957), *reprinted* 1961.	£6·75
244	**The South English Legendary,** Vol. III, Introduction and glossary, ed. C. D'Evelyn. 1959 (*for* 1957), *reprinted* 1969.	£4·75
245	**Beowulf:** facsimile of British Museum MS. Cotton Vitellius A. xv, with a transliteration and notes by J. Zupitza, a new reproduction of the manuscript with an introductory note by Norman Davis. 1959 (*for* 1958), *reprinted* 1981.	£15·00
246	**The Parlement of the Thre Ages,** ed. M. Y. Offord. 1959, *reprinted* 1967.	£6·50
247	**Facsimile of MS. Bodley 34:** St. Katherine, St. Margaret, St. Juliana, Hali Meiðhad, Sawles Warde, with an introduction by N. R. Ker. 1960 (*for* 1959).	£9·75
248	**þe Liflade ant te Passiun of Seinte Iuliene,** ed. S. R. T. O. d'Ardenne. 1961 (*for* 1960).	£6·75
249	**The English Text of the Ancrene Riwle: Ancrene Wisse,** Corpus Christi College Cambridge MS. 402, ed. J. R. R. Tolkien, with introduction by N. R. Ker. 1962 (*for* 1960).	£7·75
250	**Laȝamon's Brut,** Vol. I, Text (lines 1–8020), ed. G. L. Brook and R. F. Leslie. 1963 (*for* 1961).	£16·00
251	**The Owl and the Nightingale:** facsimile of Jesus College Oxford MS. 29 and British Museum MS. Cotton Caligula A. ix, with an introduction by N. R. Ker. 1963 (*for* 1962).	£8·00
252	**The English Text of the Ancrene Riwle,** British Museum MS. Cotton Titus D. xviii, ed. F. M. Mack, and the Lanhydrock Fragment, Bodleian MS. Eng. th. c. 70, ed. A. Zettersten. 1963 (*for* 1962).	£7·75
253	**The Bodley Version of Mandeville's Travels,** ed. M. C. Seymour. 1963.	£7·75
254	**Ywain and Gawain,** ed. Albert B. Friedman and Norman T. Harrington. 1964 (*for* 1963), *reprinted* 1981.	£7·75
255	**Facsimile of British Museum MS. Harley 2253,** with an introduction by N. R. Ker. 1965 (*for* 1964).	£20·00
256	**Sir Eglamour of Artois,** ed. Frances E. Richardson. 1965.	£7·75
257	**The Praise of Folie by Sir Thomas Chaloner,** ed. Clarence H. Miller. 1965.	£7·75
258	**The Orchard of Syon,** Vol. I, Text, ed. Phyllis Hodgson and Gabriel M. Liegey. 1966.	£16·00
259	**Homilies of Ælfric, A Supplementary Collection,** Vol. I, ed. J. C. Pope. 1967.	£16·00

OS 260	**Homilies of Ælfric, A Supplementary Collection,** Vol. II, ed. J. C. Pope. 1968.	£16·00
261	**Lybeaus Desconus,** ed. M. Mills. 1969.	£8·50
262	**The Macro Plays:** The Castle of Perseverance, Wisdom, Mankind, ed. Mark Eccles. 1969.	£8·50
263	**The History of Reynard the Fox translated from the Dutch Original by William Caxton,** ed. N. F. Blake. 1970.	£8·50
264	**The Epistle of Othea translated from the French text of Christine de Pisan by Stephen Scrope,** ed. C. F. Bühler. 1970.	£8·50
265	**The Cyrurgie of Guy de Chauliac,** Vol. I, Text, ed. Margaret S. Ogden. 1971.	£15·00
266	**Wulfstan's Canons of Edgar,** ed. R. G. Fowler. 1972.	£4·75
267	**The English Text of the Ancrene Riwle,** British Museum MS. Cotton Cleopatra C. vi, ed. E. J. Dobson. 1972.	£13·25
268	**Of Arthour and of Merlin,** Vol. I, Text, ed. O. D. Macrae-Gibson. 1973.	£10·00
269	**The Metrical Version of Mandeville's Travels,** ed. M. C. Seymour. 1973.	£8·50
270	**Fifteenth Century Translations of Alain Chartier's Le Traite de l'Esperance and Le Quadrilogue Invectif,** Vol. I, Text, ed. Margaret S. Blayney. 1974.	£9·50
271	**The Minor Poems of Stephen Hawes,** ed. Florence Gluck and Alice B. Morgan. 1974.	£8·00
272	**Thomas Norton's The Ordinal of Alchemy,** ed. John Reidy. 1975.	£8·50
273	**The Cely Letters, 1472–1488,** ed. Alison Hanham. 1975.	£10·75
274	**The English Text of the Ancrene Riwle,** Magdalene College Cambridge MS Pepys 2498, ed. A. Zettersten. 1976.	£8·00
275	**Dives and Pauper,** Text Vol. I, ed. Priscilla H. Barnum. 1976.	£11·00
276	**Secretum Secretorum,** Vol. I, Text, ed. M. A. Manzalaoui. 1977.	£20·00
277	**Laȝamon's Brut,** Vol. II. Text (lines 8021–end), ed. G. L. Brook and R. F. Leslie. 1978.	£20·00
278	**The Ayenbite of Inwyt,** Vol. II, Introduction, Notes and Glossary, ed. Pamela Gradon. 1979.	£10·75
279	**Of Arthour and of Merlin,** Vol. II, Introduction, Notes and Glossary, ed. O. D. Macrae-Gibson. 1979.	£9·50
280	**Dives and Pauper,** Text Vol. I, Part 2, ed. Priscilla H. Barnum. 1980.	£11·00
281	**Fifteenth Century Translations of Alain Chartier's Le Traite de l'Esperance and Le Quadrilogue Invectif,** Vol. II, Introduction, Notes and Glossary, ed. Margaret S. Blayney. 1980.	£10·75
282	**Erasmus Enchiridion Militis Christiani, an English Version,** ed. Anne M. O'Donnell. 1981.	£20·50
283	**The Digby Plays,** ed. Donald C. Baker, J. L. Murphy and L. B. Hall. 1982.	£15·50
284	**Hali Meiðhad,** ed. Bella Millet. 1982.	£10·00
285	**John Capgrave's Abbreuiacion of Cronicles,** ed. Peter J. Lucas. 1983.	£32·00
286	**The Old English Herbarium and Medicina de Quadrupedibus,** ed. H. J. de Vriend. 1984.	£25·50
287	**Aelred of Rievaulx's De Institutione Inclusarum: Two Middle English Translations,** ed. J. Ayto and A. Barratt. 1984.	£6.50

OS 288	**The Pilgrimage of the Lyfe of the Manhode,** Vol. I, ed. A. Henry. 1985.		£26·00
289	**Octovian,** ed. F. McSparran. 1986.		£11·00
290	**Barlam and Iosaphat,** ed. J. C. Hirsh. 1986.		£13·00
291	**The Liber Celestis of St Bridget of Sweden,** Vol. I, ed. R. Ellis. 1987.		£30.00

SUPPLEMENTARY SERIES

SS 1	**Non-Cycle Plays and Fragments,** ed. Norman Davis with an appendix on the Shrewsbury Music by F. Ll. Harrison. 1970.	£9·50
2	**The Book of the Knight of the Tower translated by William Caxton,** ed. M. Y. Offord. 1971.	£8·00
3	**The Chester Mystery Cycle,** Vol. I, Text, ed. R. M. Lumiansky and David Mills. 1974.	£13·25
4	**The Winchester Malory,** a facsimile with introduction by N. R. Ker. 1976.	£74·00
5	**Ælfric's Catholic Homilies,** Series II, Text, ed. Malcolm Godden. 1979.	£22·00
6	**The Old English Orosius,** ed. Janet Bately. 1980.	£22·00
7	**Seinte Katerine,** ed. S. R. T. O. d'Ardenne and E. J. Dobson. 1981.	£22·00
8	**Curye on Inglysch** (Middle English recipes), ed. C. B. Hieatt and S. Butler. 1985:	£6·50
9	**The Chester Mystery Cycle,** Vol. II, ed. R. M. Lumiansky and David Mills. 1986.	£15·00

FORTHCOMING VOLUMES

OS 292	**The Pilgrimage of the Lyfe of the Manhode,** Vol. II, ed. A. Henry (1988).
293	**Richard Rolle: Prose and Verse, from MS. Longleat 29,** ed. S. Ogilvie-Thompson (1988).
OS 294	**Lollard Sermons,** ed. G. Cigman.
OS 295	**Alan Chartier: A Familiar Dialogue,** ed. M. Blayney.
SS 10	**The Wars of Alexander,** ed. H. Duggan and T. Turville-Petre.

LIST 2

ORIGINAL SERIES 1864–1954

OS 1	**Early English Alliterative Poems** . . . from MS. Cotton Nero A. x, ed. R. Morris. 1864, *revised* 1869, *reprinted* 1965.	£7·50
2	**Arthur,** ed. F. J. Furnivall. 1864, *reprinted* Kraus 1984. *Paper.*	*
3	**William Lauder Ane conpendious and breue tractate concernyng ye Office and Dewtie of Kyngis,** ed. F. Hall. 1864, *reprinted* 1965.	£3·00
	Also available reprinted as one volume with OS 41.	$11·00
	William Lauder The Minor Poems, ed. F. J. Furnivall. 1870, *reprinted* Kraus 1973.	
4	**Sir Gawayne and the Green Knight,** ed. R. Morris. 1864. Superseded by OS 210.	
5	**Alexander Hume of the Orthographie and Congruitie of the Britan Tongue,** ed. H. B. Wheatley. 1865, *reprinted* 1965. *Paper.*	£3·00
6	**The Romans of Lancelot of the Laik,** re-ed. W. W. Skeat. 1865, *reprinted* 1965. *Paper.*	£6·50
7	**The Story of Genesis and Exodus,** ed. R. Morris. 1865, *reprinted* Kraus 1973.	$20·00
8	**Morte Arthure** [alliterative version from Thornton MS.], ed. E. Brock. 1865, *reprinted* 1967.	£4·50
9	**Francis Thynne Animadversions uppon Chaucer's Workes** . . . **1598,** ed. G. H. Kingsley. 1865, *revised* F. J. Furnivall 1875, *reprinted* 1965.	£8·00
10, 112	**Merlin,** ed. H. B. Wheatley, Vol. I 1865, Vol. IV with essays by J. S. S. Glennie and W. E. Mead 1899; *reprinted as one volume* Kraus 1973. (See OS 21, 36 for other parts.)	*
11, 19, 35, 37	**The Works of Sir David Lyndesay,** Vol. I 1865; Vol. II 1866 The Monarch and other Poems, ed. J. Small; Vol. III 1868 The Historie of . . . Squyer William Meldrum etc., ed. F. Hall; Vol. IV Ane Satyre of the Thrie Estaits and Minor Poems, ed. F. Hall. *Reprinted as one volume* Kraus 1973. (See OS 47 for last part.)	$39.00
12	**Adam of Cobsam The Wright's Chaste Wife,** ed. F. J. Furnivall. 1865, *reprinted* 1965. (See also OS 84.)	£2·50
13	**Seinte Marherete,** ed. O. Cockayne. 1866. Superseded by OS 193.	
14	**King Horn, Floriz and Bauncheflur, The Assumption of our Lady,** ed. J. R. Lumby. 1866, *revised* G. H. McKnight 1901, *reprinted* 1962.	£7·75
15	**Political, Religious and Love Poems,** from Lambeth MS. 306 and other sources, ed. F. J. Furnivall. 1866, *reprinted* 1962.	£9·75
16	**The Book of Quinte Essence** . . . Sloane MS. 73 *c.* 1460–70, ed. F. J. Furnivall. 1866, *reprinted* 1965. *Paper.*	*
17	**William Langland Parallel Extracts from 45 MSS. of Piers Plowman,** ed. W. W. Skeat. 1866, *reprinted* Kraus 1973.	$12.00
18	**Hali Meidenhad,** ed. O. Cockayne. 1866, *revised* F. J. Furnivall 1922 (*for* 1920), *reprinted* Kraus 1973.	$11.00
19	**Sir David Lyndesay The Monarch and other Poems,** Vol. II. See above, OS 11.	
20	**Richard Rolle de Hampole English Prose Treatises,** ed. G. G. Perry. 1866, *reprinted* Kraus 1973. *Paper.*	*
21, 36	**Merlin,** ed. H. B. Wheatley. Vol. II 1866, Vol. III 1869; *reprinted as one volume* Kraus 1973.	*
22	**The Romans of Partenay or of Lusignen,** ed. W. W. Skeat. 1866, *reprinted* Kraus 1973.	*
23	**Dan Michel Ayenbite of Inwyt,** ed. R. Morris. 1866, *revised* P. Gradon, *reprinted* 1965.	£8·25

OS 24	**Hymns to the Virgin and Christ** . . . and other religious poems, ed. F. J. Furnivall. 1867, *reprinted* Kraus 1973.	$12.00
25	**The Stacions of Rome, The Pilgrims Sea-Voyage** etc., ed. F. J. Furnivall. 1867, *reprinted* Kraus 1973. *Paper*.	$12.00
26	**Religious Pieces in Prose and Verse** from R. Thornton's MS., ed. G. G. Perry. 1867, *reprinted* Kraus 1973.	$26.00
27	**Peter Levins Manipulus Vocabulorum,** ed. H. B. Wheatley. 1867, *reprinted* Kraus 1973.	$28.00
28	**William Langland The Vision of Piers Plowman,** ed. W. W. Skeat. Vol. I Text A 1867, *reprinted* 1968. (See OS 38, 54, 67, and 81 for other parts.)	£6·00
29, 34	**Old English Homilies of the 12th and 13th Centuries,** ed. R. Morris. Vol. I. i 1867, Vol. I. ii 1868; *reprinted as one volume* Kraus 1973. (See OS 53 for Vol. II.)	*
30	**Pierce the Ploughmans Crede etc.,** ed. W. W. Skeat. 1867, *reprinted* Kraus 1973. *Paper*.	$12.00
31	**John Myrc Instructions for Parish Priests,** ed. E. Peacock. 1868, *reprinted* Kraus 1973.	$15.00
32	**Early English Meals and Manners:** The Babees Book etc., ed. F. J. Furnivall. 1868, *reprinted* Kraus 1973.	$36.00
33	**The Book of the Knight of La Tour-Landry** (from MS. Harley 1764), ed. T. Wright. 1868, *reprinted* Kraus 1973.	$20.00
34	**Old English Homilies of the 12th and 13th Centuries.** Vol. I. ii. See above, OS 29.	
35	**Sir David Lyndesay The Historie of . . . Squyer William Meldrum** etc., ed. F. Hall. 1868, *reprinted* 1965. *Also available reprinted as one volume with* OS 11, 19, and 37. See above, OS 11.	£3·00
36	**Merlin,** Vol. III 1869. See above, OS 21.	
37	**Sir David Lyndesay Ane Satyre** . . . Vol. IV. See above, OS 11.	
38	**William Langland The Vision of Piers Plowman,** ed. W. W. Skeat. Vol. II Text B 1869, *reprinted* 1972. (See OS 28, 54, 67, and 81 for other parts.)	£6·50
39, 56	**The Gest Hystoriale of the Destruction of Troy,** ed. G. A. Panton and D. Donaldson. Vol. I 1869, Vol. II 1874; *reprinted as one volume* 1968.	£16·00
40	**English Gilds** etc., ed. Toulmin Smith, L. Toulmin Smith and L. Brentano. 1870, *reprinted* 1963.	£13·75
41	**William Lauder The Minor Poems.** See above, OS 3.	
42	**Bernardus De Cura Rei Famuliaris,** with some early Scottish Prophecies ed., J. R. Lumby. 1870, *reprinted* 1965. *Paper*.	£3·00
43	**Ratis Raving,** and other Moral and Religious Pieces in prose and verse, ed. J. R. Lumby. 1870, *reprinted* Kraus 1973.	$12.00
44	**Joseph of Arimathie:** the Romance of the Seint Graal, an alliterative poem, ed. W. W. Skeat. 1871, *reprinted* Kraus 1973.	$12.00
45	**King Alfred's West-Saxon Version of Gregory's Pastoral Care,** ed. H. Sweet. Vol. I 1871, reprinted with corrections and an additional note by N. F. Ker 1958, *reprinted* Kraus 1973. (See OS 50 for Vol. II.)	$23.00
46	**Legends of the Holy Rood,** Symbols of the Passion and Cross-Poems, ed. R. Morris. 1871, *reprinted* Kraus 1973.	$20.00
47	**Sir David Lyndesay The Minor Poems,** ed. J. A. H. Murray, 1871, *reprinted* Kraus 1973. (See OS 11, 19, 35, 37 for other parts.)	$17.00
48	**The Times' Whistle,** and other poems: by R. C., ed. J. M. Cowper. 1871, *reprinted* Kraus 1973.	$17.00
49	**An Old English Miscellany:** a Bestiary, Kentish Sermons, Proverbs of Alfred and Religious Poems of the 13th Century, ed. R. Morris. 1872, *reprinted* Kraus 1973.	$23.00
50	**King Alfred's West-Saxon Version of Gregory's Pastoral Care,** ed. H. Sweet. Vol. II 1871, reprinted with corrections by N. R. Ker 1958, *reprinted* Kraus 1973. (See OS 45 for Vol. I.)	$18.00

OS 51	þe Liflade of St. Juliana, ed. O. Cockayne and E. Brock. 1872. Superseded by OS 248.	
52, 72	Palladius On Husbandrie, ed. B. Lodge and S. J. Herrtage. Vol. I 1872, Vol. II 1879, *reprinted* as one volume Kraus 1973.	*
53	Old English Homilies of the 12th Century etc., ed. R. Morris. Vol. II 1873, *reprinted* Kraus 1973. (See OS 29, 34 for Vol. I.)	$30.00
54	William Langland The Vision of Piers Plowman, ed. W. W. Skeat. Vol. III Text C 1873, *reprinted* 1978. (See OS 28, 38, 67, and 81 for other parts.)	£8·25
55, 70	Generydes, a romance, ed. W. A. Wright. Vol. I 1873, Vol. I 1873, Vol. II 1878; *reprinted as one volume* Kraus 1973.	*
56	The Gest Hystoriale of the Destruction of Troy. Vol. II. See above, OS 39.	
57	Cursor Mundi, ed. R. Morris. Vol. I Text ll. 1-4954, 1874, *reprinted* 1961. (See OS 59, 62, 66, 68, 99, and 101 for other parts.) *Paper.*	£6·00
58, 63, 73	The Blickling Homilies, ed. R. Morris. Vol. I 1874, Vol. II 1876, Vol. III 1880; *reprinted as one volume* 1967.	£11·00
59	Cursor Mundi, ed. R. Morris. Vol. II ll. 4955-12558, 1875, *reprinted* 1966. (See OS 57, 62, 66, 68, 99, and 101 for other parts.) *Paper.*	£7·75
60	Meditations on the Supper of our Lord, and the Hours of the Passion, translated by Robert Manning of Brunne, ed. J. M. Cowper. 1875, *reprinted* Kraus 1973. *Paper.*	*
61	The Romance and Prophecies of Thomas of Erceldoune, ed. J. A. H. Murray. 1875, *reprinted* Kraus 1973.	*
62	Cursor Mundi, ed. R. Morris. Vol. III ll. 12559-19300, 1876, *reprinted* 1966. (See OS 57, 59, 66, 68, 99, and 101 for other parts.) *Paper.*	£6·00
63	The Blickling Homilies, Vol. II. See above, OS 58.	
64	Francis Thynne's Emblemes and Epigrames, ed. F. J. Furnivall. 1876, *reprinted* Kraus 1873.	$12.00
65	Be Domes Dæge, De Die Judicii: an Old English version of the Latin poem ascribed to Bede, ed. J. R. Lumby. 1876, *reprinted* 1964.	£4·75
66	Cursor Mundi, ed. R. Morris. Vol. IV ll. 19301-23826, 1877, *reprinted* 1966. (See OS 57, 59, 62, 68, 99, and 101 for other parts.) *Paper.*	£6·00
67	William Langland The Vision of Piers Plowman, ed. W. W. Skeat. Vol. IV. 1 Notes, 1877, *reprinted* Kraus 1973. (See OS 28, 38, 54, and 81 for other parts.)	*
68	Cursor Mundi, ed. R. Morris. Vol. V ll. 23827-end, 1878, *reprinted* 1966. (See OS 57, 59, 62, 66, 99, and 101 for other parts.) *Paper.*	£6·00
69	Adam Davy's 5 Dreams about Edward II etc. from Bodleian MS. Laud Misc. 622, ed. F. J. Furnivall. 1878, *reprinted* Kraus 1973.	$12.00
70	Generydes, a romance. Vol. II. See above, OS 55.	
71	The Lay Folks Mass Book, ed. T. F. Simmons. 1879, *reprinted* 1968.	£13·25
72	Palladius On Husbandrie, Vol. II. See above, OS 52.	
73	The Blickling Homilies, Vol. III. See above, OS 58.	
74	The English Works of Wyclif hitherto unprinted, ed. F. D. Matthew. 1880, *reprinted* Kraus 1973.	$44.00
75	Catholicon Anglicum, an English Latin Wordbook 1483, ed. S. J. H. Herrtage and H. B. Wheatley. 1881, *reprinted* Kraus 1973.	*
76, 82	Ælfric's Lives of Saints, ed. W. W. Skeat. Vol. I. i 1881, Vol. I. ii 1885; *reprinted as one volume* 1966. (See OS 94 and 114 for other parts.)	£9·50
77	Beowulf, autotypes of Cotton MS. Vitellius A. xv. 1882. Superseded by OS 245.	
78	The Fifty Earliest English Wills . . . 1387-1439, ed. F. J. Furnivall. 1882, *reprinted* 1964.	£8·25
79	King Alfred's Orosius, ed. H. Sweet. Vol. I Old English Text and Latin Original (*all published*) 1883, *reprinted* Kraus 1974.	$21.00

OS 80	**The Life of Saint Katherine,** from Royal MS. 17 A. xxvii etc., ed. E. Einenkel. 1884, *reprinted* Kraus 1973.	$20.00
81	**William Langland The Vision of Piers Plowman,** ed. W. W. Skeat. Vol. IV. 2 General Preface and indexes. 1884, *reprinted* Kraus 1973. (See OS 28, 38, 54 and 67 for other parts.)	$45.00
82	**Ælfric's Lives of Saints,** Vol. I. ii. See above, OS 76.	
83	**The Oldest English Texts,** ed. H. Sweet. 1885, *reprinted* 1966.	£16·00
84	[Adam of Cobsam] **Additional Analogs to The Wright's Chaste Wife,** ed. W. A. Clouston. 1886, *reprinted* with OS 12, Kraus 1973.	$15.00
85	**The Three Kings of Cologne,** ed. C. Horstmann. 1886, *reprinted* Kraus 1973.	$23.00
86	**The Lives of Women Saints** etc., ed. C. Horstmann. 1886, *reprinted* Kraus 1973.	*
87	**The Early South-English Legendary,** from Bodleian MS. Laud Misc. 108, ed. C. Horstmann. 1887, *reprinted* Kraus 1973.	*
88	**Henry Bradshaw The Life of Saint Werburge of Chester,** ed. C. Horstmann. 1887, *reprinted* Kraus 1973.	$20.00
89	**Vices and Virtues** [from British Museum MS. Stowe 240], ed. F. Holthausen. Vol. I Text and translation. 1888, *reprinted* 1967. (See OS 159 for Vol. II.) *Paper.*	£6·00
90	**The Rule of S. Benet,** Latin and Anglo-Saxon interlinear version, ed. H. Logeman. 1888, *reprinted* Kraus 1973.	$18.00
91	**Two Fifteenth-Century Cookery-Books,** ed. T. Austin. 1888, *reprinted* Kraus 1981.	*
92	**Eadwine's Canterbury Psalter,** ed. F. Harsley. Vol. II Text and notes (*all published*) 1889, *reprinted* Kraus 1973.	*
93	**Defensor's Liber Scintillarum,** ed. E. W. Rhodes. 1889, *reprinted* Kraus 1973.	*
94, 114	**Ælfric's Lives of Saints,** ed. W. W. Skeat. Vol. II. i 1890, Vol. II. ii 1900; *reprinted as one volume* 1966. (See OS 76, 82 for other parts.)	£9·50
95	**The Old English Version of Bede's Ecclesiastical History of the English People,** ed. T. Miller. Vol. I. i 1890, *reprinted* Kraus 1976.	$32.00
96	**The Old English Version of Bede's Ecclesiastical History of the English People,** ed. T. Miller. Vol. I. ii 1891, *reprinted* Kraus 1976. (See OS 110, 111 for other parts.)	$32.00
97	**The Earliest Complete English Prose Psalter,** ed. K. D. Bülbring. Vol. I (*all published*) 1891, *reprinted* Kraus 1973.	*
98	**The Minor Poems of the Vernon MS.,** ed. C. Horstmann. Vol. I 1892, *reprinted* Kraus 1973. (See OS 117 for Vol. II.)	*
99	**Cursor Mundi,** ed. R. Morris. Vol. VI Preface etc. 1892, *reprinted* 1962. (See O.S. 57, 59, 62, 66, 68, and 101 for other parts.)	£5·50
100	**John Capgrave The Life of St. Katherine of Alexandria,** ed. C. Horstmann, forewords by F. J. Furnivall. 1893, *reprinted* Kraus 1973. *Paper*	*
101	**Cursor Mundi,** ed. R. Morris. Vol. VII Essay on manuscripts and dialect by H. Hupe. 1893, *reprinted* 1962. (See OS 57, 59, 62, 66, 68, and 99 for other parts.) *Paper.*	£5·50
102	**Lanfrank's Science of Cirurgie,** ed. R. von Fleischhacker. Vol. I Text (*all published*) 1894, *reprinted* Kraus 1973.	*
103	**History of the Holy Rood-tree,** with notes on the orthography of the Ormulum etc., ed. A. S. Napier. 1894, *reprinted* Kraus 1973.	$12.00
104	**The Exeter Book,** ed. I. Gollancz. Vol. I Poems I–VIII. 1895, *reprinted* Kraus 1973. (See OS 194 for Vol. II.)	$22.00
105, 109	**The Prymer or Lay Folks' Prayer Book,** ed. H. Littlehales. Vol. I 1895, Vol. II 1897; *reprinted as one volume* Kraus 1973.	$18.00
106	**Richard Rolle The Fire of Love and The Mending of Life** . . . translated by Richard Misyn. ed. R. Harvey. 1896, *reprinted* Kraus 1973.	$22.00
107	**The English Conquest of Ireland,** A.D. **1166–1185,** ed. F. J. Furnivall. Vol. I Text (*all published*) 1896, *reprinted* Kraus 1973.	*

OS 108	**Child-Marriages, Divorces and Ratifications** etc. in the Diocese of Chester 1561–6 etc., ed. F. J. Furnivall. 1894 (*for* 1897), *reprinted* Kraus 1973.	$25.00
109	**The Prymer or Lay Folks' Prayer Book,** Vol. II. See above, OS 105.	
110	**The Old English Version of Bede's Ecclesiastical History of the English People,** ed. T. Miller. Vol. II. i 1898, *reprinted* 1963.	*
111	**The Old English Version of Bede's Ecclesiastical History of the English People,** ed. T. Miller. Vol. II. ii 1898, *reprinted* 1963. (See OS 95, 96 for other parts.)	*
112	**Merlin,** Vol. IV. See above, OS 10.	
113	**Queen Elizabeth's Englishings of Boethius, Plutarch and Horace,** ed. C. Pemberton. 1899, *reprinted* Kraus 1973.	$18.00
114	**Ælfric's Lives of Saints,** Vol. II. ii. See above, OS 94.	
115	**Jacob's Well,** ed. A. Brandeis. Vol. I (*all published*) 1900, *reprinted* Kraus 1973.	*
116	**An Old English Martyrology,** re-ed. G. Herzfeld. 1900, *reprinted* Kraus 1973.	$28.00
117	**The Minor Poems of the Vernon MS.,** ed. F. J. Furnivall. Vol. II 1901, *reprinted* Kraus 1973. (See OS 98 for Vol. I.)	*
118	**The Lay Folks' Catechism,** ed. T. F. Simmons and H. E. Nolloth. 1901, *reprinted* Kraus 1973.	*
119, 123	**Robert of Brunne's Handlyng Synne** [and its French original], ed. F. J. Furnivall. Vol. I 1901, Vol. II 1903; *reprinted as one volume* Kraus 1973.	$29.00
120	**The Middle-English Versions of the Rule of St. Benet** and two contemporary rituals for the ordination of nuns, ed. E. A. Kock. 1902, *reprinted* Kraus 1973.	*
121, 122	**The Laud Troy Book,** Bodleian MS. Laud Misc. 595, ed. J. E. Wülfing. Vol. I 1902, Vol. II 1903, *reprinted as one volume* Kraus 1973.	$40.00
123	**Robert of Brunne's Handlyng Synne,** Vol. II. See above, OS 119.	
124	**Twenty-Six Political and other Poems** . . . from Bodleian MSS. Digby 102 and Douce 322, ed. J. Kail. Vol. I (*all published*) 1904, *reprinted* Kraus 1973.	$18.00
125, 128	**The Medieval Records of a London City Church** (St. Mary at Hill), 1420–1559, ed. H. Littlehales. Vol. I 1904, Vol. II 1905; *reprinted as one volume* Kraus 1973.	*
126, 127	**An Alphabet of Tales,** an English 15th-century translation of the Alphabetum Narrationum, ed. M. M. Banks. Vol. I 1904, Vol. II 1905; *reprinted as one volume* Kraus 1973.	*
128	**The Medieval Records of a London City Church.** Vol. II. See above, OS 125.	
129	**The English Register of Godstow Nunnery** . . . *c.* 1450, ed. A. Clark. Vol. I 1905, *reprinted* Kraus 1971.	$29.00
130, 142	**The English Register of Godstow Nunnery** . . . *c.* 1450, ed. A. Clark. Vol. II 1906, Vol. III 1911; *reprinted as one volume* Kraus 1971.	$36.00
131	**The Brut,** or the Chronicles of England . . . from Bodleian MS. Rawl. B. 171, ed. F. W. D. Brie. Vol. I 1906, *reprinted* Kraus 1981. (See O.S. 136 for Vol. II.)	*
132	**The Works of John Metham,** ed. H. Craig. 1916 (*for* 1906), *reprinted* Kraus 1973.	$17.00
133, 144	**The English Register of Oseney Abbey** . . . *c.* 1460, ed. A. Clark. Vol. I 1907, Vol. II 1913 (*for* 1912); *reprinted as one volume* Kraus 1971.	$22.00
134, 135	**The Coventry Leet Book,** ed. M. D. Harris. Vol. I 1907, Vol. II 1908; *reprinted as one volume* Kraus 1971. (See OS 138, 146 for other parts.)	$43.00
136	**The Brut,** or the Chronicles of England, ed. F. W. D. Brie. Vol. II 1908, *reprinted* Kraus 1971. (See OS 131 for Vol. I.)	*

OS 137	**Twelfth Century Homilies in MS. Bodley 343**, ed. A. O. Belfour. Vol. I Text and translation (*all published*) 1909, *reprinted* 1962. *Paper*.	*
138, 146	**The Coventry Leet Book**, ed. M. D. Harris. Vol. III 1909, Vol. IV 1913; *reprinted as one volume* Kraus 1971. (See OS 134, 135 for other parts.)	$35.00
139	**John Arderne Treatises of Fistula in Ano** étc., ed. D'Arcy Power, 1910, *reprinted* 1968.	£6·75
140	**John Capgrave's Lives of St. Augustine and St. Gilbert of Sempringham and a sermon**, ed. J. J. Munro. 1910, *reprinted* Kraus 1971.	$40.00
141	**The Middle English Poem Erthe upon Erthe**, printed from 24 manuscripts, ed. H. M. R. Murray. 1911, *reprinted* 1964.	£4·75
142	**The English Register of Godstow Nunnery**, Vol. III. See above, OS 130.	
143	**The Prose Life of Alexander** from the Thornton MS., ed. J. S. Westlake. 1913 (*for* 1911), *reprinted* Kraus 1971.	$12.00
144	**The English Register of Oseney Abbey**, Vol. II. See above, OS 133.	
145	**The Northern Passion**, ed. F. A. Foster. Vol. I 1913 (*for* 1912), *reprinted* Kraus 1971. (See OS 147, 183 for other parts.)	$20.00
146	**The Coventry Leet Book**, Vol. IV. See above, O.S. 138.	
147	**The Northern Passion**, ed. F. A. Foster. Vol. II 1916 (*for* 1913), *reprinted* Kraus 1971. (See OS 145, 183 for other parts.)	$17.00
148	**A Fifteenth-Century Courtesy Book**, ed. R. W. Chambers, and **Two Fifteenth-Century Franciscan Rules**, ed. W. W. Seton. 1914, *reprinted* 1963.	£4·75
149	**Lincoln Diocese Documents, 1450–1544**, ed. A. Clark. 1941, *reprinted* Kraus 1971.	$28.00
150	**The Old English Versions of the enlarged Rule of Chrodegang**, the Capitula of Theodulf and the Epitome of Benedict of Aniane, ed. A. S. Napier. 1916 (*for* 1914), *reprinted* Kraus 1971.	$10.00
151	**The Lanterne of Liȝt**, ed. L. M. Swinburn, 1917 (*for* 1915) *reprinted* Kraus 1971.	*
152	**Early English Homilies from the Twelfth-Century MS. Vespasian D. xiv**, ed. R. D.-N. Warner. 1917 (*for* 1915), *reprinted* Kraus 1971.	$16.00
153	**Mandeville's Travels** . . . from MS. Cotton Titus C. xvi, ed. P. Hamelius. Vol. I Text 1919 (*for* 1916), *reprinted* Kraus 1973. *Paper*	$18.00
154	**Mandeville's Travels** . . . from MS. Cotton Titus C. xvi, ed. P. Hamelius. Vol. II Introduction and notes. 1923 (*for* 1916), *reprinted* 1961. *Paper*.	£6·00
155	**The Wheatley Manuscript**: Middle English verse and prose in British Museum MS. Additional 39574, ed. M. Day. 1921 (*for* 1917), *reprinted* Kraus 1971.	$12.00
156	**The Donet by Reginald Peacock**, ed. E. V. Hitchcock. 1921 (*for* 1918), *reprinted* Kraus 1971.	$22.00
157	**The Pepysian Gospel Harmony**, ed. M. Goates. 1922 (*for* 1919), *reprinted* Kraus 1971.	$15.00
158	**Meditations on the Life and Passion of Christ**, from British Museum MS. Additional 11307, ed. C. D'Evelyn. 1921 (*for* 1919), *reprinted* Kraus 1971.	*
159	**Vices and Virtues** [from British Museum MS Stowe 240], ed. F. Holthausen. Vol. II Notes and Glossary, 1921 (*for* 1920), *reprinted* 1967. (See OS 89 for Vol. I.) *Paper*	£4·25
160	**The Old English Version of the Heptateuch** etc., ed. S. J. Crawford. 1922 (*for* 1921), reprinted with additional material, ed. N. R. Ker 1969.	£10·00
161	**Three Old English Prose Texts** in MS. Cotton Vitellius A. xv, ed. S. Rypins. 1924 (*for* 1921), *reprinted* Kraus 1971.	$13.00
162	**Pearl, Cleanness, Patience and Sir Gawain**, facsimile of British Museum MS. Cotton Nero A. x, with introduction by I. Gollancz. 1923 (*for* 1922), *reprinted* 1971.	£30·00

OS 163	**The Book of the Foundation of St. Bartholomew's Church in London,** ed. N. Moore. 1923, *reprinted* Kraus 1971. *Paper*	$12.00
164	**The Folewer to the Donet by Reginald Peacock,** ed. E. V. Hitchcock. 1924 (*for* 1923), *reprinted* Kraus 1971.	$25.00
165	**The Famous Historie of Chinon of England by Christopher Middleton,** with Leland's Assertio Inclytissimi Arturii and Robinson's translation, ed. W. E. Mead. 1925 (*for* 1923), *reprinted* Kraus 1971.	*
166	**A Stanzaic Life of Christ,** from Harley MS. 3909, ed. F. A. Foster. 1926 (*for* 1924), *reprinted* Kraus 1971.	*
167	**John Trevisa Dialogus** inter Militem et Clericum, Richard Fitzralph's 'Defensio Curatorum', Methodius' 'þe Bygynnyng of þe World and þe Ende of Worldes', ed. A. J. Perry. 1925 (*for* 1924), *reprinted* Kraus 1971.	*
168	**The Book of the Ordre of Chyualry** translated by William Caxton, ed. A. T. P. Byles. 1926 (*for* 1925), *reprinted* Kraus 1971.	$13.00
169	**The Southern Passion,** Pepysian MS. 2334, ed. B. D. Brown. 1927 (*for* 1925), *reprinted* Kraus 1971.	*
170	**Boethius De Consolatione Philosophiae, translated by John Walton,** ed. M. Science. 1927 (*for* 1925), *reprinted* Kraus 1971.	$40.00
171	**The Reule of Crysten Religioun by Reginald Pecock,** ed. W. C. Greet. 1927 (*for* 1926), *reprinted* Kraus 1971.	*
172	**The Seege or Batayle of Troye,** ed. M. E. Barnicle. 1927 (*for* 1926), *reprinted* Kraus 1971.	*
173	**Stephen Hawes The Pastime of Pleasure,** ed. W. E. Mead. 1928 (*for* 1927), *reprinted* Kraus 1971.	$30.00
174	**The Middle English Stanzaic Versions of the Life of St. Anne,** ed. R. E. Parker. 1928 (*for* 1927), *reprinted* Kraus 1971.	*
175	**Alexander Barclay The Eclogues,** ed. B. White. 1928 (*for* 1927), *reprinted* 1961.	£8·00
176	**William Caxton The Prologues and Epilogues,** ed. W. J. B. Crotch. 1928 (*for* 1927), *reprinted* Kraus 1973.	$22.00
177	**Byrthferth's Manual,** ed. S. J. Crawford. Vol. ·I Text, translation, sources, and appendices (*all published*) 1929 (*for* 1928), *reprinted* 1966.	£9·75
178	**The Revelations of St. Birgitta,** from Garrett MS. Princeton University, ed. W. P. Cumming. 1929 (*for* 1928), *reprinted* Kraus 1971.	*
179	**William Nevill The Castell of Pleasure,** ed. R. D. Cornelius. 1930 (*for* 1928), *reprinted* Kraus 1971.	$12.00
180	**The Apologye of Syr Thomas More, knyght,** ed. A. I. Taft. 1930 (*for* 1929), *reprinted* Kraus 1971.	*
181	**The Dance of Death,** ed. F. Warren. 1931 (*for* 1929), *reprinted* Kraus 1971.	$10.00
182	**Speculum Christiani,** ed. G. Holmstedt. 1933 (*for* 1929), *reprinted* Kraus 1971.	*
183	**The Northern Passion** (Supplement), ed. W. Heuser and F. A. Foster. 1930, *reprinted* Kraus 1971. (See OS 145, 147 for other parts.)	$12.00
184	**John Audelay The Poems,** ed. E. K. Whiting. 1931 (*for* 1930), *reprinted* Kraus 1971.	$22.00
185	**Henry Lovelich's Merlin,** ed. E. A. Kock. Vol. III. 1932 (*for* 1930), *reprinted* Kraus 1971. (See ES 93 and 112 for other parts.)	$22.00
186	**Nicholas Harpsfield The Life and Death of Sr. Thomas More,** ed. E. V. Hitchcock and R. W. Chambers. 1932 (*for* 1931), *reprinted* 1963.	£15·00
187	**John Stanbridge The Vulgaria and Robert Whittinton The Vulgaria,** ed. B. White. 1932 (*for* 1931), *reprinted* Kraus 1971.	$15.00
188	**The Siege of Jerusalem,** from Bodleian MS. Laud Misc. 656, ed. E. Kölbing and M. Day. 1932 (*for* 1931), *reprinted* Kraus 1971.	$12.00
189	**Christine de Pisan The Book of Fayttes of Armes and of Chyualrye,** translated by William Caxton, ed. A. T. P. Byles. 1932, *reprinted* Kraus 1971.	$22.00

OS 190	**English Mediaeval Lapidaries,** ed. J. Evans and M. S. Serjeantson. 1933 (*for* 1932), *reprinted* 1960.	£7·75
191	**The Seven Sages of Rome** (Southern Version), ed. K. Brunner. 1933 (*for* 1932), *reprinted* Kraus 1971.	$18.00
191A	R. W. Chambers: **On the Continuity of English Prose** from Alfred to More and his School (an extract from the introduction to OS 186). 1932, *reprinted* 1966.	£4·00
192	**John Lydgate The Minor Poems,** ed. H. N. MacCracken. Vol. II Secular Poems. 1934 (*for* 1933), *reprinted* 1961. (See E.S. 107 for Vol. I.)	£11·00
193	**Seinte Marherete,** from MS. Bodley 34 and British Museum MS. Royal 17 A. xxvii, re-ed. F. M. Mack. 1934 (*for* 1933), *reprinted* 1958.	£7·75
194	**The Exeter Book,** ed. W. S. Mackie. Vol. II Poems IX–XXXII. 1934 (*for* 1933), *reprinted* Kraus 1973. (See O.S. 104 for Vol. I.)	$20.00
195	**The Quatrefoil of Love,** ed. I. Gollancz and M. M. Weale. 1935 (*for* 1934), *reprinted* Kraus 1971. *Paper.*	*
196	**An Anonymous Short English Metrical Chronicle,** ed. E. Zettl. 1935 (*for* 1934), *reprinted* Kraus 1971.	$20.00
197	**William Roper The Lyfe of Sir Thomas Moore, knighte,** ed. E. V. Hitchcock. 1935 (*for* 1934), *reprinted* Kraus 1976.	$26.00
198	**Firumbras and Otuel and Roland,** ed. M. I. O'Sullivan. 1935 (*for* 1934), *reprinted* Kraus 1971.	*
199	**Mum and the Sothsegger,** ed. M. Day and R. Steele. 1936 (*for* 1934), *reprinted* Kraus 1971.	*
200	**Speculum Sacerdotale,** ed. E. H. Weatherly. 1936 (*for* 1935), *reprinted* Kraus 1971.	$21.00
201	**Knyghthode and Bataile,** ed. R. Dyboski and Z. M. Arend. 1936 (*for* 1935), *reprinted* Kraus 1971.	$20.00
202	**John Palsgrave The Comedy of Acolastus,** ed. P. L. Carver. 1937 (*for* 1935), *reprinted* Kraus 1971.	$20.00
203	**Amis and Amiloun,** ed. MacEdward Leach. 1937 (*for* 1935), *reprinted* 1960.	£7·75
204	**Valentine and Orson,** translated from the French by Henry Watson, ed. A. Dickson. 1937 (*for* 1936), *reprinted* Kraus 1971.	$28.00
205	**Early English Versions** of the Tales of Guiscardo and Ghismonda and Titus and Gisippus from the Decameron, ed. H. G. Wright. 1937 (*for* 1936), *reprinted* Kraus 1971.	$22.00
206	**Osbern Bokenham Legendys of Hooly Wummen,** ed. M. S. Serjeantson. 1938 (*for* 1936), *reprinted* Kraus 1971.	$22.00
207	**The Liber de Diversis Medicinis** in the Thornton Manuscript, ed. M. S. Ogden. 1938 (*for* 1936), *revised reprint* 1969.	£6·50
208	**The Parker Chronicle and Laws** (Corpus Christi College, Cambridge MS. 173); a facsimile, ed. R. Flower and H. Smith. 1941 (*for* 1937), *reprinted* 1973.	£21·50
209	**Middle English Sermons,** from British Museum MS. Royal 18 B. xxiii, ed. W. O. Ross. 1940 (*for* 1938), *reprinted* Kraus 1981.	*
210	**Sir Gawain and the Green Knight,** re-ed. I. Gollancz, with introductory essays by Mabel Day and M. S. Serjeantson. 1940 (*for* 1938), *reprinted* 1966.	£4·50
211	**The Dicts and Sayings of the Philosophers:** translations made by Stephen Scrope, William Worcester, and anonymous translator, ed. C. F. Bühler. 1941 (*for* 1939), *reprinted* 1961.	£11·75
212	**The Book of Margery Kempe,** Vol. I, Text (*all published*), ed. S. B. Meech, with notes and appendices by S. B. Meech and H. E. Allen. 1940 (*for* 1939), *reprinted* 1961.	£11·00
213	**Ælfric's De Temporibus Anni,** ed. H. Henel. 1942 (*for* 1940), *reprinted* 1970.	£7·00

OS 214	**Forty-Six Lives translated from Boccaccio's De Claris Mulieribus by Henry Parker, Lord Morley,** ed. H. G. Wright. 1943 (*for* 1940), *reprinted* 1970.	£8·00
215, 220	**Charles of Orleans: The English Poems,** Vol. I, ed. R. Steele (1941), Vol. II, ed. R. Steele and Mabel Day (1946 *for* 1944); *reprinted as one volume with bibliographical supplement* 1970.	£9·75
216	**The Latin Text of the Ancrene Riwle,** from Merton College MS. 44 and British Museum MS. Cotton Vitellius E. vii, ed. C. D'Evelyn. 1944 (*for* 1941), *reprinted* 1957.	£6·75
217	**The Book of Vices and Virtues:** A Fourteenth-Century English Translation of the *Somme le Roi* of Lorens d'Orléans, ed. W. Nelson Francis. 1942, *reprinted* Kraus 1984.	$63.00
218	**The Cloud of Unknowing and The Book of Privy Counselling;** ed. Phyllis Hodgson. 1944 (*for* 1943), *corrected reprint* 1981.	£7·75
219	**The French Text of the Ancrene Riwle,** British Museum MS. Cotton Vitellius F. vii, ed. J. A. Herbert, 1944 (*for* 1943), *reprinted* 1967.	£8·00
220	**Charles of Orleans: The English Poems,** Vol. II; *see above* OS 215.	
221	**The Romance of Sir Degrevant,** ed. L. F. Casson. 1949 (*for* 1944), *reprinted* 1970.	£7·75
222	**The Lyfe of Syr Thomas More, by Ro. Ba.,** ed. E. V. Hitchcock and P. E. Hallett, with notes and appendices by A. W. Reed. 1950 (*for* 1945, *reprinted* 1974.	£9·75
223	**The Tretyse of Loue,** ed. J. H. Fisher. 1951 (*for* 1945), *reprinted 1970*.	£7·00
224	**Athelston: a Middle English Romance,** ed. A. McI. Trounce. 1951 (*for* 1946), *reprinted* Kraus 1984.	$34.00
225	**The English Text of the Ancrene Riwle,** British Museum MS. Cotton Nero A. xiv, ed. Mabel Day. 1952 (*for* 1946), *reprinted* 1957.	£7·75
226	**Respublica:** an interlude for Christmas 1553 attributed to Nicholas Udall, re-ed. W. W. Greg. 1952 (*for* 1946), *reprinted* 1969.	£4·75
227	**Kyng Alisaunder,** Vol. I, Text, ed. G. V. Smithers. 1952 (*for* 1947), *reprinted* 1961.	£11·75
228	**The Metrical Life of St. Robert of Knaresborough,** together with the other Middle English pieces in British Museum MS. Egerton 3143, ed. Joyce Bazire. 1953 (*for* 1947), *reprinted* 1968.	£7·00
229	**The English Text of the Ancrene Riwle,** Gonville and Caius College MS. 234/120, ed. R. M. Wilson with an introduction by N. R. Ker. 1954 (*for* 1948), *reprinted* 1957.	£5·50
230	**The Life of St. George by Alexander Barclay,** ed. W. Nelson. 1955 (*for* 1948), *reprinted* 1960.	£6·50
231	**Deonise Hid Diuinite** and other treatises related to *The Cloud of Unknowing,* ed. Phyllis Hodgson. 1955 (*for* 1949), *reprinted with corrections* 1958.	£7·75
232	**The English Text of the Ancrene Riwle,** British Museum MS. Royal 8 C. i, ed. A. C. Baugh. 1956 (*for* 1949), *reprinted* Kraus 1984. *Paper.*	$14.00
233	**The Bibliotheca Historica of Diodorus Siculus translated by John Skelton,** Vol. I, Text, ed. F. M. Salter and H. L. R. Edwards. 1956 (*for* 1950), *reprinted* 1968.	£12·00
234	**Paris and Vienne translated from the French and printed by William Caxton,** ed. MacEdward Leach. 1957 (*for* 1951), *reprinted* 1970.	£7·00
235	**The South English Legendary,** Corpus Christi College Cambridge MS. 145 and British Museum MS. Harley 2277, with variants from Bodley MS. Ashmole 43 and British Museum MS. Cotton Julius D. ix, ed. C. D'Evelyn and A. J. Mill. Vol. I, Text, 1959 (*for* 1957), *reprinted* 1967.	£9·75
236	**The South English Legendary,** Vol. II, Text, ed. C. D'Evelyn and A. J. Mill. 1956 (*for* 1952), *reprinted* 1967.	£9·75
237	**Kyng Alisaunder,** Vol. II, Introduction, commentary and glossary, ed. G. V. Smithers. 1957 (*for* 1953), *reprinted with corrections* 1969.	£7·75

OS 238	**The Phonetic Writings of Robert Robinson,** ed. E. J. Dobson. 1957 (*for* 1953), *reprinted* 1968.	£4·75
239	**The Bibliotheca Historica of Diodorus Siculus translated by John Skelton,** Vol. II, Introduction, notes and glossary, ed. F. M. Salter and H. L. R. Edwards. 1957 (*for* 1954), *reprinted* 1971.	£4·75

EXTRA SERIES 1867–1920

ES 1	**The Romance of William of Palerne,** ed. W. W. Skeat. 1867, *reprinted* Kraus 1973.	$35.00
2	**On Early English Pronunciation,** by A. J. Ellis. Part I. 1867, *reprinted* Kraus 1973. (See ES 7, 14, 23, and 56 for other parts.)	$17.00
3	**Caxton's Book of Curtesye,** with two manuscript copies of the treatise, ed. F. J. Furnivall. 1868, *reprinted* Kraus 1973. *Paper.*	$10.00
4	**The Lay of Havelok the Dane,** ed. W. W. Skeat. 1868, *reprinted* Kraus 1973.	$20.00
5	**Chaucer's Translation of Boethius's 'De Consolatione Philosophiæ',** ed. R. Morris. 1868, *reprinted* 1969.	£6·00
6	**The Romance of the Cheuelere Assigne,** re-ed. H. H. Gibbs. 1868, *reprinted* Kraus 1973. *Paper.*	*
7	**On Early English Pronunciation,** by A. J. Ellis. Part II. 1869, *reprinted* Kraus 1973. (See ES 2, 14, 23, and 56 for other parts.)	$17.00
8	**Queene Elizabethes Achademy** etc., ed. F. J. Furnivall, with essays on early Italian and German Books of Courtesy by W. M. Rossetti and E. Oswald. 1869, *reprinted* Kraus 1973.	$20.00
9	**The Fraternitye of Vacabondes** by John Awdeley, Harman's Caveat, Haben's Sermon etc., ed. E. Viles and F. J. Furnivall. 1869, *reprinted* Kraus 1973.	*
10	**Andrew Borde's Introduction of Knowledge and Dyetary of Helth,** with Barnes's Defence of the Berde, ed. F. J. Furnivall. 1870, *reprinted* Kraus 1973.	$35.00
11, 55	**The Bruce by John Barbour,** ed. W. W. Skeat. Vol. I 1870, Vol. IV 1889; *reprinted as one volume* 1968. (See ES 21, 29, for other parts.)	£9·75
12, 32	**England in the Reign of King Henry VIII,** Vol. I Dialogue between Cardinal Pole and Thomas Lupset, ed. J. M. Cowper (1871), Vol. II Starkey's Life and Letters, ed. S. J. Herrtage (1878); *reprinted as one volume* Kraus 1973.	$40.00
13	**Simon Fish A Supplicacyon for the Beggers,** re-ed. F. J. Furnivall, A Supplycacion . . . Henry VIII, A Supplication of the Poore Commons and The Decaye of England by the great multitude of shepe, ed. J. M. Cowper. 1871, *reprinted* Kraus 1973.	$15.00
14	**On Early English Pronunciation,** by A. J. Ellis. Part III. 1871, *reprinted* Kraus 1973. (See E.S. 2, 7, 23, and 56 for other parts.)	$28.00
15	**The Select Works of Robert Crowley,** ed. J. M. Cowper. 1872, *reprinted* Kraus 1973.	*
16	**Geoffrey Chaucer A Treatise on the Astrolabe,** ed. W. W. Skeat. 1872, *reprinted* 1968.	£6·00
17, 18	**The Complaynt of Scotlande,** re-ed. J. A. H. Murray. Vol. I 1872, Vol. II 1873; *reprinted as one volume* Kraus 1973.	$35.00
19	**The Myroure of oure Ladye,** ed. J. H. Blunt. 1873, *reprinted* Kraus 1973.	$40.00
20, 24	**The History of the Holy Grail by Henry Lovelich,** ed. F. J. Furnivall. Vol. I 1874, Vol. II 1875; *reprinted as one volume* Kraus 1973. (See ES 28, 30, and 95 for other parts.)	$45.00
21, 29	**The Bruce by John Barbour,** ed. W. W. Skeat. Vol. II 1874, Vol. III 1877; *reprinted as one volume* 1968. (See ES 11, 55 for other part.)	£13·25

ES 22	**Henry Brinklow's Complaynt of Roderyck Mors,** The Lamentacyon of a Christen agaynst the Cytye of London by Roderigo Mors, ed. J. M. Cowper. 1874, *reprinted* Kraus 1973.	*
23	**On Early English Pronunciation,** by A. J. Ellis. Part IV. 1874, *reprinted* Kraus 1973. (See ES 2, 7, 14, and 56 for other parts.)	$33.00
24	**The History of the Holy Grail** by Henry Lovelich, Vol. II. See above, ES 20.	
25, 26	**The Romance of Guy of Warwick,** the second or 15th-century version, ed. J. Zupitza. Vol. I 1875, Vol. II 1876; *reprinted as one volume* 1966.	£11·25
27	**John Fisher The English Works,** ed. J. E. B. Mayor. Vol. I (*all published*) 1876, *reprinted* Kraus 1973.	*
28, 30, 95	**The History of the Holy Grail by Henry Lovelich,** ed. F. J. Furnivall. Vol. III 1877; Vol. IV 1878; Vol. V The Legend of the Holy Grail, its Sources, Character and Development by D. Kempe 1905; *reprinted as one volume* Kraus 1973. (See ES 20, 24 for other parts.)	$29.00
29	**The Bruce by John Barbour,** Vol. III. See above, ES 21.	
30	**The History of the Holy Grail by Henry Lovelich,** Vol. IV. See above, ES 28.	
31	**The Alliterative Romance of Alexander and Dindimus,** re-ed. W. W. Skeat. 1878, *reprinted* Kraus 1973.	*
32	**England in the Reign of King Henry VIII,** Vol. II. See above, ES 12.	
33	**The Early English Version of the Gesta Romanorum,** ed. S. J. H. Herrtage. 1879, *reprinted* 1962.	£15·00
34	**The English Charlemagne Romances I: Sir Ferumbras,** ed. S. J. H. Herrtage. 1879, *reprinted* 1966.	£8·00
35	The English Charlemagne Romances II: **The Sege of Melayne, The Romance of Duke Rowland and Sir Otuell of Spayne,** ed. S. J. H. Herrtage. 1880, *reprinted* Kraus 1973.	$20.00
36, 37	The English Charlemagne Romances III and IV: **The Lyf of Charles the Grete,** translated by William Caxton, ed. S. J. H. Herrtage. Vol. I 1880, Vol. II 1881; *reprinted as one volume* 1967.	£8·00
38	The English Charlemagne Romances V: **The Romances of the Sowdone of Babylone,** re-ed. E. Hausknecht. 1881, *reprinted* 1969.	£7·75
39	The English Charlemagne Romances VI: **The Taill of Rauf Coilyear, with the fragments of Roland and Vernagu and Otuel,** re-ed. S. J. H. Herrtage. 1882, *reprinted* 1969.	£6·50
40, 41	The English Charlemagne Romances VII and VIII: **The Boke of Duke Huon of Burdeux** translated by Lord Berners, ed. S. L. Lee. Vol. I 1882, Vol. II 1883; *reprinted as one volume* Kraus 1973. (See ES 43, 50 for other parts.)	$60.00
42, 49, 59	**The Romances of Guy of Warwick,** from the Auchinleck MS. and the Caius MS., ed. J. Zupitza. Vol. I 1883, Vol. II 1887. Vol. III 1891; *reprinted as one volume* 1966.	£15·25
43, 50	The English Charlemagne Romances IX and XII: **The Boke of Duke Huon of Bordeux** translated by Lord Berners, ed. S. L. Lee. Vol. III 1884, Vol. IV 1887; *reprinted as one volume* Kraus 1973.	$54.00
44	The English Charlemagne Romances X: **The Foure Sonnes of Aymon,** translated by William Caxton, ed. O. Richardson. Vol. I 1884, *reprinted* Kraus 1973.	*
45	The English Charlemagne Romances XI: **The Foure Sonnes of Aymon,** translated by William Caxton, ed. O. Richardson. Vol. II 1885, *reprinted* Kraus 1973.	$35.00
46, 48, 65	**The Romance of Sir Beues of Hamtoun,** ed. E. Kölbing. Vol. I 1885, Vol. II 1886, Vol. III 1894; *reprinted as one volume* Kraus 1973.	$34.00
47	**The Wars of Alexander,** an Alliterative Romance, re-ed. W. W. Skeat. 1886, *reprinted* Kraus 1973.	$45.00
48	**The Romance of Sir Beues of Hamtoun,** Vol. II. See above, ES 46.	
49	**The Romance of Guy of Warwick,** Vol. II. See above, ES 42.	

ES 50	The English Charlemagne Romances XII: **The Boke of Duke Huon of Burdeux,** Vol. IV. See above, ES 43.	
51	**Torrent of Portyngale,** re-ed. E. Adam. 1887, *reprinted* Kraus 1973.	$15.00
52	**A Dialogue against the Feuer Pestilence by William Bullein,** ed. M. W. and A. H. Bullen. 1888, *reprinted* Kraus 1973.	*
53	**The Anatomie of the Bodie of Man by Thomas Vicary,** ed. F. J. and P. Furnivall. 1888, *reprinted* Kraus 1973.	$67.00
54	**The Curial made by maystere Alain Charretier,** translated by Caxton, ed. P. Meyer and F. J. Furnivall. 1888, *reprinted* 1965.	£2·00
55	**The Bruce by John Barbour,** Vol. IV. See above, ES 11.	
56	**On Early English Pronunciation,** by A. J. Ellis. Part V. 1889, *reprinted* Kraus 1973. (See ES 2, 7, 14, and 23 for other parts.)	$66.00
57	**Caxton's Eneydos,** ed. W. T. Culley and F. J. Furnivall. 1890, *reprinted* 1962.	£7·75
58	**Caxton's Blanchardyn and Eglantine,** ed. L. Kellner. 1890, *reprinted* 1962.	£9·75
59	**The Romance of Guy of Warwick,** Vol. III. See above ES 42.	
60	**Lydgate's Temple of Glas,** ed. J. Schick. 1891, *reprinted* Kraus 1973.	*
61, 73	**Hoccleve's Works: The Minor Poems,** Vol. I ed. F. J. Furnivall (1892), Vol. II ed. I. Gollancz (1925 *for* 1897); reprinted as one volume and revised by Jerome Mitchell and A. I. Doyle 1970.	£9·75
62	**The Chester Plays,** ed. H. Deimling. Vol. I 1892, *reprinted* 1967. (See ES 115 for Part II.)	£4·50
63	**The Earliest English Translations of the De Imitatione Christi,** ed. J. K. Ingram. 1893, *reprinted* Kraus 1973.	*
64	**Godeffroy of Boloyne,** or the Siege and Conqueste of Jerusalem by William, archbishop of Tyre, translated by William Caxton, ed. M. N. Colvin. 1893, *reprinted* Kraus 1973.	*
65	**The Romance of Sir Beues of Hamtoun,** Vol. III. See above, ES 46.	
66	**Lydgate and Burgh's Secrees of old Philisoffres:** a version of the Secreta Secretorum, ed. R. Steele. 1894, *reprinted* Kraus 1973.	$15.00
67	**The Three Kings' Sons,** ed. F. J. Furnivall. Vol. I Text (*all published*) 1895, *reprinted* Kraus 1973.	*
68	**Melusine,** ed. A. K. Donald. Vol. I (*all published*) 1895, *reprinted* Kraus 1973.	$40.00
69	**John Lydgate The Assembly of Gods,** ed. O. L. Triggs. 1896, *reprinted* Kraus 1976.	$20.00
70	**The Digby Plays,** ed. F. J. Furnivall. 1896, *reprinted* 1967.	£3·50
71	**The Towneley Plays,** re-ed. G. England and A. W. Pollard. 1897, *reprinted* Kraus 1973.	*
72	**Hoccleve's Works: The Regement of Princes and fourteen minor poems,** ed. F. J. Furnivall. 1897, *reprinted* Kraus 1973.	$21.00
73	**Hoccleve's Works: The Minor Poems,** Vol. II. See above, ES 61.	
74	**Three Prose Versions of the Secreta Secretorum,** ed. R. Steele and T. Henderson. Vol. I (*all published*) 1898, *reprinted* Kraus 1973.	$22.00
75	**Speculum Gy de Warewyke,** ed. G. L. Morrill. 1898, *reprinted* Kraus 1973.	$22.00
76	**George Ashby's Poems,** ed. M. Bateson. 1899, *reprinted* 1965.	£4·75
77, 83, 92	**The Pilgrimage of the Life of Man,** translated by John Lydgate from the French by Guillaume de Deguileville, Vol. I ed. F. J. Furnivall (1899), Vol. II ed. F. J. Furnivall (1901), Vol. III introduction, notes, glossary, etc. by K. B. Locock (1904); *reprinted as one volume* Kraus 1973.	$90.00
78	**Thomas Robinson The Life and Death of Mary Magdalene,** ed. H. O. Sommer. 1899. *Paper.*	£4·75
79	**Dialogues in French and English by William Caxton,** ed. H. Bradley. 1900, *reprinted* Kraus 1973. *Paper.*	*
80	**Lydgate's Two Nightingale Poems,** ed. O. Glauning. 1900, *reprinted* Kraus 1973.	*

ES 80A	**Selections from Barbour's Bruce (Books I–X),** ed. W. W. Skeat, 1900, *reprinted* Kraus 1973.	$39.00
81	**The English Works of John Gower,** ed. G. C. Macaulay. Vol. I *Confessio Amantis* Prologue–Bk V. 1970. 1900, *reprinted* 1978.	£9·50
82	**The English Works of John Gower,** ed. G. C. Macaulay. Vol. II *Confessio Amantis* V. 1971–VIII, *In Praise of Peace.* 1901, *reprinted* 1978.	'
83	**The Pilgrimage of the Life of Man,** Vol. II. See above, ES 77.	
84	**Lydgate's Reson and Sensuallyte,** ed. E. Sieper. Vol. I Manuscripts, Text, and Glossary. 1901, *reprinted* 1865. (See ES 89 for Part II.)	£7·75
85	**The Poems of Alexander Scott,** ed. A. K. Donald. 1902, *reprinted* Kraus 1973.	$12.00
86	**The Poems of William of Shoreham,** ed. M. Konrath. Vol. I (*all published*) 1902, *reprinted* Kraus 1973.	$25.00
87	**Two Coventry Corpus Christi Plays,** re-ed. H. Craig. 1902; *second edition* 1957, *reprinted* 1967.	£4·75
88	**Le Morte Arthur,** a romance in stanzas, re-ed. J. D. Bruce. 1903, *reprinted* Kraus 1973.	*
89	**Lydgate's Reson and Sensuallyte,** ed. E. Sieper. Vol. II Studies and Notes. 1903, *reprinted* 1965. (See ES 84 for Part I.)	£5·25
90	**English Fragments from Latin Medieval Service-Books,** ed. H. Littlehales. 1903, *reprinted* Kraus 1973. *Paper.*	$12.00
91	**The Macro Plays,** ed. F. J. Furnivall and A. W. Pollard. 1904. Superseded by OS 262.	
92	**The Pilgrimage of the Life of Man,** Vol. III. See above, ES 77.	
93	**Henry Lovelich's Merlin,** ed. E. A. Kock. Vol. I 1904, *reprinted* Kraus 1973. (See ES 112 and OS 185 for other parts.)	*
94	**Respublica,** ed. L. A. Magnus. 1905. Superseded by OS 226.	
95	**The History of the Holy Grail by Henry Lovelich,** Vol. V. See above, ES 28.	
96	**Mirk's Festial,** ed. T. Erbe. Vol. I (*all published*) 1905, *reprinted* Kraus 1973.	*
97	**Lydgate's Troy Book,** ed. H. Bergen. Vol. I Prologue, Books I and II, 1906, *reprinted* Kraus 1973. (See ES 103, 106, and 126 for other parts.)	$31.00
98	**John Skelton Magnyfycence,** ed. R. L. Ramsay. 1908 (*for* 1906), *reprinted* Kraus 1976.	$30.00
99	**The Romance of Emaré,** ed. E. Rickert. 1908 (*for* 1906), *reprinted* Kraus 1984.	$32.00
100	**The Middle English Harrowing of Hell and Gospel of Nicodemus,** ed. W. H. Hulme. 1908 (*for* 1907), *reprinted* Kraus 1976.	$20.00
101	**Songs, Carols and other Miscellaneous Poems from Balliol MS. 354,** Richard Hill's Commonplace-book, ed. R. Dyboski. 1908 (*for* 1907), *reprinted* Kraus 1973.	$25.00
102	**The Promptorium Parvulorum:** the First English-Latin Dictionary, ed. A. L. Mayhew. 1908, *reprinted* Kraus 1973.	*
103, 106	**Lydgate's Troy Book,** ed. H. Bergen. Vol. II, Book III, 1908; Vol. III, Books IV and V, 1910; *reprinted as one volume* Kraus 1973. (See ES 97, 126 for other parts.)	$45.00
104	**The Non-Cycle Mystery Plays,** ed. O. Waterhouse. 1909. Superseded by SS 1.	
105	**The Tale of Beryn,** with a Prologue of the Merry Adventure of the Pardoner with a Tapster at Canterbury, ed. F. J. Furnivall and W. G. Stone. 1909, *reprinted* Kraus 1973.	$25.00
106	**Lydgate's Troy Book,** Vol. III. See above, E.S. 103.	
107	**John Lydgate The Minor Poems,** ed. H. N. MacCracken. Vol. I Religious Poems. 1911 (*for* 1910), *reprinted* 1961. (See OS 192 for Vol. II.)	£10·75

ES 108	**Lydgate's Siege of Thebes,** ed. A. Erdmann. Vol. I Text. 1911. *reprinted* Kraus 1984. (See ES 125 for Vol. II.)	$40.00
109	**The Middle English Versions of Partonope of Blois,** ed. A. T. Bödtker. 1912 (*for* 1911), *reprinted* Kraus 1973.	$45.00
110	**Caxton's Mirrour of the World,** ed. O. H. Prior. 1913 (*for* 1912), *reprinted* Kraus 1978.	*
111	**Raoul Le Fevre the History of Jason,** translated by William Caxton, ed. J. Munro. 1913 (*for* 1912), *reprinted* Kraus 1973.	$17.00
112	**Henry Lovelich's Merlin,** ed. E. A. Kock. Vol. II 1913, *reprinted* 1961. (See ES 93 and OS 185 for other parts.) *Paper.*	£6·75
113	**Poems by Sir John Salusbury and Robert Chester,** ed. Carleton Brown. 1914 (*for* 1913), *reprinted* Kraus 1973.	$13.00
114	**The Gild of St. Mary, Lichfield:** Ordinances and other documents, ed. F. J. Furnivall. 1920 (*for* 1914), *reprinted* Kraus 1973. *Paper.*	$10.00
115	**The Chester Plays,** ed. Dr. Matthews. Vol. II 1916 (*for* 1914), *reprinted* 1967.	£4·25
116	**The Pauline Epistles** in MS. Parker 32, Corpus Christi College, Cambridge, ed. M. J. Powell. 1916 (*for* 1915), *reprinted* Kraus 1973.	$35.00
117	**The Life of Fisher,** ed. R. Bayne. 1921 (*for* 1915), *reprinted* Kraus 1973.	$12.00
118	**The Earliest Arithmetics in English,** ed. R. Steele. 1922 (*for* 1916), *reprinted* Kraus 1973.	$12.00
119	**The Owl and the Nightingale,** ed. J. H. G. Grattan and G. F. H. Sykes. 1935 (*for* 1915), *reprinted* Kraus 1973.	$14.00
120	**Ludus Coventriæ,** or The Plaie called Corpus Christi, Cotton MS. Vespasian D. viii, ed. K. S. Block. 1922 (*for* 1917), *reprinted* 1961.	£9·50
121	**Lydgate's Fall of Princes,** ed. H. Bergen. Vol. I 1924 (*for* 1918), *reprinted* 1967.	£9·75
122	**Lydgate's Fall of Princes,** ed. H. Bergen. Vol. II 1924 (*for* 1918), *reprinted* 1967.	£9·75
123	**Lydgate's Fall of Princes,** ed. H. Bergen. Vol. III 1924 (*for* 1919), *reprinted* 1967.	£9·75
124	**Lydgate's Fall of Princes,** ed. H. Bergen. Vol. IV 1927 (*for* 1919), *reprinted* 1967.	£13·25
125	**Lydgate's Siege of Thebes,** ed. A. Erdmann and E. Ekwall. Vol. II Introduction, Notes, Glossary etc. 1930 (*for* 1920), *reprinted* Kraus 1973.	$22.00
126	**Lydgate's Troy Book,** ed. H. Bergen. Vol. IV 1935 (*for* 1920), *reprinted* Kraus 1973. (See ES 97, 103, and 106 for other parts.)	$50.00

University Printing House, Oxford